DEFENCE OF HOPE

DEFENCE OF HOPE

DOUG LAVERS

PARTRIDGE
A Penguin Random House Company

To order additional copies of this book, contact
Toll Free 800 101 2657 (Singapore)
Toll Free 1 800 81 7340 (Malaysia)
orders.singapore@partridgepublishing.com

www.partridgepublishing.com/singapore

Contents

Acknowledgement

THIS BOOK COULD NEVER HAVE BEEN written without the tolerance and support of my wife Gill. Comments by Dr Lona Brown were also greatly appreciated.

Melbourne, October 2015

Author's Note

THIS NOVEL IS A SEQUEL TO the Rejuvenation Trilogy. However, it is designed to stand on its own, and comprises what I hope is an interesting mixture of science fiction and real history.

Rejuvenation Series ©

Backdrop

IN THE SCIENCE FICTION NOVEL IN the Rejuvenation Trilogy, "Fulfilment of Hope", Katie Shepherd successfully established the Outer Arm Federation with the assistance of a collective intelligence known as The Bearing and three separate artificial intelligences. Her female descendants who resembled her were known as Shepherds and shared a strange chromosome.

During the establishment process, she was forced to return to old Earth in order to assist in the protection of the Calai Federation from an expansion minded and xenophobic species known as the Qui. To their great regret, The Bearing had eventually been forced to resort to genocide of the Qui because the latter would not negotiate with any other species and change their behaviour.

Katie returned to her Federation, and resumed her comfortable and relatively anonymous lifestyle on the planet Europia. The changes to her physiology initiated by The Bearing moved to completion, and she was increasingly drawn into their community which existed entirely within foldspace. She was beginning to plan how she would completely withdraw from the Federation after appointing a successor.

Unfortunately, the extinction of the Qui had consequences unforeseen even by The Bearing ....

Prelude

THE QUI HAD EXISTED AS COMMUNITIES within which all the members had been linked telepathically to each other. The links between the Qui Queens had been strong, and they were genetically conditioned to assist each other when threatened. The workers and soldiers in their hive societies were in turn telepathically linked to their own Queens.

Many generations previously, an exceptional Queen of their species called Aon had been transformed into a member of The Bearing.

When the decision to exterminate the Qui had been debated, she had been the only entity to strongly oppose the proposal. When it had been implemented, the breakage of the mental links to the Qui species had destroyed Aon's psychological stability. She removed herself from the collective, and planned vengeance.

Chapter 1

INTRODUCTION TO FOLDSPACE

A s the changes initiated by The Bearing moved towards completion, Katie found she needed less and less sleep, and she spent more and more time in foldspace engaging with the Bearing Community. To her surprise, she had found that seniority within the community seemed to partially depend on how closely any being had interacted with the central entity of the community.

She had asked about this, and the response was; "Katie, we do not understand the nature of our most senior member. It appears that the entity is the most ancient member of our community, and may have been present when it first formed. It rarely interacts directly with anyone apart from acknowledging presence, and is known as the Oldest. We are absolutely convinced that it is completely ethical and completely supports our protection of the galaxy, but otherwise it does not open to us. In our opinion, it seems to be more female than male in your psychological terms, but such a distinction is probably meaningless.

"Occasionally, it engages in a 'conversation', and the recipient or recipients of the conversation gain status within our community. It is extremely rare for it to react at all to apprentice members such as yourself.

"There have been other members of our community in the past, but in all those cases, after a long period they have disengaged themselves completely and disappeared. The Oldest is the only remnant of our far distant past."

Out of curiosity, Katie had ascended to the upper fold space level where the Oldest existed. The process was somehow analogous to moving from the outer reaches of a solar system towards the central sun. As she approached, she could feel a sense of ancient wisdom and almost a weight of knowledge. She was also surprised to feel a distant sense of familiarity, and sadness.

She had the absolute conviction that the entity knew everything about her.

Not expecting any interaction, she watched for a while, letting her senses collect a more complete impression.

She was surprised when a thought formed in her mind; "Greetings, Katie. I request that you undertake an important task, as a problem has arisen which was not foreseen by the Community.

"I should mention that my comments are being shared with our more senior members, as they will need to assist.

"The historical database about Earth maintained on Nova has started to diverge from similar information held on Earth. This can only happen through manipulation of the past. As a vast simplification, when a temporal change is made, the changes radiate outwards like three-dimensional ripples in a pond. As these "chronons" move outwards in space and forwards in time, the effects weaken. The changes take a perceptible time to take effect.

"The database on Nova is sufficiently far from Earth that it is effectively unchanged.

"You are familiar with the quantum mechanical concept of Schrödinger's Cat, where a multitude of states are possible until something causes one to coalesce into reality.

"An analogous temporal process is occurring, except that the chronons are now coalescing into a slightly altered state. In other words, history is being changed on Earth.

"This is occurring because a previous Qui derived member of our community called Aon is now moving back in time on Earth, and altering key historical events. Vast quantities of energy are required to operate the process, and the timeshift can only be done with small bodies. About 100 kg represents the limit. The further into the past the movement, the greater the power requirement. Aon is effectively tapping part of the energy output of a supergiant star using a banned and suppressed technology. Unfortunately she derives from an era before the restrictions were applied.

"Changing history anywhere in the galaxy is extremely undesirable, as unpredictable follow-on effects can occur far into the future. In general, we have even prohibited the sending of messages into the past for the same reason.

"Aon has the same problem with respect to her own species; she cannot simply return to her own past and make alterations.

"As a species, the Qui nearly exterminated themselves before they learnt mutual cooperation.

"She would not know the effects that she might create, and could easily erase herself completely. She has to make do with far less assistance than you would control.

"She does not have the same problem with Earth, as from her point of view any change is a possible improvement, considering the regrettable genocide we undertook.

"The changes that Aon has/will make would have a catastrophic effect if they are not countered, and not only on Earth.

"The method that she is using is subtle. In general, history is difficult to change as most alterations involve vast numbers of people and tend to be statistical in nature. However there are a few critical branch points where the action of an individual can move the flow. These individuals are known as divertants.

"Aon is making changes by influencing divertants, using the historical database from Earth.

"The task that I would like you to undertake, is to follow her back, and as far as possible nullify the changes. This will be difficult. You will have little more than your intelligence, enhanced physiology and a limited ability to provide a personal fold space shield.

"The Bearing will be able to send and receive messages, so you will have an indication when any action you have taken is successful. This feedback is important as small coincidental changes that you have introduced may have unexpected effects.

"You may have to return to a nearby but earlier point in time and make further small alterations.

"You will also have a limited view into the future for any altered timeline. Sometimes the short term results will be glorious, but unfortunately in virtually every case disaster eventually overtakes the human race, and a much wider audience. Our core timeline is the only safe path. Even that will present you with some agonising choices; on occasion you will have to ensure that truly horrible events occur.

"Fortunately, a small personal remote can also be included to assist you. That remote will give you an access point for advanced technology when you need it, and will hold a large database. The form of the remote is up to you, but it would appear likely that it will be in the shape of a cat with less conspicuous colouration than Yelli!

"If too threatened, your body will automatically move back into fold space, but in that case you will have a problem if you return and meet an earlier version of yourself – your older version will be erased. Temporal movement and placement is rather erratic. The remote would be linked to you, and would remain in contact.

"In making your decision, please bear in mind that refusal of this request will almost certainly lead to the nonexistence of everything you hold dear."

With that comment, the communication channel closed.

1a – First Alteration

Katie felt completely overwhelmed, and a terrible anxiety gripped her.

A few seconds later, she felt another communication channel open, and a Bearing individual whom she knew well and who had become a friend spoke to her; "Katie, we are as astonished as you at what the Oldest has told you. We are preparing for a comparison of the historical databases between Earth and Nova, and you will need to be involved in that process if you accept the request.

"We are sure we will find changes as suggested.

"We have no idea why you have been selected, but apparently your participation is absolutely necessary.

"Will you assist?"

Katie had the strong impression that she stood at the edge of a precipice, and the moment she moved, she would be falling irrevocably into the unknown. However the Oldest's last comment resonated in her mind. With dread spreading through her, she softly said, "Yes".

* * *

Katie was already located in the Outer Arm of the galaxy, and the Bearing group which had been seconded to assist moved themselves the vast distance to Nova before they started to study the historical databases. A small group of Bearing volunteered to stay in the vicinity of earth to assist in the collection of data. They were aware that they would be embroiled in a temporal disaster.

Katie was told by her seconded group, "Our knowledge of how time operates is not complete, and we are aware there are large gaps in physical knowledge.

"We have asked the Oldest about this. There was an acknowledgement that a more complete theory existed, but we were told explicitly that no extra information on chronons would be provided, with one exception.

"This exception was a description of a strange effect that occurs when an individual moving in time meets the same individual. This appears to be the temporal equivalent of the Pauli exclusion principle. The older copy of the individual simply disappears after a short time dependent on the original temporal displacement of the pair.

"Apparently, horrible temporal loops can be created in time, which effectively mean that history ends for that particular individual.

"Katie, you will need to be really careful to avoid this effect."

1b – Changes

Katie and her group started to study the changes.

It was immediately apparent that a large number of small changes had occurred to Earth-based history, but the main timeline seemed to be intact. The group asked for regular refreshes of the database, and soon a curious flickering effect was noticed when comparisons were made between successive receipts of databases.

Aware of the possible deliberate incompleteness of their theory of time, there was a long discussion amongst the more senior Bearing members about what was happening.

When Katie asked, they said; "We are not certain what is creating this flickering effect, but it is possible that actions you will/have taken are influencing the recorded history, which keeps changing slightly.

"In a sense, we are seeing the vibrations from a time war between yourself and Aon.

"Clearly, whatever actions you take have vast historical significance".

This made Katie feel even more uncomfortable, and still more nervous, about the project on which she had embarked.

A short period later, a further message was received from Earth.

"Investigation Group, be aware that the Oldest has disappeared. A message was left as follows; [*Members of the Bearing Community, my time is up and I am disengaging. You must assist Katie in every way possible. I leave*

*a small and suitably disguised remote to provide her with information and
assistance.*

Farewell]"

The sense of shock through the whole group was almost palpable. This was
particularly the case for the older Bearing members, for whom the Oldest had
been a fixture in their lives for as long as their community had existed. They
were aware that an epic event in their history had occurred, but were totally
uncertain about its significance.

Katie was simply terrified.

* * *

About a week later, in Bearing subjective time, the remote arrived. It
appeared in the form of a small grey tabby cat with light stripes.

A thought formed in her mind, "Katie, I am your personal remote. The
oldest named me Yelli.

"You should be aware that some of the techniques used in my construction
are unknown to the existing Bearing. We are linked in spacetime, so wherever
you move I will remain with you.

"I hold a vast database, and some small foldspace tools which the Oldest
considers will be useful."

On reflection, Katie decided that she should return to normal space and
finalise her relationship with her family and the Federation.

She told the group, "Please continue your research, and I will return in
a few days. I would hope by then you will have mapped out the first of the
historical events with which Aon has tampered. We will then decide on some
form of strategy.

"You will also have to re-introduce me to the Time Machine, for want of
a better description.

"As a sort of reward for helping with the Qui, I was allowed to visit Ancient
Egypt for a time."

One of the group members said, "That visit was allowed on the instruction
of the Oldest. At the time, we were surprised, as in general time travel has been
totally banned."

1c – Back on Europia

Katie had been Dean of the Medical School at Europia University for nearly 10 years. She had repeatedly refused to become Chancellor of the University, or accept any special privileges. She had found that with her position as Empress of the Outer Arm Federation, whenever she expressed an opinion, that opinion would prevail. Members of the faculty simply would not disagree with her.

As a result, she only rarely appeared at meetings, and restricted her input to occasionally asking a question. She had found this had the great advantage of forcing the faculty to operate as if she was effectively absent.

When she returned to Europia, Tia and her husband Commander Perry Wright were the only people who knew she had been away.

Tia asked, "Mother, where have you been? You left so suddenly that I had to make some embarrassing apologies for your absence!"

Tia saw what appeared to be tears forming in Katie's eyes, and there was no answer for a few seconds.

"Can we not talk about this, as I would just like to enjoy the next few days with yourselves and the children."

The following day, Katie took her grandchildren out to the local zoo. It was not a particularly pleasant day, but quite typical for Europia. There was a cold wind blowing, and heavy clouds filled the sky, but at least it stayed dry.

This did not worry the children at all – they always loved to go out with their grandmother, who just appeared like a big sister to them. As soon as the zoo staff saw her arrive, they immediately delegated a couple of keepers to look after the family. Some cheetah kittens had just reached the age when they could be introduced to human visitors, and the zoo staff were delighted to be able to take them into the enclosure. As they did so, Yelli appeared from the shadows and leapt onto Katie's shoulder. As they went in, she started the rasping purr characteristic of the cats. When the mother appeared with her 3 half grown kittens behind her, she leapt off Katie's shoulder, and walked up to the mother, and almost immediately all five cats seemed to be purring in harmony.

Ambria, Katie's youngest grandchild, said "Grandma, can I go up and stroke them?"

Katie answered, "Of course you can, Ambria."

Seeing that the keepers were looking a little worried, she added quickly; "Crystal is keeping a close watch on the children, and discrete shields are in place."

She added, "Children, I'm going to go and sit on that seat at the edge of the grass. I'm sure the keepers will look after all of you!"

Katie went and sat down on the corner, and her mind returned to the Bearing task confronting her.

Ten minutes later, a discreet cough from one of the keepers brought her attention back to the enclosure.

"My Lady, I think the kittens have probably had enough, and we had better move on.

"We have taken a few photographs; would it be alright if we use them in the next zoo magazine?"

Katie nodded, and the tour continued.

In the evening, Tia and Perry took the children upstairs to get ready for bed, and a little later Katie joined them to read the obligatory story.

When she was downstairs again, Katie saw Tia and Perry looking at her very thoughtfully.

She asked, "What is it, you are both looking rather concerned?"

There was a short pause, and then Perry said; "Katie, the children told us that when you were sitting in the cheetah enclosure at the zoo, they thought your eyes were glowing.

"Ambria asked; 'Mummy, when you get older, will your eyes glow like grandmother's?

"What should we tell them?"

There was a long pause, while Katie considered how to respond.

She said, "Tia and Perry, please keep what I'm about to tell you in complete confidence, particularly from the rest of the family.

"When I disappeared last week, I was called away to a meeting with the Bearing.

"I am becoming part of the Bearing community as a sort of apprentice, and only a small part of me is still human as you understand it. Unfortunately, when I'm not concentrating a part of the inner me starts to appear through my eyes, which glow.

"I have been given a task by the Bearing, for which I am apparently uniquely qualified.

"I am deeply saddened to tell you that I'm going to have to leave for a perhaps extended period.

"This task is extremely difficult, and from its nature I may never be able to return permanently."

Tia and Perry looked absolutely aghast.

Katie continued, "Accordingly, I'm going to abdicate as Empress, and one of Charlotte's grandchildren is going to be nominated as my heir.

"There is a University meeting tomorrow, when I will announce my resignation from the faculty. In about three weeks' time, I will be addressing the Federation Parliament at Nova, when my abdication will be announced.

"I expect you would like to come with me on Crystal with the children when I leave tomorrow.

"To return to Ambria's question, you will have to tell the children that I will be going to live in foldspace, where glowing eyes are needed, but they are not to tell anyone yet."

Tia started to cry, and Perry looked completely stunned.

* * *

Katie's message to the Federation Parliament that she wished to make an address caused enormous surprise. For nearly a decade, she had managed to avoid almost every official engagement.

At the same time, a message went out to all her family suggesting that they might like to attend the event as observers.

As one Shepherd husband remarked, "Somehow, I don't think anyone is going to miss this. When the Empress makes an address, it tends to be memorable."

1d – Sienna

Sienna Cordwell had just completed a degree in history and architecture at Melbourne University. She had been one of only a handful of humans at the University, whose students were generally sourced from all over the Federation. Entry was ferociously competitive. She was looking forward to entering the Federation Administration College in a few months.

She was in a coffee bar with her group of friends, who had just started discussing the forthcoming address at the Federation Parliament. They were interested in Sienna's views, as she was one of Katie's great grandchildren.

"My parents and all our other relatives have been discussing the same question. They are worried, as the Empress has tried hard to avoid any official engagements, and the announcement of her resignation from the faculty at Europia University was awfully sudden.

"We all thought she was completely settled there, looking after Tia's children and teaching.

"It has to be something pretty momentous, especially as all the family have been invited to watch."

At that moment, a small remote drifted through the entrance to the coffee bar. The group of students looked up in surprise, as it came towards them.

The remote spoke softly; "Sienna, the Empress would like to have a short talk with you. She apologises for interrupting your chat with your friends."

The girl looked up in shock, "Yes of course, but can I stop by at my rooms and put on something a bit more respectable?"

The remote said, "The Empress is entirely unconcerned at how you are dressed, so there is no need to change.

"There is a shuttle waiting outside for you. By the way, I have settled the bill for your group of friends at the bar, which will include anything else they order."

A few minutes later, the shuttle stopped in front of the Crystal Palace, and the Crystal remote appeared and said, "Sienna, please follow me".

She was taken up to the tip of the Palace, to a large open room with windows on all sides.

Katie was waiting for her, and Sienna was astonished at how young she looked. She had read that the Empress never seemed to age, but seeing her at first hand still surprised her. She only had a distant memory from when she was much younger.

Katie stood and smiled slightly, "Sienna, thank you for coming so promptly, and I apologise for the short notice. Please take a seat.

"By the way, call me Katie, as that is what I like.

"Crystal is bringing in some coffee and biscuits, as I don't think you had got as far as drinking your cappuccino.

"While we are waiting, perhaps you could tell me how you found your course at Melbourne University?"

A slightly relieved Sienna started talking about her course, acutely aware that a substantial part of the history section of that course had revolved around the woman in front of her. However, she was feeling steadily more relaxed, as it appeared that her great-grandmother simply wanted to have a chat with her. There did not seem to be much difference between talking to Katie and talking to her friends.

Coffee and biscuits arrived, and Sienna finished her description of the course after Katie filled her cup.

Katie smiled and said, "I am really glad you enjoyed the course, and congratulations on your results."

Sienna had finished at the top of her class. She had been offered one of the University Medals for most distinguished student in her subject area, but had turned it down.

She put down her own cup, and said "Sienna, I did not invite you to the Crystal Palace just for a friendly chat.

"You must keep what I'm about to tell you in complete confidence from everyone, and especially our family, until after my address to the Federation Parliament next week.

"What you decide to tell them after that will be entirely up to you. However, I would counsel discretion.

"Do you agree to this?"

Apprehension beginning to grip her again, Sienna could only nod.

Katie continued; "I am becoming an apprentice within the Bearing community, and only a small part of me is still human. For reasons which are not clear, I have been given what promises to be an immensely difficult, important and long-lasting task.

"Accordingly, I'm going to abdicate as Empress."

Sienna looked at her in shock and anguish, and wondered why she was being told. From the side of the room, a golden cat ran across and leaped onto Sienna's shoulder.

Katie looked at her with what appeared to be immense sadness, and her eyes glowed slightly.

"I am so sorry to lay this burden on you, but you will be my heir, and the new Empress of the Federation."

Sienna's anguish turned to absolute horror as she contemplated this prospect. The cat on her shoulder purred faintly and licked her ear.

Sobbing slightly she said, "Katie, do I have to accept this?"

Katie looked at her for a moment and then said, "Sheila, Yelli, Crystal and I have considered our family carefully. We think you are best fitted for the role.

"While you could refuse, you will only be laying the burden on someone else in our family, and I do not believe that your sense of responsibility would allow you to do that.

11

"It is a terrible thing to say, but I think we are equally reluctant to take up the new roles which are being thrust upon us. And we both have as little option."

Sienna nodded slowly.

Katie continued, "Yelli is transferring her attention to you. You should be aware that she is actually a junior Bearing in disguise, and you can communicate with her at any time.

"I would suggest that you freely discuss any problems you have with her, and you will find her immensely helpful, as she has been to me.

"Separately from this, Crystal will put you through the major health makeover, and give you a far more complete history of what I have been up to in the last few decades.

"I should mention that you will also become the controller of the Ghost Fleet, subject to certain restrictions. I would strongly recommend to you that you only ever use it as a last resort. You will be shocked to find out how and where it has been used, and that its size has been significantly diminished."

Katie paused for a moment, and refilled Sienna's cup of coffee. The girl really needed a moment to catch her thoughts.

"Finally, you need to recognise that for most of the time your role will be simply ceremonial. Your aunt the Governor is extremely capable, and there is nothing to stop you delegating almost everything to her!

"Your input is only critical at major decision points, or when some group in the Federation or the Parliament decides to do something stupid.

"There is also nothing to stop you completing the course at the Federation Administration College, and then moving into the community to do what you will. You can increase your anonymity by changing your hair colour from black to something of your choice. Reversing the change will make you far more inconspicuous in your ordinary life.

"You can also take on your role as Empress under a different name.

"However, you will have ultimate authority, and no one will ever forget that."

* * *

Sienna's friends had told her parents that she had been invited to the Crystal Palace. When she returned home, her mother was alarmed at how pale her daughter looked. Clearly, she had also been crying.

She asked, "Darling, what is the matter? Visits to the Crystal Palace are normally delightful."

Sienna looked at her; "Mum, I can't say anything about what I discussed at the Crystal Palace, and I really, really don't want to talk about it."

To her mother's dismay, she burst into tears again and simply went off to her room. Her parents could hear her sobbing for hours afterwards.

Although her intelligence told her the thought was ridiculous, it was worry about how her friends at the College would react which troubled her the most.

She decided that changing her "Empress" identity would have some considerable advantages. Only a handful of people would ever need to know.

She hardly said a word at supper that night. Her parents were deeply concerned, but their daughter seemed to have built a barrier around herself and would not say anything.

1e – Abdication

On the day of the ceremony, Katie's address was scheduled for early afternoon. Well before then, all the Federation members of Parliament had assembled, and it was seen that large screens had been set up in the Parliamentary gardens for the surrounding crowds to follow what was said.

All Katie's family and partners came along, and found they were given the viewing balconies normally reserved for foreign dignitaries. Sienna's parents were surprised to find their daughter had lost herself in the family group when they arrived at the Parliament. In view of her subdued mood they had expected that she would stay close to them.

At the appointed time, Crystal's shuttle appeared and stopped by the main entrance. Katie appeared, dressed completely in black.

As she took a seat inside, all rose, and the Federation anthem played.

When it finished, she stood and said "Be seated".

For about half a minute, she looked at the assembly in front of her, knowing that an audience of many billions was also watching the scene, except that distance would delay their view.

"My people, for reasons which are not clear to me, the Bearing have requested that I undertake an immensely difficult, important and long-lasting task. Apparently, I am uniquely suited to the function.

"As it is totally uncertain when, and even if, I will be able to return permanently to the Federation, I am now formally abdicating as Empress."

There was a loud collective gasp, as an almost palpable sense of shock was felt by all the people in the building, and particularly Katie's family.

"Your new Empress will hold the same position in the Federation that I held, supported by Crystal, Sheila and Avenger. She will be able to communicate with the Bearing at will, and she will control the Ghost Fleet. In the case of a Federation emergency, she can rule by decree, and she will hold a veto on current legislation. She has assured me that use of the veto will be rare."

The doors at the main entrance to the building opened, and a young girl walked in with a golden cat on her shoulder and with platinum blonde hair. When she reached Katie she turned, and the nearer members of the Parliament could see that there were tears in her eyes.

Katie said, "People of the Federation, meet Sylvia, your new Empress."

For a moment there was a blaze of light behind the girl, and when it disappeared it was seen that Katie had also gone.

There was a rustle throughout the assembly, and a background murmur as people whispered to their neighbours.

Sylvia waited until silence again spread over the Parliament.

With a slight catch in her voice, she began; "People of the Federation, I greet you".

She then went on to give the speech that she had prepared, with a considerable amount of help from Katie.

Her parents realised that they knew that voice.

Much later that afternoon, they heard a knock at the door, followed by the sound of it opening. It was their daughter, back in her familiar jeans and normal hair colour. They simply gave her a long hug, aware that her life had changed immeasurably.

A little later in the kitchen, over a soft drink, she said; "Mum and Dad, I hope you don't mind, but I have taken the liberty of asking Auntie Caroline and Admiral Jenna around for a casual supper. I think we need to have a quiet discussion, and I must get to know the Admiral.

"By the way, I'm going to try hard to stay anonymous, which is why I appeared with a different hairstyle and name".

The invited individuals were respectively the Governor of Nova and the head of the Federation armed forces.

Her parents looked at her in amazement, the full realisation of the authority their daughter now held dawning on them. Before then, in some strange manner it had not registered.

The individuals concerned were enormously busy, and normally their schedules were prepared months in advance. Sienna had just swept their current arrangements aside.

"Don't worry about any catering: Crystal is providing dinner including appropriate food for Admiral Jenna, and several remotes to assist.

"I would like you both to listen as well, as I think I am going to need a great deal of help in the months ahead.

"Although I can go and live in the Crystal Palace straight away, I would much rather stay here for the time being. I also intend to complete the Federation College course; if my great-grandmother can get away with living on Europia almost indefinitely, I'm sure I can hide myself in the College here!"

* * *

Elsewhere, while there was a sense of regret and surprise at Katie's departure, it seemed clear that in the short-term nothing was going to change for most people.

Quietly observing the position, Katie was satisfied that her young protégé would quickly learn to cope. The administrative machinery which would let her stay completely in the background had been well established.

She could turn her attention elsewhere.

Chapter 2

PLANNING FOR WAR

KATIE RETURNED TO HER BEARING PLANNING group, and asked for an update on their progress.

She was shown two timelines running side-by-side prepared from the historic and imported earth databases.

Her main friend in the group, whose name approximated to Iva, said; "Katie, the first comparisons we prepared from the two databases did not show much divergence. There was only the flickering effect we mentioned. However, as we received later databases, catastrophic changes occurred for a time, with increasing divergence. The more recent databases are now almost stable.

"We have scoured our records for more information about Earth. Unfortunately, we cannot return ourselves and physically examine earth-based paper archives as we would also be embroiled in the chronon temporal disaster.

"It is only the firm instructions we left with the Bearing group in the vicinity of Earth which has enabled us to continue to receive the updates. The latter are deeply concerned about the request.

"As with ourselves, they were alarmed at the disappearance of the Oldest, and it is clear to them that they are in the midst of a temporal disaster.

"Although they have the instructions to continue to provide the databases, the original reason for the request has been obliterated from their history."

2a – Wiemar

As she familiarised herself with the general changes which were occurring in the Earth database, Katie considered the position.

She was horrified to find that a large part of the history she knew had disappeared.

The onset in 1929 of the great depression in the United States proved economically devastating to Germany. The slow and disjointed recovery between 1924 and 1929 came to a halt.

The Weimar Republic remained in place until 1930, when it became completely dysfunctional and government by presidential decree started.

In the original history, there was frustration with the continuing foreign control of what was regarded as parts of Germany. Coupled with the pain of further reparations, economic deflation and depression this led to the rise of the Nationalsozialistische Deutsche Arbeiterpartei, better known as the Nazi party. Rule by presidential decree was a gift to this organisation; a determined charismatic leader with little regard for due process did not take long to move his eventual position as Chancellor to one of dictator. The rearmament program started to rebuild prosperity, and reoccupation of the Rhineland cemented his popularity.

In the new history, the whole process was drawn out over nearly a decade. There had been occasional threats and disturbances from both extreme left-wing and extreme right wing parties, but the absence of any driving personality had allowed some form of the rule of law to continue. In the meantime, Soviet Russia under Stalin had grown stronger. It once again invaded Finland in 1939, with a similar result to the original history.

The war put the Russians on notice that their armed forces needed major reorganisation and rebuilding from the officer purges of the 1930s. This was gradually implemented.

Russia became the dominant power in continental Europe, and began to successfully support left-wing groups in a number of countries. Most of continental Europe gradually became Communist.

By the time the United States and Britain took serious notice, it was too late.

Europe had effectively become a group of Russian protectorates.

In the Far East, Japan dominated with its brutal and fanatical armies. It managed to occupy most of China, which was greatly assisted by the lack of any Russian or Western support for the Nationalists. A takeover of Vietnam, Cambodia, and Laos followed. It then absorbed Hong Kong and attacked Burma, as it was then known.

A weak British government was unable to provide any effective resistance. It was already under nationalist threat in India, and it only held a tenuous control of Malaya.

As soon as they had consolidated control elsewhere, the Japanese had no difficulty in occupying the latter.

With control of Burmese oil, and Malayan rubber and tin, the Japanese managed to avoid antagonising or attacking the USA.

The world was effectively divided into three broad partitions – Russian, Japanese and the Americas plus Britain.

Although the Bearing had provided a Habitat equivalent, the individual selected as overseer had been completely unrelated to Katie's family and had not proved effective.

When the Calai had arrived, no proper defence had been offered, Earth had been brutally occupied and the Habitat had fled. A large part of the population had perished.

Thereafter, the transferred database had become incoherent, and no information was available.

Iva explained, "As the change chronons move forward in time, their strength diminishes and it becomes increasingly difficult for 'outsiders' to receive information which is understandable. Our theory of how this occurs is not satisfactory. We suspect that the Oldest had a much greater knowledge of the process, but for unknown reasons refused to share it with us."

2b – Search for German changes

Finally, Katie came to a decision and said to the Bearing group: "Looking at the databases, the start of the disaster seems to be located in Europe in the early 1930s. However, I suspect that its roots lie earlier, by perhaps several decades.

"I think we absolutely need more information.

"The more recent updates we have received are no longer showing major changes to the temporal pattern.

"We must risk sending a message to the Earth-based Bearing group. They must collect all the historical information which is available in Western Europe in museums, newspaper archives, or wherever, for the period from the beginning of the First World War until the middle of the 1930s.

"I'm not sure whether collecting the information, or analysing it, will be harder, but I think our communities on both sides of the temporal divide are going to be fully occupied for some time.

"I think Aon has an enormous advantage, in that she can organise some apparently inconsequential event which will take effect perhaps decades later. Finding that event is not like looking for a needle in a haystack, to use an Earth based simile, but more like finding a needle in a Prairie."

* * *

As extra information started to arrive from Earth, the enormity of the task became apparent. The Bearing group were trying to identify a small critical change from a one sided database covering millions of people. Moreover, that database was disjointed, with large gaps.

No comparable detail was available on the original database which had been taken to Nova.

After a week of research, the only conspicuous point of difference was the nonappearance of the National Socialist party in Germany, better known as the Nazis. Trying to track the lives of the approximately half million people who had possibly contributed to the party's rise was proving extremely difficult. In the age before computers, little real information was available as most data had been kept on paper records which were gone.

The next day, Iva contacted Katie; "We have found a possible search strategy which may simplify our task.

"Aon would only have had our Nova based data available when she started, and would have used that database to identify critical events or divertants. We think she will only be able to find the latter if they are identified at a particular location at an approximate time.

"We will follow the same approach, and see what is revealed. Even the poor quality of the most recent database we have received should enable us to identify the crucial points."

It did not take long to identify the divergence. *It was immediately apparent that the founder and driving force of the Nazi party had never appeared.*

With a focus for their efforts, the Bearing group soon found that Adolf Hitler had died in November 1916 in a military hospital in a small town called Beelitz about 40 km south-west of Berlin, from wounds received in the battle of the Somme.

With Aon clearly lurking in the background, it became apparent that the task of the group was to preserve Hitler's life.

The prospect of keeping alive one of the most evil men in all of history did not appeal to Katie at all, but the consequences of his premature death were worse.

* * *

Iva showed Katie the machinery of what she had described as the "Time Machine", and explained how it was linked to a supergiant star at the far side of the galaxy, from which it absorbed the required energy.

"Katie, the theoretical basis of the machine is complex, and there is no need for you to have more than a broad understanding of how it functions. Like your small remote, it has been linked to you through all of time and space. However, for reasons we do not understand, it will not go into the future beyond the time it was first used.

"What may complicate matters for you, is a note we hold from the original builders of the machine. When it is used the individual concerned is likely to initially suffer what has been described as 'temporal shock'. Subsequent usage gradually acclimatises the individual's physiology, and the shock period lessens.

"This means that it is possible that you will lose almost all of your memories when you arrive in Germany apart from basic living and language skills. These will slowly return, but the process will take up to 2 years. Extreme necessity may force a particular skill to reappear, and your body will automatically revert to foldspace if too threatened.

"However, if that happens it may take you a long time to reclaim your position in time and space, and may give Aon some warning of what is happening.

"Your remote will remain with you, and may be able to provide some limited assistance. However, it has little power at its disposal.

"As your mental facilities return, it will be able to provide appropriate advice and information.

"By the way, an important point is that when you move back in time, you will need to move from a location near the Federation to avoid being involved in the chronon disaster.

"When you have moved back far enough, you can cross over to old Earth. Your transit time will still be about a week. To return, the process is reversed.

"Fortunately, we can arrange for any queries to be handled by the same pathway, so they will be immune from interference. Adjustment of temporal placings will make any answer effectively instantaneous."

The Bearing group and Katie started to plan in detail. The critical location was clearly the military hospital, which was a converted sanatorium. She needed to be in place at the hospital in a responsible position comfortably before October 2016.

It took a large effort, but a way to ensure that she was delivered to the hospital in plenty of time to re-establish herself and ensure her memories had returned was identified.

She gave herself a refresher course in German, with a Bavarian accent. Deciding that it was most likely that Hitler had died of some form of septicaemia, she built a cheap looking necklace with a small heart shaped pendant which opened to show a picture of an attractive middle-aged woman. Hidden behind the picture, was a supply of a potent broad-spectrum antibacterial.

With an enormous feeling of apprehension, she realised she was ready to go to war.

Chapter 3

IMPERIAL GERMANY

THE BATTLE OF THE MARNE WAS not going well. After triumphant early advances in the bright September 1914 sunshine, the army had finally been halted by the combined British and French armies, and the number of casualties was rising rapidly. The initial belief of most of the German army, people and politicians thàt the war would be over in a few months was giving away to a realisation that victory would possibly need a long hard grind covering years. This was not going to be a repeat of the relatively rapid victories of the Franco Prussian War in 1870.

3a – Establishment in Germany

The old troop train carriage rattled on its tracks on the way back to Germany, and there were agonised groans from several of the soldiers lying on rough stretchers placed between the wooden seats.

There was a stench of blood, urine, and vomit.

Several nurses moved up and down the centre of the carriage, trying to make the soldiers more comfortable, and providing food, water and assistance when needed. Sometimes they were able to adjust blood stained bandages, but more often they felt it was better to leave them in place undisturbed. Some of the soldiers had already died, and others were unconscious. A dirty grey army blanket covered one of the casualties, who moaned faintly and was clearly trying to adjust his leg position. The nurse moved the blanket, and was surprised to find it covered a barely conscious woman in a nurse's uniform. There was a bloodstained bandage around her head and her arm was injured.

Blood had been seeping through the extensive arm bandages. The nurse could not fathom how the woman was on a military train, but decided a doctor at one of the rail stations had obviously decided that the individual was best dealt with elsewhere.

Looking more closely, she saw a label had been tied on to the woman's wrist. It said, "Nurse at one of our forward posts which was shelled, no identification found, patient unconscious."

There was an indecipherable doctor's signature next to the words, and a date one day earlier.

In a whisper, the woman asked for water, and then after drinking a little lapsed back into unconsciousness.

The train finally stopped at Potsdam, the casualties were unloaded and horse-drawn carriages were used to transport the survivors from the trip to the military hospital at Beelitz-Heilstätten.

A day later, the injured nurse regained consciousness. By then it was apparent that she was a girl who appeared aged in her late teens.

The middle-aged senior doctor asked for her name. She said in a weak, halting voice, "I don't remember, I don't remember anything, ...I think my name is Käthe".

The doctor said gently, "There is a locket round your neck, with a picture of a lady inside. Do you remember anything about her?"

"I think it is my mother Z.........".

The doctor realised his patient had drifted into unconsciousness again. He made a note that she was suffering from complete amnesia presumably from the shelling which had caused her injuries.

A few hours later Käthe was fully conscious, and was able to drink some water and a little soup. When her bandages had been changed, the attending doctor saw the deep and extensive wounds on her arm were healing well. The head injury was not so serious. However, it was clear that the girl had completely lost her memory, and even the memory of the name of her mother had faded. The army records were unable to make a probable identification, but as there had been a large amount of chaos and confusion in the front lines that was hardly surprising. There only remained the brief note on the label which had been attached to her wrist, the pendant round her neck, and a clearly Bavarian accent. None of these were of much assistance.

3b – Nurse

A week later, Käthe was able to move around reasonably freely. When asked, she tried hard to recall something about her background. She told the resident psychologist, "All I can remember is a big old wooden house in the mountains, with lots of stuffed animals and military portraits. There was also a large dog."

This description would fit a multitude of houses in Bavaria and Austria, and probably elsewhere. It was of no help in identifying the girl.

The psychologist told her, "As a temporary measure, I'm authorising the issue of new identity documents for you. We will use the name Käthe Marne, and the documents will note that you suffer from amnesia, and give an approximate age of eighteen."

Käthe was also getting bored. Once the bandages from the head wound had been removed, her bandaged arm was no more than an inconvenience, despite the deep wounds. She asked if she could help the nurses in the ward.

"After all, about the only thing I seem to know about myself is my first name and that I was a nurse. I might as well make myself useful."

As soon as she started helping the other nurses, it was apparent that she was highly skilled. It also soon discovered that she spoke perfect English.

Since she had no notional qualifications, she decided to take a nurses' examination which was due in about ten days. When she looked at the material, she realised that she knew it all, and far more.

When the date and time for the examination arrived, and she sat down, she realised the questions were almost trivially easy for her. She had to force herself to go back and check them properly when she had finished, but she still submitted her answers long before any of the other candidates had completed their papers.

The examining doctor looked at her in surprise, and was even more surprised when he marked the submissions and discovered she had achieved a perfect score.

Since there was a huge scarcity of trained nurses, she was immediately promoted to a staff nurse position. The senior doctor responsible for her ward was called Helmut Lang. He was surprised when she began to regularly offer quiet comments on patients to him. Initially put out, he quickly realised the suggestions were valuable.

A few days later, he was talking to his wife about this particular nurse. He told her how she was brought in unconscious and severely injured, with complete memory loss and absolutely no identification. The hospital administrator had not been able to find any details about her from the army records.

His wife looked at him, and said "The poor girl must be so distressed. You might consider suggesting that she comes and stays here at some point. However, you had better wait a week or so to make sure her memory doesn't return in that time, when she can be reunited with her family."

Käthe had initially been given a bed in the staff dormitory, but after two more weeks as a staff nurse, the senior doctor said to her; "Käthe, our son is away fighting on the Eastern front. We have a lot of spare space in our house, and my wife and I would be delighted if you would come and stay with us.

"I'm terribly sorry that none of your memories have returned, but our psychologist thinks that will happen eventually."

As the hospital dormitory was cold, draughty and impersonal, Käthe was happy to accept.

Helmut told her, "I will meet you after work with my pony and trap".

A little later, as she was getting together her few possessions, there was a piteous mew from the door of the dormitory and a small and bedraggled tabby cat came in.

Still mewing plaintively, it leapt on the bed and then, to her surprise, onto her shoulder. Its mew turned to a soft purr, and it licked her ear. There was something strangely familiar about the cat, and Käthe did not want to put the animal down and leave it in the dormitory.

It could not belong to anybody, as no pets were allowed in the building or any of the surrounds, and there were no other nearby houses.

Käthe had expected the cat to jump off her shoulder and go somewhere else when she started to leave, but the animal simply tightened its claws on her shoulder and continued to purr softly.

As she came outside, she saw that Doctor Lang was waiting.

Hesitantly, she said "Doctor, I have a large favour to ask, and I would entirely understand if you said no. This cat I have on my shoulder has just attached itself to me, and I would really, really like to look after it."

The doctor saw the girl looking at her with a terrible pleading in her eyes. He reflected that after the trauma she had been through, looking after a small animal would probably be helpful psychologically. Besides which, there was no other pet in his house and rats had started to be a problem.

He said, "That's fine, Käthe! Jump in, and we will get going. However, you had better hold the cat in your lap!

"It will take us about twenty minutes to get home, and my wife is really looking forward to meeting you. I think she misses our son terribly, and would like someone else to talk to."

His face turned sad for a moment.

"Also, our daughter died two years ago and she was about the same age as you. Please bear this in mind when you talk to her.

"Our house is in the pine forest, and it is rather isolated."

Mrs Lang was a plump, motherly hausfrau type, and was clearly delighted that someone was coming to stay. As soon as she saw Käthe holding on tightly to a small cat, all her mothering instincts came to the fore.

A little later, Käthe found herself in a comfortable upstairs room, with a good view over the forest.

Mrs Lang had said, "Sadly, our daughter died two years ago, but I kept all her clothes and things. You are welcome to use them."

Katie was really grateful for the offer, as she had almost no clothes and only one pair of shoes.

She gave herself a wash with the help of a large bowl of warm water, and for the first time she had a sense that she had found a home, and something inside her started to relax.

A little cat was sipping milk from a saucer in the corner.

She brushed and loosened her hair and changed into a dress which fitted her surprisingly well. When she came downstairs she found the doctor and his wife seated in the kitchen around a wood stove. It was late September, and at night there was a distinct chill in the air.

Doctor Lang said, "Welcome again, Käthe. You must call us Helmut and Mathilde. Would you like something to drink before supper?"

They were pleased at how different she looked. Having her hair completely pinned back and wearing the scruffy and ill fitting nurse's uniform at the hospital had done her no favours.

A proper cleanup, a little grooming, a much nicer dress, and the way she had let her hair down changed her appearance completely. She now looked like a slightly built but attractive young woman. A few minutes later, the cat reappeared. It also seemed to be completely revitalised and freshly groomed. It gave a little mew, rubbed itself against her legs, and then padded across to Mathilde and jumped on to her lap. It settled itself down, and its purrs grew louder as Mathilde stroked it.

There was an easy and unforced discussion for a few minutes, when Käthe said, "Mathilde, while Helmut did not suggest any charge for me staying here, I would like to make a reasonable contribution for my board and lodging and the use of the clothes and facilities in the room, for which I am ever so grateful. Would about half my weekly income be sufficient?"

Neither the doctor or his wife had thought about this at all, and were both aware that nursing salaries were a pittance. Mathilde immediately said, "Käthe, that would be fine. If you find that does not leave you enough to live on, please let me know and we will reduce the figure."

After supper, the family usually retired to the living room. There was an unfinished chess game laid out on a table in the centre. Helmut saw Katie looking at it with interest. He said, "Several of the senior staff at the hospital play, and we have formed a small chess club. That is an unfinished game from when one of the younger doctors came over last week. I am afraid he is gradually breaking down my defence."

He was surprised when she answered, with a voice in a different timbre and with a level of authority he had never heard in it before, "From your position, the game is easily winnable. Your opponent has left a serious flaw in his own defence. You need to move your bishop to K6, when his position will be hopeless."

The doctor saw Käthe shake her head slightly, and she said in her ordinary voice, "Did I just say something?"

Helmut did not respond for a moment. His mind was concentrating on the move which had just been suggested, and he saw that the suggestion was completely valid.

"Your voice changed, and you made a move suggestion which in all likelihood will easily win the game for me.

"Can you remember anything else?"

The doctor saw Käthe concentrating for a moment, when she looked at him with a depth of anguish in her voice. "I'm sorry, Helmut; I now have a complete memory of how to play chess, but I can't remember even talking to you. It's as if most of my mind has been walled off from me, and there is so much more that I ought to know and remember. You have no idea how awful this is for me."

He decided to try and raise her spirits a little.

"Never mind Käthe, at least something is starting to come back. By the way, that young doctor I mentioned is coming back tomorrow evening to finish the game. He is going to be surprised.

"I think I am going to suggest to him that he plays a game with you. I suspect he is in for a shock."

3c – Erwin

The following evening, the young doctor that Helmut had mentioned arrived on his horse just in time for supper. When Käthe entered the room, he did not recognise her as a nurse at the hospital. As a member of the Junkers class, he had regarded nurses as little more than servants, and had tended to simply look through them and avoid any conversation apart from professional necessities. He had all the arrogance of youth, wealth and a high social position.

Helmut said, "Käthe, can I introduce you to Doctor Erwin von Hessen.

"Hans, this is Käthe Marne, whom you will remember was brought in desperately injured about a month ago."

The young doctor looked in astonishment at the slightly built and attractive young woman in front of him. Unusually he remembered her case, as casualties with her level of injuries rarely survived. If from nothing else, they usually died from septicaemia. Also, her complete memory loss had been the focus of some interested discussion in the doctors' common room.

Over supper, despite his initial disdain he discovered the young nurse had a lively and interesting personality. Her manners were perfect, and he quickly realised that she had to have had at least a prosperous middle class background.

After supper, the group moved into the lounge area, where Helmut had the distinct pleasure of demolishing his guest's chess position. The game was over in five minutes.

He followed this up by saying, "Erwin, I understand that Käthe also plays. If she agrees, would you like to play a demonstration game with her? You normally defeat me easily, and I was fortunate to have found a hole in your defence."

Erwin nodded, and when asked, Käthe also agreed. She wanted to play for real as she felt this might help her memory recover.

However, as the board was being set up, she received a clear thought in her mind.

"Käthe, it is important that you mask your true ability at this game. You will annoy the young doctor if you defeat him too easily, and that will be most undesirable."

It seemed to her a strange thought for her subconscious to dredge up, and she had not expected to even give the doctor a serious game. However, the thought made sense if she really was that good.

As the game started, Katie found that as she concentrated, the whole position on the board became clear to her. Half a dozen moves into the game, she realised it would not take long to checkmate her opponent.

She decided she had to prolong the agony, and deliberately made some bad moves.

On the other side of the table, Erwin had been disconcerted by the sheer ability being demonstrated by his opponent. Embarrassing as it was to him, he realised his position was falling into a heap when the girl made some poor moves. This enabled him to recover his positional advantage.

However, it still took him nearly half an hour before Käthe toppled her queen.

Later on, as he was being escorted to his horse, he said "I was impressed with Käthe, Helmut. If she has a husband somewhere, I think he is a lucky man."

His host laughed. "Erwin, I can assure you that Käthe is not married. I had to examine her very carefully when she first came in, and she is ……… intact."

When he went back indoors, Käthe had the cat on her lap, and was telling Matilda how much she had enjoyed the supper. She asked how the dessert course had been prepared.

When the pair had stopped talking, Käthe saw Helmut looking at her rather strangely.

"Käthe, I hate to say this, but I think you pulled the game with Erwin. If you had gone on playing at the level you demonstrated in the first half dozen moves, the game would have been over in short order. I hope he does not realise that, when he thinks about the match.

"You don't have to answer the implied question, but I think you were sensible."

Käthe decided she better not play any more games of chess for the time being. The doctor was just too perceptive.

* * *

Helmut had insisted on a final look at her arms before he certified her as completely fit. He was surprised to find that the terrible wounds on her arm had not only healed perfectly, but the associated scars were starting to fade away. He realised that in a few weeks, at the current rate of progress they would disappear completely. Most injuries of the sort the girl had suffered would have led to permanent scarring.

Käthe was also feeling a need for far more exercise. She discovered that Mathilde's daughter had also owned a pair of old running shoes, and she asked if they could be borrowed.

Initially, she had only gone a short distance. However her endurance seemed to be recovering so fast that she quickly extended her early morning runs.

Mathilde had been surprised at how long she was taking on these excursions. It was now October, and there was normally frost in the mornings. Staying out for an hour in nothing but running shorts would leave Käthe dangerously cold.

The girl would not have run continuously, as she would probably have dropped to a walk for most of the time. A week after the runs had started, Mathilde casually asked Käthe how far she had gone.

"About 10 km I think, to the village and back."

Mathilde looked at her in astonishment.

That evening, Helmut had been browsing in a drawer at the back of the lounge, and to get at the back he had pulled out various items.

Amongst these was an old flute. Käthe looked at it, and a fleeting memory tugged at her. She could not help asking if she could borrow it.

As she picked it up, a strangely familiar tune came into her mind, which she started to play.

Helmut and Mathilde listened with some amazement. The girl was clearly an extraordinary flute player, playing a tune they had never heard before.

When she finished, Mathilde said, "Käthe, that was played beautifully. I have never heard that tune before. What is it called?"

Käthe answered, once again in a voice with a completely different timbre, "That is the Anthem of the Outer Arm Federation, which I wrote."

As before, Hans saw her look confused for a moment. "What did I just say? There seems to be another hole in my memory."

Hans answered; "You said 'That is the Anthem of the Outer Arm Federation, which I wrote.' We assume that you have as little idea as we do of what that actually means."

Käthe could only look at her kindly hosts with a sense of despair gripping her. She hoped that her memory would repair itself in the future, and that she was not going insane. She also realised that a large repertoire of music had opened up in her mind.

* * *

Despite himself, Doctor Erwin von Hessen had been more than impressed with the girl at the Lang household. Something about her had really intrigued him, despite her lowly position as a nurse.

He woke in the small hours of the morning with a niggling thought in his mind; the contrast in the way the girl had played in the first half dozen moves in the game, with her much weaker subsequent performance.

He managed to get himself invited back several times over the next two weeks, using chess as the excuse. The reason for the visits had not fooled Helmut for one moment.

Käthe had firmly refused to play any more chess games, but could not resist being an observer.

At the end of the third session she had watched, Helmut had managed to win the game.

Erwin asked, "Käthe, I saw you watching closely. Where do you think I went wrong?"

When she replied, the timbre of her voice changed, and her soft comment had enormous authority. "Erwin, you went wrong four moves from the end."

To the astonishment of the two men, Käthe rearranged the board.

"This was the position at that point, and you should have castled your king. Helmut could still win if he had immediately brought up his bishop like this, but otherwise the game would have been wide open."

Käthe indicated where the bishop should move.

She then looked confused, and said in her normal voice, "Helmut, what have I just said, and how did the board get like that?"

Questioned, once again she had absolutely no memory of the last few minutes. Erwin was fascinated.

Later on, when Helmut had returned after seeing Erwin back to his horse, he found Käthe looking at some of his more advanced surgical textbooks. Mathilde was knitting in the chair opposite her.

"Käthe, those books are much too difficult for you – if you are interested why don't you look at some of the more introductory medical texts?"

She answered without thinking, "Helmut, I know all of this, but so much of what is written here is wrong."

She looked up in anguished surprise, "Please Helmut, I am sure what I said is true, but how can I possibly know it?"

He said, "I'll tell you what, I will ask you questions about some of the sections and we will see if you really do understand".

Mathilde had put down her knitting, and was listening with interest. She had become rather attached to the girl, who was becoming a sort of substitute daughter to her, and she was also hoping that some form of insanity was not creeping in.

As Helmut started to question Käthe on various points in the book, it became obvious that she really did know the material except in two cases when her answers were different.

When asked she said, "I know Helmut, my answers were different from the text, but I'm sure I'm right."

She then told him the textbook answers to the questions.

Later that evening as they were preparing for bed, Mathilde asked him, "Helmut, when Käthe was answering your questions, she was answering as if she absolutely knew the material.

"How on earth is that possible?"

Helmut looked at her and said, "If I had asked the doctors at our hospital those questions, most of them would not have answered as accurately as Käthe, which is extraordinary. She also has those strange lapses, when she speaks like someone else with vastly greater knowledge and authority, but can't remember afterwards what she has just said. It may be that her real personality is starting to break through.

"However, I think you should keep those comments to yourself."

Mathilde smiled slightly. "I have noticed that Erwin keeps coming over, and I'm sure he is becoming really interested in the girl despite his Junkers background.

"I hope Käthe appreciates his interest."

3e – Move to domesticity

The following Sunday morning, Erwin was taking his horse for a dawn ride. He was surprised to see a girl in shorts running towards him down the path which skirted the pine forest. Even at a distance of several hundred meters, she was clearly a natural athlete, and was moving easily and quickly. As she approached, he suddenly realised it was Käthe.

She pulled up when she reached him, and greeted him cheerfully despite her panting.

"Good morning Erwin, it is so nice to see you here. I didn't think there would be anyone else around at this ungodly hour of the morning!"

He smiled, and said "Good morning to you as well, Käthe. I had no idea you were so athletic!

Without thinking at all he added, "My stable and house are about half a kilometre back along the path. It's a bit forward of me, but would you like to come in for a coffee before you continue?"

"The staff always have a pot ready for me when I return."

Käthe laughed, "Thank you, that sounds like a lovely idea. I hope you have an old coat I can borrow as soon as I get in, as otherwise I will be a bit cold. I can run behind you as long as you don't ride too quickly."

The housemaid was surprised to see Doctor von Hessen return with a girl in running shorts, but recovering quickly she found a thick old coat. It was many sizes too large for Käthe, and a little smelly, but also warm. As she put it on, he noticed that the terrible scars on her arm had almost disappeared.

She chatted happily to Erwin for about twenty minutes while she finished her coffee and then said, "Erwin, thank you for the coffee. I must get back now, as Mathilde will be wondering where I have got to, and we are going to church later on this morning.

"Auf wiedersehen!"

As she ran back to the path, Erwin watched her go. He was realising that he was deeply attracted to her, but wondered how his parents would react to a girl with a totally unknown background if they were introduced.

* * *

It had become obvious that the war was going badly on the Western front. The government had increased taxation levels, and ordinary goods as well as luxuries were becoming scarce. More and more of the local men were being called up for Army service. There were also a growing number of deserters and refugees from the East to be found in the bigger towns.

Hardship and impoverishment were spreading rapidly, even amongst the wealthier sections of the community.

Casualties amongst officers had been particularly high, and social distinctions were being levelled downwards.

The hospital had been under increasing pressure. A number of the male cleaners and maintenance staff had gone to war, while the number of casualties was growing rapidly. To try and cope, local girls and women from the age of 17 to middle age were being recruited to help. Käthe had been promoted to the position of matron of a new ward. A substantial part of her time had been given over to training the new nurses, including those from elsewhere. It had been found that she was an effective lecturer. For some of the classes on battlefield injuries, even some of the doctors had attended, ostensibly to assist with more difficult questions. Their services had not been required. The new matron seemed to have a complete knowledge of the subject, to a level which even some of the doctors found interesting.

By late November, Erwin had long since given up any pretence that he was just coming over for a game of chess, and had invited Käthe out for dinner several times. With her promotion, it did not seem to him that there was any longer any associated social stigma. It had been quietly recognised that the hospital's newest matron was remarkable.

One Saturday evening, he had taken her to Potsdam to watch a play. Afterwards, they were walking back to the horse and trap discussing the performance; Käthe was displaying a detailed knowledge of acting. They were startled when three roughly dressed men ran out of a side lane and threatened them with knives.

Erwin was paralysed for a moment, as he had no experience of this sort of situation, but the girl next to him stepped forward straight away and said in that strangely different and authoritative voice, "Depart immediately, or you will find yourselves severely injured."

The men had looked frightened, and turned on their heels and fled.

Erwin was astonished; he did not know that the men had seen a woman in front of them with brightly glowing eyes.

Käthe had stepped back, and looked dazed for a moment. She held on to him tightly, and said with a normal but shaky voice, "What happened?"

Carefully omitting to describe what Käthe had done or said, he said, "Three men threatened us with knives and then suddenly ran away."

The girl said, "Oh Erwin, you must have been so brave!", and he found himself on the receiving end of a most passionate kiss. He felt no inclination whatsoever to say what had really happened.

As she reluctantly finished kissing him, Käthe suddenly realised that she had acquired a large knowledge of hand to hand combat, and knew she could have easily disarmed the men. As she pondered this, a thought came into her mind, "It would be a bad idea to tell anyone about your unarmed combat skills".

Erwin was remembering that Helmut had mentioned that every time he had seen Käthe go into one of these changed voice episodes, she seemed to come out with a new set of skills. He wondered what had really happened.

Realising their relationship had changed irreversibly, the pair walked back to the trap in silence.

On the way back, holding his hand under the thick blankets in the trap, she said to Erwin, "Darling, you have no idea how disconcerting it is for me to keep having these strange memory lapses. Also, I really hoped someone from my unknown family would have asked the Army about me by now, as I have been 'missing' for several months.

"By the way, I have decided to give a series of little concerts at the hospital over Christmas. A singing group has been organised, and we will go around the wards with Christmas carols. I will be playing the accompanying flute as I seem to have remembered a lot of music."

Erwin smiled, "You will also get to meet my parents, as they are coming over here for the last ten days in December. They realised that I would not be able to get away to see them otherwise.

"I apologise, but I think I mentioned in my last letter that I was taking someone out regularly. They are probably rather curious!"

In fact his parents were more than curious. Their son had been too intelligent and supercilious for all of the girls they knew he had seen, and relationships had not prospered. With a dangerous war in progress, they were feeling an understandable desire for grandchildren. Up to that point, there had seemed little prospect of these, and they had agreed between themselves to be welcoming to almost any girl to whom Erwin wished to introduce them.

* * *

Over breakfast the following morning, Käthe was telling Helmut and Mathilde about the play, leaving out the subsequent more dramatic action.

She blushed slightly and added, "Erwin's parents are coming over for Christmas. He wants me to meet them."

Matilda gave her a big smile, "I don't know what the customs are in whatever part of Germany you came from, Käthe, but for Erwin to want to introduce you to his parents is a big step.

"As a Christmas present, you and I will visit a dressmaker in Potsdam next week."

3f – Emergence

Just before Christmas, an exceptional number of casualties started arriving from somewhere called Givenchy.

On the assumption that there would be a lull in the fighting over Christmas, the hospital administrator had given a number of the nurses and doctors leave to go home for a week.

As a result, the hospital was ill-prepared for the influx.

Helmut and Erwin were the two doctors remaining for most of the weekend. The latter had worked all night and most of the day, and had been forced to go home from sheer exhaustion. His parents had been shocked at his condition when he returned, and despite having only just arrived simply told him to go and sleep.

Käthe had distributed the few nurses around the various wards, and she and Helmut constituted the surgery team who were to look after three desperately injured soldiers. There was no one else available.

Helmut had patched up the first soldier, but Käthe could see he was nearing total exhaustion.

As he prepared for the second unconscious soldier, who needed a leg amputated as it was already gangrenous, she could see his hands shaking.

Something inside her made a decision, and he heard her say in the entirely different voice timbre with which he had become familiar, "Doctor, let me take over. I have vastly more experience than you in surgery, even in these primitive conditions. Käthe will not be aware of what has happened, but when this operation is finished the surgical memory segment I have unblocked will remain with her. You must not allow her to conduct any other operations even though she will have the capability, as she will become too conspicuous.

"You may tell Mathilde about this conversation, but absolutely no one else."

Helmut was so tired and shaken, that he simply change places with Käthe. She started by wiping dilute Lugol's solution over everything.

"The dilute potassium tri-iodide will help sterilise the area. I'm going to remove the leg just below the knee. Be ready with the clamps."

The girl used the quick and precise cuts of an expert surgeon, and where major blood vessels were exposed they were efficiently handled. Every few seconds, the Lugol's solution was dripped over everything. The bones were severed and the flesh folded over. Helmut had never seen quicker or neater sutures tied. Finally, yet more iodide was wiped over the whole area which was bandaged.

Helmut also noticed that Käthe's eyes were glowing slightly, and wondered if he was hallucinating.

Käthe moved on to the third soldier, and then they wheeled the three patients up to the only ward which still had spare beds.

An hour later, another doctor arrived to handle the night shift.

After they had formally handed over control, the entity who had been helping him said, "Doctor, you and Käthe must go home now. I will release her when she is about halfway there. She will be confused as there will be a large memory gap. Just tell her she assisted you. Remember – you may only tell your wife."

Mathilde had been horrified at the condition of the pair when they returned, totally exhausted and with heavily bloodstained clothing. She made them eat a quick meal, and then helped Käthe up to her room and out of her clothing. The girl just collapsed into her bed and was clearly falling asleep even as Mathilde pulled over the covers. The cat jumped on to the bed next to her and lay down.

She was about to make a further re-arrangement of the cover, when the cat hissed at her. It clearly wanted no further disturbance.

Mathilde looked at the cat, and murmured "Protective little monster, aren't you. Very well, I'll leave her alone!"

The cat changed its hiss to a purr.

Downstairs, Helmut had just finished his meal. Although utterly exhausted, he could not stop himself relating to Mathilde what had happened.

She said to him, "My dear, in your current condition there was a chance you were hallucinating. Whether or not that is the case, we will not say anything to anyone.

"Perhaps the strangest thing of all, was that this apparent being used the expression 'primitive conditions'.

"Primitive conditions compared to what?"

At that, Mathilde helped put her husband to bed as well.

The following morning, neither Helmut or Käthe were fully recovered from their exhaustion, but dragged themselves to the hospital as soon as possible.

The night doctor was most relieved to see them, as it had been a harrowing night. A dozen soldiers had died, but that group did not include the three operated on by Helmut and Käthe. The latter were still unconscious, but appeared as stable as could be hoped.

Soon after they arrived, Erwin came down from another ward. He had returned some hours before them.

He asked if he could leave a little earlier that afternoon, "My parents have just arrived, and I have hardly seen them for two days. I must attempt to be sociable."

Helmut was called urgently to another ward, and Käthe was about to wish Erwin goodbye, when he said, "Käthe, tomorrow is Christmas Eve. Would you like to come over for supper, and meet my parents?

"I would pick you up at about 6 o'clock in the trap."

Käthe nodded after a moment, adding; "I would love to meet them Erwin, but you must promise to get me home by 11 o'clock as I will have to be up early the following morning."

* * *

At home that evening, Erwin's parents were delighted that they were at last able to talk to him on a reasonable basis over supper. They were beginning to appreciate the extreme pressure he was under at the hospital. In their view, it was improving his character as he was far more civil to his servants at the house than he had been at the ancestral home.

After the first course, his mother asked; "Erwin, you have not said a word about this girl you have been seeing, according to your last letter. Could we have just a little more information about what she is like?"

Erwin had been rather dreading this moment. "Well ………. You see I first met her when she came in as a desperately injured and unconscious nurse three months ago from the Western front.

"She recovered amazingly well, except that she suffered complete amnesia. Moreover, the army has been unable to identify her. This is not surprising as there was complete chaos at the front when she was shelled at a forward nursing post. Strangely, no one seems to have come forward from her family to identify her.

"She is extremely upset about that, as well as her memory lapse.

"She has proved such an excellent nurse that she has been promoted to be matron of one of the wards despite being too young for the position.

"The administrator was at first a little uncertain about whether she would be able to cope, as there were some pretty hard-bitten nurses in the group. He needn't have worried …………. In three days she had that ward running like clockwork. The other nurses are not exactly scared of her; totally overawed might be a better description. That seems to include some of the young doctors who have only just come from medical school."

At this point, his parents were getting the impression of a heavily built woman with a formidably strong character. This was unusual as their son had normally favoured slim girls.

His mother smiled encouragingly. "We're not so worried about the amnesia – I read somewhere that it normally clears itself after a while. I hope she is bright enough to take you on!"

To their surprise, their son blushed slightly.

"She plays chess, and although she has never beaten me in a game, I strongly suspect that she could wipe the floor with me if she wanted to. I don't know why, but she has been careful to avoid that."

His mother reflected to herself that this woman was showing a considerable understanding of her son.

"Anyhow, I have invited her over tomorrow evening so you will be able to form your own impression."

He looked anxious for a moment.

"Please try hard to give her a good impression of you both".

Bearing in mind their position in society as large-scale landowners, that seemed to be a strange statement for their son to make. Both parents decided that Erwin must be really serious about this girl.

* * *

It was snowing lightly the following evening when Erwin arrived to collect Käthe. She came out immediately he arrived wearing a heavy greatcoat with a hood, and long leather boots. She was also carrying a small bag, obviously for shoes.

Giving him a quick kiss she said, "We better hurry Erwin, as it's so cold I'm not sure how long I will stay warm in this coat.

She looked rather nervous for a moment, "I admit I'm a bit scared about meeting your parents for the first time. I'm sure you've told them I'm an amnesiac with an unknown family!"

Erwin laughed, "I'm absolutely certain you will cope really well. Be warned, I also told them to be on their best behaviour with you!"

When they arrived, Erwin's parents could not see much of the girl as she hurried up to the front porch in a snow covered and hooded greatcoat.

Inside, as the greatcoat was peeled off her, both Erwin and his parents were astonished. She was wearing a beautiful slim fitting dress with a small necklace that Erwin realised Mathilde must have lent her. Slightly built and attractive, she was completely different from what his parents had expected from the description.

Erwin said, "Käthe, meet my mother Hilda and my father Doctor Albrecht von Hessen."

Over dinner, the family group quickly relaxed and conversation was lively and unforced.

Owen's father said to Käthe, "We understand you speak English. I speak it well as I have commercial connections in America and elsewhere. Try speaking a little to me, and I might be able to identify where you learnt."

The girl happily obliged, and the two chatted away for a few minutes.

When they finished talking, Albrecht thought for a moment. "It is strange, your English is perfect but your accent is not like any I've heard before. You sound a little like an Australian I once met, but it is different from that.

"I'm sorry Käthe, but I really don't think I can help."

When Erwin had left to take Käthe home, Albrecht said to his wife "I have to admit the girl made a considerable impression on me."

Hilda replied, "I hope we have just seen a future daughter-in-law. We were handled beautifully, and the girl must have an at least equivalent social background to our own.

"I'm looking forward to listening to the singing group that Käthe has apparently organised for tomorrow."

When Erwin returned, his father said to him "We were impressed."

His son looked at him for a moment; "I'm glad to hear it."

"She just agreed to be my wife."

* * *

Erwin had to leave for the hospital early on Christmas morning. He told his parents there would be a short carol service at about 5 o'clock in the afternoon, just after dark. He would then take Käthe back to Doctor Lang's house for a Christmas dinner.

"I'll be back as soon as possible after dropping Käthe off, but I expect Mathilde will insist I have a drink and some titbits before I leave."

Just after lunch, Käthe and her small group of nurses put on completely cleaned uniforms, with some festive additions. For once, Käthe let her hair run long and loose over her shoulders.

They then visited each of the wards in turn, singing a little selection of Christmas carols. Käthe provide the accompanying flute music, with a little solo performance at the end. For many of the soldiers, it was almost heartbreaking, and especially for those who knew they were dying.

One of the soldiers murmured to his comrade in the adjacent bed, as the little group of nurses left, "That was a magical performance, especially with matron as the flute player. I must be hallucinating, but I would swear that her eyes were glowing slightly as she played."

When the singing group had finished with the wards they had a short break to recover, and waited for darkness to descend completely.

Outside, it was clear and cold, and crystals of fresh snow glittered in the faint light from a crescent moon.

All the hospital staff who could be spared including the doctors and administrators, assembled in the hospital outside forecourt, which was illuminated with soft lighting around the edges. This included Erwin's parents. They were greatly looking forward to greeting Käthe as their future daughter-in-law.

The nursing group filed out, this time wearing heavier coats and gloves, and started their performance.

For about twenty minutes, they sang their way through all the favourite German Christmas carols, accompanied by that magical flute.

At the end, Käthe stepped forward and said. "We would like to thank everyone for coming to listen to us. I would like to finish by playing our national anthem."

One of the other doctors, who was an excellent amateur musician, said softly to one of his colleagues, "I don't think I've ever heard flute playing of that standard before."

As she finished, she said "Merry Christmas", as her group was enthusiastically applauded.

One of the other matrons who had been listening, stepped forward and said, "Käthe, you and your little group have put on the most beautiful performance. We have had words of appreciation from the soldiers in every ward you visited.

"As an encore, could you please play us one more tune?"

Käthe smiled and said, "All right, I will play one final tune, which is one of my favourites."

As she started, Helmut recognised the tune called the 'Anthem of the Outer Arm Federation'. It was clearly important to her, as tears started to slide down her face.

When she finished, Erwin and his family rushed up to her and his mother gave her a big hug.

"We are so pleased to hear of your engagement to Erwin, Käthe. That was a wonderful performance!"

She smiled, but then her face went blank, and the flute fell from her hand. Erwin was just quick enough to catch her as she fainted.

Helmut and Mathilde rushed up as well. The two doctors looked at each other, then Helmut said "We had better get her home straight away; Käthe appears to have fainted."

Erwin looked at his parents, "I will go with Helmut, I will be back home as soon as possible."

Käthe was put on the back of the carriage, wrapped in blankets, and when they reached home she was carried up to her room, undressed and placed in the bed. The small cat was very much in evidence, making soft distressed mews.

Mathilde went downstairs to make up a hot water bottle. As she left the room, Käthe's eyes flickered open and she said in her strange timbre voice, "Käthe has gone into another episode of temporal shock. This was brought on by playing the Anthem, for which she has powerful buried emotions. It will be a few hours before she is fully conscious again, and when that happens she will be completely disorientated. She will have regained some more of her memories.

"Helmut, as Erwin is her fiance you may tell him everything you know about her. She loves him dearly, and is the most ethical person you will ever meet.

"You must also know that she is from the distant future. I will block her from revealing any future history, as that would have catastrophic consequences.

"Take good care of her; she is extremely important."

The two doctors looked at each other in astonishment.

Erwin had the presence of mind to say, "What are you?"

The strangely timbred voice continued, "Käthe can exist in two states. The normal one is the girl you know and love. The other state which I represent is completely different, and in that form she is the most ruthless and dangerous person on this planet. Käthe does not like that state at all.

"At the moment, I have full control over our memories, but that will slowly change."

At that, Katie's eyelids shut, and she was clearly unconscious again.

Helmut said, "Those are amazing statements, but it makes her abilities as a surgeon understandable.

"Erwin, you will remember those three surgery cases that happened the other night when I was the only doctor on duty. You commented on how well they were faring this morning.

"In two of those cases, Käthe was the surgeon. I had reached the point of total exhaustion, and she just took over. Her ability is much greater than mine.

"I might add, that she understands all my medical textbooks. She made the observation that so much that is written in them is wrong."

Erwin was shaken to the core, and thought about what Helmut had said for a few minutes.

"I will return home for an hour or so, then I would like to come back here if that is all right with you.

"Could you ask Mathilde to make up a bed for me in the spare room?"

While Erwin was gone, Helmut told Mathilde what had happened.

She looked at him, worry evident in her face. "Either we are hallucinating, Käthe is insane, or something really important for the future must be happening here.

"Our young lady does not strike me as likely to suffer from insanity, and this hallucination feels altogether real."

About half an hour after Erwin returned, the two doctors were watching her when she started to show signs of waking again.

Her eyes opened, and she said in her normal voice; "Where am I, what has happened?"

She continued disjointedly, "Doctor at Oxford, surgeon in Kenya in the Egyptian Southern War;

"Lecturer at the Space Academy".

Horror and alarm leapt onto her face, "I remember, I'm in Germany in the early twentieth century as a nurse.

"How did I get here, and why do I feel it is so terribly important?"

She looked desperately at the two doctors, "There is so much I still don't remember – oh Erwin, I am so glad you're here!"

Helmut decided this was a good time to leave the couple on their own.

A small cat lay on the end of the bed, purring softly.

3g – Marriage

Käthe and Erwin were married six weeks later. Long engagements had gone out of fashion with a horrible war in progress. Also, the marriage would help ensure that they both could stay at the military hospital.

Helmut and Mathilde were happy to act as surrogate parents, and the wedding was quick and simple. It was increasingly difficult for medical staff to be away from the hospital.

They were terribly worried about their son, who was fighting somewhere in Eastern Europe in an area called the Masurian Lakes. It was clear that battles every bit as nasty as on the Western Front were being fought in the region.

1915 was an awful year for Germany. Food rationing had been imposed, and shortages of basic goods made life difficult. Horrifying casualties were being incurred.

Whenever major battles occurred, the hospital attempted to cope with waves of badly injured soldiers. In many cases, this included victims of gas attacks. Sometimes, care even had to be taken by nurses in undressing wounded soldiers, as traces of gas sometimes remained on clothing.

The hospital was operating with a minimum number of staff, as many had been transferred to the front lines.

Erwin and Helmut were amongst the few doctors remaining, and struggled to cope. Twelve hour days became the norm.

On several occasions when they came into Käthe's ward, they saw her holding the hand of a desperately injured soldier. Where the injury came from gas attacks, there was often little that could be done apart from making the soldier's death as comfortable as possible. They saw the tears in her eyes, and absolute fury on her face.

The other nurses had learnt to tread warily around her when she had that look.

The doctors frequently had to operate with only one nurse in attendance, the latter handling the crude anaesthesia arrangements. Some of the nurses noticed that in many of the most desperate cases, the surgical sutures were closer together and neater. A surprising number of those cases survived.

Nobody asked any questions.

Erwin's parents visited occasionally, but travel was becoming difficult and dangerous. They did what they could to help, but they knew their son and daughter-in-law were struggling to cope.

One Sunday afternoon in late autumn, Erwin came back from making a short walk. He was finding a terrible need to put some sanity back in his life by going out for walks in the open countryside.

When he returned, he found his wife sitting in a chair looking fixedly at the wood fire. Her cat was sitting on her lap, hissing faintly.

"What's the matter, Käthe?", he asked, pondering the many things that could be upsetting her.

She turned and looked at him for a moment, and he realised that something had changed. She was somehow older and more mature.

She stood up and came over to him, wrapping her arms around his neck.

"Darling, I'm afraid I have just recovered all my memories. I now know what I am, and why I came here.

"In order to do this, I abdicated from my position as Empress of the Outer Arm Federation. I was ruler of approximately 30 billion sentients, spread across dozens of planets thousands of light-years from here.

"I renamed as Käthe the tiny part of me which is still human. That is the woman you love and married."

Erwin saw the woman, if that was the correct description, look at him with what appeared to be enormous sadness, and he saw that her eyes were glowing slightly.

Shocked, he said, "What happens now?"

The entity that called itself Käthe said, "We must continue as we are for perhaps another year. Towards the end of that period, a seriously injured soldier will come here.

"An alien being called Aon will try desperately hard to ensure he dies. She must be stopped from succeeding in this."

Recovering a little, Erwin said "This soldier must have achieved a great deal to need such care".

The sorrowful answer was, "He became one of the most evil men in all of history, responsible for many tens of millions of deaths. And somehow, I must keep him alive.

"If he dies, most of the human race will also die in the not too distant future.

"You must never repeat this conversation, even to Helmut and Mathilde. They have more or less accepted me as I am, and that is sufficient."

Erwin thought about this for a few seconds. He desperately hoped that Käthe was not insane or that he was not hallucinating.

"Have you any idea what this alien will look like?"

She looked at him. "None at all, and it will only become apparent when I confront her, as any shape can be taken.

"My only possible help will be my cat, who is far more than it appears.

"Human assistance would be futile. Vast forces are balanced on edge here.

"In the meantime, it is imperative that I blend in as a matron of the hospital and your wife. Aon will be alert for anything or anyone who does not fit in perfectly. She could then attack at an earlier date, which might be difficult for me to stop."

* * *

A month later, an instruction came from Berlin that Doctor and Mrs von Hessen should visit the senior officer in charge of army hospital administration.

Once they had reached Berlin, the day had turned cold and foggy but fortunately it did not take long to find the grey old stone building.

Inside, there were ushered into a comfortable waiting room. A few minutes later, a middle-aged soldier in a grey uniform limped out of an office; one of his legs was clearly artificial. He wore an Iron Cross 2nd Class.

"Good morning, Doctor Erwin von Essen and Matron Käthe von Essen.

"I am Oberst Fritz von Klausen. You may remember me, as I was one of the casualties you treated at the end of last year.

"I'm sorry for dragging you away from the hospital, but I would like to have a discussion with you. As it is close to lunchtime, may I invite you to a restaurant across the road? I'm afraid the food is not up to the usual standard, due to wartime exigencies, but I hope you will find it acceptable."

Erwin was delighted to accept, and a little later they were all seated in a comfortable small restaurant. The Oberst was clearly well known to the staff.

After a little casual conversation, and serving of some drinks, Käthe saw that Fritz von Clausen was looking at her with some interest.

"You will not know this, but before the war I was a statistics lecturer at a Berlin university. When I took over my current position, I instituted a process whereby the mortality and injury figures of each of the hospitals under my control were collected. This enables me to monitor what you might describe as their quality of service.

"By whatever criteria I use, your hospital has an outstanding record. Soldiers who come to you are significantly more likely to survive than elsewhere. This is particularly the case when they have suffered severe injuries, like my own.

"Separately from this, a friend of mine is a senior surgeon at our best Berlin hospital. He was interested in the way my leg had been amputated, and asked if he could look."

There was a long pause. The soldier was aware that the two people in front of him were looking more and more concerned at the drift of the conversation.

"What I'm about to say to you, is entirely off the record. I am profoundly grateful for what you have done for me, and for a large number of the people you have treated.

"When this surgeon friend of mine examined the amputation, he was astonished. Apparently the way the wound had been bound over and stitched was completely different from current practice. He also said that the very small scars from the sutures indicated they had been made with extraordinary delicacy and precision. In his words, 'I doubt that my best handiwork would have been anywhere near as neat and precise.'

"There is also a persistent rumour that one of the surgeons at your hospital is …less than formally qualified."

There was a long pause in the conversation. Erwin looked nervous, and the colonel saw that the young and attractive matron was clearly thinking deeply as she sipped a glass of wine.

Finally Käthe said, and her voice had completely changed its timbre; "Oberst, Käthe and I have considered this, and we have decided to rely on your integrity and sense of gratitude.

"You are right in your supposition that we were one of the surgeons. As I have told Erwin, we are from the distant future, and we are here to ensure that one of your future casualties survives."

To his astonishment, the colonel saw that Käthe's eyes were glowing softly.

"We will not go into further details, but if a certain soldier dies, so will almost all of the human race through a causal chain.

"As for your comment about formal qualifications, with due modesty we can say that in the era from which we derive, we were considered as one of the great surgeons. Our knowledge and qualifications vastly exceed those of anyone currently alive on this planet."

The colonel was astounded, as the conversation had moved in a totally unexpected direction. Strangely, he believed what he was hearing, as the young woman's glowing eyes watched him.

He said, "I'm recommending that you both receive an award for services to medicine. I was also considering having you moved to one of our hospitals in Berlin.

"Matron, from what you have just said I assume that you know the future to some extent. This means that you know this soldier you have mentioned will be taken to your hospital when injured. I was also curious to note that you seem to have a ... binary type of personality.

"From this, I assume that you would not want to be moved?"

Erwin decided it was time he entered the conversation. He had been alarmed by Käthe's frank admissions. She would be jailed or worse if the colonel took action on the comments. However he also had a level of responsibility.

"Oberst, I absolutely stand by my wife's comments. I also admit complicity in her surgery. Her skills are much greater than mine. We have tried to ensure that she only handles the most difficult cases. It has been difficult to keep her role concealed, and obviously rumours have leaked.

"Käthe has absolutely refused to discuss future history with me, which on reflection I think I understand. She knows how this war, and presumably any number of future wars, will end.

"We would be truly grateful for two things.

"First, we would simply like to be left in place at the hospital, with as little fuss as possible. This will include your minimisation of publicity for the good results from our hospital, and cancellation of any awards for us. Käthe has told me that it is important that we remain utterly inconspicuous if we are to prevent the death of this certain soldier. Apparently, another entity will try hard to ensure this happens and must not suspect her identity.

"Secondly, we would like you to completely suppress any record of this conversation. We may need to ask you for additional assistance in the future, and we would like to be able to enlist your help."

Käthe added, and her voice had returned to normal, "Do you agree to this, Herr Oberst?"

He nodded, and added "And now, perhaps we can enjoy our lunch and talk about more pleasant things!"

On the way back, Erwin asked Käthe "Will he abide by his agreement?"

Käthe did not say anything for a few minutes. "Yes, he will. I have a way of testing that."

She had sent a short message to the future, and received that confirmation.

Her husband asked her, "What would you have done if he had decided to take action?"

Käthe answered, and it was in her strange timbred voice; "I would have killed him".

Erwin was horrified.

3h – Defence of a soldier

In early 1916, Käthe began to think seriously about how she was going to organise her ward for the coming October.

She began to arrange for her area to be staffed only by nurses she had known more or less since her arrival. She was pondering how else to improve her position.

In February 2016, Helmut and Mathilde were shocked to hear that their son had been badly injured. He had received a bullet wound in the arm, which had shattered the bone. The splint had not been positioned well, and his left hand was going to be permanently disabled. Fortunately, he had not suffered any of the bacterial infections which had been so common, and lethal.

He had met Käthe on a few occasions when he was on leave, and regarded her in many ways as a sort of surrogate sister.

After enjoying a 'family' Sunday lunch at the Lang household, Erwin realised that Käthe was unusually silent going home.

Eventually she said, "I think I have just realised how I can solve a further problem."

They had met Fritz von Clausen several times socially in the months since the first meeting, and they now regarded him as a good friend.

"I will ask Fritz if I can come up and visit him at the back end of the week after next, for lunch.

"Unfortunately, I think from your schedule you will be too busy to come as well, but I think I'm going to be unusually well supplied with nurses on that Thursday."

* * *

On the day, Käthe had taken the train to Berlin in the morning, and walked into the army office just before midday.

The Oberst greeted her with respect and great pleasure. She suspected that if he had not known she was already married, he would have tried to move their relationship to a much more intimate basis.

"Good morning Käthe, I am delighted to see you. I am sorry that Erwin cannot come, but that will allow me to take you out on your own!"

She answered, "Not this time Fritz; as I imposed myself on you for a change, it is my treat!

"Shall we go?"

After the first course, he saw her put down her glass.

"Fritz, as you may have surmised, this is not entirely a social call. We have all carefully avoided ever talking about my first conversation with you, but I need to start putting defensive arrangements in place.

"For a starter, our chief hospital administrator is going to be retiring in two months. He has not been well recently, and is already comfortably passed his retirement age. He has turned a satisfactorily blind eye to some of my .... arrangements, but it is important that his replacement is equally amenable.

"You may not be aware, but Doctor Lang has a son who was a captain on the Eastern Front. He has been seriously injured, and given a medical discharge from the army. He has only limited use of his left arm, and is wondering what to do with himself.

"I think he would make an excellent replacement for our chief administrator."

Fritz laughed; "I will agree to this, Käthe, provided you satisfy my curiosity on some points. I realise that you will not talk about the future, but I find you a most interesting personality."

In the privacy of their small booth in the restaurant, Fritz saw that the eyes of this ostensibly young woman were glowing slightly.

She did not say anything for about a minute. He did not know that she had just requested a much more detailed in-depth study of his future. Despite the search taking many hours of subjective time, the response came back almost immediately.

She nodded.

Fritz continued, "Are you really human as I understand it?"

Käthe smiled slightly, "I was once, when young, an entirely human doctor on earth. For reasons I cannot go into, I was moved elsewhere by a group called The Bearing, who are the overarching intelligence of this galaxy. They started adapting me after I became the ruler of a vast Federation of species in another quadrant.

"Only a small part of me is still human, and that is the part you know as Käthe.

"In my own time and space, I have nearly unlimited power.

"In this era, my position is entirely changed. You would not believe the energy requirement to move me back in time. Unfortunately, one of the results is that I have little more than my intelligence to solve my future problem of how to keep a particular soldier alive.

"You must understand that a time war is being waged. We were forced to exterminate a species that had effectively become a cancer on the galaxy. Unfortunately, one of our members was derived from the species, and once we committed genocide she went insane.

"She is now determined to eradicate the human species. The flow on effects will have devastating consequences elsewhere as well."

Käthe added, "What I have just told you is skirting the boundaries of what it is safe for you to know. Fortunately it is so incredible that you would not be believed if you told it elsewhere.

"I have reasons to be confident that you will not breach my trust."

Fritz considered this. The comment about unbelievability appeared accurate.

He smiled. "There are also other interesting implications in your comment. For example, it implies interstellar travel and other species. However, I think out of politeness I must back off on questioning.

"If Captain Lang is agreeable, I will ensure he is the replacement chief administrator at the hospital. In any event, from what you have said he might have been considered for the position anyway.

"Sadly, casualties amongst army officers have been so high that we are finding it difficult to find people for senior positions outside direct fighting units.

"Perhaps we should now talk about dessert?"

* * *

Erwin was relieved to see her when she returned, as apparently another gigantic battle had started at a place called Verdun. Sickening casualty rates were being reported, which were becoming obvious to the German population despite heavy censorship. There had been so many deaths and injuries that the extent of the slaughter could not be hidden.

Käthe described to him the results of the meeting with Fritz.

Erwin smiled slightly, which pleased her as he had been looking most unhappy when she first returned. "I'm glad that went okay, and Helmut's son will be just right for the position.

"Mind you, I rather think that Fritz will do almost anything to please you! That's probably why you went on your own!"

The timbre of Käthe's voice changed; "Erwin von Essen, I'm going to make you regret that comment!"

* * *

Her cat told Katie that it had sufficient power available to provide a weak foldspace shield. "It will not stop serious weaponry, but I will be able to shield the human for a few minutes. This will be enough for you to come and assist. We will be able to resist Aon in normal space, where his Bearing ability will be a little muted."

Katie thought about this for a while. Introducing the cat as a pet might go a long way to making sure the ward was covered at all times.

The retiring administrator, whom Käthe had grown to know and like, baulked a little at her proposal as he was not certain that any form of pet was allowed under the rules.

He finally consented when Käthe said, "You know we have a growing rodent problem in parts of the hospital, which represent a serious health risk. Apart from the direct risk of introduced rodent-based diseases, there have been cases where unconscious patients have been gnawed. A few cats sprinkled around the wards will go a long way to solving this problem. They are remarkably clean animals.

"Moreover, I think their presence will be good psychologically for many of the soldiers."

Unfortunately, two weeks after the cats had been introduced, one of the army generals in charge of procurement decided to inspect the hospital.

On the day, he arrived with several officers, and proceeded to demonstrate all the worst features of an army bureaucrat.

He started his performance by berating a nurse who had just finished re-bandaging a severely injured soldier, as a result of which she had some blood on her uniform.

"Nurses must maintain an absolutely clean uniform at all times. Lieutenant, take the name of this nurse and ensure she is reprimanded."

He next launched into Helmut, "Doctor, you are the senior medical representative here. Far too many bandages and dressings are being used in this hospital. You don't seem to be aware that there is a war on and we need to economise!"

Helmut was so surprised by this, that for a moment he was unable to think of a suitable retort.

A young matron who had been examining a soldier's wounds turned round swiftly and said with considerable annoyance in her voice, "General, you may know a great deal about Army administration for soldiers.

"However, in the medical area, your knowledge is clearly lamentable. If we don't regularly change bandages and dressings and ensure the replacements are clean and sterile, the death rate from septicaemia will climb rapidly. I have absolutely forbidden the reuse of such items unless they are put through a rigorous sterilisation process. That is why so many are being used.

"As it is, parading your staff through the wards is a major distraction and most unhygienic."

There was a shocked silence round the ward. No one present had ever heard a general of the army criticised in such strong terms from someone as junior as this matron.

The general was stunned by the comments, simply glared at the matron, and then stomped towards the exit doors of the ward. As he was nearing these, he looked down and saw a cat being stroked by an injured soldier.

He stopped, and looked even angrier.

"That is the last straw. I intend to see that the senior staff of this hospital are severely reprimanded and demoted. Cats should be absolutely banned from these premises!

"Lieutenant, make notes of the ward number, and the names of the senior staff."

At that he left, with the staff and many of the injured soldiers looking at the exit with horror.

Helmut said to his matron, "Käthe, I agree totally with your comments but you do not score high marks for diplomacy. This is going to cause a major problem."

Erwin then appeared, and looked alarmed when told what had happened.

He took Käthe aside and said, "Darling, how are we going to fix this? That general is an oaf, but he is most senior and has the ear of the Kaiser."

At that moment, there was another disturbance at the ward entrance. A nurse appeared and said, "We need help immediately by the front gate. It appears that a tree fell on the general's carriage, and there are several dead and injured."

That was indeed the case; both the general and his lieutenant were dead. Several other officers had been severely injured.

On the way home that evening, Erwin said to Käthe; "That accident was remarkably convenient."

There was a short pause, and then she answered in her strange timbred voice, "On my instruction our cat arranged for the tree to fall on the carriage and made sure the general and the lieutenant were dead. Their notes of today's visit have gone missing. I might add that Käthe is most upset with me, but I think she will agree it was necessary when she considers the position more calmly."

Erwin started to appreciate an earlier comment about how ruthless and dangerous this alternate state of Käthe could be when required. He wondered how the tree fall had been engineered.

When they were not far from their home, he said, "I will not bring up the subject again, as it is distressing to Käthe, but how were the deaths arranged?"

Käthe's alter ego said in her strange voice, "The cat introduced air into the vascular systems of the soldiers. In this era and with wartime conditions, post-mortem examinations are not careful enough to pick up air embolisms as the cause of death."

Back at the hospital, Käthe's comments had been widely repeated. Even some of the doctors regarded her with awe. She had quietly become the unofficial leader of the group of matrons.

* * *

According to the historical record, Hitler had been injured in the left thigh on 7th October, but the record was silent on exactly when he had been admitted to the hospital in Beelitz. A reasonable assumption was during the following week.

It was three days later when he arrived. Käthe was quite relieved. As she remarked to Erwin, "If Aon had been able to access him before now, nothing could have been done to save this man. She is obviously operating under severe data constraints, and has no future backup team.

"My cat will now always be in his vicinity. It can immediately detect Aon in whatever form she is using or has suborned."

The wound on Adolph Hitler's leg was clearly slightly infected. In such cases, soldiers generally recovered. However, it would only take the introduction of some infected material or use of an infected bandage to tip the infection into full-blown septicaemia. When no-one was watching, she sprinkled the wound with the antibiotic from her locket, to make sure he would recover.

Käthe was at the other end of the ward when Erwin entered. As he approached Hitler's bed, the cat suddenly growled, and stood up. Erwin stopped.

The cat thought at Käthe, "Aon has arrived, and has taken over Erwin's mind. I am shielding Hitler, but provide help immediately."

She ran over, and stood by the bedside. She could supplement the cat's shield for an indefinite period.

To other casualties and nurses, everything seemed quiet, but a furious conversation was occurring.

Aon thought, "Katie Shepherd, of all the Bearing, to be here. I should have guessed. You were a prime factor in the destruction of my species.

"Release this man to me immediately."

She replied, "My sole purpose here is to prevent you harming this divertant".

There was a pause for a few seconds, as Aon savagely attacked the cat's supplemented shield. The alien had insufficient power to break it.

To Käthe's horror, Aon added, "I see from this man's mind that you are linked. He has resisted my probing his memories for a remarkable period. Release the soldier to me, or he dies!"

Grief almost overwhelmed her for a moment, then her other self interposed.

"We will not release our shields. Aon, depart."

Käthe felt the attack on the shield cease.

Aon made one last comment, "The man dies", and her thought presence vanished.

Erwin crumpled onto the floor, dead.

Käthe rushed across to him, and felt his pulse.

Her cat said, "Erwin's brain has been destroyed."

She collapsed across him, sobbing.

Käthe's alter ego sent off a message to the future, asking how history was changing. A few seconds later, the answer came back "History is reverting to the safe path". This also meant that Aon would make no further attempt to kill the soldier, and Hitler would recover.

The other nurses crowded around, but they saw their matron was clearly distraught. One of them located Helmut, who came quickly.

He recognised complete emotional collapse and said to one of the nurses, "Take my horse and trap and get Käthe to my house immediately. Tell my wife what has happened."

* * *

The funeral was a sombre affair. Erwin's parents had arrived, also deeply distressed. When it was over, a still grief stricken Käthe returned to the Lang house.

In the evening, when their son was out of the room, she said to Helmut and Mathilde, "I'm going to volunteer to serve on the Western Front. From there, I will disappear as mysteriously as I arrived. I am enormously grateful for what you both have done for me here.

"When this war is over, I strongly recommend that you and your son move to North America, and change your names. Europe is about to enter a most unhappy period. You might suggest this to Fritz von Clausen as well.

"To assist, may I give you these?"

Käthe handed over a cloth bag, whose contents felt like small pebbles.

"Those are uncut diamonds. When you reach America, sell them and use the proceeds to re-establish yourselves."

For her cat, with some tools and access to foldspace, diamond synthesis was easy.

* * *

A few weeks later Käthe was on her way to the Western front. Not that far from the front, the nurses on the train were allowed to get off for a short walk. She was seen to be wandering onto a field, when there was a large explosion. When the smoke and dust had cleared, no trace of Käthe could be found. It was assumed that a large mine had somehow found its way onto the field.

Chapter 4

RELATIVITY CRACKED

BACK IN FOLDSPACE IN THE VICINITY of Nova, Katie still felt emotionally drained. There was considerable speculation on what Aon's next move would be, and the regular database updates from earth were watched carefully. There was a realisation that it might be a considerable period before anything happened again.

Katie decided to visit New Melbourne, and see how Sienna was faring.

The Federation's new Empress had decided that the best way to make herself inconspicuous was to announce that she was going to make a tour of the outlying planets of the Federation.

The Crystal Palace duly vanished one night, together with Sylvia. In fact the Palace was concealed on Nova's moon, with some assistance from Sheila.

Sienna was able to quietly become a student at the Federation Administration College. Her decision to remain anonymous was already paying dividends. She only told three of her closest female friends, her parents, the Governor of Nova, and Admiral Jenna.

The Governor had looked at her with considerable amusement when told, "Having 'disappeared' Empresses is becoming a tradition in this Federation!"

Sienna found it easy to merge back into the student population. The only privilege she awarded herself was the allocation of better than usual student accommodation, which included a rather ordinary small striped cat.

A year into the course, she was in a cafe having a coffee with two other students. One of them called Iain Taylor had become her first serious boyfriend.

She saw another girl who was clearly a Shepherd on the other side of the room. Recognising the family resemblance, Sienna invited her over.

The newcomer introduced herself as Katie Hertzberg, and there was an astonishing resemblance between the two girls.

Iain said, "Shepherds are rare even on Nova, and to have 2 of them at the same table is fun! Do you know each other?"

The two girls looked at each other and laughed. Katie said, "I'm sure we have met in the past, before Sienna joined this college."

A few minutes later, the conversation turned to the whereabouts of the Empress.

Iain asked, "Are there any good rumours as to which planet our new Empress has visited? There has been an astonishing silence in the press, which I assume means no one has caught sight of her recently."

Katie smiled and said, "Iain, you need to appreciate that while our Empress is young, she has an epic level of responsibility and almost unlimited power. I think it is important that she lives as normal a life as possible. She only needs to intervene when critical decisions have to be made, which we all hope are rare.

"I hope that all her friends cooperate actively to maintain her privacy.

"Oddly enough, I think that most people in the Federation like the current setup. There are lots of checks and balances, which is good."

Iain was surprised at how authoritative Katie's words sounded. He wondered if she was actually Sylvia in disguise.

10 minutes later, the conversation having reverted to a discussion on clothing and jewellery, he excused himself saying, "Sienna, I will see you this evening at the college club. I've got a couple of essays on contract and tort law to prepare."

The other student at the table also left.

Sienna said, "Katie, you can stop acting now. Why don't we go back to my flat, and have a chat."

As they walked back, she continued "I think you need to be a little more careful with your eyes. When you were not concentrating, they started to glow softly. Fortunately, no one else noticed.

"By the way, I thought you also looked terribly sad and worn at that moment."

Katie said, "For your ears only, Sienna, I'm going to tell you what I have been up to. Strangely, I think I need to talk to a real human being as things have been ……… difficult………….. for me."

Back at the apartment, when Katie had finished talking, Sienna said softly, "Katie, thank you for telling me this. You realise of course, that you may be the most critical 'divertant' of all.

"You are far more than I am, but please consider me your friend."

Katie smiled, perhaps a little sadly, and said "And now, have you considered when you are going to tell Iain your real occupation?"

* * *

Iain had known Sienna for some time, but had never heard her talk about her family, which he found a little odd.

However, two weeks later as they were chatting after supper in Sienna's flat, she said, "Iain, would you like to come and meet my parents this weekend?"

He answered "Of course Sienna, I'd really like to meet them. I'm a little nervous about this – I've always wondered about them as you have said virtually nothing about your family!"

Sienna did not say anything for a moment, and looked rather uncertain. Iain thought this was strange, as although quiet and softly spoken, she always spoke with great authority and was almost never hesitant. He had noticed that when she had a view on something, other students tended to move to that view after a discussion. Personally, while he realised that he had totally fallen for Sienna, he was slightly in awe of her.

She continued, "My family is prominent in the Federation, and it was thought much better that I keep pretty quiet about them."

4a – Meeting the relatives

On the Saturday, he collected Sienna early in the evening, and she directed him to a house in the suburbs of Melbourne which was clearly one of the 'originals'.

As they walked in, Sienna's parents Robert and Anna cheerfully greeted him. He was surprised – for a 'prominent' family they looked completely ordinary. Anna was a Shepherd, and looked similar to her daughter.

A little later, they admitted their professions were hydraulic engineer and vet respectively.

Anna looked at Sienna, and said "I am sorry dear, but Caroline has invited herself over for coffee after supper. I told her about Iain, and she is rather curious!"

A possible future partner of the Empress would be of extreme interest to the Governor of Nova.

Sienna realised some explanation was needed, and said, "Auntie Caroline is Mum's sister. It is hard to say 'no' to her!"

Iain could still see no sign of the prominence which justified Sienna living so quietly at the College.

'Auntie Caroline' duly arrived after supper, and was greeted cheerfully by the parents. Iain noticed that her greeting of Sienna was oddly respectful.

The conversation moved elsewhere. A little later, Iain casually mentioned that another Shepherd called Katie Hertzberg had appeared at the College.

He was surprised at how interested Caroline suddenly became, together with Sienna's parents.

The former said, "Sienna, you did not mention this to me last week!

"Was she?"

Sienna looked acutely uncomfortable, to Iain's surprise. He had also been curious to hear that Caroline talked to his girlfriend occasionally. That was something else she had never mentioned.

She nodded. "All I can say, is that Katie is actually worried and upset at present. I will not say anything about what she has been doing, but we had better really, really hope she is successful."

There was a sombre silence for a moment. Iain could not understand the thread of the conversation, and was puzzled.

A little later, the family were all chatting happily over coffee, when he suddenly realised what had been prodding his memory.

"Caroline, am I right in thinking you are our Governor?"

Sienna's aunt looked at him for a moment and nodded, and then a look of astonishment passed over her face.

She turned to her niece, "Sienna, you haven't told him!"

She paused for a moment. "As Governor, I strongly advise you to take Iain into the kitchen, and do that straight away!"

She had decided that Iain was just right for Sienna, and her young Empress needed a partner.

Iain noticed that Sienna looked a mixture of alarmed, embarrassed and nervous.

She stood up, took his hand, and almost dragged him out of the room, shutting the door behind her.

As they moved into the room, he was the beneficiary of a most enthusiastic kiss from his girlfriend, but tears were dripping down her cheek.

"Tell me what, Sienna?", he asked softly, but he realised he already knew the answer.

The girl looked at him, and burst into tears. Between sobs, she said "I'm the missing Empress".

"And this Katie?"

Sienna wiped her eyes and said, "Don't repeat this, but she is my great grandmother. That was why Caroline was so interested!"

A feeling of protectiveness for Sienna came over him, and he just hugged her tightly.

An authoritative thought came into his mind, "Ask Sienna to marry you, with my good wishes".

Katie listened to the subsequent conversation with satisfaction. Another loose end was being tied. Her human support group was getting established.

When Iain and Sienna re-emerged from the kitchen, the latter said with a blush, "By Imperial Decree we are getting married next month."

* * *

As her wedding day approached, Sienna had several discussions with Katie.

She was increasingly convinced that staying completely anonymous was the right policy.

During one of her talks to Katie, after the latter had described what would happen if she met herself, she asked "How different do you have to be to avoid the 'older version disappearance' effect?"

With their existing knowledge, there was no obvious answer to this question.

Sienna also decided that it was time she had a slightly more formal talk with Admiral Jenna.

She contacted him at the headquarters on Lunar Base and agreed a time.

The following day, the Lieutenant in charge of the main entrance at Lunar Base was surprised to see a shuttle approach, with no interference from any of the surrounding patrol vessels. A young girl in civilian clothes and with platinum blonde hair exited, and came up to him.

"Lieutenant, I've come to see Admiral Jenna. Please let him know I have arrived. One of the remotes can escort me through to him."

Something about the girl stopped the Lieutenant saying any more, or even asking her name, and he simply rang through to the Admiral's office.

The Flag Lieutenant who answered the call said, "Lieutenant, escort the girl to the office, but you are not to say anything about her visit to anybody. Do not use any military formality, but treat her with great respect."

The other staff at the office were surprised to see a young woman escorted straight towards the Admiral's suite.

The marine guards at the entrance doors were about to intervene and question whether she should be there, when the Admiral came out with a smile on his face and said, "Sylvia, it is good to see you again; please come straight in.

"Lieutenant, organise some coffee and biscuits and bring them in."

When they were seated, Sienna said, "Admiral, I think it would be a good idea if the Base Commander, his Executive Officer, and your Lieutenant also joined us."

Some coffee was served, and when the other senior officers had arrived, they were invited to take seats.

The Admiral said, "Nothing that is said in this room is to be mentioned or discussed elsewhere. Sylvia, the young lady sitting opposite you, is our missing Empress, and has made it clear that as far as possible she wishes to remain anonymous."

The two officers from the Base immediately started to rise, when Sienna said "Please remain seated."

She continued, "Admiral, it has not been reported, but I'm getting married in two weeks' time. There will be absolutely no publicity for the event, as I have decided that as far as possible I'm going to remain completely inconspicuous. Our Federation has developed a tradition of 'missing' Empresses, which I have every intention of continuing!

"Aunty Caroline is comfortable with this.

"You will always be able to contact me, and Sheila and Crystal are keeping me completely informed about what is happening.

"My great-grandmother has told me what she has been doing, and all I will say is that she is fighting a war with the support of the entire Bearing Community. She has already suffered terribly. You should be aware that the Ghost Fleet has been significantly diminished in size in activities related to this war. I was shocked to discover how it has been used."

Sienna had decided that a little misinformation was a good idea, and would move any speculation away from sensitive areas.

"I will only ever use that Fleet as a last resort, and you will need to quietly get the message across to the politicians that going soft on funding the Federation Fleet would be most unwise. You can mention my comment. Even frightful casualties and the loss of planets will not change my view on this.

"As a weapon, it is simply too tempting, and too terrible."

The Admiral and the staff were surprised at the underlying steel in Sylvia's voice, but there was satisfaction that the Empress was totally committed to maintaining their position.

However they were deeply concerned that a war was being fought without their knowledge, and could not imagine what level of threat could even challenge the Ghost Fleet.

Admiral Jenna asked, "Are we likely to become involved militarily in this war?"

His young Empress looked at him, and it was clear that she was deeply worried.

"Nothing we can do will have any impact. Matters are utterly beyond our level. As I said to Caroline, we had better really, really hope that Katie is successful."

The worry on her face became even more evident, with a suspicion of tears. There was a long pause.

"And now, I would like to hear your views on the Fleet, the Federation, and any other military issues which may be relevant."

The officers were surprised at how carefully Sylvia listened to their comments, and her questions were frequent, and to the point. The discussion lasted for several hours, to the dismay of the administrative staff outside who had to change a number of appointments. There was a great deal of speculation as to the identity of the girl.

The Admiral was impressed, especially after she had picked him up on a couple of points where he had glossed over problems. He made a mental note to never, ever underestimate his new Empress despite her young age.

He also continued to wonder at the level of threat which would cause the Ghost Fleet to be significantly diminished in size; if the guesstimates made by his officers were correct, the number of its vessels approached or exceeded seven figures.

Katie, observing from her position in fold space, was satisfied that her protégé was setting up the required direct but informal links. She was also pointedly making clear to her military arm that she had ultimate control, and had sources of information to which they were not privy.

As Sylvia was about to leave the Admiral's office, all the officers and the Admiral came to attention and saluted her.

She smiled and said, "Thank you, but please do your best to keep me anonymous!"

This did not stop rumours circulating in the Fleet that their new Empress had quietly visited the Admiral.

Katie withdrew, still pondering the question which Sienna had asked.

* * *

For several months, Katie was able to resume her human form and take a quiet holiday in some of her former haunts. Her island on Stortin was used as a base. She also reintroduced herself to her old boss at HMC, Dar Stan.

One weekend at lunchtime, after making sure he was relatively free of engagements, she simply walked up to the front door of his house and knocked.

When he answered, she said "Dar, it is so nice to see you again. Can I take the liberty of inviting myself to join you and Cora for lunch?"

For a moment, Dar had been nonplussed, then his brain kicked into gear; "Katie – My Lady – I would be delighted if you would join us."

Katie laughed, "Dar, please abandon the formality and just call me Katie!"

His wife had been delighted to see her, and was not stressed at all as she had never realised that she was the former Empress.

4b – WWII derailed

3 months later, Katie's holiday came to an abrupt halt. She received a message from the Bearing Community that the databases had again skewed wildly.

History seemed to be running very much on the safe track until almost the end of the Second World War.

However, in this version of history, the United States had not produced a nuclear weapon, and this had necessitated the invasion of Japan.

The Japanese Navy and Air Force had already been obliterated, but the Army fought with fanatical courage. The American landing on the southern shores of Japan had been successful, but thereafter the fighting had turned into a bloodbath. Not only had the Japanese Army fought with desperate courage, but masses of civilians had hurled themselves at the invader. In some places, the population of whole towns and villages had suicided.

As the fighting bogged down on Kyushu, the southern island of Japan, the people in the rest of Japan had started to starve. Without the overwhelming psychological effect that the two nuclear weapons had achieved in the "safe" historical path, the Japanese Emperor had been unable to persuade the militarist government to allow him to surrender.

While this was happening, the Russians had taken the opportunity to invade Northern Japan as well as Manchuria and Sakhalin, and had occupied Hokkaido. This had been achieved quickly as the Japanese Army had been totally preoccupied with fighting in the South. The Soviet Army had crushed any military and civilian resistance with overwhelming force and utter brutality.

It took about 4 months after the initial invasion, before the Japanese government accepted the inevitable, and the Emperor was allowed to sue for peace.

By then another five million Japanese were dead, and their economy was totally ruined. Allied casualties had also been enormous.

In Europe the Soviet armies had taken the opportunity to sweep much further West. The transfer of almost all of the British and American armies to the war in Japan had left many countries wide open. Without the threat of nuclear weapons, Stalin had felt entirely unconstrained and saw no reason why he should not occupy a large part of Europe. The Scandinavian countries and Denmark were "freed" by Soviet armies, and they had "liberated" a substantial part of Italy.

Another large slice of Germany had been absorbed, well beyond what might have been known as East Germany.

There had been no withdrawal from Austria.

Protests from the Western allies were simply ignored, and where their troops had been in place, they were simply placed on trains and sent to North Sea ports. American and British numbers had been too low to even contemplate fighting the large Russian forces.

Britain was totally exhausted, and the US had withdrawn too many troops and had been too distracted by the war in Japan to be able or willing to react militarily.

The absence of the subsequent Marshall Aid program which had buttressed Europe in the 'safe' historical path led directly to stagnation and depression.

Left-wing governments loosely associated with Russia came to power in most of the countries not directly controlled by Soviet armies, with the exception of Britain.

In China, a vicious civil war was in progress between the Nationalists and the Communists. Assistance from Russia and the use of Manchuria as a safe base was contributing to the rapid destruction of the Nationalists.

However, after the Chinese Communists had destroyed the latter, who had been unable to retreat to Taiwan, the Russians had refused to return Manchuria to Chinese control.

Moving further up the timeline, most developed and semi-developed countries had suffered economic depression, and horrible unemployment rates coupled with devastating poverty were common. In many areas, huge numbers of people were dying of disease and starvation.

It took about another 30 years before some aspects of the special theory of relativity were discovered, and Russia and the United States started to experiment with the precursors of nuclear weapons.

Several decades after that, the Calai arrived, and nationalism and most of the population of Earth ceased to exist.

Katie contemplated all of this with horror.

4c – Value of weapons

Once again, the historical databases were studied in detail.

It was immediately apparent that it was the introduction of nuclear weapons in 1945 by the United States which had completely altered history.

Their totally unexpected use to produce complete destruction of 2 Japanese cities had halted the war in Japan. The immediate and unconditional surrender by the Emperor had not given the Russians enough time to occupy Hokkaido.

The latter's shock at discovering that a weapon existed that completely negated the huge size and efficiency of their armies in Western Europe and Asia had psychologically stopped Stalin in his tracks, and he had acted with great caution. The Soviet armies had even retreated from Austria, but not the rest of Eastern Europe.

Alarmed at what might happen to Europe if recovery was not implemented, to their enduring credit the United States had implemented the major aid program called Marshall Aid.

In Japan, apart from the reforms and new constitution engineered by General MacArthur, the onset of the Korean War had given Japan a huge economic boost which had accelerated its recovery.

Katie and the Bearing group realised that they would need to uncover what had stopped production of nuclear weapons. On further study, it was apparent that a large part of 20th-Century physics had failed to appear on schedule. The enormous contribution that Albert Einstein had made to the discipline in the first two decades of the 20th century was missing, together with the physicist.

The primary scientific loss was found to be an obscure paper called, in German, "On the Electrodynamics of Moving Bodies".

Einstein's Special Theory of Relativity had never appeared.

In Katie's view, the editor of the 1905 September issue of the Annalen der Physik had shown extraordinary courage in even publishing the paper. She sourly reflected that the peer review process when she was at university would have almost certainly blocked its publication. A friend of Einstein's called Besso was the only acknowledgement of assistance, and the usual host of references to previous papers was absent.

The subsequent addendum to the paper which defined the relationship between matter and energy demonstrated the huge energy potential of destruction of matter.

Understanding that potential eventually led to nuclear weapons.

In a surprising twist, possibly the single most important scientific paper published in the 20th Century sat on the shelves almost unnoticed for 6 months. It then slowly dawned on the community of physicists that their subject had been revolutionised.

However, without the focussing effect of the original paper, not to mention Einstein's other contributions, physics had floundered for another 40 odd years before special relativity had been reconstructed. By then a host of unexplained problems had come to light. One of the most embarrassing had been the failure of synchrotrons to work as expected. Without special relativity, the design physics was simply wrong.

With a defined target for research, a search of the local newspapers and university archives of the Polytechnic Institute in Zurich soon revealed a simple one line headline in the university student newsletter.

"Promising young student dies in boating accident."

It transpired that Einstein loved sailing, although he could not swim. He had joined a student boat club, and frequently took a dinghy out on Lake Zürich. According to the article, the boat had capsized and since Einstein never bothered with a buoyancy aid, he was found drowned near the waterlogged craft.

Katie was starting to focus on how she would organise enough protection for Einstein, when a thought interrupted her reverie. It was from a junior Bearing, who had been given the task of trying to identify exactly how Aon had built her version of the Time Machine.

"Katie, I may have some good news for you. The type of machine that Aon would have been able to build has been defined closely.

"First of all, it will not have the stored energy capacity for keeping her on a planet surface for more than at most 3 of your days. It can only accumulate supergiant solar energy while it is moving back in time, and has no capability for moving forward in time towards the present.

"Secondly, because Aon does not possess any support group in current time, she cannot know the effects of whatever she achieves. She can only aim at well-defined divertants, and try and move them from the safe path.

"Finally, she will not be able to move more than about 80,000 years into the past."

Katie thanked the junior Bearing warmly. "You have made my task much easier by defining Aon's constraints. Presumably this means that if we block one of her efforts at any moment in time, any later repeat of an attack is unlikely, and she will have to spend several years in foldspace moving backwards before another attempt can be made."

4e – Zurich

Zürich in 1896 was a busy, prosperous city. With good educational institutions and an advanced engineering industry, the Swiss had taken to electrical engineering and its associated products with enthusiasm.

Katie had read all the material she could find about Einstein. It was apparent that as a young student, he was already attractive to women, and a substantial proportion of the literature about him revolved around his marital affairs and disasters. It seemed that the reading public were fascinated by the contrast between the physics genius, and the all too human male. A touch of eccentricity only added flavour to the mix.

She decided that while it was important to get to know him personally, at all costs she would have to ensure that he did not become attracted to her.

Accordingly, she remoulded herself into a short dumpy woman, with an unattractive complexion. She greyed and tied back her hair, and roughened her voice.

When she arrived, it was to a vacant apartment in a poor suburb. It was as well that enough local currency had been provided to cover the week she suffered from temporal shock.

It was late on a Sunday afternoon in August when she walked into the student sailing club, and introduced herself to the elderly supervisor.

"Good morning, sir. I see you are busy, and I think you need some help. I am now retired, but a long time ago I was able to do some sailing with my son.

"I would be happy to assist you at no charge, except for an occasional coffee and a chance to use a boat when the club is not busy.

"My name is Katie."

Henri, the supervisor, was feeling distinctly harassed as the weather had been good and demand for the dinghies had been brisk. He was not looking forward to bringing them in from where most of them had been carelessly pulled up on the shore by the students.

He said, "Well, you can give me a hand in getting the boats stowed away. If I think you are strong enough to do the work, and you still want to come here when we have finished, we will talk about this tomorrow."

Henri was surprised at how strong Katie proved, and she clearly demonstrated some knowledge of small boats.

2 hours later, as the last of the dinghies was pulled onto a light trolley and stowed, he said "Thank you for your help, Katie. My coffee is not of a good standard, but let me get you a cup."

Katie found the supervisor unexpectedly interesting, which seemed to be reciprocated. He had been a mathematics teacher before he retired, and since he enjoyed sailing and needed to supplement his income, the position at the boat club suited him well.

He asked, "What did you do for a living, Katie?"

She said, "I worked at government, Henri. That is, when I was not looking after my children."

Henri thought she had just misstated the phrase, and then he noticed she looked rather forlorn for a moment.

She continued: "I have been married twice; both my husbands died tragically."

He moved the conversation onto safer ground. "We will be busy tomorrow morning, if you are still interested in coming here. After this sort of weekend, a complete clean of the premises is required."

Katie found herself working hard the following morning. She had forgotten that mundane tasks like wiping down tables, sweeping floors, and cleaning out the basic kitchen were taxing.

However, by mid-afternoon, the tasks were done, and Henry said, "If you would like to go for a short sail, Katie, I would suggest the small dinghy on the left-hand side of the beach. It is comparatively stable and the sail has been made too small for the boat. Also, it would probably be a good idea if you use some sort of buoyancy aid, and do not venture far from the shore for your first outing for a while!"

While fully conversant with the theory of sailing, Katie found the practice somewhat more difficult. Light winds and a little surreptitious help from Yelli stopped her capsizing. When she came ashore half an hour later she said ruefully, "That was great fun Henri, but I seem to be badly out of practice."

Henri laughed, "Never mind, you at least avoided capsizing.

"Would you be available tomorrow?"

Over the next few months, Katie established her position at the boat club, to the point where most of the students who came thought she was a permanent appointment.

Regular sailing sessions meant she improved rapidly.

The club owned a pair of larger sailing boats, which required several crew as well as a helmsman.

When the club was not busy, and an extra crew member was required, she sometimes volunteered for the position.

4f – Sailing Student

On an unusually warm weekend early in Spring, a student came to the club with two friends.

After some coffees had been ordered, he came up to Katie and asked, "Sailing looks rather exciting. Is it possible to hire a boat, and perhaps get some basic lessons? There must be someone in the club who can teach me."

The elderly grey haired woman looked at Albert Einstein with almost disturbing intentness.

"Since I assume you are a student at the Polytechnic, you can join the sailing club for a nominal fee.

"For a few lessons, provided you use weekdays, I can take you out in the afternoon. I assume you can stand a woman teaching you?

"I won't charge you anything, as I just like sailing."

Albert had never much enjoyed being taught by anyone, yet alone a woman, but he appreciated that this was as good an offer as he was likely to receive. He nodded.

"I'm called Albert Einstein. Your name, please?"

Katie smiled, and he was surprised at how her face seemed to light up with character; "You may call me Katie.

"I will introduce you to Henri in a moment, as he will fix the formalities. He is in charge of running the club.

"When would you like your first lesson?"

Albert answered, "How about tomorrow afternoon?"

Katie said, "That's fine. I suggest you bring a towel and a spare set of clothes. Light shoes which do not mind getting wet would be good. Get here about 4 o'clock."

Katie introduced the young student to Henri, then left to serve some orders at the counter.

Albert completed a form, and provided the nominal joining fee.

He asked Henri, "I have been offered some lessons by the woman at the counter, for free. Is she any good?"

Henri laughed, "You're lucky. She might be the best sailor in this club, although for some reason she does not seem to want to push it. She is also interesting to talk to, if you can spare some time from the lesson."

Albert arrived the following afternoon, dressed as suggested.

Katie greeted him cheerfully, and then said, "Before we start, I think it would be a good idea to explain some basic sailing theory to you. That will help you grasp exactly what you're doing."

With a pencil, and some scrap paper, Katie explained the general concepts of tacking, gybing, and the advantages of what she described as a broad reach.

"As a mathematical physicist, you might also find the workings of the sail interesting."

Katie explained how the air on the outside of the sail had a longer distance to travel, and therefore had to move faster than air that moved on the inside of the sail.

Albert was clearly interested. "That means that the air on the outside is effectively stretched ……. In other words its volume must be increased."

Katie listened to this with fascination, aware that the best physics mind for several centuries was coming to grips with the problem.

Albert continued, "Of course……… that means its pressure must be reduced, and the higher inside air pressure effectively pushes the sail!"

Katie replied, "Exactly! A mathematician called Bernoulli tackled this about a century ago. You might find his flow equations interesting. Of course, the sail is not particularly efficient as an aerofoil because there is a large amount of turbulence on the inside. Wings on birds work much more efficiently.

"Bernoulli approached the problem using incompressible fluids, and conservation of energy, but the physical result is the same.

"Anyhow, these are all the different pressures working on the boat, and it is why you need a centreboard to stop the boat being rapidly pushed sideways."

Katie then drew a little diagram showing the different pressures and effects on the boat from the centre board, sail, rudder and wind pressure.

She concluded by saying, "Any particular boat can only sail to a limited extent into the wind. The long distance clippers of the last century were efficient. The dinghy we are about to practice on, is awful!

"Here are 2 flotation devices, one each, and we will get going."

After putting the sail up and pushing the dinghy out a little way, Katie told Albert to get in. She then spent 5 minutes explaining the names of the principal ropes, the boom, and other features of the boat. She explained that the centreboard needed to be pushed down fully as soon as there was enough water depth.

Jumping in, she said; "We are lucky, there is only a light breeze today. I will take the boat a little way out, demonstrating a couple of tacks and a gybe.

"You can then take over! Watch your head as the boom swings!"

Albert was rather nervous when he started. Strangely, he was already slightly overawed by his sailing teacher. For once in his life, he had the impression that he was meeting someone who really did know a great deal more than he did.

His first attempt at a tack was horrible. He was nowhere near decisive enough in turning the rudder, and found the boat floundering head to the wind, sail flapping uselessly.

Slightly to his annoyance, Katie laughed.

"This is what being in irons means! Let the bow fall away, and let the boat pick up speed again. When you try again, turn the rudder much more quickly!"

Albert was delighted when he followed the instructions, and he had his first successful tack. He only just remembered to duck his head in time as the boom passed above him.

Katie said, "Well done! Let's do it again a few times, and then I will risk all by letting you do a gybe, which is a much more dangerous manoeuvre!"

Albert find himself really enjoying the sailing experience, and managed to narrowly avoid a couple of capsizes.

An hour later, Katie called a halt. "That's enough for today. I think you're getting a little tired, and your concentration is wavering. I think I would rather avoid going for a swim today in these clothes!"

Back on shore, Albert thanked her profusely. He also added, "I think I am going to be looking up Bernoulli this evening. I was fascinated by your description of the different forces working on the boat, and the way it responded to those pressures. The way the apparent wind direction changed as you went faster was also interesting.

"When could I have my next lesson, please?"

Katie set a time, and watched him walk away, his feet leaving slightly damp footprints.

Her cat thought at her, "You do realise that you may just have started him thinking about movement and parallax; those thoughts will eventually lead to special relativity!"

Katie was shocked. She realised that she might have inadvertently jolted history. She sent a message back up time querying this, but the answer came back that nothing had changed.

That was also strange.

Albert was indeed thinking about parallax and movement. He was also wondering how a middle-aged assistant in a sailing club could summarise a complicated physics theorem. Somehow, he doubted whether more than a tiny fraction of all the sailors who had ever lived really understood what was happening physically when they sailed a boat.

He also wondered how Katie had known he was studying physics.

Over the next 2 months, Albert had regular sailing lessons from Katie, and rapidly turned himself into a capable dinghy sailor.

When he started going out on his own, it was no surprise to her that he nearly always avoided wearing any sort of flotation device.

When he returned, he frequently asked her over for a coffee. He had found her a useful sounding board when he had a problem.

4g – Student Upset

One day, several months later, he explained to her that he had just been to a lecture on photo electricity; when light was shone on a clean metal surface, various electrical effects had been observed.

"My lecturers were uncertain about what was happening. I'm sure there is some fundamental physics involved in this. Do you have any ideas, Katie?"

Katie looked at him, aware that giving the correct answers might have a noticeable impact on scientific history.

"Albert, as a simple sailing club assistant I am not going to give you the answers to that sort of comment."

She smiled, "And now, I think we should drink our coffee as I need to go and clear the tables."

* * *

A few hours later, a message came from the far future. "Katie, the databases have again altered wildly. You need to return immediately to the vicinity of Nova, and consider the position."

Returning, she was shown the problem. Her friend Iva said, "It seems that in this version of history, Einstein lost focus. He became more absorbed with his friends and enjoyment. He failed to matriculate from the Zurich Polytechnic, and was never given a position at the patent office.

"In fact, we had a great deal of difficulty tracing any information about him at all. After he left the Polytechnic, he faded into obscurity. Obviously, passing his matriculation was critical, as was the patent office position. We theorise that it was the training in grasping essential details, plus a fair amount of free intellectual time at the office, which enabled him to produce his major papers in 1905.

"Obviously, he never died in a boating accident. There was no reason for Aon to ever even consider him as a candidate divertant."

Katie was terribly concerned about this turn of events.

She asked her cat to prepare an accurate summary of the relevant parts of the last days in Zurich.

Her Bearing group considered the information carefully. However, as far as they could see, she had not made any mistakes.

After brooding over this for several days, Katie decided she needed a human view on the position.

Sienna and Iain had just returned from a skiing honeymoon, and they had managed to "fortuitously" acquire a small house just outside Melbourne.

Iain answered a knock at the door, and was surprised to see Katie standing there with her cat on her shoulder.

He hesitated for a moment and then said, "Katie – My Lady – please come in."

Raising his voice he shouted, "Sienna, we've got a visitor!"

Sienna was surprised – Crystal almost always warned her when people were about to arrive.

A little later, after some light refreshments, Katie said; "I've got a problem, and I suspect that I need a human view point to find the solution. My Bearing colleagues are stumped, and I suspect that it is something else which I did or didn't do which has caused the difficulty.

"In strict confidence, I located myself back in time at the end of the 19th century. My purpose was to ensure that Albert Einstein survived a boating accident. Unfortunately, the accident never occurred, and Einstein never emerged as a mathematical physicist.

"I will run the summary hologram of all the significant portions of the last few days in Zürich".

The two young humans watched the slightly blurred hologram with fascination. When it had finished, Sienna requested a repeat.

When it had finished, there was a long silence.

Iain said hesitantly, "I'm trying to put myself in Einstein's shoes. I'm only a year or so older than he was at the time.

"Katie, I hate to say it, but I think it was almost the last comment you made to Einstein which might be the key. You know, the one where you said; 'Albert, as a simple sailing club assistant I am not going to give you the answers to that sort of comment.'

"I think, consciously or subconsciously, he might have taken it badly. In some strange way, he has begun to look up to you. Knowing your real background somewhat better than he does, I can't say I'm surprised!

"Us males, with fragile egos to be preserved, would tend to be disconcerted by the phrase in those circumstances.

"It might have acted as a subconscious putdown."

There was another long silence as Katie considered this.

Finally, she said "I've put my psychologist hat on, and it looks like I might have made a mistake. Iain, you could be right.

"I think I'm going to have to have a long discussion with my foldspace colleagues. How this is going to be solved is not at all obvious to this junior Bearing."

After that, there was a friendly discussion about family and other local issues, and then Katie returned to the Bearing community.

When Iain's suggestion was described, there was general concern.

Iva said, "We are in danger of creating more problems than we solve, if the suggestion is correct.

"Which is possible.

"Katie, you are becoming involved with history to an alarming extent. This is not your fault, but we need to carefully think through the consequences of what we do next."

4h – Meddling with time

For the foldspace equivalent of a week or so, there was an active debate. Even normally placid and logical Bearing members came close to the metaphorical equivalent of blows in some cases.

There was a recognition that fundamental issues were involved. Also, having spent millions of years doing everything possible to avoid altering the past, they were being forced to intervene directly, and no-one was certain of the outcome.

A great deal of regret was expressed that the Oldest was no longer with them. There was a realisation that the being had exercised inconspicuous but firm leadership for aeons.

Eventually a consensus was reached about what Katie needed to say.

However, there was still the fundamental problem that a message had to be passed to her younger version to change the comment.

Initially it had been thought that the easiest way to achieve this would be for another Bearing to return to the past and simply tell her.

After thinking about the suggestion, Iva had told her Bearing group; "The difficulty with that approach is that it will effectively leave two "versions" of Katie in existence, one of whom has moved out of the local time stream."

There was an uncomfortable pause after this comment.

The Bearing theory of time was incomplete, but it did theorise that the chronon equivalent of quantum entanglement existed between past and future versions of an individual.

If the changes were minor, and history had been continuous, there would simply be a small ripple in the historical chronology, and not much would happen. That is what generally occurred when a time traveller met an individual in the past and no chronologically dramatic change had been made. If the meeting had been significant, the chronons would reset all subsequent history, but the outcome would still be logically consistent.

However the existence of a second version of an individual who had moved completely out of the local time stream was likely to lead to chronological chaos as that individual might not be included in the reset. The outcome was totally uncertain, and the Bearing as a whole were not prepared to risk the experiment.

After much discussion, it appeared there was one possible solution that might work. If Katie met her younger self, she had a few seconds, literally, before she would be historically obliterated. She had to use that interval to pass a message to her younger self.

* * *

For Katie [older version] it was the morning before she had made her last comments to Einstein which had changed the future.

Katie [younger version] had just finished breakfast when a duplicate of herself appeared.

The duplicate said "Just listen. When Einstein asks you about the photoelectric effect later on today, say the following;

'What might happen if light was considered as a particle rather than a wave?'

'What energy effects might be relevant for this theoretical particle?'

"Don't move in time before then. This is so important ....''

As the duplicate finished the word 'important' she simply vanished. Strangely, a small area where her feet been touching the ground had also vanished.

Katie was deeply troubled by this, realising that some form of disastrous time loop had been established which a future version of herself was trying to correct.

RESET

Later on that day, Einstein had come in and was talking to her before he went out for a sail.

He explained to her that he had just been to a lecture on photo electricity, when light was shone on a clean metal surface and various electrical effects had been observed.

"My lecturers were uncertain about what was happening. I'm sure there is some fundamental physics involved in this. Do you have any ideas, Katie?"

Katie realised that this was the moment that her future self had needed to alter.

She said, "I can't directly answer your question, Albert.

"What I will do, is ask you a couple of questions which you might consider at your leisure.

"The first one is; what might happen if light was considered as a particle rather than a wave?

"The second is; what energy effects might be relevant for this theoretical particle?"

Albert had the uncanny impression that the woman in front of him knew exactly the answers to his questions, but would simply not tell him. Both points were most peculiar.

However, the questions she had asked were fascinating.

When he had left to go sailing, Katie sent a message to the future asking if any changes had occurred.

The answer came back, "History has reverted to the safe path".

* * *

Two hours later, Katie and Henri went for a walk along the lake. This had become a habit, especially on quiet, warm evenings.

He said, "I think Albert Einstein has become a fan of yours. I hate to say this Katie, but if you were a few decades younger I think he would have gone after you!

"Mind you, I've taken the liberty of listening to some of your little chats with him. As an ex-teacher, I have noticed that you are careful to only ever ask him questions. Socrates would have been proud of you!

"If you don't mind me saying so, I have the strong impression that you know far more than you ever reveal. You don't have to say anything, but I would like to know why you're so interested in Albert. You have never offered sailing lessons to anyone else.

"Another point, which I will never repeat elsewhere, is that once or twice in the evening when you were on your own, your eyes seemed to glow.

"I completely respect your right to privacy, Katie, but I can't help being curious."

Katie walked for a few minutes in complete silence. Henry was getting concerned that he might have wrecked his relationship with this strange woman.

In fact, Katie had requested a check on Henri from the far future. It revealed nothing untoward.

"Henri, you will keep what I'm about to tell you in complete confidence from anyone.

"You are right that I am extremely interested in Albert. I am from the far future, and I'm here to prevent his death in about a month from drowning. He is critical to the future of science on this planet, and an alien entity is determined to kill him. I must prevent that, or almost all the human race will die.

"If you would bear with me, I will revert to my ordinary human appearance for a little while."

To Henri's astonishment, the woman walking beside him morphed into a slim young girl with black hair.

She said in a soft teenage girl's voice, "A small grey tabby cat is about to take up residence in the clubhouse, with your concurrence. It will provide critical protection for Albert. I will also need to stay nearby, as the cat can only provide protection for a short period on its own."

Henri said, "Thank you for telling me, and I won't tell anyone. I suppose I will have to restrain my curiosity about the future! By the way, I think you need to be more careful with your eyes – they are glowing again!"

Katie answered soberly, "I am far more than I appear, and only a part of me is still human. It is dangerous to you personally to know more, as terrible things tend to happen to people who get too close to me. I am engaged in a time war, and many bystanders have already become casualties.

"Let us finish our walk, and then I think I would like to play my flute for a while. It helps remind me of what I'm trying to protect."

When they returned to the clubhouse, Henri prepared two coffees. Katie had produced a flute from somewhere, and sitting on a low wall just outside the clubhouse, started to work her way through her repertoire.

Henri realised he was listening to almost magical flute playing.

4i – Sailing Accident

Her cat had taken the form of a seagull, and Einstein had been surprised to discover that every time he went out, a seagull seemed to materialise and fly along with the boat.

On the third time he had seen this, he said to the bird rather facetiously, "You do have permission to come aboard if you like, seagull!"

A few seconds later, the bird swooped down, squawked, and landed on the bow. It fussily folded its wings, and proceeded to completely ignore him.

Albert laughed.

After that, whenever he went out the bird would swoop down and repeat the performance.

Two weeks later he went out again at the weekend. The lake was busy, and he noticed a sailor in a dinghy on port tack bearing down upon him. He shouted loudly as he was on starboard tack and had right of way, and then tried to swerve the boat downwind away from a collision course.

Unhappily, the other dinghy swerved as well, and crashed into Einstein's dinghy on the windward side. The dinghy capsized, and began to sink, and Albert was tipped out and away from the boat. The other craft simply sailed away.

The gull had immediately taken to the air, screeching loudly. Albert threshed about wildly and his head was about to slip below the surface when he felt an arm slide around him from behind.

A familiar voice shouted, "Albert, don't struggle! It will make it more difficult for me to hold you."

He almost froze with surprise, which momentarily stopped him struggling. As this happened, he realised he was being safely supported with his head above the surface.

Katie sounded annoyed; "Perhaps this will teach you to use a buoyancy aid in future!"

She tightened her grip around him, and started the long backstroke swim to the shore.

A very subdued Einstein kept quiet and still as he was towed back. He noticed the arm around him looked like it belonged to a girl.

As he felt his feet touch bottom 20 meters from the shore, Katie said, "Its' shallow enough now for you to get ashore safely. I'm going to have a proper swim for a little while.

"Get yourself dried and changed, and then you can buy me a coffee!"

Albert felt Katie's grip release, and he cautiously went inshore, with the depth rapidly decreasing.

Looking around, he saw that Katie was already 15 meters away and swimming strongly with her face down.

Strangely, what little he could see of her looked young and athletic.

Half an hour later, she waded out of the sea opposite the clubhouse. For an elderly woman who must have been swimming for several hours, she looked surprisingly fresh.

Albert and Henri were waiting for her as she came out of the water.

She was handed a towel, and Albert thanked her profusely. He said, "Why were you out there, Katie?"

She answered, "I often swim well out from the shore. When I was young I was a good swimmer. You were lucky I was close by when the other boat crashed into you.

"By the way, the other boat was entirely in the wrong, and you did everything right. I don't think the other boat is identifiable. We will try to retrieve the dinghy tomorrow; it is waterlogged and on its side, so it should not have moved too far.

"I will get changed quickly, then I would really like a hot coffee and perhaps a bun!

"I think you may find Henry insisting that you use a float when you go sailing next time!"

Albert looked rather subdued at this comment. It was dawning on him that he had nearly drowned, and it was only Katie's almost miraculous appearance which had saved him.

Later on that evening, Henri said, "I assume that was the accident that you referred to, Katie".

She answered, "Yes. I don't think that the alien entity will try again, but I will stay around for another three days to make sure, and then I will need to leave.

"By the way, I am most grateful for the help you have provided. You will find that your bank account has been substantially increased next week, and you will remain healthy and mobile for a long time to come."

* * *

Albert came into the clubhouse just before her departure. Katie told him that she had to leave permanently, about which he was most disappointed.

He said, "I'll really miss you, Katie. By the way, if I was not an agnostic I would suspect you to be some sort of goddess. I can't help remembering how young you appeared when you rescued me, from what little I saw of you."

Katie smiled, a little sadly. "A famous playwright once said, 'There are more things in heaven and earth than are dreamt of in your philosophy'. He was right."

He never saw her again.

Chapter 5

DOMESTIC CONSIDERATION

F ROM SIENNA'S POINT OF VIEW, SHE was finding that her 'anonymous' approach to being Empress was working well. She was really enjoying her time at the Federation Administration College, with a realisation that it was filling out many critical gaps in her knowledge. Moreover, because almost every planet in the Federation had members attending, she was able to familiarise herself with most of the races.

She realised that she was never going to like some of them – in particular the Xicon still displayed a considerable level of arrogance towards other species. However she was amused to note that humans made them nervous, particularly if they were young Shepherds who looked eerily like the previous Empress.

Within the student body of the FAC, there was continuing speculation about which planets had been visited by the Empress Sylvia. Surprise was expressed that no one from anywhere had actually heard any relevant news.

Sienna realised that at some point, some real visits were going to be required.

Apart from this, she was also enjoying being married, and was coming to rely more and more on Iain as a sounding board.

When Katie mentioned this with a cautionary comment, in a rare flash of temperament she said rather crossly; "I am never going to keep any secrets from my husband!

"I seem to remember, Katie, that NOBODY knew about the Ghost Fleet until it arrived! I don't have your penchant for secrecy!"

Considering that Sienna had managed to make herself almost invisible, Katie thought that the last comment was a little inaccurate. Moreover, she doubted whether, when more difficult realities intruded, her young Empress was actually going to be able to stick to her script.

However, she was happy to let things ride for the moment.

She also noticed that Sienna had only told a tiny number of people that she was Empress, and that included almost no one of her generation in the family.

Iain was finding his young wife rather more of a handful than he had expected. Sienna had discovered that Nova, as a still extremely sparsely populated planet, had all sorts of interesting and exotic locations which could be quickly reached by shuttle. Having the latter shielded meant that privacy could be almost completely guaranteed, especially with a little assistance from Sheila.

Frequently at weekends, she hauled Iain off for a walk and swim at one of those locations.

Her latest find was on the Equator. It was a small remote island about 2 km across, on the other side of the planet from Melbourne. It was now surrounded by a coral reef, with a sandy protected cove fringed with coconut trees. The latter was probably a partly submerged caldera. A hilly interior, which looked like the remnant of a small volcano, led to some streams meandering down in the valleys with deep freshwater pools. It was rocky nearly everywhere, but the terrain was gradually being covered by tropical vegetation and trees. The probable reason it was uninhabited was that it had no agricultural value.

After a reasonably long walk along the beach, Sienna had led him to one of the freshwater pools which had a sandy beach on one side and a grassy strip.

As they reached it, she laughed and said, "I'm going for a swim!"

Stripping off all her clothes she had rushed in with much splashing. Iain had followed in a few seconds, equally nude. A little later some energetic open-air sex followed.

Discreetly observing this, Katie was happy that such activities were high on the young couple's agenda. She believed strongly that it helped cement marriages, and she was surprised to find that she wanted her family to keep growing in size; she still loved looking after children.

She realised she could provide a distinct prod in that direction.

Sienna asked "Sheila, does anyone actually own this island?"

A slightly amused sounding Sheila answered; "No, but I suspect that will change shortly!"

Sienna said, "In that case, register a claim for it in the name of the Empress. I would also like a small cottage built near the coral bay overlooking the sea.

"Please make it off-limits to anyone without our permission."

Seeing a rainbow from a large thunderstorm on the horizon, she added; "Also, call it Thunder Island."

Sheila said, "The cottage will be built by next week. By the way, I will include some heavy defences for your new property. The associated shields will make it cyclone proof."

There was considerable curiosity on Nova when the alterations to the island were noticed, together with the name of the owner. It suddenly became fashionable to acquire remote uninhabited tropical islands.

This came as a surprise to Sienna. She had forgotten that there would always be a slight element of almost superstitious awe surrounding the Federation Empress, even one obviously trying to remain anonymous. Katie's comment that no-one would ever forget that they had a ruler, with enormous concealed power, seemed exactly correct. It also meant that her public face and statements when she appeared would have to be carefully controlled. They would be subject to searing scrutiny.

Two months later, she discovered that she was pregnant.

Caroline laughed when she heard. "I think it would be a good idea to actually go on that tour to the other planets in the not too distant future, before you are too far gone. You will also have to ask Crystal to arrange that Iain's name and face doesn't appear on any news program!

"Discovering that their Empress is pregnant but still incognito, is really going to stir up the press!"

5a – History debate

A week later, Katie came to dinner at the cottage on the island. She was waiting for the next temporal disaster to occur, and had again been effectively on holiday.

After the first course, Sienna asked; "Katie, has your Bearing group tried to anticipate where this alien entity would attack next?

"I have been thinking about this, and some possibilities immediately occurred to me.

"Apart from Hitler, the other absolute standout for the Second World War was a British Prime Minister called Winston Churchill.

"In 1940, the British were bundled out of Norway after an unsuccessful attempt to assist that country and then the British and French armies were routed in France. There was a successful evacuation of most of the British Army by sea, but all its equipment was lost. All that remained to defend the country were 25 squadrons of fighters, and a badly overstretched navy.

"I seem to remember that the British Cabinet was about to throw in the towel, when the newly elected Prime Minister Winston Churchill persuaded Parliament to fight on with some rousing speeches. A few of the more powerful members in the Cabinet were ready to open negotiations, which would only have had one result- the total demotivation the British people and effective surrender.

"Churchill had had a pretty chequered political career, and was on few lists at the beginning of the war as someone who would be critically important.

"When he was elected Prime Minister, it seems that he was not even certain he would keep the job for long. However, he was utterly determined to keep on fighting.

"If the British had capitulated in the summer of 1940, Hitler would have been able to throw the total might of his army and air force at Russia in the autumn of that year, undistracted by battles elsewhere. It is probable that Moscow would have been taken, and the Russians would have sued for peace.

"At that point, the Germans would have been almost undefeatable militarily. In the unlikely event of the Americans entering a war against them, landing an invasion fleet somewhere in Europe in the face of a completely focused German army and air force would have been impossible.

"Europe would have entered a new dark age.

"Apart from Churchill, I also thought that the President in the American Civil War would qualify. If I remember right, he was called Abraham Lincoln.

"All the historical reports I read seemed to think he was amongst the best Presidents to have ever held that position. The American Civil War was an epic affair, and casualties were staggering. The Southern States bitterly defended what they regarded as their way of life. While we regard slavery as completely obnoxious, I don't think in reality it was anywhere near as bad as it was made out to be, except for rare exceptions which were horrific. As far as I can tell, while the white men from the estates were fighting, management of the estates by the slaves continued in an orderly fashion. I don't recall any revolts, which might have been expected.

"Anyhow, I believe that by the end of the war, one in three of the eligible southern men of military age had become casualties.

"Abraham Lincoln was instrumental in ensuring the North prosecuted the war effectively.

"If the war had ended differently, or had never started, which was a possibility, that would certainly have affected a large part of history.

"Katie, those were the first of the possibilities I considered.

"The other one is slightly more obscure. In the 15th century, the Chinese were learning to send major expeditions a long way from China. They certainly reached the East Coast of Africa, and possibly much further. I can't remember exactly what happened, but they suddenly withdrew from exploring elsewhere, and I believe all their major shipyards were destroyed.

"If this had not happened, it might have been Chinese junks sailing up the rivers of Europe in the 16th century, rather than British gunboats sailing up Chinese rivers 300 years later.

"Certainly, the history of the world would have changed dramatically."

Katie looked thoughtful for a few minutes.

She said, "I suspect that your knowledge is more up-to-date than mine, Sienna, as you are a history major. I will have a look at the databases and see what I think.

"At the moment, my more immediate list includes Napoleon Bonaparte, the Duke of Wellington, a man called John Churchill who became the Duke of Marlborough, and then Isaac Newton.

"Curiously, Churchill was a distant relative of the British Prime Minister of that name."

A week later she returned.

Katie came to the point as soon as Iain had provided a coffee.

"I have been doing some serious research on your suggestions, Sienna.

"With respect to the British Prime Minister Winston Churchill, I think you are absolutely right that he was a key historical figure. If he had not been in place in 1940, history would have changed completely.

"As to why this alien Aon does not appear to have targeted him, I can only speculate. The first possibility is that she was simply too close in time to the other disruption she planned for the era. Energy limitations might have prevented her from taking on more than one historical figure. Otherwise, it is possible she simply never noticed. In her eyes, Churchill may have made enough mistakes to make him less than distinguished as a leader.

"It would be easy to miss the fact that he was the swing factor in several absolutely crucial decisions.

"I have vast research resources at my disposal; Aon has only a rather disjointed database."

Sienna and Iain could only nod thoughtfully.

"Abraham Lincoln is certainly a possibility. You are correct in suggesting he was one of the great leaders of the United States. The problem I have, is that I think that war between the North and South was probably inevitable. Even if he was eliminated from history, I don't think the end result would have been different. He would not have been a key divertant.

"For your Chinese case, again I think you are absolutely right. If the Chinese had not abandoned – no, destroyed – their shipyards, and all the associated exploration, they would have dominated the planet.

"Once again, I suspect that the decision was probably inevitable. As far as I can see, Chinese politics at the time was dominated by factions. The faction that wanted to explore lost out to the faction that wanted to turn more attention towards facing the Mongols and other developments. There is no one person whom history has labelled as responsible.

"Having said that, our database is full of gaps. There might have been such a key individual, but he or she is not identifiable from the historical record.

"Aon does not have the luxury of being able to spend a large amount of time searching for that person."

Siena laughed. "I am glad our alien enemy can make mistakes and does have some limitations!

"By the way, we are planning our long delayed tour of the outer Federation planets for next month. Which ones do you think we should visit?"

There was a lengthy discussion on this.

At the end of it, Iain said, "Sienna, something has just occurred to me.

"When you start appearing in the news videos slightly pregnant, it is not going to take your other Shepherd relations any time at all to figure out your identity. If I remember correctly, there are only about 30 of you in the right sort of age group. Statistically speaking, only a few of those will be just visibly pregnant, and they will still be in Melbourne!

"We better start telling them what is happening, and figure out how to maintain your camouflage. Sheila may have to start obscuring the database!"

Sienna did not say anything for a few minutes.

Then she remarked, "Crystal, I think you will have to reappear in the sky about two weeks before we leave. All my close relatives will be invited to a big party, where I will admit my identity."

5b – Re-introduction

The reappearance of Crystal caused considerable excitement in Melbourne, and there was astonishment that once again, the Empress remained entirely inconspicuous.

However, an invitation was issued to all Federation Ministers, other senior government figures, and Federation military representatives to meet her on Crystal for dinner. There were no apologies.

A similar invite went out to Sienna's close relatives two days afterwards, for another gathering a week later.

She asked her husband, "Iain, would you like to attend the official party?"

He looked startled for a moment –he had almost forgotten he was the consort of the Federation's most senior member.

"Darling, I would stand out like a sore thumb at that party. If we want to be able to continue some sort of normal life in Melbourne, it's really important that I stay out of the way!

"As it is, I hope your relatives are as close lipped as you think, when they discover your real position!"

Sienna was nervous as she met her guests as they entered the Crystal Palace for the official party. She had a golden cat on one shoulder, and her aunt the Governor stood on the other side. In fact Caroline was pleased. Her young Empress was actually most impressive in a long silvery dress matching her blonde hair and white gloves. Crystal murmured the name of the guests as they came in, so Sienna was able to greet them with their own names directly.

She gave Admiral Jenna an especially warm greeting when he arrived with two vice admirals.

As the group walked away, the Admiral said to his colleagues, "I expect Sylvia will try and talk to you during the evening. Operate on the assumption that she is extremely well informed despite her young age. I made that mistake when I first met her, and she picked me up sharply. After that, I promised myself that I would never, ever underestimate her again.

"She is keenly interested in how we are performing, and frequently drops in on me without notice. She seems to have no problem at all in avoiding our security measures, which I put down to assistance from Crystal and Sheila!"

This was news to the two vice admirals; they had heard rumours that the Admiral had met Sylvia a few times, but this was the first concrete confirmation they had heard.

He continued rather apologetically, "I'm sorry not to have kept you informed about this, but our Empress is determined to stay as inconspicuous as possible. She simply ordered me not to tell anyone!"

During the casual drinks, Sylvia and Caroline circulated as widely as possible, and then the formal dinner started.

Caroline noticed that the Empress was looking much more relaxed – it was clear that in many cases the guests were nervous talking to her, and Sylvia was going out of her way to make them feel more comfortable. The realisation was clearly dawning on her that she was the real controller, and these were her people to be guided and assisted.

After the first course, Sylvia stood.

Silence spread like a wave across the room.

"My people, I am delighted to see you all here tonight.

"I am trying hard to keep a distance from my private life and my persona as Empress. I asked my husband if he would like to come this evening, but he was adamant that he wanted to stay out of the limelight. Our identity will eventually become known, but we would like to defer that process for as long as possible.

"If you accidentally find out about me, I ask you to keep silent.

"I would like the twins which I am expecting to be several years old before they have any exposure to the glare of publicity."

There was a slightly excited murmur as Sylvia said this. These were two items of news – marriage and children – which would set the news services alight.

Guests who tried to access electronic items discreetly found that transmissions were blocked.

"More seriously, I am concerned about reports that some of the more outlying planets of the Federation have been relatively slow to implement critical health programs. Some of the legal systems also seem to have maintained a large element of inequity or perhaps criminality. In one case, other problems are becoming apparent.

"I shall be visiting some of those planets over the next few months, and I will be interested in hearing how those problems are going to be resolved.

"For resolved, they will be."

The realisation swept over the audience that their young Empress had no intention of just being a figurehead for most of the time.

When the speech finished, Sylvia asked for questions. The representative from Xicon raised his hand. "My Lady, your speech was most illuminating. As a matter of interest to my people, have you heard from the former Empress Katie at all?"

Across Xicon, Katie had been regarded with hatred or reverence depending on the location of the viewer. She remained the one being who had truly awed the species.

Sylvia looked at him for a moment. "She is fighting a war with the support of the Bearing Community. She has already suffered terribly. As I said to Admiral Jenna once, we had better really, really, hope she is successful. Nothing our Federation can do will help her, and defeat would represent disaster on many levels.

"She is vastly more than I am, but she does talk to me regularly. I will not say any more on this matter."

Nearly everyone in the audience looked at her in shock, and for a few seconds there was complete silence in the room.

Later in the evening, after the guests had left, Caroline said to Sienna "Most of the people in the audience this evening left with the strong impression that you intend to do something about some of the outer planets. Rumours that I have heard indicate that your concerns are well founded.

"Before she abdicated, Katie said that one of my most important functions would be to provide advice. I can't do that, if I have no idea of your intentions!"

Sylvia laughed, "All right, this is how I am going to approach the issues."

She proceeded to explain the tentative plans that she, Iain and Katie had agreed.

Her Governor made some pertinent suggestions, and was happy when Sylvia agreed immediately

The family party that Sienna had organised was a much more cheerful affair.

Once again, the Empress was conspicuous by her absence when they arrived. However, her speech and comments had been widely circulated, and a large proportion of Sienna's family had a strong suspicion of her identity.

One Shepherd girl was talking to another Shepherd about this.

The latter said, "Sylvia really wants to try and lead an ordinary life for as long as possible. She is beginning to feel comfortable with her role as Empress, which needs the support of her family. That's why this party was organised.

"By the way, it's nice to meet you. My name is Katie."

The other girl said, "I thought the family had more or less agreed a long time ago to never use that name again?"

Katie laughed, "I don't think that applies to me!"

The other girl looked at her in surprise, as she realised the meaning of the comment.

Katie continued, "It looks like Caroline and Crystal are organising the reception!"

There was a low stage at the end of the room, and Caroline and the Crystal avatar had moved to the front of the stage.

Caroline said, "My Lady, would you and your husband care to join us!"

Iain and Sienna threaded their way through the family up to the stage. A small golden cat ran from the side and jumped on her shoulder.

Sienna said, "Everyone, thank you for coming this evening. As you will have gathered, Iain and I have been reluctant to abandon our cloak of anonymity. I apologise for not telling you all sooner, although I have a suspicion that many of you actually knew my position!"

She paused for a moment.

"As I am now pregnant with twins, this was hardly a tenable position going into the future.

"Sheila and Crystal are obscuring the databases, and enquiries about our family will not go anywhere from now onwards.

"I have assured Iain, that none of you will tell the wider community our private identity.

"We are going to be touring some outer Federation planets for the next two months.

"I'm sure that Aunty Caroline will get on with running the Federation in my absence, with her customary efficiency!

"And now, let us just enjoy the party!"

5c – Cheetah

When proceedings had finished, Katie had a short talk with Iain and Sienna.

"As a belated wedding present, I am giving you a somewhat modified scout which will look like a luxury interstellar cruising yacht. Even the engine room area will appear ordinary to a cursory look. It will have its own artificial intelligence, called Cheetah, at the same level as Crystal, but obviously without the extensive facilities and manufacturing capabilities.

"Cheetah will be faster than any Federation ship, with formidable shields, but with only limited offensive capability. There will be two small attached shuttles and some combat remotes.

"He can house two couples comfortably, with a couple of spare bedrooms.

"Also, Cheetah will be able to operate an emergency remote transfer capability.

"This will enable you to move around the outer planets much more anonymously. As additional protection, I suggest that Crystal stays in fold space near you, which will please her. She will give Cheetah some real protection if he needs help."

Sienna looked happy at the gift and this comment, but Katie saw that Iain was frowning a little.

"What's the problem, Iain?"

He said, "Thank you for the present, Katie. What I wondered, was whether it would be helpful to Sienna to bring some other people along? This might also make us less conspicuous, and provide some company!

"Even Sienna's scintillating conversation will start to pall if we are on our own for too long!"

His wife replied, "That was a low blow, but you are probably right!

"I'm sure there must be a young naval couple somewhere who would like to come along. I will ask Admiral Jenna. Also, I will just describe Cheetah as a super scout, without mentioning any of his additional capabilities or Crystal's hidden presence."

Her Admiral was happy with the idea; he had been concerned about his Empress travelling around the outer planets anonymously and with no assistance.

"Sylvia", he said after a few minutes thought, "I think that is an excellent idea. There must be a few military couples who might fit the bill. I will get back to you shortly."

Unbeknown to him, Katie influenced the selection.

* * *

Lieutenant Peter Moore had recently married a Lieutenant in the Marines. They were surprised to find themselves ordered to report to Admiral Jenna.

Arriving at the office, he told the Flag Lieutenant; "Lieutenant Peter Moore and Lieutenant Louise Moore reporting as ordered."

They were ushered straight into the Admiral's office, where they smartly came to attention while trying to disguise their nervousness. A coffee service with biscuits stood on a tray at the edge of the Admiral's desk, and a wisp of steam writhed from the pot.

Admiral Jenna's smiled slightly, "At ease, and please take seats."

The Admiral was familiar with the two Lieutenants' careers, which he had looked at carefully.

They were both about 23 years old, had seen action against pirates, and had received commendations. Peter Moore was an intelligence expert, and Louise Moore had specialised in small arms and unarmed combat in the Marines.

The only negatives in their career reports were that they had both shown signs of an addiction to practical jokes, and had been slightly disrespectful to some senior officers. The Admiral had pulled up details of the latter, and decided that he would probably have been disrespectful as well.

Peter was slightly built, but his wife was large and solid.

The Admiral said, "This conversation is entirely off the record and informal. Louise, would you mind serving the coffee and biscuits, please?"

When this had been done, he continued "Under no circumstances are you to repeat any of the conversation we will have in the next few minutes to anyone. Is that clearly understood?"

"Yes, Admiral" was the immediate and almost simultaneous response. Both officers were becoming still more apprehensive.

He said, "I need to send two married officers on a long term detached duty."

"Peter, you would be captain of what has been described as a super scout, with Louise as your first officer. There would be no other crew, but I'm assured that the scout is rather sophisticated.

"You would be responsible for escorting and protecting two civilians, for an indefinite period.

"Do not for one moment think this is any detraction from your careers. You are amongst the best young officers in my fleet, and you would be given additional authority to co-opt help if needed. The civilians are under Imperial Protection, of which you would form a part.

"Before I proceed further, do you accept this detachment?"

Two young officers looked at each other. Louise nodded almost imperceptibly. She was more observant than her husband, and the assignment had to be important for the Admiral of the Fleet to be asking them to volunteer.

Peter said, "Yes Admiral, we volunteer."

Admiral Jenna said, "Good. You will receive promotions to commander and major respectively, dated from when your voyage starts."

Both the young officers looked startled at these considerable promotions.

"I will issue formal written orders to you covering these points. Other sealed orders will be issued which will enable you to co-opt assistance from any Federation military or diplomatic arm, and the co-opted personnel must follow your instructions whatever their rank."

Peter said, "Admiral, may we ask the identity of the civilians, and who will provide the instructions as to destinations?"

The Admiral said "I have been told not to give you their names or other details of what they will be doing, and you will accept their instructions as to when and where to travel. Be prepared to stand up to them on security matters, which may be difficult. Having said that, I think you will find them interesting. While you will need some formal uniforms made up to your new ranks, I suggest you take a good supply of civilian gear. That is what your passengers will expect you to wear for most of the time. After this meeting, see the armoury officer on this vessel, and select what you might need for personal weaponry with his assistance. He can also organise the uniforms. He has been ordered to be absolutely discrete, and everything will be delivered to the scout.

"A shuttle will collect you at your base at midday in three days. If anyone asks, just say you're being assigned for training. Your commanding officers will have been informed that you are being transferred to undertake other duties.

"Be very wary about saying anything to anyone; this detachment is extremely important. Good luck.

"Dismissed."

When they were well outside anyone's hearing, Louise said "Peter, there are only a handful of people in the Federation who can give instructions to the Admiral of the Fleet.

"Moreover, it sounds like our sealed orders will give us enormous authority."

* * *

Their fellow officers had been surprised to hear about the Moores' sudden transfer for 'training purposes'.

However all the pair would say was, "We have no idea where we are being sent ultimately."

When the small shuttle appeared to take them to the scout, they wore their old uniforms, but the bystanders were a little puzzled at the amount of luggage the young officers were taking, which appeared to include all of their civilian gear.

As they approached their new vessel, they saw that it was similar in size and shape to a scout, except the rear half appeared distinctly larger.

There were no obvious weapons blisters.

It was a polished silver colour except for black viewing windows around the front. A large picture of a leaping cheetah was painted on each side.

There was a class of luxury interstellar yachts which looked similar.

After the shuttle entered the scout and landed, a door slid open on the side and steps folded down. As they walked out, Sienna and Iain were waiting. Two remotes passed them, clearly intent on collecting their luggage.

To Louise, the waiting couple looked remarkably like university students, one of them clearly a Shepherd.

The latter said, "Peter and Louise, welcome aboard. We are called Sienna and Iain; and the ship is called Cheetah.

"Your luggage will be transferred while we show you around. I expect my cat will put in an appearance at some stage."

The scout was a surprise. The living areas were luxuriously appointed throughout, with a large common room and dining area, and a small gymnasium, kitchen, and surgery. The latter looked surprisingly well equipped and included paediatric equipment.

There was a compact shooting range.

Louise particularly approved of her large bedroom, with attached ensuite. She gathered that Sienna and Iain's quarters were similar.

There were two spare single bedrooms, which shared a bathroom.

The control room at the bow was conventional. There were large windows, viewing screens to cover all surrounding space, and four command chairs, with the captain and co-pilots' seats slightly lower and forward.

The captain's position was equipped with navigation and viewing screens, and standard throttle and direction joysticks, while the co-pilot seat appeared to control weaponry, shields, and more screens.

Peter said, "Iain, why only one set of flight controls?"

It was the ship who answered in an accent free male voice; "Commander, no extras are required. I control all functions including the engine room. You simply specify where you wish to go, and any other requirements, and these will be arranged. You can use the controls if you wish, but that is unnecessary."

Peter was taken aback for a moment, and then said; "Cheetah, please call us Peter and Louise.

"For my own curiosity, what is your level of sophistication?"

Louise was interested to note that Sienna looked a little uncertain – she clearly did not realise or had forgotten that Peter was an intelligence officer – and she had a sense that a communication process was occurring.

Sienna said, "You might as well know. Sentience."

Peter looked thoughtful for a moment. "Up to now, I was only aware of three sentient AIs in this part of the galaxy. They have only ever been connected with one identity.

"My Lady, what is our first destination?"

Cheetah said, "You are quick off the mark, Peter. Sienna – as you so rightly surmised, better known as the Empress Sylvia – had a bet with Iain that you would take at least an hour to figure it out.

"Sienna, the washing up liquid is awaiting your attention after the first meal!

The young Empress laughed, "Okay, I concede. Peter and Louise, it is hard to make a worthwhile bet on this scout when the remotes will provide everything given half a chance. Unpleasant realities like washing up are about the only way we can provide some penalties! Elsewhere, the bets can be more purposeful!

"To get back to your question, Peter, we are going to Datura, where it looks like problems are beginning to emerge. The government seems to be acting increasingly like a criminal gang rather than a democratic organisation, and there is suspected complicity in extortion and kidnapping.

"A number of tourists have gone missing. A few have been released after substantial ransoms were paid. The police appear quite ineffective.

"The opposition parties have been muzzled, and although the press is still free this is unlikely to last.

"The trip will take about two weeks.

"Please come through, and have a coffee. After that, I suggest you unpack and get out of those uniforms. This ship runs casual, and we plan to stay as anonymous as possible. That is becoming my trademark. This means we must look like tourists, and you need to adopt that camouflage as well.

"Iain and I will then explain our plans. Cheetah, please get underway, and cut to a normal speed when we start to approach Datura."

Peter and Louise gradually relaxed over supper. Conversation was intelligent and light hearted.

As Sienna and Iain outlined their plans, the full importance of their role dawned on the two officers. They asked a large number of questions, and were pleased to note that Sienna was happy to change her plans when those questions exposed likely difficulties or led to possibly better outcomes.

They moved to the common room for coffee after the meal. A nondescript tabby cat was sprawled over a sofa, and it meowed softly as they entered. As soon as Louise had sat down, the cat transferred itself to her lap.

At the end of the meal, Sienna washed and rinsed the plates and glasses. She would not allow anyone to help. When she had finished, the remotes moved in to load the dishwasher with the cleaned plates.

Before she went to bed, Sienna said; "Cheetah, please link Peter and Louise into our communications network, and train them to speak subvocally".

Later on, Peter and Louise gravitated towards the control room, eager to find out more about the craft.

Louise said, "Cheetah, apart from sentience, how does your performance differ from an ordinary scout craft?"

The answer was, "Katie had me built at the main Bearing manufacturing centre. I can outrun any Federation craft, my screens are equivalent to those on a Federation battleship, but I have little in the way of weaponry. I have some small conventional and fusion missiles and some mercury guns. There are also three combat remotes.

"None of the weaponry is visible to casual inspection as I am designed to look like a civilian yacht.

"My surveillance probes are practically undetectable, and I have two small shuttles which have strong shields.

"Running is my preferred option in case of trouble, while we organise some more substantial help.

"The main reason for having a control room, was to help disguise my capabilities. This is important with Sienna intending to play galactic tourist while she investigates the problems in the outer planets.

"When those are reached, I hold override codes which will enable control of the computer complexes.

"Peter, that should give you enormously enhanced information capability. I can handle the information processing requirements."

There was a short pause, then Cheetah continued; "You and Louise are my Captain and First Officer. However I will act independently if I believe that Sienna is endangered or it is warranted for other reasons. Also, it is my opinion that you should be prepared to argue with Sienna and Iain if you don't agree with their view at any point. I'm afraid our Empress can be a little headstrong, and I will need assistance in reining her in sometimes!

"She needs someone to disagree with her occasionally".

5d – First planetary visit

Over the next two weeks, the couples begin to get to know each other.

Peter and Iain quickly became friends, but Sienna found it more difficult to get along with Louise. While she realised that having another woman on board would be a great help when she reached the more uncomfortable parts of pregnancy, she found the major a little too military for her taste. On her side, Louise found that with her training and temperament as a soldier, it was difficult to adjust to a woman who totally fitted her mental model of a rather indolent student.

A slightly stiff formality remained between them.

When they reached Datura, the space authority gave them a parking orbit about 100,000 km from the surface.

As with all Federation planets, a Fleet detachment was in place. On the flagship, a bored communications officer made a routine query to the computer complexes about the new yacht's registration, and last known owners and passengers.

He was startled to be told, "The registration of the vessel Cheetah is in order, but you are not authorised for further information."

With his curiosity piqued, the captain of the flagship ordered a destroyer to make a close in scan of the luxury yacht.

About two in the morning, Cheetah woke Peter and Louise.

"I'm sorry to disturb you, but a problem has arisen.

The AI sounded embarrassed, "I made a mistake when we first entered this solar system. The computer complexes were left to run as normal.

"The fleet detachment queried my identity and passengers. Unfortunately, part of the automatic response was to tell the Fleet officers that they were not authorised for the latter information.

"Since it is hard to imagine anything more likely to arouse their curiosity, they sent a destroyer for a close in scan. Naturally, that failed.

"I apologise for the mistake, which will not be repeated.

"In the meantime, we need to prepare a response."

On the battleship, the results of the routine scan from the destroyer were received with some consternation.

The captain had roused his Admiral and was explaining, "Apart from being told by the computer complexes that we are not authorised to know the identity of the owner or passengers, our close in scan bounced completely. That civilian luxury craft has military grade anti-surveillance screens. More to the point, neutrino emission analysis indicates that the engines of that craft are at least an order of magnitude more powerful than is possible for its size."

The Admiral thought about this for a moment. "Invite the captain and first officer of the vessel to shuttle over and see us. If they demur, quietly suggest that we will impound them under anti-smuggling regulations."

Back on Cheetah, Iain and Sienna had also been woken.

Sienna was quite bad tempered. Louise hoped that pregnancy hormones were responsible.

Fortunately, Iain took his wife in hand rather firmly.

"Sienna, it is not Louise's fault that she had to wake you. Also, this is the first time that Cheetah has actually travelled to another planet, and he is entitled to make one mistake!

"We need to quickly decide how to respond."

A short time later, a message was sent to the Federation flagship that the captain and first officer would come over immediately on a shuttle.

The two young officers remembered not to salute as they arrived, but Peter could not restrain himself from saying "Permission to come aboard, Lieutenant?"

After it was determined that they carried no weapons, armed marines escorted them to the room where the Admiral, the captain and his executive officer were waiting. Before they arrived, they received a message from the Lieutenant, "Captain, I strongly suspect that the two people on the shuttle have a military background. They were quite familiar with procedures, and did not show any curiosity about the flagship surrounds."

Two soldiers parked themselves in the corner of the room.

The Admiral said, "Please introduce yourselves."

Peter said, "I am Peter Eden, and my first officer is Louise Eden.

"Admiral, I request that all personnel apart from yourself withdraw from this room. If you are concerned about your safety, we will consent to being restrained in the seats."

The captain started to say something, but the Admiral stopped him with a gesture.

"Everyone leave."

As the doors were shut by a concerned looking marine, the Admiral said; "Explain."

Peter took a microchip from his shirt pocket.

"Admiral, our real names are Commander Peter Moore, and my first officer is Major Louise Moore.

"These are sealed orders, which I request that you verify and read."

The Admiral took the microchip, which was inserted into a reader on the desk.

"Ship computer, verify this microchip, check the results with the computer complexes, and print out the sealed orders."

There was silence in the room for a minute, when the computer said, "Orders verified with the computer complexes. Printing."

The Admiral took the single sheet, and started reading. When he had finished he said, "These are extraordinary orders, Commander.

"Let me see. You arrive in a vessel with an impossible specification. We don't have a sufficient security clearance to be told the name of the passengers. You hold orders which effectively make you both the senior officers on any planet on which you arrive, and a certain young lady made a widely publicised speech about five weeks ago. I don't need you to complete the dots."

Louise spoke for the first time, "Admiral, the identification and security clearance response was a mistake, which we will not repeat in future. I have to confess I'm alarmed at how quickly you drew certain conclusions."

The Admiral laughed, "I'm glad my brain is not completely atrophied!

"Commander and Major, what are your instructions? By the way, I would suggest that the captain of this ship and his XO also be made a party to these orders."

Peter said, "Please invite them in, Admiral".

The Admiral pressed a button on his desk, and said "Captain, please join us with your XO".

The officers quickly entered, clearly relieved that nothing untoward had happened.

"Gentlemen, the real names of our guests are Commander Peter Moore, and Major Louise Moore, which I assume means they are married.

"Before we go any further, please read these orders, which have been verified."

The Captain read the single sheet of paper, his eyebrows rising as he finished.

He passed it over to his subordinate, and said, "Admiral, I have never seen orders like this!

"An obvious conclusion can be drawn from them."

Peter laughed, "Another sharp mind at work. Gentlemen, at the moment all we can ask is that you back off and make us look as inconspicuous as possible. If anyone queries why our vessel was scanned, please provide a reassuring answer, even if it is less than honest.

"I suspect we may need some help a little further down the track. Please be ready to act very quickly if that happens!"

Just before they left, the Admiral said; "Commander, I do have one request. Before you leave the system, I would like to host a dinner for you and your passenger with the senior officers from the Fleet. Could you try and persuade her to say 'yes'?"

Chapter 6

NAPOLEONIC CHANGES

THREE DAYS LATER, KATIE HEARD THAT the databases had once again skewed wildly.

As she and the Bearing group looked at the new historical record from Earth, it was clear that the Napoleonic wars had ended in a rather different manner.

Napoleon had been victorious at Waterloo in 1815. The Duke of Wellington had been killed, and a large part of his army destroyed.

Blucher and the Prussian army had been routed, and the French armies had reoccupied Belgium and Holland. The UK government fell, and a Whig government was installed.

However, all the countries involved with the war were exhausted and almost insolvent.

A truce was arranged, and fighting more or less stopped everywhere. Napoleon returned to Paris, and concentrated on trying to restore France.

In September, a general peace treaty was signed.

Mount Tambora in Indonesia erupted catastrophically in April 1815, and the 1815/16 winter was bad. The following months were worse, and 1816 became known as the "Year without a summer". European, North American and Asian harvests were disastrous, and terrible famines developed all across the Northern Hemisphere.

Napoleon tackled famine in his country with great efficiency. Compared with the rest of Europe, the death rate was much lower. Despite the climate ravages and the nearly one million people killed in the Napoleonic wars, France became the dominant European power. There was an appreciation in the country of how much was owed to the Bonaparte dynasty, which became completely entrenched with popular support. When Napoleon died in 1823, his son inherited his position without noticeable dissent.

Britain was successful in dominating overseas areas, and a "British Empire" appeared which was not too dissimilar to that which had occurred in the original history.

Another major historical change was in North America, where France re-engaged with its ex colonies on the Gulf of Mexico. A short and vicious war was fought with states further North, despite France having had a loose alliance with the United States during the Napoleonic wars. A separate country was carved out which called itself "The United Southern States."

This mostly comprised what would have been known as Louisiana, Mississippi, Alabama, Georgia, and Florida. With continued robust support from France, the new state survived.

Texas retained its independence, and managed to expand westwards at the expense of Mexico.

Effectively the United States was partitioned into three countries.

In Europe, the Low Countries and a large part of what would have been known as Italy effectively became French satellites.

Prussia, Hungary and Austria, were forced to merge in order to retain their independence from France.

Russia absorbed a large part of Poland and then concentrated on expanding eastwards.

The net result of this was a world utterly different politically from the "safe" history.

This ended badly when the Calai arrived, and no defence was offered.

* * *

Once again, Katie and her group started to examine the detail on the databases. It was quickly apparent that it was in June 1815 that history had split.

In particular, the two battles immediately before the Battle of Waterloo seemed to be critical.

The Battle of Ligny and the Battle of Quatre Bras both took place on the same date, 16th June, two days before the Battle of Waterloo.

In the "safe" history, the battle at the crossroads of Quatre Bras was more or less a draw, but the allies held the advantage in that they controlled the crossroads at the end of the day.

In the case of the Battle of Ligny, the Prussians were defeated after a day's fierce fighting and forced to retreat. However, the French lacked sufficient strength to make the battle crushing, and the retreat was in relatively good order.

A curiosity of these two battles, was that the Compte d'Erlon, with 20,000 men and about 40 guns, had almost reached Napoleon at the Battle of Ligny when he received a most urgent order from Marshall Ney to return. In practice, this meant that his Corps spent the entire day marching without contributing to any of the battles, which were only about 10 km apart.

In the "new" history, the recall order was not received or ignored. The arrival of 20,000 relatively fresh French troops turned the Prussian defeat into a rout. Blucher was seriously injured, and as well as taking huge casualties his army lost all its guns and was widely dispersed. D'Erlon was given a detachment of 10,000 men and plenty of cavalry to continue to vigorously pursue the Prussians.

Napoleon had the further advantage that he no longer needed to peel off 33,000 men under Marshall Grouchy to keep the Prussians off his back. That had failed in the "safe" history, when amazingly, Grouchy had managed to lose contact with them.

In the new version of history, Napoleon was in a position to defeat his enemies in detail.

The result at Quatre Bras was unchanged, but when Wellington heard what had happened to the Prussians, he considered retreating all the way to Brussels. It would now be impossible for the Prussians to come to his aid. The problem with this strategy, was that this was likely to destroy the morale of his troops, and in all likelihood a large part of his Dutch-Belgian contingent would desert. Since Belgium had been a French department since 1995, while before that it had been controlled by Austria, the loyalties of a large part of its people were suspect. Retreat would also be a political disaster for the United Kingdom; there was a possibility that the government at Westminster would fall, and the Dutch might surrender.

Wellington felt that that he had no option but to stand and fight at Waterloo, although he had severe misgivings about the outcome. At least it was an area he had reconnoitred in depth, and offered a strong defensive position.

In practice, his misgivings were totally justified. Napoleon, who was feeling rather ill on the morning of 18 June, put off attacking until the following day. Not only was he feeling better, but the ground had sufficient time to dry properly.

With French morale at a new high, and with considerably more troops than Wellington, a much fitter Napoleon outflanked and outfought his opponent and destroyed the British squares with artillery. Wellington died inside one of the squares.

The Allied Army disintegrated, and Napoleon occupied Brussels. Holland sued for peace, the British government fell, and a new Whig government called for a truce.

For Katie, the most important point was that the messenger from Marshall Ney had failed to make the Compte D'Erlon turn his Army Corps around and march back to Quatre Bras before it could assist Napoleon at Ligny.

That was the swing point from which everything followed.

Talking to her group she said, "I must practice my rather poor French, and then park myself in Brussels well before June 2015. I'm not entirely sure at the moment how we make sure D'Erlon turns back. What is certain is that I need to be there in good time, free from jump shock and well integrated with the local population."

Her Bearing friend Iva said, "Something has just occurred to me.

"Neither you or Aon can afford to make the local Bearing aware of your presence. Aon might find herself meeting her sane past version, causing elimination.

"That would create an utterly unpredictable time loop as the local group became aware of the future.

"If I was a part of the Bearing Community of that time, I would then study the Qui carefully. At that stage they had not started their dramatic expansion. It is possible they could be fenced into the home planet, and stripped of their technology. Another possibility would be immediate extermination, although I am not certain how that would sit with an earlier version of Aon. The result might be the same.

"Anyhow, to return to my theme I do not believe that she can afford to embark on a killing spree. Neither can she afford to hang around for any length of time as she might be noticed. Moreover, the death of the messenger will immediately start to change the future. Aon will realise that she could also be caught up in a chronon disaster, with unpredictable consequences.

"Katie, I think we need to consider the position carefully before your plans are finalised. You should enlist your human group to help. I noticed that your new Empress has been joined by two officers for whom European history was a specialist study!

"As the Bearing, we are too powerful and too detached. We need some human input to make sure we are handling human psychology correctly.

Katie decided to move to Sienna's location, and pay a visit.

6a – Visiting Datura

Back on Cheetah, Sienna decided her little group should start to play tourist while the planetary databases were investigated by the AI.

Most of the kidnappings had occurred in a particular area which was historically interesting. It was summer in the region, which enjoyed a Mediterranean climate. She asked Peter and Louise which town in the area they thought they should visit first, as they had been studying the local geography.

Louise said with a smile, "A small town called Caplin looks interesting. It has the local equivalent of Greek tavernas, and a famous swimming beach. In the hills behind the town, the architectural ruins are apparently spectacular."

The Daturans were hominoid, with regional differences in colouration. With some rare exceptions, their food was edible to humans. As the Federation language, English was widely spoken.

The group enjoyed touring the town, and Iain irritated everyone slightly by stopping to take photographs of anything he thought might be interesting.

Sienna indulged in a somewhat imprudent level of shopping. Peter and Iain were struggling a little with the load when they came to a small cafe overlooking the beach, where they decided to eat.

Peter was just starting on his second course when he looked up and saw another human woman about 50 meters away.

Sienna saw her at almost the same time, gave a happy laugh as she stood up, rushed towards the woman, and gave her a vigorous hug.

Louise murmured to Peter, "What do think the odds are of randomly meeting a human woman, no - another Shepherd - 200 light years from Nova on an obscure planet?!"

Holding hands, the two girls came back.

"Louise and Peter, please meet Katie, one of my favourite relatives!"

After a few minutes casual and cheerful conversation, another place was laid by the cafe owner and some more food ordered.

Katie saw that the two officers were looking at her with great interest.

She looked at them with unexpected seriousness. "As you two have surmised, meeting here was not an accident. I need the input of this group into my next project.

"Peter and Louise, you are now being included in a small and absolutely exclusive circle. Without Sienna's permission, you must never tell anyone that you have met me here or what I am about to tell you."

There was a moment's pause, then Sienna added with an authoritative voice they had never heard before. "Consider that an Imperial command."

Louise was surprised; the rather casual student like figure she had known was gone, instantly replaced by a deadly serious young Empress who radiated power. She realised that she had completely misinterpreted Sienna, with consequences which might have been catastrophic.

She said formally, "My Lady, I apologise for not appreciating you properly. I will never make that mistake again."

Sienna relaxed, and laughed. "Apology accepted. Please, also remember that we are playacting as tourists, and avoid that form of address completely down here.

"Katie, I think you need to do some explaining."

To the astonishment of the two officers, Katie described who and what she was, and where she had been fighting her war. She gave a quick summary of what had happened so far. She also explained the limitations of time travel, and how a chronon disaster worked.

She continued, "Part of the reason you were chosen to escort Sienna and Iain, was that one of your hobbies is European military history.

"I now need to draw on that knowledge. When you return to Cheetah, look at the historical databases and the major battles at the end of the Napoleonic wars, and think about some suggestions.

"We will have a discussion at breakfast tomorrow morning."

The conversation turned casual again.

Iain remarked, "It's just as well we had to stop for lunch. At the rate Sienna was emptying the shops, we would have had to call down the shuttle rather than Peter and I acting like pack-horses!"

Louise said, "Someone had to watch our surroundings unencumbered, and the males of the species have to have some utility!"

Both the soldiers carried concealed arms. Cheetah had arranged for them to be authorised by some deft forging of certificates with the help of the computer complexes.

Sienna smiled, and looked at Louise with a fresh understanding. She also realised that she had misunderstood the major.

Over the next 20 minutes, they finished the meal, and Katie stood up.

"You might be interested to know that you are being watched. Enjoy the afternoon."

Katie walked away. With that hint, Cheetah quickly found the watchers, and started to observe and record.

The group enjoyed a swim in the afternoon, and then returned to the yacht.

While they were on the planet, a small group of Daturans had been studying the human tourists from a distance with powerful binoculars.

The Prime Minister of the planet was contacted. When the luxury yacht Cheetah was described, he said, "It would be a good idea if this group was discovered with a quantity of *thaka* in their possession when they next return to the ground. This will enable us to legally confiscate their yacht, which will make a good addition to my private fleet."

Thaka was a highly addictive drug, with severe penalties for possession.

6b – Waterloo considerations

Back on Cheetah, as soon as they had washed and changed serious study of the Napoleonic era started, with particular reference to the 1810 to 1815 period.

Louise was concentrating on the period just before the Battle of Waterloo. She noticed something strange, and made a list of the relevant items.

She called everyone together.

"You all know I was concentrating on the Waterloo campaign. The Battle of Waterloo is actually a slight misnomer, as it really consisted of three battles. The battles of Quatre Bras and Ligny occurred on 16ᵗʰ June 1815, and the battle of Waterloo on 18ᵗʰ June, all in the same general area. The first two battles happened only about 10 km apart.

"In my view as a professional soldier, Napoleon was exceedingly unlucky to lose.

"Point one: After being defeated at Ligny, Gneisenau, the Chief of Staff of the mauled Prussian Army, unexpectedly retreated North rather than East. The latter direction would have been much safer. It meant the Prussians stayed within striking distance of Wellington. Eventually, this was critically important.

"Point two: How did Marshall Grouchy manage to "lose" the Prussian Army? He had a large cavalry detachment. All he had to do was despatch them in all possible directions to find out which way Blucher was retreating.

"Point three: Why on earth did d'Erlon turn around with his men to return to Ney at Quatre Bras when he was within sight of Napoleon at Ligny? He had been ordered to assist the Emperor. He must have known he would arrive too late to help Ney, and his corps would have enabled Napoleon to annihilate Blucher.

I might add, that if Ney had attacked Wellington as he was trying to retreat to Waterloo the following day, the Duke would have been in real strife. He was in no position to fend off the French cavalry as he was marching!

"Point four: Suffering a major thunderstorm on the night of 17th June just before Waterloo was really unlucky for Napoleon.

"Point five: A fit Napoleon would never have waited until after 11 o'clock to start the battle at Waterloo, knowing that Blucher was lurking nearby. Also, he didn't really get moving for another hour or so. While I can understand his artillery general's point about the ground being too sodden from the previous night's storm to move guns easily, it was simply an excessive delay. Wellington would have collapsed if he had started two hours earlier.

"Napoleon was most unfortunate in both feeling unwell in the morning, and also in having to retire sick later in the afternoon. That left Ney free to order unsupported cavalry to attack the British squares, which almost never worked in all the Napoleonic wars. Why didn't Ney just bring up a few light guns, and carve up the squares with grapeshot? The British cavalry had been dispersed and could not have interfered. The British guns might even have been useable for this.

"Once the squares were broken, the cavalry would have had a field day running down the soldiers.

"In contrast, Wellington was at the top of his game, and managed his side of the battle brilliantly.

"Point six: Grouchy could hear the guns at Waterloo. Why didn't he get his troops moving in that direction as soon as possible, instead of enjoying a very late breakfast? It's not clear what would have happened, but one possibility is that he would have collided with the lead elements of Blucher's army. That would have definitely delayed Blucher, perhaps crucially. The area the Prussians were marching through was ideal for a defensive posture. If he had reached the area first, Grouchy could have stopped the Prussians easily.

111

"Point seven: when Blucher started marching to support Wellington, his Chief of Staff really did not like this idea. He directed the Prussian march through congested areas, which slowed them down. What this meant was that when they did arrive, Napoleon's army was so tangled up with Wellington that it could not withdraw in good order. It was destroyed.

"He could have regrouped with the aid of Grouchy's 33,000 men.

"There are a few other points which I could mention. For example, despite all the battles in which they were involved, neither Wellington nor Napoleon were ever significantly hurt. Also, Wellington's early career was less than stellar, and it was surprising that his career progressed in India. On the other side, Napoleon seems to have led a charmed life in his Egyptian campaign, and in evading the British squadrons to return to France."

Louise paused for a moment, and took a sip of coffee.

"What I'm trying to say rather longwindedly, is that it is strange that matters panned out the way they did. That was a low probability outcome."

Sienna was impressed. Her opinion of Louise rose a few more notches.

"That is a rather brilliant, but quite disturbing, piece of analysis, Louise. I can't help wondering if there is another player in these time games!

"Now, what are we going to suggest to Katie tomorrow morning as some sort of plan?"

* * *

Over breakfast the following morning, Peter summarised the group's conclusions.

Katie was concerned at what Louise had said. The comment that the "safe" history result at the Battle of Waterloo was a low probability outcome seemed exactly right.

"If I read what you're suggesting correctly, you think that we should let Aon do her worst, and let history trundle into the new path for a week or so.

"This time, we know within a tiny period of time exactly where history was diverted. I can minimise the time needed to embed myself in the culture, and hide from Aon.

"Thinking that she has successfully derailed the future with no interference, she will retreat further into the past to do yet more damage. She has no possible way of knowing what will happen subsequently, and cannot return.

"At that point, I should move in and make some subtle alterations depending on exactly what happened.

"I will have to move myself to Brussels at least six months before Waterloo, to ensure that I am completely cured from any jump shock. Apparently, how long that will take is highly variable.

"Also, I think I would like to go to the Duchess of Richmond's Ball on the night before Waterloo. So much fiction has been written about that event, that I would love to see it for real!"

6c – Detainment on Datura

The following day, it was decided to revisit the taverna in Caplin where the group had eaten two days previously. The food, service, and general ambience had been most enjoyable.

They were just finishing coffee, when a group of police arrived. They marched up to the table and told them, "You must come with us to the police station. We have received advice that you are dealing in drugs."

Peter and Louise looked furious, and were starting to rise and reach for their weapons, when Sienna said firmly, "Nobody do anything. We will go along with the police and find out what this is about."

When they reached the station, their bags were confiscated and taken elsewhere. They were roughly escorted down a flight of stairs, and towards the bottom Iain was given a rather forceful push.

He stumbled and fell heavily on the stone floor. He was motionless for a moment, groaning slightly.

Sienna rushed up to him, and kneeling down was relieved to find he was conscious.

Iain said in a voice full of pain; "Darling, I think I have broken my wrist and my knuckles are grazed badly!"

The police officers saw the young girl looking back at them with absolute fury; she radiated …something… and without thinking they recoiled slightly.

Sienna snarled at them: "You will deeply regret this!"

Iain said quickly, "Darling, back off please, and don't do anything! I'm not that badly hurt, and it was partly an accident."

The senior police officer was interested to note that all members of the party were focused on the girl, rather than the injured man.

"Is that a threat?" he asked, sounding annoyed. "Making threats to police officers is a serious crime on this planet."

The girl looked at him, her recent fury replaced by what was clearly a cold anger, "No, it is a prediction. In the meantime, I want a human doctor here as soon as possible, and contact the Nova embassy at your capital immediately."

Meanwhile, the group's baggage was taken into a separate room. A few minutes later, the senior police officer came in with a subordinate and ordered the other police in the room to leave.

As soon as they were gone, he produced a substantial quantity of *thaka*, and placed it in the bottom of one of the bags.

The bag was closed again. He called in the officers who had just left, and said "Search these bags. Record the process."

Meanwhile, the human group had been searched, and the concealed weapons held by Peter and Louise had been discovered.

The police were quite gleeful, until Peter said "These weapons are held legally. Our copies of the documentation are in our bags and on file with your authorities."

The search upstairs was concluding, and a commercial quantity of *thaka* had been discovered. The police had enthusiastically photographed the whole process.

They did not realise that two tiny remotes were also making complete recordings.

The drugs had been found in Sienna's bag, and the police chief enjoyed explaining to her what had happened, the serious penalties for possession, and charging her. The rest of the group were charged as accessories.

None of the humans said anything, but they were all clearly furious.

Sienna looked at the senior police officer with a cold intentness. "When will the human doctor arrive?"

She was told, "In about one hour. He has been told your husband has probably suffered a broken wrist and some grazing. Your embassy has also been informed, and a representative will arrive at the same time."

The officer was surprised that none of the other members of the group seemed concerned about the charges; they appeared far more worried about the woman and how she was reacting. For a moment, a little frisson of worry ran through him. This behaviour was not normal.

When the doctor arrived, Iain was attended to immediately. The doctor's instruments showed that his wrist was indeed broken, and it was set and plastered. His other grazes were bandaged.

The other human who arrived was the second ranking member of the Nova embassy.

He told Sienna, Peter and Louise, "These charges are most serious. If commercial dealing in the amount of *thaka* allegedly discovered in Mrs Taylor's bag can be proved, there is an associated death penalty.

"I've taken the liberty of arranging for a well-known lawyer to represent you. He will be arriving in about forty minutes. In the meantime, please let me know if there is anything else I can do. I will also try and get you moved to a more comfortable set of cells. Unfortunately, these charges preclude any possible bail."

Sienna said, "Thank you for your help. We accept the help of the lawyer. Can you please advise the Federation fleet in orbit, and tell them in exactly these words 'Do nothing for the time being, until you receive a message from our yacht Cheetah. When that happens, follow the instructions.' Note those down please."

The hidden communications network had enabled Cheetah to tell all the group exactly what was occurring. High-quality recordings of all the police activities and phone calls they had made were available. This included the prime minister's comments on the telephone to the police chief.

There was consternation on the Federation battleship when the embassy official relayed the message from Sienna.

However, the instructions were clear, and for the time being the Admiral realised his hands were tied.

He had a discussion with his captain and the executive officer.

There was a realisation that these arrests could blow up into a huge diplomatic row.

The XO remarked, "Sir, the Empress could have claimed diplomatic immunity. It seems to be possible that her response was deliberate. The embassy official remarked that she seemed absolutely furious, but it is conceivable that was connected with her husband being injured.

"She may be like her great-grandmother; not a person to annoy."

When the human doctor had finished with Iain, he insisted that he examine all the other members of the party. Peter and Louise were clearly in perfect health, but his instruments immediately revealed to him that Sienna was pregnant. Both her wrists were bruised, presumably from rough police handling.

He was concerned. "Mrs Taylor, this is not a good environment for someone in your condition. The cells are not comfortable, you will not get enough exercise, and the food is unlikely to have enough human nutrients.

"I can provide you with supplements for the vitamins and missing amino acids, but you must make sure you spend at least an hour a day walking."

He saw the young woman looking back at him rather grimly. She said, "Don't worry, doctor. I don't think I'm going to be in jail for long. I will take supplements as instructed.

"Thank you for coming so promptly, and for your competent assistance. I will remember that.

"By the way, am I right in thinking you come from Europia?"

The doctor was surprised. "Yes, but how did you know?"

Sienna smiled, which was a pleasant contrast to her previous demeanour; "I have an aunt living there. I recognised the accent!"

* * *

Cheetah collated all the information from his surveillance.

He contacted his human group and said through the hidden communications net, "I have packaged all my surveillance recordings. They will suffice to jail quite a number of the officers for a long time, and the career of the Prime Minister should come to a quick end.

"Following up some of the leads, I have located almost all of the missing tourists. They are being kept in a set of caves in the hills near your town, under armed guard.

"I have also broken the encryption on a number of the computers used. The data files were interesting, to say the least.

"It appears the corruption on this planet is limited to this area of the police force and some of the heads of the current ruling party. However, they are planning to rapidly extend their control.

"How do you think we should proceed from here?"

There was an active discussion for about an hour, and a plan was agreed.

Cheetah sent a message to the Admiral in charge of the Federation fleet. It contained quite specific instructions for action in the case of certain eventualities.

In the evening, Sienna's lawyer had arrived. He reviewed the police evidence carefully, and then went down to see the human group. They were all present when he talked to Sienna.

"The police evidence is quite strong. They have no evidence that you were actually dealing in the drug.

"Personally, I am surprised that any human tourist group would be even able to obtain the amount which was found."

Peter said, "We think the drugs were planted in Sienna's bag by the police."

The lawyer looked at them. "Attacks on the police tend not to be received well on this planet.

"I might add, that the judge assigned to this case has been notoriously fierce in such cases. I do not think that would be a good argument. You would do much better to plead ignorance and throw yourself on the mercy of the court."

The lawyer saw the young human who was his principal client looking at him. There was a controlled fury in her voice. "I suspect what has happened here is what happened to several other tourists. I respect your opinion as a lawyer, sir, but you will put in a plea of Not Guilty on all the charges. Please also arrange for maximum publicity for this case."

The lawyer looked quite troubled. "As those are your instructions, Mrs Taylor, I will comply. I do not think I need to repeat my advice.

"I will see you again in three days' time. The case will start the day after that."

When he had gone, Louise said; "Those comments about the judge were interesting. I think we should ask Cheetah to do an in-depth study of him as well."

The area in which the kidnapped tourists were being held was just inside the border of another police jurisdiction. The police chief of that area had not been complicit in any criminal activity.

He received an anonymous tipoff that some hidden caves in a particular area would contain items of interest. He was warned that the gang concerned was numerous and heavily armed. It was also suggested that he only pick police members from his own staff, and under no circumstances pass the information elsewhere before the raid. "There is a risk that the information will leak to the criminal gang involved".

The data file that contained the information also provided some detailed maps of the area and the underground caves. The file was professionally formatted.

He arranged a raid for the following morning. Fifteen members of his armed response unit reported to him well before dawn. He gave them a detailed summary of the information he had received. He had decided in view of the leakage warning to leave a minimal time gap between briefing and action.

There were only two roads out of the area, and both would be sealed. The caves had two entrances, one of which was clearly an escape route. Three officers would cover the latter, and the remainder would assault the main entrance with guns and flash grenades.

Unbeknown to the police, Cheetah had deployed and concealed her three combat remotes. One would discreetly protect the captives, and the others would make any response from the gang members much less effective. The latter were more numerous and heavily armed than had been realised by the police.

The attack started precisely at dawn, and the police successfully stormed into the cave despite almost immediately returned gunfire.

The police firing had been effective, and the return gunfire had ceased after about 30 seconds. The officers did not realise that Cheetah had arranged lethal injuries for the two entrance guards.

When the human group had been discussing the plan, Iain had been quite disturbed at one of Sienna's instructions.

She had said; "Cheetah, my primary interest is in protecting the police and the captives. The death or serious injury of gang members is not of concern."

The AI had taken the comment at face value.

Peter and Louise had also been surprised; there was a ferocious side to the Empress which they had not appreciated.

Meanwhile, a fierce gunfight was occurring in the maze of underground caves. The police found that the maps that had been provided with the tipoff were exact, which was a considerable help. They were surprised at how few injuries they were receiving, and the unexpected effectiveness of their own gunfire.

Deep in the cave complex, the head of the gang was considering the position.

He told the one of the two guards of the kidnapped captives, "Activate the disaster plan, and follow us to the hidden exit. There seems to be too many police for us to resist. We must destroy all evidence."

The 'disaster plan' involved detonating hidden explosives to destroy the entire cave complex.

The two gang members fled down a side tunnel, while the third moved to the switches which controlled the timed detonating mechanisms. He was killed by a ricochet a meter before he reached the control box.

Five minutes later, the police chief and three of his officers burst into the area. They saw the gang member sprawled in front of a large switchbox. In the corner of the cave there were a number of barred doors to what were clearly holding cells. When the police looked, they found the cells contained about a dozen captives of various races. Most were huddled wimpering on crude beds. The officer who looked at the switchboard was horrified.

"Sir, these look like detonating switches. There are obviously explosives deployed throughout these caves."

Looking at the dead guard, he added; "It was most fortunate that this carrion was killed before they could be activated."

The police chief said grimly, "Look after the captives. I must call in more police, the forensic people and some explosives experts."

The chief of the gang and his subordinate were captured as they left the second exit. They were the only gang members left alive.

Half an hour later, the kidnapped tourists were gently escorted from the caves into waiting shuttles, and a serious search of the complex started after the explosives had been deactivated.

It was found to be highly organised, with bedrooms, kitchens, toilet facilities and offices.

Next to one of the computers in those offices, a quantity of data chips were placed in a drawer. They were taken away for analysis. A large amount of cash was found, together with nearly a tonne of *thaka* and what amounted to a large armoury.

Meanwhile, the planetary press had become aware of the operation, and rumours that a major gunfight had occurred spread quickly.

Police chiefs on Datura had a considerable level of autonomy. In this case, the officer concerned decided to clamp down on any release of information until his investigation concluded. He realised that this complex could not have been assembled without considerable help from state or national authorities.

The Prime Minister of the planet had immediately intervened when he heard, and demanded access for his representative to all the information which had been obtained, and that control of the investigation be transferred immediately to his nominee.

At that moment, a message was received from the Admiral of the Federation fleet orbiting the planet.

"We have received information that interplanetary drug smuggling and kidnapping of members of other planets has occurred. Under the Federation

Constitution protocols, this entire investigation must now be controlled by the Federation Fleet.

"We are sending down marine detachments to take control of the whole area."

The local police chief was furious when these detachments started to arrive.

The major in charge took him aside. "Sir, you will remain in charge of this investigation. For your private information, we have reason to believe that it will be compromised politically at an early date. We are here to ensure that you will not suffer any interference. We have also sent a detachment to guard the laboratory where the analysis of the data chips is occurring. This also includes two technicians to assist."

The police chief wondered how the Federation fleet had heard about his operation so quickly; he thought he had been successful in controlling the release of almost all information. He did not know that the same question was being discussed on the Federation flagship.

The XO on the latter summed up the position; "The information that we have received, not to mention the tipoff to the police chief on the surface, smacks of the level of technology controlled by Sheila or Crystal. I might be wrong about this, but I can see no sign of either of them around here.

"Sir, I have a suspicion that we are only pieces in this game, which our Empress is controlling covertly."

His Admiral and Captain could only agree.

The Prime Minister of Datura was becoming desperate. He was advised by his own military and his legal office that the Federation fleet did indeed have the power to intervene. Kidnapping of other species definitely empowered them to interfere. He hoped all traces of a connection to his own group had been erased.

In the laboratory where the data chips were being carefully copied and analysed, with the assistance of the two Federation technicians and with all steps carefully recorded, there was fascination at the information being revealed.

There was data on the drug trafficking which had occurred, identification of the suppliers and complete information on the relevant bank accounts.

There was data on how wealthy tourists had been identified and kidnapped. There was information about how some of those tourists had effectively bribed officials to enable their release.

There was extensive evidence of how opposition parties and the press were slowly but surely being muzzled. Preliminary plans for a complete political and military takeover were included.

Lastly, there were high-quality recordings of how the human group from Cheetah had been framed.

The police chief and his senior staff studied the information which had been gathered with a mixture of fascination and horror. He realised that without the intervention of the Federation Fleet, their investigation would have been stopped.

He decided that a press conference and release of the information should occur concurrently with the arrest of identifiable individuals.

Journalists from every major news outlets were invited, together with a number of planetary officials and members of Parliament. All noticed the large Federation detachments guarding the area when they arrived. Two Federation destroyers hovered several kilometres above the area.

Armed police arrived at the police station where Sienna and their human group were held. They were accompanied by a detachment of marines.

Most of the officers at the station were arrested. Peter and Louise collected their personal arms, and the group's baggage. As the marines escorted the human group out of the station, Cheetah's shuttle descended.

The detainment of the Prime Minister and several senior ministers with convincing evidence of criminal and treasonable activity led to collapse of the government.

In Datura as a whole, a sense of shame started to permeate the population. There was a realisation that the planet's fledgling democracy had almost been destroyed.

Elections were called.

Back on their yacht, the human group considered the position. Iain had been most concerned that their personal identification seemed inevitable.

Sienna smiled grimly. "Darling, you do not have to worry. This is what is going to happen."

"Katie has volunteered to take on my appearance, which will not be difficult for her, and she will come in with you. As we have met almost nobody from here, that will suffice to separate us from my "Sylvia" identity.

"Iain and Katie will appear in some of the film of my speech. That should be enough to convince people that I am not the Empress!"

Cheetah left orbit and Sienna transferred across to Crystal at a rendezvous far from the planet. The yacht immediately returned.

An announcement was made that in three days the Empress would arrive.

A large number of dignitaries and press representatives from Datura were invited to attend a formal dinner in the Crystal Palace, together with a number of officers from the Federation Fleet.

A certain police chief, human doctor and their wives were included.

There was a large square in front of the planetary parliament building, where Crystal landed after the surface had been suitably reinforced.

At the start of the formal dinner, Sylvia greeted her guests as they entered. She had a golden cat on her shoulder, and the Nova Ambassador and Crystal's remote on each side. Once again, the invitee's name and function were murmured in her ear as they arrived.

The Ambassador had worried how someone as young as the Empress would cope, but soon realised his fears were groundless. She might have been many decades younger, but her silver outfit suited her absolutely, and her personal presence was overwhelming. She radiated confidence and authority.

The Admiral of the Federation Fleet had been most confused. He had sat at the table with the Empress Sylvia, the four members of the group from Cheetah, the senior political representatives from Datura, and the Nova Ambassador. He had been convinced that it was the Empress who had been rescued from the surface, but it appeared that he had been wrong.

He had watched the Empress questioning Iain Taylor and his wife Sienna Taylor at length about their treatment on the planet.

Halfway through the first course, she stood up. Silence spread like a wave through the entire Hall.

Sylvia smiled slightly, "My people, I am delighted to be visiting this area, and it is with great relief that I hear that matters on Datura have been resolved.

"My understanding is that the local police, with valuable help from the Federation fleet, fixed the problems."

There was a short pause, then she continued, "I am most upset that two members of my family were mistreated in Caplin."

The camera had panned to where Iain and his wife had been sitting at the high table.

"I am furious that members of other species were equally badly treated when they visited the planet at an earlier date.

"All such cases will be re-investigated carefully, with compensation where appropriate.

"In future, I shall be annoyed to hear of any mistreatment of visiting tourists on any planet."

She had gone on to make some complimentary comments about how well the local economy was integrating with the rest of the Federation, and the improvement in local health statistics. She had remarked that from recordings made by a shuttle which she had seen, Datura was an astonishingly beautiful planet.

These comments greatly pleased the local population.

During the second course, the Empress had walked around and sat at a number of the tables, talking for a little while at each.

Peter and Louise had watched in fascination, aware that their young Empress was displaying enormous political skill. She was acquiring a fanatically loyal following on Datura, and ensuring that any guilt feelings from the previous political missteps were quelled.

At one table, she had talked briefly to a young human doctor and his wife. Just as she was about to move on, he murmured; "I notice your bruises have nearly faded, My Lady."

She looked at him, and smiled. She said softly, "You are observant, doctor. Please don't tell anyone! When you return to Nova, contact Crystal. I would like to meet you and your wife again."

On the shuttle back to Cheetah, Katie's eyes had started to glow.

She said; "It was interesting to pretend to be Sienna. Peter and Louise, you are fitting in well, good luck in the future."

Katie vanished.

Recordings of the evening spread across the Federation at foldspace speed.

There was no mention of the luxury yacht Cheetah, and Iain and Sienna Taylor were not named.

Detailed pictures of the Empress Sylvia and the Crystal Palace were the main items of interest, together with a recording of her speech.

Next day on the Federation Flagship, the Admiral had called in the Captain and XO for a brief discussion.

He said, "I have to send a report on this whole affair back to Admiral Jenna and the Governor of Nova.

"I would like to hear your comments."

The Captain nodded to his XO, "I think you can start, John".

The latter collected his thoughts for a moment.

"Admiral, we have to assume that the Empress has taken our superiors on Nova into her confidence.

"I think we should stay exactly with the script as we know it, and leave out anything about the parts we don't understand.

"The source of the data chips which were found is a complete mystery. Apparently, the head of the criminal gang was aghast when confronted with some of the contained information. He denies any knowledge of much of the contents.

"Not that it will make much difference to him – with nearly a tonne of *thaka* in the caves, he will be treated harshly.

"For my part I wonder about the yacht Cheetah. It may be far more than we realise.

"That might explain the accuracy of the local tipoff.

"Strangest of all is the position of the Taylors. I think we were all convinced that Sienna Taylor was the Empress, but that was visibly impossible!

"Overall, I have the impression of a beautifully orchestrated operation, and we are up against a 'need to know' barrier.

"Personally, I am awestruck by our young Empress. Somehow, she has pulled off a political master stroke on Datura - her handling of the dinner was perfect - and she has kept her hands completely clean with no apparent direct involvement!

"I have heard rumours that some of the other outer planets who were thinking of playing a little fast and loose, are re-assessing their priorities.

"Nearly all of the polities who have stepped over the line, are fixing things quickly. Masun and Coblan are visible exceptions! I think I can predict where our Empress will show up next!"

The XO looked at his Captain, who nodded. "An excellent summary, John.

"Admiral, may I suggest we keep any speculation about how things were engineered strictly within this group?"

Just before Cheetah was due to leave orbit, Peter and Louise paid a courtesy visit to the Admiral to say goodbye, and thank him for acting with such efficiency.

The Admiral looked at the pair of officers, with a faint smile of amusement.

"Thank you for the courtesy visit, and the compliment. Somehow, I am sure that you two know far more about what actually occurred than you are allowed to admit.

"I still wonder about your two passengers."

Peter replied, and there was absolutely no levity in his voice, "Admiral, please keep any speculation to yourself.

"That is most important to our tourists."

6d – Early 19th Century Brussels

Brussels in 1814 was a town with an approximate population of 70,000. It rated as a small provincial capital and by the standards of the age was quite prosperous and well-kept. Even in those days, it had a somewhat polyglot population, with the Dutch region starting North of the town and the French speaking region to the South.

Katie decided that she might as well arrange to appear in the town itself late in the year.

The Church of St. Michael and St. Gudula was built on the Treurenberg Hill, the fashionable upper part of Brussels. Built over centuries in a mixture of Baroque and Gothic architecture, the building and its two towers was acclaimed as an architectural masterpiece.

Abbé Jean Rodan was middle-aged, overweight and rather sedentary. He took many of his duties rather casually, but he never failed to enter his church first thing in the morning to say a brief prayer before breakfast.

It was still dark on a damp and cold late October morning when the Abbé raised the bar at the entrance. As he walked up the centre aisle he noticed a limp bundle near the altar, but the poor light kept him from realising until he was quite close that it was a body in a filthy greatcoat, either dead or unconscious. In the dim light from his candle, the hooded face looked dirty and pinched, but quite young. Unusually, there were none of the smallpox pockmarks which disfigured a high proportion of the population.

Even in relatively prosperous towns, vagrants or refugees from the wars which had swirled around Europe were quite common, as was their death by starvation or disease.

Kneeling down, it was clear that the boy was still alive. There was a small cat next to him, making piteous mews.

The previous day, the Abbé had been talking to a couple who ran a bakery about 100 meters away. They were relatively prosperous, but quite depressed as their teenage only son had recently died.

He decided that they might be willing to help, and hurried over to the shop.

"Marie, I have an unconscious boy lying in the church. Would you be willing to look after him for a bit? I will make a contribution to his welfare."

The baker's wife immediately said she would help, although the priest noticed that her husband looked a little more reluctant.

He said, "Marie, you will be blessed for this; can you come over and help carry the child?"

Marie was heavily built, and the pair of them had no difficulty carrying the semiconscious boy back to the house. As his clothes appeared quite dirty, an old blanket was spread on the bed, before the boy was laid down.

They were surprised that the small cat followed them all the way to the room.

The boy's shoes were surprisingly well made, and although the greatcoat was filthy and wet on the outside, the inside was dry.

As they carefully removed it, the boy's eyes flickered open, and he said in German "Where am I, I can't remember anything."

Marie's eyes narrowed – the voice was quite female, which was confirmed when the shirt was loosened.

Looking more closely, she realised that much of the dirt and grime on the girl's face looked like it had been deliberately applied. Considering the number of soldiers from different groups circulating in the area, it was sensible for a single girl to disguise herself as a boy.

Marie asked in German, "You are in a room in our bakery. What's your name, and where are you from?"

The girl frowned, and looked puzzled; "I think…. I am called Käthe. I can't remember …. I can't remember anything.

"Which town is this?"

The Abbé, who had been listening with interest, said; "This is Brussels. I suppose you have no idea how you came to be here?"

The girl looked desperately anxious; "I'm sure it's really important, but my memory is a ….. complete blank".

Marie finished taking off the girl's slightly damp outer garments, and wiped the more obvious grime off her face. She gave her a thick cloak and slippers to wear. It was apparent that the girl was slightly built but attractive, albeit somewhat thinner than normal. After being carefully helped down a rather steep staircase, Käthe was taken into a room next to the main bakery. The small cat which seemed to be attached to her followed behind.

The Abbé said, "Marie and Käthe, I must get back to the church. I will come in later on today and have a talk with you."

He disappeared through a side door, which was closed quickly to stop the blast of cold air from outside.

A wonderful aroma of freshly baked bread swirled through the room, and it was beautifully warm. Käthe was given a bowl of soup and a hunk of bread. The latter was still quite hot, and needed a fair amount of chewing to be digestible.

Marie decided from the rate that the food disappeared – despite her warning to Käthe not to eat too fast – that the girl must have been close to starving.

As the food and warmth took effect, Käthe looked around. Through the door, she saw a bustle of activity as the main bake for the day was organised. Instructions were being shouted in French. There was a large woodfired oven, from which metal trays of cooked loaves were regularly being withdrawn, to be replaced by fresh trays with attached lumps of dough.

Käthe asked in strangely accented and slightly broken French, "Marie, thank you greatly for me helping. Since I have no idea where I have come, or anything, would it possible to stay with you for few days. I can help in bakery in meantime. Now I've had food, I feel quite strong enough work."

Marie smiled, "That'll be absolutely fine. I will tell my husband that you are staying with us until further notice!"

Käthe went to bed soon after. She was asleep almost as soon as her head hit the pillow and slept for several hours. The small cat which seemed to be attached to her slept on the bed as well.

When she heard her stirring, Marie came up. "I have brought up some girl's clothes for you, Käthe. Your other clothes will be cleaned up when we start washing tomorrow.

"As you are still probably quite weak, I will help you put them on."

She saw the girl looked puzzled as the garments were laid out.

"Marie, could you tell me names of garments in French please? Also …. I seem have no memory of how to wear them!"

The first item was a "shift" which ran from her shoulders to just above her knees like an overgrown vest – she had no idea where the word "vest" came from, except she understood it.

She could understand the thick rough stockings which went on, but Marie had to explain how the gaiters were used to hold them up, as they almost reached her knee.

Her shoes – with the more obvious mud wiped off – went on next.

The skirt was familiar, but the petticoat and stays that went on after that seemed terribly uncomfortable to her.

A voice said in the back of her mind, "Käthe, do not expect to be given a bra or mention the word. It is not understood here."

Marie was baffled by the girl. She seemed intelligent and perceptive, but clearly had absolutely no idea of the clothes. Her origin seemed more puzzling than ever.

For the rest of the day, apart from a short break for lunch, Käthe helped in the bakery. The people working there kept their distance, probably because she represented an outsider to them.

Marie's husband Claude Joubert had been surprised when the boy had turned out to be a girl. During the day, he normally supervised deliveries of the bread, and during his visits to the baking area he saw that the girl worked hard. While clearly not familiar with the process, she was obviously learning quickly. He decided that his wife might have made a good decision to look after the girl.

In the evening, the Abbé Jean returned. Two of the senior assistants at the bakery who were nephews of Marie and Claude also came in for the evening meal.

Marie introduced Käthe, and said she would be staying for a while. She noticed her nephews were looking at the girl with interest.

She added, "Forgive me Käthe, but I have started to clean your greatcoat. There was a hard object stitched in a pocket on the side. When I looked, I found this."

She produced a flute. The Abbé was familiar with musical instruments – he had once taught music in Paris – but he never seen a flute quite like the one displayed.

Something in Käthe's mind clicked, and she took it with a happy smile; "My flute – I thought I lost it!"

She fingered it expertly, raised it to her lips and played a short trill.

"Monsieur Joubert – Claude – would you mind if I played short tune?"

Claude nodded, "Go ahead".

Käthe then proceeded to play a wonderful lilting tune. It clearly meant something to her, as the group saw tears start drip down her face. A minute or so later she had to stop, as she had started crying.

The group had been entranced by the quality of the music. To have the girl break down into tears made it even more dramatic.

Marie rushed over and put her arms round the girl, "Käthe what is it, what has upset you so much?"

The girl looked at her, and between sobs said, "I love this tune – I think I wrote it – but I can't remember where or when, or anything!"

Marie decided that serving supper would be a good idea, as it would enable the girl to recover her composure.

Jean Rodan was fascinated. He had immediately recognised that Käthe was expert. He had no idea of the material from which the flute had been made, but recognised that its sound quality was superb.

An idea was forming in his mind.

The following morning when Marie went down to the kitchen and started to prepare breakfast, Käthe's cat appeared holding a dead rat. It approached her and dropped it, purring enthusiastically.

Marie laughed, "All right, you can stay provided you earn your keep by killing the rats!"

* * *

Over the next week, Käthe completely mastered the art of breadmaking. Her French improved rapidly.

It was noticed that all the rats in the area had disappeared. Käthe's cat took on a sleek and well-fed look.

The Joubert bakery produced several types of bread, depending on the proportions of wheat, rye, and barley utilised. The grains were stone ground at a watermill several kilometres away. Salt and baker's yeast were also needed.

It was recognised as a quality bakery, as unusually it did not adulterate the product with sawdust or other materials.

The main oven was normally fired up at about 4 o'clock in the morning, and baking started at about 5. The process was a little convoluted, as dough had to be mixed and left to rise in a warm area near the main furnace in a batch process. As each batch finished rising, it was baked.

As Käthe integrated herself into the household she saw the Abbé Jean Rodan regularly. He had apparently always been a frequent visitor, and she found him interesting with a fund of knowledge about Europe's politics and the local community. In turn, he remained intrigued by the girl's completely unknown background, and her clearly keen intelligence.

There was always a break mid-morning, with a light snack and some drinking water. Käthe frequently used the opportunity to spend 10 to 15 minutes practising on her flute. When she had first started playing, she realised that she remembered a large volume of music.

One morning unbeknown to her, the Abbé had entered a few minutes before with a friend of his who was responsible for a private orchestra.

When Käthe had finished her little repertoire, the friend nodded at the priest. "You were right Jean, she is an absolutely brilliant musician. I would like to have her in my orchestra."

Käthe was talking to Marie when the musician approached, followed by the Abbé. He introduced himself, and said "Käthe, I manage a small orchestra. Listening to you, I believe that you would fit in well. Would you consider this?"

Käthe looked at Marie and said, "Marie, you and Claude have been so kind to me, and I really feel at home here. Would it be possible for me to play with the orchestra, perhaps 2 nights a week?"

Marie considered for a moment. The girl had become more and more like a daughter to her, and she was convinced that she could make far more of herself than a bakery offered.

"Sir, provided that you can guarantee that Käthe will always be escorted to and from the bakery, I would be happy for her to play in your orchestra. Of course, she will need enough money to buy the proper clothes!"

Käthe began to play regularly in the orchestra. As the orchestra received invitations to play for social events, she began to know the insides of some of the grand houses of Brussels.

Madame van der Capellan was the middle aged widow of a wealthy clothier. She lived in a large house quite close to the bakery, and over the years she had become friends with Marie Joubert despite the large difference in their social standing.

She had come in one morning for a baguette, but had lingered talking to Marie. In the morning break, she saw a girl playing a flute beautifully.

"Who is the girl, Marie?", she asked.

"Valerie, she was found almost unconscious in the church about a month ago. She has completely lost her memory. I decided to look after her for a little while. It is a pleasure to have her in the house and she works hard for part of the time in the bakery. She also plays in our local orchestra for a few evenings each week.

"She speaks fluent German and English, but her French is not so good. No-one who has talked to her can identify her accents, but they say they sound well educated. That fits in with her flute playing, which I'm told is of a professional standard."

Madame Capellan thought about this for a few seconds.

"Marie, you know I have my 24 year old nephew Andre staying. This is probably for the foreseeable future as his parents died, unless the army move him somewhere else.

"Would you mind if I asked her if she would teach him some English? I'm having some difficulty finding anyone who is fluent in the language here.

"The way things may go in the future, knowing how to speak English properly would be a huge advantage for him.

"I don't know what she gets paid in the bakery, but I will improve on it!"

Marie laughed. "She does it in return for food and lodging. However, I am sure she would be delighted to work with your nephew! I think it is a really good idea – she is much too bright to go on working in the bakery."

Käthe was called over and introduced. When the suggestion was explained, she immediately said to Marie, "Marie, I would enjoy doing that, but what about the bakery?

"Actually, thinking about that, I can always stand in if you are short of staff. Also, if I accept I would like to pay some rent for my room!"

From what little she had seen of the girl, Madame Capellan was impressed. Although only slightly built, the girl had a surprisingly strong presence, and looked intelligent. She had very bright eyes. For that day and age, she had an amazingly good complexion and teeth.

* * *

The following morning Käthe knocked on the door of the van der Capellan townhouse. It was an imposing three-storey building built in the local stone. She noticed that the door was unusually solid, and all the windows were barred.

A maid answered, and led her down a long and rather gloomy corridor to a much better lit room at the back. This looked over a vegetable garden with quite high walls on all sides.

Madame Capellan rose to greet her as she walked in. She saw a solidly built man in a military uniform standing by the fireplace.

She said in German, "Käthe, welcome to our household. This is your pupil, Lieutenant Andre van der Capellan of the Dutch army."

The Lieutenant had been expecting a solidly built Flemish girl, with few social graces. His aunt had told him the girl was working at the bakery. He had expressed some reservations about whether she would be able to speak sufficiently polite English. He had a basic grounding in the language, and was concerned that he might learn a lower class version. This might subject him to ridicule from his English officer contacts.

However his aunt had overruled his objections rather firmly. As he was greatly beholden to her for looking after him, he had accepted the planned lessons.

The girl looked at him, and said in soft, fluent and educated German; "I'm very pleased to meet you, Lieutenant. I am called Käthe."

He saw that she looked distressed for a moment.

"I don't know whether your aunt told you, but I have completely lost my memory and I have no idea of my origin or surname.'

She switched into English.

"Anyhow, from now onwards, English is the only language which is going to be spoken here."

Madame Capellan was pleased. Her nephew had a dominating character, but she had a feeling that this girl was quite capable of handling him.

She said, in rather poor English, "That is good, Käthe. I order chocolate and small biscuits."

She added rather mischievously, "Make work hard my nephew!"

After she had left the room, Käthe said, "My lessons are going to be divided into two parts. The first is conversation, when we will talk about - anything you like. The second part is learning words and writing. Since I assume you are serious about studying the language, the home work will be hard. I will expect you to learn at least 50 words every day, and we will find some text for you to translate into English.

"Every day, I will test you on the words, and I expect you to have learnt most of them properly. Occasionally, I will retest you on previous vocabulary.

If your aunt is willing, I will ask her to help you in that. I will then mark your written text in front of you each morning, and I will explain where changes are needed."

The Lieutenant was astonished. He had been expecting the girl to be quite diffident at first, but she was completely taking control of the program.

He asked, "Käthe, I told you speak well German, English. Which learn first?"

She answered after a moment, "I think I learnt English first. Now, what you should have said is …..", and the conversation lessons started.

From just outside the door, Madame Capellan listened with satisfaction. The girl had made a promising start.

A few minutes later, the chocolate and biscuits arrived. The drink was a luxury, only affordable by the wealthy, and the Lieutenant was surprised at how casually the girl received it. She tasted the cup, and said "I can't remember when I last tasted chocolate, but this is good. A little sugar, please."

Putting the cup down, the lesson continued. After an hour and a half, Käthe called a halt.

"That is enough for today, Lieutenant. You're getting tired and losing concentration."

Madame Capellan had supplied some scrap paper. Käthe quickly wrote down 50 English words, and the German translation.

She glanced up at the line of books on the shelf. There were several volumes of a military nature, including one by Vauban.

She handed him the list and said, "I will test you on this list tomorrow morning. Also, choose a page of the Vauban, and translate it. It might have some appropriate vocabulary!

"If there are words or a phrase you don't understand, copy the text and I will translate it when I mark it, and explain."

The Lieutenant looked at her. He was impressed with the quality of the teaching. He said, "Thank you, Käthe. Please call me Andre."

Madame Capellan appeared just before she left.

Käthe said, "Thank you so much for the chocolate, Madame. I have arranged to come back the same time tomorrow. It would be good if you could help Andre learn some of the words."

When she had gone, the Lieutenant said to his aunt in German; "Käthe is an amazingly good teacher. I think my English is going to improve quickly."

She answered, "Good. Sit down and start to learn those words before lunch. I will come in and give you a sort of preliminary test a little later."

* * *

A week later, Andre's English was clearly improving rapidly. He noticed that in the word lists she supplied, she never repeated a word.

The Abbé had arrived just before Käthe, and she was surprised to see a chess game being arranged in the drawing room.

Andre saw her looking through the door. He said, "The priest and my aunt have known each other for a long time. They are the best chess players in this area, and often play.

"By the way, you would be most welcome to stay for lunch today. I took the liberty of checking with Marie earlier on, and she said that would be fine."

When they had finished the lesson, Marie and Andre went into the drawing room. A second game was in progress, and Madame Capellan was looking a little vexed.

Seeing the glance from her nephew, she said, "Jean is thrashing me today, and he has me in real difficulty at the moment!

To the surprise of all present, Käthe said in a voice with a completely different timbre, "Madame Capellan, if you move your bishop along the diagonal to the 5th row, the Abbé will be under real pressure. You should win easily from that position."

Andre saw that his aunt looked astonished, and then pleased as she contemplated this suggestion. "Thank you, Käthe. I did not realise you played chess!"

Käthe looked really confused, and said in her ordinary voice, "Did I say something? My memory is a complete blank."

Everyone looked at her in astonishment.

Over lunch, the group discovered that Käthe had perfect manners, and the conversation ranged widely.

When they had finished the first course, the Abbé asked Käthe, "Have you any idea where you learnt some of your music? Some of the tunes I have heard you play are not at all familiar."

Käthe looked quite confused for a moment, "I am trying to remember .... Oh...."

At that, her eyes shut and she appeared to faint. Andre just caught her before she fell out of the chair.

As he laid her down on the couch, her eyes flickered open. She said in that strangely timbred voice, "Käthe has gone into an episode of temporal shock. She will be quite confused when she recovers."

At that, her eyes shut and she was clearly unconscious. No one knew what 'temporal shock' meant.

10 minutes later, she regained consciousness and said in a slurred voice in English. "Doctor in England, lecturer at the Space Academy, and Overseer of the Outer Arm Federation…"

She added a few more words in German which were difficult to understand, and something in a language none of them had ever heard before.

She stopped, and then looked around her surroundings more cogently, "Madame Capellan, I'm so sorry. What happened, and what was I saying?"

When the few understandable words she had said were repeated, Käthe looked puzzled. She said, "I have no idea what I meant. I think the unknown language was …. *Stortin*, but I don't know how I know that."

Anyhow, the group was relieved that she seemed to have recovered completely.

Andre walked her back to the bakery afterwards.

Two weeks later, at the end of the lesson, Andre said; "Käthe, we are having a small dinner party next Saturday. Both my aunt and I would like you to come. Would you be interested?"

A thought came into Käthe's mind, "This would be a good idea. Accept graciously."

She said, "That is so nice of you both. I would be delighted to accept."

Andre said, "I will collect you at 6 o'clock. By the way, guests are normally asked to give a small party piece after supper. This can be a short talk, some poetry, music or dancing."

Käthe laughed quite merrily, "All right Andre, I will bring my flute! I suspect that I have never been asked to play so subtly!"

Marie was delighted when she heard that Käthe was going to a dinner party with the Capellan family. Since Käthe's only respectable outfit was the dress she wore for the orchestra, she insisted that she borrow her pearl necklace.

When Käthe arrived on the Saturday escorted by Andre, she discovered that the affair was rather more elaborate than had been explained. The colonel and a major from Andre's regiment was present, together with their wives, and two senior army officers from England.

Over dinner, Madame Capellan was astonished at how easily Käthe fitted into the group. Somehow, she seemed completely at ease with the senior people present.

Andre's colonel was impressed that his lieutenant was speaking in good English to the two visiting officers, whose German and French were poor.

The principal reason for their visit to Brussels was to identify possible future liaison officers.

They also enjoyed talking to Käthe.

Andre asked one of the officers, "Käthe is actually my English teacher, but she has completely lost her memory. Can you identify her accent?"

The English captain was something of an expert on regional language – his regiment had men from all parts of the British Isles in its ranks.

He paused for a moment. "Her English is completely fluent and sounds highly educated, but its usage is slightly unusual. I am embarrassed to admit that I really can't identify her origin."

After dinner, Madame Capellan asked her guests if they would like to put on some form of party piece.

The older of the two English officers said, "I can sing two songs from Herr Handel's Zadok the Priest."

He was surprised to hear Käthe say, "Sir, I know that music. I can accompany you on my flute if you so wish. There is a short introduction before the singing part, which is where I could begin."

The officer was so surprised, he just nodded.

Käthe collected her flute, and the pair stood in the centre, as everyone else seated themselves in the large drawing room.

At a nod from the officer, she started playing. He realised immediately that she was expert.

He really enjoyed singing the two songs, accompanied by that almost magical flute.

As he finished, there was a loud round of applause.

Turning to Käthe, he bowed. "Fraulein, I have never heard flute playing of that standard before. Singing with your assistance was a pleasure."

Käthe curtsied, and smiled; "Sir, your singing was even better than your compliment!"

To his own surprise, Andre felt a little surge of jealousy.

Madame Capellan was pleased; the dinner was proceeding well.

She asked; "Käthe, would it be too much to impose on you to play one more tune?"

She answered, "I will play one tune which is dear to me, and then I will play the British National Anthem as a compliment to your guests."

When she had finished, there was an astonished silence for a moment. The group had seen tears run down the side of her face as she finished the first tune.

The British major said, "Käthe, that was magnificent. If I may ask, what was the first tune you played? It obviously meant a great deal to you.

The girl said in a strangely timbred voice, "It is the Anthem of the Outer Arm Federation, which I wrote."

She then looked confused, saying in her normal voice; "I know that is true, but I have no idea why I said it. I just can't remember …I just can't remember anything, although I feel it is so important."

Overall, the evening was a great success. When they were alone, Madame Capellan dropped a broad hint to Andre that he should pursue Käthe seriously, which met no resistance.

The following day, a letter was sent to London suggesting to the Duke of Wellington that Lieutenant Andre van der Capellan together with two other officers would be suitable liaison officers between the Dutch Army and the British Army in the unlikely event of any future conflict.

6e – Andre Capellan

About a week before Christmas, Marie was pleased to receive an invitation from Madame Capellan to Christmas lunch for herself, her husband and Käthe. The last time that had happened had been three years previously, just before Monsieur Capellan's untimely death.

She sent a short note back saying the family would be delighted to accept, and adding she would bring some bread, nice pastries, and a pudding.

On the day, Marie inspected her little group before they went over. Claude was told to change into a more respectable shirt, but she was pleased to note that Käthe was wearing a new dress and shoes. The regular income from the lessons and the orchestra was being well applied, in her view.

She was aware that Andre Capellan's growing interest in Käthe had a great deal to do with the invitation. She and her friend had discussed this seriously the previous day.

It was an interesting situation from a social point of view. Käthe's completely unknown past and lack of any visible fortune or relatives would normally have made any marriage to a Lieutenant in the Army impossible. Andre himself had little money, but it was known that he was his aunt's heir. At some point in the future, he would likely become extremely eligible.

Marie decided that Valerie van der Capellan valued Käthe's keen intelligence and character far above visible wealth,

A strong north-west wind was blowing, with a hint of sleet. It was a relief to enter the Capellan household, where a roaring fire was more than welcome. The other guests were the Abbé, the housemaid, and her husband. The latter were old family retainers and lived in the house.

Usually by late December, for most people food was of poor quality and becoming scarce. The fruit and vegetables of summer were long gone, and sauerkraut, beet and turnips would be served frequently. Except for a privileged minority, meat was a rarity.

The Capellan family belonged to the latter group, and the food was plentiful, including some rather stringy chicken. Wine was offered with the main course, but Käthe only tasted it once. She decided that the flavour was closer to vinegar than wine, and reverted to the weak beer which was on offer. It was not a drink she liked but in the early 19th century, water quality was problematical, and weak beer was much safer for most people.

Conversation was cheerful, and light hearted. The Abbé in particular had a fund of stories; his somewhat irreverent descriptions of the Vatican, which he had visited a decade previously, left most of the group almost helpless with laughter.

Dessert was a plum pudding surrounded with flaming brandy, which Valerie Capellan brought in from the kitchen in a large dish. A little holly sprig on the top was threatening to catch fire.

She said, "This was Marie's contribution to the lunch!"

After the meal was finished, all the men went off to the drawing room for a smoke, brandy and serious conversation.

The four women in the group were seated around the fire in the lounge, each having accepted a sweet liqueur.

Käthe saw Marie look at Madame Capellan and nod slightly.

The latter said, "Käthe, this seems as good a time as any to bring up the matter. My nephew is interested in making an offer of matrimony to you.

"Would you be prepared to consider this?"

Matrimony in the early 19th century rarely had anything to do with romance, and the families of prospective partners often had a large part in its organisation. Life was too hard, and it was generally a pragmatic commercial decision for the alliance of families and preservation and extension of wealth. It was also important in that day and age to produce plenty of children quickly, as both infant and adult mortality rates were horrific.

Käthe realised that in her circumstances, this was a most favourable offer.

A clear thought intruded on her mind, "Provisionally accept, but suggest that you would like at least three months to see if your memory will return."

She said, "Madame Capellan, Andre does me great honour to suggest this.

"May I provisionally accept, with a delay of at least three months before a formal engagement. The reason is, I would like a little more time to see if my memory will return."

The women in the group saw the anguish on her face.

"I think I was sent here to do something terribly important; you have absolutely no idea how awful it is for me to have lost my memory and my past. It would also be much better for Andre to have a clearer understanding of his future wife.

"For what little the impression is worth, I have a feeling that I was influential in my prior existence."

Madame Capellan smiled, "Käthe, please call me Valerie."

About 20 minutes later, Andre came into the room on his own, looking anxious.

Käthe stood up, walked across to him, and put her arms round his neck. She kissed him gently.

"Andre, I have provisionally accepted your proposal. I told your aunt that I would like to wait at least three months before any formal engagement, to give my memory a little more time to return.

"I think it would be much fairer to you, if I was able to let you know what you are letting yourself in for!

"If my memory does not return, too bad. We will just announce our engagement."

Andre look delighted. He took Käthe in a crushing hug, and gave her a really enthusiastic kiss. It was apparent that he really wanted her.

When the couple finally looked around, they found the room was empty and the door closed.

* * *

In the days after Christmas, Käthe continued Andre's English lessons, but always stayed on for lunch afterwards.

About two weeks later, Käthe had just put down a cup of chocolate after the meal, when Andre and Valerie saw her shudder slightly and collapse back into the sofa. The small cat which nearly always came with her gave a distressed mew and leapt onto her lap.

Valerie felt Käthe's forehead, which felt hot and damp. She said, "Andre, go and find a blanket and another pillow."

As he left the room, Käthe's eyes flickered open and she said in her strange timbred voice, "Madame Capellan, Käthe has gone into a final bout of temporal shock. When she recovers consciousness, she will find she has regained all her memories.

"Look after her carefully as she is important. I am most grateful for the help that people in this town have given her, which will not be forgotten."

Valerie saw that Käthe's eyes seemed to be glowing slightly, before they closed again.

Andre returned soon afterwards, and the girl was positioned comfortably and covered by the blanket.

Andre looked extremely anxious. His aunt wondered about the comment she had heard.

About half an hour later, Käthe stirred again, her body twitched, and her eyes flickered open. Just for a moment, they glowed.

She said in her strange timbred voice, "Andre and Valerie, we have now recovered all our abilities and memories.

"I am a sort of binary personality, and you are talking to Käthe's alter ego. Käthe does not like me at all, as I am the most intelligent, ruthless and dangerous being on this planet. In a few minutes, she will recover sufficiently to take over again.

"She is from the far future, and came here to complete an immensely important task.

"You will be shocked to hear that shortly a new war is going to start, and she must ensure that the French are defeated once and for all in this era.

"Andre, you and Käthe will need to discuss your relationship. She is far more human than I am, and is the most ethical person you will ever meet."

Her eyes shut for a few seconds, and then opened again.

She said in her normal voice: "Andre and Valerie, I'm so sorry for collapsing. Give me a few minutes, and I will be myself again."

Andre pulled up a chair, and took her hand. She looked at him, and smiled. Somehow, she looked far older and more mature.

Her arms came up and she pulled him down on herself in a crushing hug. Andre was surprised at her strength.

Sitting up after a minute, she said; "My alter ego has told you the elements of why I'm here. You will have gathered that we do not get on well. She has made decisions in the past which I regarded as appalling, although I have had to accept them as done deeds."

Valerie was looking at her with a mixture of shock and amazement. Although she only looked like a teenager, her words had enormous authority. They represented a speech pattern that expected to be obeyed.

Käthe continued, "Before I came here, I was the Empress of the Outer Arm Federation. I was ruler of approximately 30 billion sentients, with a level of wealth and power beyond what you can possibly imagine.

"I am much older than I look, and have been married twice. I have brought up seven children. Both my husbands died tragically.

"Andre, you have become precious to me. I'm prepared to continue our engagement, and eventually marry you, but you need to understand that the importance of my task overrides everything. If I fail, a causal chain will lead to the death of almost all the human race, and terrible effects on other species.

"I should mention that I have an adversary, and being close to me is dangerous. When she appears, my ability to protect the people around me is limited. I am far more than I appear, and only a small part of me is still human.

"I know this is hard, but you and your aunt need to make a decision. If you decide not to continue the engagement – and that is entirely your decision and for which no blame can be attached – I will depart and you will not see me again.

"I will leave you both alone for a few minutes, and will wait in the drawing room".

She walked out with her cat on her shoulder, and shut the door behind her.

In the room, there was a long silence. Valerie had a lifetime's experience in dealing with people, and despite the strangeness of Käthe's explanation, it had a ring of credibility.

She also remembered her strangely glowing eyes, and the comment about Käthe being completely ethical.

Andre was in many ways quite straightforward, and he completely trusted his aunt.

"Valerie, what do you think I should do?"

The Capellans came into the drawing room a few minutes later.

Käthe was standing by the fire, and tears were sliding down her cheeks. She looked sad and forlorn.

Neither Capellan had really known what to do, and in the end Valerie had said to him; "Andre, this is your decision. I will support your choice."

As he looked at Käthe, his heart went out to this strange being and her evident misery.

He went up to her, took her in his arms, and said "May I suggest we announce our formal engagement?"

Käthe's eyes glowed brilliantly for a moment, and she hugged him tightly.

"Andre, I am so pleased. I was convinced you would say no! Having you by my side will be wonderful!"

Valerie had been listening to this intently; she felt strangely relieved, and had also noticed the glowing eyes.

She said, "In the circumstances, an extremely short engagement would be appropriate. I will persuade Jean to marry the pair of you next week".

Andre took Käthe in his arms and gave her an enthusiastic kiss.

At minute or two later, Käthe's cat appeared. It was carrying a bag in its mouth, and gave a muffled mew.

Käthe laughed. "My cat is also far more than it appears, and I think it just brought in my dowry!"

She picked up the bag, and handed it to Valerie.

"These are uncut diamonds. Could you arrange for their sale, please. 5% of the proceeds should be split between Marie, Claude and the Abbé for looking after me, and have a nice necklace made for yourself with some of the stones.

"Give the rest of the proceeds to Andre – I think our finances need some assistance!"

Two days later, Valerie took a carriage to Bruges. Andre arranged through his regiment for it to be escorted by a small cavalry patrol, plus three private armed guards. The colonel of the regiment had agreed after Andre indicated that a substantial contribution to the regimental funds would be made. He also told his aunt to have a second necklace quickly made for Käthe.

Valerie had arranged for the senior partners of two of the most prestigious jewellers in the town to meet her.

She had known both of them for a long time, but they could not help gasping in astonishment as the bag was opened, and the contents tipped onto a soft cloth. There were nearly 100 rough diamonds, ranging from pea size to a dozen which were the size of large acorns.

While their client sipped a coffee, they made a rough preliminary appraisal. The stones appeared to be colourless and flawless.

The older of the two jewellers said to her; "Madame, this is an amazing collection of stones. It would keep our diamond cutting centres busy for a long time, and greatly increase their prestige.

"What are your instructions?"

Valerie had spent much of the rather uncomfortable carriage journey considering exactly this question.

"Albrecht, can you make a guess at what the stones are worth?"

The jeweller considered. "I think – and this is only a guess – that they would be worth at least 100,000 English pounds."

"They may be worth much more."

Valerie smiled. "First of all, I would like to take home with me a quarter of your valuation in gold coins, the contribution being split between your two companies.

"Secondly choose two sets of the stones - perhaps five in each - and make me a pair of necklaces with gold chains."

"Thirdly, arrange the sale of all the other stones. This must be completed by the end of February."

Käthe had warned her that war would start in early March.

"Your joint commission on this will be 10% of the total value of all the stones, split equally. Charge me a fair amount for fabricating the necklaces. As you make the sales, take out your commission, costs and the consignment monies you have provided first, and then send the rest to my company office in Bruges in gold."

The two jewellers bowed deeply. "We will have the cash ready in about an hour, together with the contract. Thank you for your business, Madame, and you will hear from us regularly."

With the financial side of their marriage well organised, the Abbé married Käthe and Andre the following Sunday. It was a low-key wedding at Käthe's request, and only about 30 guests attended.

Marie, Claude and the Abbé had been amazed when they found themselves the recipients of a huge sum of money for those days.

* * *

Andre was given two weeks' leave of absence from his regiment. He had also been promoted to captain. His colonel had decided that being a lieutenant was too junior a rank for someone who might become a liaison officer with another army.

After a week in a luxury hotel in Antwerp, he decided that he needed to know more about his wife's long-term plans.

"Darling, you have been absolutely delightful in and out of bed for the last week, but I think I would like to know more about this project of yours."

Käthe looked at him, and she looked fiercer and darker than he had ever seen her.

"Andre, you must not repeat this conversation to anyone.

"In the beginning of March, Napoleon will escape from Elba, and a new war will start.

"I am fighting a time war to preserve the future, and my adversary Aon is determined, as an act of vengeance, to destroy the human race. Other species will also be seriously damaged.

"I am here to frustrate her actions: history must be kept on what my group regard as the 'safe' path.

"In this era, I have little power apart from my intelligence, some strange abilities, and my cat.

"The latter is far more than it appears – for example it controls tools which enabled it to quickly make my dowry.

"By the way – and this is going to make you most annoyed – I have made a decision that you will be nowhere near me when I confront my adversary.

"I don't know how I am going to arrange this yet, but I expect something will turn up."

Andre was, as she had expected, most annoyed at this.

"I will not allow you to stop me being involved! I should be helping to protect you!"

Katy took his hands, "As I have said before, vast forces are balanced on edge here. I have no way of even explaining the energy requirement – crudely, heat in your terms – required to return me to this era in words you would understand. All the heat this world could produce for millions of years, would not even be noticeable in that total!

"Aon is much older and more experienced, and I am not sure I can hide you from her probing my mind. Killing a human is trivially easy for her."

"You need to be somewhere well out of sight, and where I am not certain of your location. Otherwise, you will just die. My dear captain, there is no courage involved in this. My war is being fought at a level where humans are just bystanders."

Andre considered this. Although not happy, he reluctantly accepted the position.

He asked, "When you said 'my group', what did you mean?"

He saw Käthe's eyes were glowing slightly; "There is a group called The Bearing who are the overarching intelligence controlling all the stars you can see in the sky, and many more. I am a junior member of this group, and Aon is a renegade member.

"The Bearing have exterminated species who have crossed them. It is also vitally important that I make sure they are not aware of my existence in this era. Our theory of time is not complete, but we believe the consequences would be awful."

Andre was fascinated and appalled. "Does that mean you can visit other worlds on different stars?"

Käthe looked at him. "I've lived for most of my life on a world so far from here, that you could not even see the star which it circles with the best telescope which can be made."

* * *

That evening, Käthe and Andre dressed up for a formal dinner downstairs.

During the dinner, Andre rather nervously pulled a beautiful diamond necklace out of his pocket.

"Käthe, this is a belated wedding present!"

He reached over and put it round her neck, fixing it on with a small clasp.

He saw her eyes fill with tears. She came round the table, and gave him a whole-hearted kiss, which embarrassed him horribly. In that day and age, public displays of affection were rare.

Afterwards, they wandered into the hotel ballroom, at one end of which was a large group of officers from various armies.

A senior officer was playing chess at one of the tables. Käthe decided he fitted the fabled image of a Prussian exactly; he was overweight, florid and loud-mouthed.

He had just arrogantly checkmated another Prussian.

Andre knew one of the Dutch officers who had been watching the game. "Who is he, Hans?"

His friend answered, "He is Oberst Berghof, one of Marshall Blucher's staff officers.

"He is an excellent chess player."

Surprisingly perhaps, the Prussian's eye fell on Andre. "Ah, a Dutch captain! Do you play chess?"

Andre rather hesitantly admitted that was the case – in fact he was a fairly good player from practice with his aunt.

The Prussian Colonel said, "In that case you will play with me. Take a seat."

Seeing no way of backing out without embarrassing himself and the other Dutch who were present, Andre reluctantly started playing.

The Prussian was indeed an excellent player, and demolished Andre in the space of fifteen minutes.

He said, "I'd hoped for a better game; it seems to be true that the Dutch are no match for the Prussians!"

Andre was quite irritated, but as a relatively junior officer he was in no position to say anything.

He discovered his wife had other ideas. In fact, Käthe had been annoyed with the whole episode.

She said, "Herr Oberst, I rather take exception to your remarks to my husband.

"I will challenge you to a game. If you win, I will agree he is inferior to the Prussians. If I win – and I am only a simple Flemish girl – you will apologise to him for your remarks."

The Prussian Officer was rather taken aback by this. This young but clearly wealthy young woman had no place challenging him in this manner. He decided to teach her a lesson.

"Take a seat Madame, and you may begin."

To his surprise, the young woman said, "Oberst, I challenged you, so you should start."

The Colonel expected this to be a quick and easy match. He made a conventional opening.

His opponent seemed to hardly hesitate, as she moved her piece.

After a minute's consideration, he made another move. The woman moved her bishop, almost without thinking.

After four moves, the Oberst realised that he was outclassed. The woman opposite him seemed to hardly hesitate when it was her turn, which was unnerving, while his pauses became longer and longer.

Andre had been aghast when Käthe had issued the challenge, but together with the other officers present began to watch the match with increasing fascination.

Even relatively inexperienced players realised how one-sided the match had become.

After a dozen moves, Käthe checkmated him.

He said, "That was a fluke and I was not trying."

Käthe answered, "Fine. Please start again, with the same conditions."

After 10 minutes, the result was the same – the Colonel found his position had been obliterated. Käthe had hardly hesitated between moves.

She smiled sweetly, "Your apology please, Herr Oberst!"

Neither Andre or Käthe had realised that the group of army officers had been accompanying the Duke of Wellington, who was on his way to a meeting with some German and Austrian politicians. He was trying to engineer a political framework for Europe which would suit England.

As the red-faced German stuttered out an apology, the Duke appeared and invited Käthe and Andre to come and sit at his table.

Andre was nervous and concerned; he saw the Duke and his wife study each other in silence for a moment.

"That was extremely impressive chess, Madame, if I can be rude enough to venture an opinion", said the Duke, in English.

Käthe answered, "Thank you, Sir. I'm afraid I was annoyed at the behaviour of the Oberst a little earlier."

The Duke continued, speaking to Andre, "What is your name, captain?"

Andre replied, "I am Captain Andre van der Capellan, and this is my wife Käthe."

The Duke frowned, "Let me see… weren't you one of the officers recommended to me as a liaison officer?"

"Yes, My Lord, I believe that is the case."

Wellington smiled, "Oh yes, I enjoyed my officer's description of the evening at your aunt's house. I am obliged at the courtesy and assistance she provided.

"I will make sure you are named as the liaison officer to one of my brigades if required, as a standing arrangement."

He took out a small notebook and wrote in some details.

Andre could only say, "Thank you, My Lord."

Käthe then added, to his surprise, "If you are in Brussels, My Lord, please look us up. Andre's aunt Madame Valerie van der Capellan is well known socially in the town."

"I look forward to that, Madame. And now, if you could excuse me, I need to go and pacify the Prussian Colonel whom you demolished!"

As he walked away, Käthe wondered if there was another player in her temporal war. There was an emerging pattern of convenient assistance. She had applied a little gentle compulsion to the Duke to get Andre appointed, but it still seemed too satisfactory to be chance.

In fact the Duke had no intention of pacifying the Prussian.

"Oberst, you have managed to embarrass someone in another army quite junior to yourself, and in so doing demonstrated that you are not fit to act in a liaison capacity. I will request Marshall Blucher to move you elsewhere."

As they left the ballroom, Andre sourly remarked, "That was rather neat, Käthe. I think that the Duke was more than impressed with you!"

"By the way, there is something which has been worrying me greatly."

Käthe held his arm more firmly, and looked at him, some concern evident on her face.

He continued, "When you have finished doing whatever you need to do in the next few months, what happens with us? Will you just go somewhere else?"

Käthe paused for a minute. "Darling, when I have frustrated Aon in this era, I fully intend to live out my married life with you.

"When I eventually return to my own time, it does not matter how long I stayed here – I will return to approximately when I left."

This left Andre feeling much more comfortable, except that he wondered why Käthe seemed so little concerned about her own life span.

The group of officers surrounding Wellington were most curious about the Duke's interest in the Dutch officer and his wife.

All they could discover about the latter, was that she had mysteriously appeared in late 1814 in Brussels, and had given the officer an enormous dowry when they married.

The Duke's extra-marital affairs in Paris over the past 12 months were quite notorious, and the general view was that Käthe was a previous mistress.

6f – Waterloo Campaign

In the beginning of March, the news swept Europe that Napoleon Bonaparte had escaped from his exile in Elba, and landed in the south of France.

Marshall Ney had been ordered to take a regiment and arrest him.

"I shall return Napoleon in a steel cage", he had sworn to the French King.

That had proved an accurate statement; Ney and the regiment had immediately deserted to Napoleon when they reached him, and then returned to Paris in something of a triumphal procession.

The "steel cage" was a rapidly expanding army.

The Bourbons and their Court had fled north, and the reinstalled Emperor rapidly organised his defences.

Politically, a new coalition was formed between Britain, Prussia, Austria and Russia to unseat him again, with other minor national and provincial participants.

It was recognised that the Duke of Wellington had to be the leader of the army that Britain, Holland, Brunswick & Hanover formed, and the overall political liaison point.

In fact Wellington's difficulties were considerable. The army that had been formed was nowhere near the quality of the Peninsular Army which he had built, and of dubious reliability. Britain had a long tradition of swiftly dismantling armies after any war, which is what had occurred in 1814.

Moreover, apart from the overall objective of defeating Bonaparte, Wellington also wanted to ensure that France remained sufficiently viable to act as a counterweight on the Continent to Prussia.

The latter had organised an army under Marshall Blucher. While not in agreement with Wellington about the long term future of France, the Marshall was wholeheartedly in favour of co-operation when it came to fighting the Emperor.

During April and May, the Coalition armies were organised. Andre found himself posted as the Dutch liaison officer with Wellington's reserve brigade in Brussels. Although still disgruntled at his apparent removal from the main army, as a result he did enjoy far better accommodation than most of his regiment.

During their short engagement, and after asking Valerie and Käthe, he had decided they should live in an unused floor of Valerie's house.

Valerie was delighted with this decision – she really liked Käthe, who was effectively her daughter-in-law. It also meant that her house rapidly became one of the social centres of the reserve brigade, when the senior officers discovered her position in the Brussels social hierarchy.

It was convenient that Andre was not in their direct line of command, as that would have been awkward. The story of how his wife had discomfited a certain Prussian Colonel had circulated widely, from which she had acquired a certain notoriety.

In May and early June, Wellington was a frequent visitor to Brussels, and quickly introduced himself into Andre and Käthe's social circle.

Together with two of his senior staff officers, he had enjoyed lunch at the Capellan household a number of times.

After one of these meals, the Duke said to Andre, "Captain, would you mind if I took a turn round the garden with your most charming wife?"

Andre agreed cheerfully. Five minutes later in the garden, Wellington said "Käthe, I took the liberty of getting one of my officers to investigate your past.

"He was surprised to find absolutely nothing except that you arrived mysteriously last October.

"You then married Andre, and provided what is alleged to be a most impressive dowry. You are now in the centre of a social circle involving a number of my officers, and myself.

"You will appreciate my concerns".

Käthe looked at him for a moment, and he saw that her eyes were glowing slightly.

"My Lord, I will not take offence, because I was aware of the investigation.

"I have also taken a liberty, and have placed a block on your mind which will stop you repeating this conversation with anyone.

"I am from the far future, and I am fighting a time war with another entity who is not human.

"If certain actions are not reversed, a causal chain will cause the extinction of the human race.

"My presence here is critical."

Käthe looked at him for a moment. "I cannot discuss the future with you as this would have terrible repercussions. Everyone needs to act out their own parts in this drama, uninfluenced by that knowledge.

"Fortunately, Andre will be based in this town when certain events occur. When I meet my enemy, my ability to protect bystanders is limited. If this alien entity detects that Andre is my husband, he will be killed out of spite if he is anywhere near me.

"I am most grateful to you for making him a liaison officer."

The Duke looked at her and smiled rather grimly. "Katie, I suspect that in some way you are here to protect me.

"If you need anything, please ask. I do not think you will have any difficulty in access, as most of my officers believe that you were my mistress in the past. I regret that is not true!

"And now, I think we had better return".

It was evident to the staff officers that Käthe had become a great favourite of their commander.

This was reinforced when he told them, "If Madame van der Capellan ever wishes to talk to me, contact me immediately wherever I am located."

Later on that afternoon, Andre asked his wife about this conversation.

She smiled slightly and said, "You have no reason to be jealous, my love. I placed a block on his mind to stop him repeating what I said.

"He was concerned that I might be a spy in view of my unknown past!

"The Duke now knows I'm here for a purpose. I refused to tell him exactly what I have to do, but he guessed that it is necessary for his protection.

"If only that was all."

Käthe looked away into the distance, and she would not say any more.

* * *

In early June, the French armies moved north. Bonaparte had decided to attack Brussels. He wanted to force Holland out of the war, and possibly engineer a political revolt in London.

A decisive victory would also reinforce his position in France.

Wellington and Blucher had expected to have to attack Bonaparte on French soil, and they were strategically surprised by the advance. Their armies were more dispersed than required by the situation.

As both were still uncertain where he would strike, they were forced to keep their brigades well apart.

On the night of the 15th June, the Duke and Duchess of Richmond had organised a ball to be held in a large hall in Brussels.

It was a glittering affair, with a tense undertone as most of the guests knew a major battle was in the offing. The army officers in particular showed a great deal of bravado, reflecting an underlying nervousness. Perhaps fortunately for them, they did not know that nearly half of them would be dead within three days.

As a captain in a liaison capacity to the British Army, Andre and Käthe were invited although he was almost certainly the most junior officer present. The Duchess had known of Wellington's interest in Käthe, which influenced the decision. They greatly enjoyed themselves, as they had many friends and acquaintances among the guests.

In the middle of the evening, a filthy and exhausted army officer appeared at the entrance, and demanded to be taken immediately to the Duke of Wellington.

There was a brief conversation on the floor of the ballroom, and then the Duke left for the Duke of Richmond's dressing room with the latter and the officer. He said to his ADC as he walked out, "Collect all the staff officers you can find, and send them straight in to me."

Käthe and Andre watched the process from the other side of the room: dancing and social chatter had stalled as this drama played out. Distress and horror started to appear on the faces of the guests as stories circulated about what had happened.

Käthe murmured; "And so it begins. Believe me, this Ball will be remembered!

"Later this evening, I will disappear for a week or two. Make sure you move from our house and billet yourself with the reserve brigade immediately. I must not know where you are located."

Andre just nodded, "Take care, my dear. I have no idea whether you can be killed or injured, but I suspect you can be defeated. Valerie and I love you dearly, and would be most distressed if you do not return."

In the side room, the Duke had been studying a map.

He dispatched one messenger with orders to take some cavalry for protection, and then find Marshall Blucher and advise him what was occurring.

"Tell him I am concentrating at Quatre Bras, to deny the French the crossroads.

"If we lose that crossroads, the French will be in a position to drive a wedge between our armies and we will be unable to concentrate our forces.

"I will try to assist him, but it is imperative we link up as soon as possible."

Other officers were dispatched to different parts of Wellington's dangerously dispersed army.

Barracks all around Brussels began to seethe with activity, as the Coalition regiments prepared to march.

Andre said, "I must attach myself to the Reserve Brigade immediately."

He gave Käthe a crushing hug, murmuring in her ear; "Good luck, My Lady".

Looking distressed, he quickly left the room.

Meanwhile, the Duke realised that he had set everything he could in motion.

He said to his host; "Sir, we might as well return to the Ball to thank the Duchess. I've done all I can at this stage, and I doubt I will get much sleep as news comes in."

When the pair walked out into the room, the number of men present had diminished significantly. Many army officers were already on their way to their regiments.

The Duke saw Käthe talking to the Duchess of Richmond, and hastened to join them.

The Duchess signalled a waiter; "Tell the orchestra to play a waltz."

The Duke looked enquiringly at Käthe, who gave him her hand in acceptance. The Duke of Richmond paired up with his wife.

At the end of the dance, which took place while surrounded by people making distressed farewells, Käthe murmured "My Lord, we must both be about our tasks. We will not meet again. Farewell."

The Duke regretfully nodded to the most interesting woman he had ever met.

Wellington excused himself to the Duchess and went off to deal with a growing stream of messages. It was clear that he was less than happy with what was occurring.

That was more or less the end of the Ball. Käthe thanked her hostess and slipped out of the room. As soon as she was in a corridor out of sight, she changed form and moved south with her cat to observe what was happening.

6g – Three battles

On the morning of 16 June, dawn was about 5 o'clock. By that time, a number of Wellington's regiments were already on the move. They had been ordered to concentrate at a crossroads called Quatre Bras.

Marshall Ney had been ordered to capture the crossroads. Napoleon was quite confident that Wellington would not be able to muster enough troops quickly enough to stop the Marshall from succeeding, and effectively fortifying the position. He was so confident about this, that he had ordered the Comte d'Erlon to take his Corps of 20,000 men and 40 odd guns and march to help him at Ligny. The latter was only about 10 km due east of the crossroads.

Marshall Ney was most concerned that he was marching into a trap as he approached. There was remarkably little activity. The troops of the brigade commanded by the Prince of Orange were apparently all that defended the crossroads.

He stopped the advance, and sent some cavalry out to investigate. At that moment some of Wellington's regiments started to appear.

The battle was a messy long drawn out affair, with Wellington effectively fighting a delaying action as he waited for more troops to arrive. As this happened, he was able to plug holes in his defence and continue to hold the crossroads.

Katy knew that this was no minor battle – in the historical records the allied forces had suffered nearly 9000 casualties, and the French a similar number.

Ney realised that he had blundered by not immediately occupying the crossroads and ejecting the brigade holding it. As the Coalition defence was rapidly solidifying, he wrote a panic stricken note to d'Erlon to return immediately.

He handed it to a staff officer, who galloped off to get to the Comte to return as soon as possible.

In the altered history which Katy had studied, the messenger had reached d'Erlon when he was only about three quarters of a kilometre from the battle at

Ligny. Napoleon had seen his advancing corps, and immediately sent messages directing him where to attack the Prussians to most effect, which over-rode the instruction from Marshall Ney.

As a result, the battle had turned into a rout for the Prussians. Marshall Blucher was seriously injured, which disrupted the Prussian command, and their army fled in complete disorder with enormous casualties. All its guns were lost, and the soldiers were scattered mainly eastwards.

Katy realised that all she needed to do was to stop the messenger, alter the message slightly, and get it to d'Erlon more quickly so he would be further away from Ligny.

That would prevent orders from Napoleon arriving which would override those from Ney.

She and her cat swept down on the messenger, and rendered him unconscious. The message was altered to make it more imperative. There was a cavalry detachment a kilometre behind d'Erlon. Those troops were also knocked out. Katy morphed her image into that of the messenger, whom she had known was called Major Henri de Feran.

Taking one of the cavalry mounts, she rapidly overtook the Corps and found the Comte d'Erlon.

Saluting, she handed over the message. She added, "Sir, Marshall Ney requests your most urgent assistance; he was under severe pressure when I left."

To emphasise the point, she applied a compulsion to the Comte. This was essential, as if he thought about the idea for too long, he would realise that he could not possibly return in time to give Ney any assistance.

He looked slightly dazed for a moment, and then nodded.

Calling up the staff officers, he said; "Marshall Ney is in severe difficulties. He has ordered us to return. We must tell all the regiments to reverse the march."

Katy saw that the general in charge of the staff function was about to protest, so she applied a further compulsion. He did not say anything.

20 minutes later, the entire corps had reversed course.

Katy made herself scarce, and watched the whole process with fascination.

It troubled her greatly that neither she nor her cat had detected any sign of the presence of Aon.

She sent a message to the future explaining what she had done, the absence of any sign of Aon, and asking whether the path of history had changed.

The message came back a few seconds later.

Her friend Iva said, "Katy, we understand what you have done. History has reverted to the safe path. Your comment about the absence of Aon is most disturbing.

"As far as we can tell, Aon did not change history; you did.

"We do not understand what is happening, and we will discuss this further when you return."

For the next four days, Katy watched the safe history play out as expected.

When Wellington heard that the Prussians had been heavily defeated at Ligny, he was forced to abandon the crossroads at Quatre Bras and retreat to the more defensible position on the ridge at Waterloo.

The battle on the 18th of June was particularly trying for Katy; the doctor in her writhed in horror when it saw the terrible injuries and deaths. Dying on the battlefield was incredibly slow and painful for many of the soldiers.

Up to that time in the Napoleonic Wars, the Battle of Borodino three years previously between the Russians and French had caused the worst casualties of any battle, with a total of about 70,000. If the three battles around the middle of June were considered collectively, the total was much greater and approached 100,000. Nearly a third of the soldiers involved ended up as casualties.

When she returned to her house on the 20th of June, Andre and Valerie were appalled at her appearance. She looked and felt utterly traumatised, and kept breaking down and crying. This was not helped by the sight of cartloads of injured soldiers being brought through the town as they were taken to whatever accommodation could be found. She knew that only the moderately injured soldiers had a good chance of recovery, unless they had suffered amputations carried out immediately by competent surgeons. In that era, gangrene and other infections carried away most of the injured.

After a day watching her in this state, Andre said, "Käthe, we are going to a small house near Copenhagen which is near a sandy beach. It is owned by some relatives.

"You need to be a long way from here while you recover.

"I am resigning my commission."

It took Käthe nearly 3 months to recover. When they returned, she and Andre decided to open an orphanage.

The marriage lasted happily for nearly 10 years, with Käthe suppressing the Bearing side of her personality.

At the end of that period, Andre died suddenly from an aggressive sarcoma. His wife was forced to watch the disease unfold, knowing that in her era he would have been cured. In the end, she hastened his death to curtail his suffering.

She returned to Nova with a heavy heart, with the date only a few days after she had originally left.

Chapter 7

MASUN

W HEN KATY RETURNED TO THE VICINITY of Nova, in local time it was only a few days after her message had been received.

In her absence, the statements and known history had been analysed and reanalysed. The additional recordings from her cat were studied with enormous interest.

Two salient facts were obvious; Aon had not put in an appearance, and Katie's actions had changed history back to the safe path.

The original safe path could not have existed without Katie's intervention, but the Nova historical records indicated this was the case. This left an unresolved logical quandary.

Katie said to her friend Iva, "What is really disturbing us, is the awful thought that we may not be in total control of history. Our theory of time is incomplete, and there may be more subtlety to this than we realised."

Iva agreed; "The disengagement of the Oldest is bitterly regretted. We are certain it possessed a more complete theory of time, but for some reason this was never shared with us.

"Katie, there is nothing more you can do here for the time being, until the next historical divergence appears.

"May I suggest you investigate the progress of your young Empress in the meantime."

* * *

Masun was similar to earth in many respects. It was slightly older, and its moon was larger and further away from the planet, but the composition of its atmosphere and the proportion of the surface covered by water were comparable.

Unlike Earth, most of the continental land was located round one of the poles, and there were a large number of islands in the same general region.

Overall the environment was quite cold. Masun's sentient inhabitants were slightly larger than humans, and their bodies were covered in fur. According to the anthropologists, both of these features were adaptations to the climate.

Allowing the planet to join the Federation had been a difficult decision. All the polities on the planet were effectively run by rulers controlling what was essentially a feudal system. Realising they faced a choice between becoming a protectorate of the Federation or a member planet, the groups had managed to come together and arrange a political system which was just representative enough to be acceptable.

Unfortunately, religious differences and internal rivalries inherited from centuries of warfare were threatening to push the planet back into civil war.

The Federation diplomats and Fleet had managed to keep the peace so far, but the reports that Sienna had seen suggested that it was only a matter of time before their efforts would fail.

Cheetah slowed as he approached the system, and on emergence he took control of the planetary computer complexes.

This time, when officers in the fleet requested details of the vessel, the information looked completely normal. The response suggested the passengers were wealthy interplanetary tourists and a group tourist visa was requested.

From Cheetah's parking orbit, the planet was studied.

After half a day, Sienna assembled her group.

"Peter, would you like to summarise what we have found."

He said, "As the reports received on Nova suggested, the planet's politics are a total mess. The system the Masuna - the collective name of the species - cobbled together in order to obtain entry into the Federation is falling apart.

"There is insufficient give-and-take in the system, and the smaller groups feel they are simply being elbowed aside when major decisions have to be made.

"Another problem is that culturally, any Masuna individual in a position of authority is expected to give preference to his relatives and group.

"This is a huge inducement to nepotism and corruption.

"As a result, loose alliances among minority nations and related religious groups are being rapidly cemented, and they are starting to rebuild stockpiles of conventional weapons.

"They are aware that the Federation will take action directly if nuclear or fusion weapons are used, and they are bypassing the HMC manufacturing complexes when it comes to building military shuttles. They have worked out that the Federation would simply shut down all shuttle based transport if anyone attempts to use HMC shuttles in a war.

"Part of the problem is that some of the groups have hated each other for so long, that there is no one they trust to arbitrate.

"The Federation diplomats attempted this process, but the moment any group perceives itself disadvantaged, they walk out of negotiations.

"From my point of view, it is not at all obvious how we are going to fix this system."

The rest of the group looked at Peter, and tried to think of any flaws in his analysis.

Unfortunately, Peter's training as an intelligence analyst was apparent, and his summary was completely consistent with their information.

Eventually Iain said, "Perhaps we need to get a better impression of the place from ground level. When we start talking to individuals, it is possible we will get some ideas.

"However, we had better be fairly discreet about our questioning. It would not be good to be labelled as spies.

"Unless anyone has any better suggestions, might I suggest we start with the town called Arun on that peninsula on the western side of the main continent. Apparently the forests are spectacular, and the guidebooks said it had an interesting museum".

No-one had any better suggestions.

Sienna, rather grumpy from her first bout of morning sickness, said; "I can understand why few people come here as tourists. Most places seem to be a mixture of cold, wet, or cold and wet."

Just before they were due to leave, Cheetah received a message from the Federation fleet.

An officer on the Flag battleship talked to Peter direct; "We understand that you are planning to visit various areas as tourists.

"We are concerned about this, as there have been a number of reports of disturbances. We do not think that as humans, you will be directly targeted, but be careful and sensitive to religious and political issues.

"We would strongly recommend that you avoid any discussion of the latter points."

Peter replied, "Thank you for the advice. We will tread carefully."

In fact, most of the officers on the battleship had been incredulous that anyone would wish to visit the planet surface. The climate was unattractive, interesting sites were scarce, and the Masuna had acquired a reputation for being rather xenophobic.

The Nova Embassy staff were advised to keep an eye on this group.

7a – Arun

When they disembarked at Arun, both Peter and Louise were wearing large rucksacks containing human food, and were carrying their personal arms and the appropriate paperwork. Iain had been excused from carrying anything because of the sling and cast on his wrist.

The database about the planet advised that many local foods, while not toxic, were likely to cause severe indigestion to humans. However, the local equivalent of coffee, called *arn*, was recommended.

The shops in the town were quite nondescript, and had been built mainly in the local stone with little view to planning coherence. More modern roofs were in corrugated metal, which clashed rather badly with the slate or tile construction of older houses. Deep open gutters ran along the sides of all the roads, presumably to handle the rain from the gales which frequently swept the area.

Louise and Sienna found a shop selling furs, which they entered. The tradition in the country was that in the more expensive shops, potential customers would be offered a small cup of *arn*. The tourist guides advised that this was quite safe, and it was acceptable to drink it with no obligation to purchase.

A young female assistant appeared with the cups, and the proprietor invited them to take fur covered seats next to a rough wooden table.

"I am called Er, and please accept the *arn* with my compliments."

The humans were surprised to find the Masuna spoke good, but guttural, English.

They explained that they were visiting tourists, and were interested in seeing more of the country.

The proprietor grunted, which was the local equivalent of laughing.

"I believe that you will find the countryside around here similar to the less attractive parts of Nova. Because our lands are close to the pole, frequent ice ages in the past stopped the evolution of large vegetation and much else. Our people discovered that trees and some types of fish from your planet would grow well here.

"There are salmon and trout in our rivers, which we find excellent eating, and cold climate trees from Nova are spreading rapidly.

"Culturally as a people, I regret that we do not like outsiders, but being human you will find you are more acceptable than most!"

Sienna asked, "I thought the Federation, which my species founded originally, was not particularly popular here?"

Er looked at her thoughtfully. "I don't think our leaders have any particular dislike of the Federation, although the alternative was to join or become a protectorate. However, at this point national and regional differences are beginning to take priority.

"We know the Federation is averse to taking part in local politics, but if nothing happens it is easy to predict local wars starting again.

"The news that the Federation Empress – I suppose our Empress as well – is concerned and planning to visit has temporarily stalled developments, but I believe that war will break out if nothing happens in the near future."

He paused, feeling that he had said enough.

"Anyhow, I would like to show you my furs, derived from some of our larger sea creatures. They are warm and waterproof."

Er had already decided that Sienna was his best potential customer. He had noticed that the group seemed to revolve around her.

"Young lady, I received a small coat yesterday which I believe will fit you perfectly."

Sienna smiled, "Yes, I would like to try it. Also, my friend Louise would probably be interested."

For these foreign tourists, Er had automatically doubled the already steep price for the garments, which only the wealthiest people on Masun could afford. They were a speciality of the area.

Louise looked horrified when she saw the price tag on the admittedly beautiful fur coat she had tried.

She said subvocally to Sienna, "I can't possibly afford this coat, Sienna!"

The relaxed reply came back, "Don't worry, I need to generate some financial goodwill here! Consider the coat a present."

Sienna had decided that she really liked the coats, but it would be bad form to take them without some form of haggling.

"Er, these are beautiful coats, and I would like to buy one, but I think the price you're suggesting is a little high."

The proprietor had expected some sort of haggling; "I could take 20% off if you would take both coats."

Sienna looked at Louise, "Didn't I see another fur shop just down the road?"

She raised an eyebrow at Er. He didn't understand the human gesture, but the message was plain.

He said hastily, "As they fit you both so well, I will take 40% of the price for both of them!"

Siena laughed, "Agreed! Iain, could you pay please."

The young female assistant had reappeared, and taken the coats.

Louise said, "Many thanks, Sienna," and turning to the assistant, she said; "Please package the coats carefully. We will send down a shuttle later on today to collect them."

Just as they were leaving the shop, Sienna said to the proprietor; "Thank you for showing us the coats, and I would like to talk to you again. I think your look of distress at the price discount was quite artistic – I'm sure you double the price for visiting tourists!"

Er grunted loudly.

For the next hour, they wandered down the main street, buying a few small souvenirs. It was an unusually warm and sunny day for that area, with the temperature nearly reaching 20 degrees.

On the other side of the town, which was beginning to look much more poverty stricken, they saw a small park, with some clean looking benches and tables. "How about some lunch, and it looks like there are some public toilets over there."

While relatively primitive in some respects, Masun had a reputation for being spotlessly clean. With their ancestry as hunter gatherers, the Masuna had superb smell, hearing and sight; keeping themselves and their surroundings really sanitary was ingrained into them.

Peter and Louise had just unhitched their rucksacks, when four rough looking Masuna appeared wielding heavy clubs. They had decided the group of foreign tourists, one injured, would be easy prey.

Peter said, "Louise, no guns. I'll keep the pair on the left busy while you fix the other two."

The assailants were surprised when two of the humans came straight towards them.

Peter took on the first, who came at him carelessly with a sweeping blow of the club. The human stepped inside the reach of the club, and punched him hard in the stomach and then violently twisted his arm taking the club as the Masuna fell to the ground gasping for breath. Peter was just in time to raise his captured club to fend off the Masuna's partner, who had approached more circumspectly.

Unfortunately Peter did not know much about fighting with clubs, and was forced to retreat slowly as the rather larger Masun attacked furiously.

This ended when Louise, who had had little difficulty with the other two as she was an unarmed combat expert, came to his assistance.

Two of the Masun were on the ground with what appeared to be broken limbs, when the local shopkeepers and police arrived. The other two had fled.

The police were most apologetic, but insisted that the human group come to the station to give more details.

They were astonished and respectful when they discovered that Peter and Louise were armed, but had made no attempt to use the weapons.

Iain and Sienna were sitting at a table at the side, and were not enjoying being inside a police station again. Sienna was snacking on a muesli bar as she was hungry.

The police chief looked at them, and suddenly a memory came back to him prompted by the white cast on the human's arm. The video of the dinner at Datura had been widely circulated and watched, and he realised that Iain and Sienna were the people at the Empress's table.

He stood up and walked across. "You two people were in the film of the Empress at Datura, at her table.

"You were described as her relatives.

"Is that correct?"

Iain said, "Yes."

The police chief continued, "Do you know the Empress well?"

Iain smiled a little wryly, "I speak to her frequently. She is not always happy with my comments, but she does sometimes listen!"

He was kicked underneath the table. His wife's sense of humour had gone missing with the absence of lunch, and the kick was harder than really intended.

Wincing, he continued, "You need to be aware that my wife is the close relative."

On Masun, family and family connections were far more important than on Nova, but the police chief was not aware of this. He had automatically assumed some similarities in social structure between humans and Masuna. He had also been considerably impressed that the humans had not used their lethal weapons when threatened. They were clearly courageous and had a sense of honour. An idea had occurred to him.

He said, "Could you wait here for a few minutes, please."

One of the curious features of the culture on Masun was that an individual in the senior ranks of any group or nation could make a contract on behalf of that group or nation without reference. This was known as a Contract of *Sirt*.

Unless the agreement was totally irrational, the contract would be regarded as binding by the individual's group. This was a hangover from the days when the species operated in hunter-gatherer groups. When a foraging group met strangers, boundaries and foraging areas had to be immediately agreed as they would be far from the main parties.

However, if this contract was regarded as less than reasonable by the individual's superiors, he or she might be invited to "take a swim".

The individual would be taken to the nearest beach, and would simply swim away from the shore. Cold and exhaustion or one of the local sea predators would soon end his or her life.

Contracts of *Sirt* were rare.

The police chief had the vague notion in his mind, that a close relative of the Empress might be willing to help on a *Sirt* basis.

On returning, he said, "I have talked to the head of this province, who is a relative of mine. He would like to meet your group as soon as possible."

This time it was Sienna who answered, "That would be fine. However, we need to have some lunch and get changed into more appropriate clothing. Also, we need to collect some coats.

"Would this evening be possible? We would bring some of our own food and drink."

An hour later, the humans were back on Cheetah and enjoying a belated lunch.

Peter suggested that a background search be made on this provincial chief. The result was surprising – it appeared that he was actually the informal leader of a small confederation of nations at that end of the continent.

He was also on record as expressing extreme concern at the militarisation that was occurring, although this had not stopped his own group from doing the same.

Sienna thought about this for a while, then said; "Peter and Louise, for once I think it would be appropriate if you wore your uniforms, but don't take any guns. This meeting may be important. This is a status orientated and militaristic society, and I think we need to shed part of our tourist image. Iain and I will also dress formally.

"Cheetah, I think we should bring along a combat remote, the excuse being that it will carry our food and drink for the evening. From what I have seen, those remotes don't look much different from ordinary remotes, except they are somewhat larger.

"I'm sure you will watch our surroundings carefully, and the remote can protect us if there is trouble."

The AI was happy with these instructions.

In the evening, the shuttle was directed to what was clearly an old fort on the top of a hill. Part had been rebuilt to make large and comfortable living quarters. It also appeared to be a regimental base, and numerous patrols were visible.

At regular intervals around the fort, advanced missile weaponry was visible. Cheetah advised that a powerful defensive shield had been installed.

Back on the Federation Fleet, the destination of the shuttle had been noted, and it was known that other shuttles had arrived at the same point from a number of different national capitals a little earlier.

The local Admiral was incensed; "These are not tourists as we understand the term; they were told to keep clear of local politics and the exact opposite appears to be occurring. Advise our embassy, and send these people an instruction to return to their yacht immediately.

"Send a cruiser over to the yacht, and prohibit it from moving until it has been searched."

When the message was sent to the yacht, an immediate reply was received. "This is the yacht Cheetah's computer complex. The captain is on the planet below and has issued instructions that no-one is to board until he has returned. Screens will be activated if this is attempted, but the yacht will comply with the instruction not to move."

Since blind adherence to instructions is a characteristic of computer systems, and a forcible breach of the screen would probably result in the destruction of the vessel, the Admiral reluctantly accepted the position.

Cheetah was quite happy with the instruction not to move. He was within range of Sienna and could immediately remove the human party if danger threatened.

However, the Admiral's mood was not improved when a message from the cruiser was received. "The yacht has military grade anti-surveillance screens. Also, neutrino analysis of the idling engines indicates they are far more powerful than is possible for the yacht size. Its main screens may be much stronger than we anticipated."

For the human party, there was no response to the instruction to return.

Sienna said curtly, "Ignore it. We will worry about the Fleet later on."

At the Nova Embassy, there was consternation. The Ambassador said; "Bloody tourists. Don't they know there is a civil war in the offing, which we are trying to stop?

"Robert, take a shuttle over there and order them to leave at once. Tell them the Fleet will be instructed to impound their yacht if they do not comply."

His deputy said, "The Fleet can certainly do that, although the yacht's captain might challenge the legality. However I agree that might be the quickest way to get them out of there. Can you advise the province that a diplomatic shuttle is arriving? Otherwise I might get shot out of the sky!"

7b – Contract of *Sirt*

Other nations on Masun were watching the movement of the shuttles to the headquarters of the local confederation. Although not large, historically the area had a reputation for being efficient militarily. The approach of a shuttle from an interstellar yacht, followed by a shuttle heading to the same destination from the local Nova Embassy began to attract considerable interest.

When Sienna's group arrived, they had been surprised to discover a small honour guard was drawn up.

Peter and Louise left the shuttle first followed by the combat remote, and then Sienna and Iain. A small cable from the remote was supporting a transparent plastic box clearly containing foodstuffs and liquids.

The appearance of two officers dressed in Federation uniforms caused a considerable stir.

The Masuna who met them said, "I'm called Ergan, and I am the leader of the small confederation in this area. Please introduce yourselves, and explain why you are dressed in what are plainly Federation Fleet uniforms."

Peter said, "I am Commander Moore and my colleague is Major Louise Moore. The other two members of our party are Sienna and Iain Taylor.

"The Federation Fleet in orbit above us is not aware that we are here. We are on detached duty, with responsibility for protecting the two civilians behind us. The latter are closely related to the Empress."

Ergan nodded, quite satisfied. His relative in the police force had made a good decision to introduce the human group. Senior officers would not be detached for protection duties unless the civilians were really important. Also he had taken a risk in inviting his opposite numbers from other parts of their small confederation, and it would have been embarrassing if these humans were insignificant. He was becoming deeply concerned at the way the planetary politics were moving, and desperately wanted to find a solution which avoided war.

He greeted Iain and Sienna with great respect.

Inside, there were a number of Masuna waiting. Introductions made it clear they were senior representatives from all the members of the local confederation. The large remote from the shuttle moved to the side of the room, where it hovered motionless.

At that moment, there was a stir at the entrance, and the diplomat from the Nova embassy entered. He was greatly perturbed and disconcerted at the array of senior Masuna in the room, some of whom he recognised.

He said, "My name is Robert Gatsby from the Nova Embassy. I need to talk to the human group here urgently."

Sienna's group detached itself and came over to him, with quick introductions.

He said, "What the hell do you lot think you are doing! You were warned before you came that this planet is heading towards a flashpoint, and you seem to have directly involved yourselves in local politics!

"The Nova Ambassador instructs you to immediately depart, otherwise your yacht will be impounded.

"I'm sure the Admiral will be furious to discover Federation officers are involved."

The young and slightly built woman in the group, whom he recognised as a Shepherd, said "Give him your data chip, Peter."

The commander pulled out his data chip and said, "Mr Gatsby, use your reader on these, and rest assured that the chip is genuine."

The chip was inserted in the reader which everyone carried, which acted as a combined database, information source and mobile communication device.

The diplomat looked quite astonished as he studied the contents.

Peter took back the chip and said, "You need to contact your Ambassador and tell him that the situation here is more complex than it appeared at first sight.

"The tourists will not be able to return immediately."

Sienna added, "Also, Mr Gatsby, I think we may need your help here. Tell your ambassador you will also not be returning immediately, and make sure he is clear that you're not under any duress.

"Apart from my request, of course. Send everything in clear, so all the parties who are listening in, know exactly what is happening."

The Ambassador was horrified when his deputy's call came through. "Robert, have you gone insane! If we have read our entrails correctly, nearly every senior figure in the local confederation is present. This is a diplomatically explosive situation, and if you don't get those humans out of there quickly, expect to become a Third Secretary somewhere unpleasant!"

His deputy paled slightly, but held his ground. "I'm sorry sir, but you're not in possession of the full facts. I will be staying here, and so will the tourists. I must go now."

He shut off his reader.

He saw the Major looking at him with considerable respect. "Well done, Robert. Don't worry, your career will be fully protected. Right now, forget about the Embassy, and concentrate on helping us when you have seen what is happening."

Back at the Nova Embassy, a furious conversation was occurring between the Ambassador and the Federation Fleet Admiral.

The Admiral was tempted to send down a detachment supported by a cruiser, but the diplomat stopped him.

"I think that would be a bad idea, and would be regarded as a most hostile act. I don't know what the hell is going on in that building, but my offsider is normally remarkably level headed. That's why he was sent here. If he says the situation is more complex than we think, we have to assume he is better informed than we are. There were no stress words included in the conversation, so he is not under duress.

"If I am wrong about this, his career will be finished."

The Admiral added, "And the planet may be in flames."

Back in the fort, Ergan watched the human group return.

Peter apologised, "I'm sorry about that, but our Embassy was concerned. Robert Gatsby is the Deputy Ambassador, and has reassured them there is no problem. Assuming you have no difficulty with this, he would like to remain. He knows a number of the people in this room."

The Masuna leader was fascinated. With excellent hearing and eyesight, he had seen the data chip that the senior human officer had extracted, which had led to complete compliance by the junior diplomat. He had also been able to hear one side of the conversation with the Embassy; the human had clearly been resisting strong pressure from his superior.

The Masuna quickly realised that the young human woman who was related to the Empress controlled the group. They were experienced politicians, and had lifetimes of practice in identifying relationship structures.

A short time later, dinner was announced. The human food and drink brought in by the remote had been suitably arranged on the tables.

At one table, Sienna was talking to a group from the most distant part of the confederation.

She said, "We were quite disturbed when we read about your planet, and the way your political systems seem to be fraying.

"I would very much like to understand how you see the problems, and whether you think there is a solution."

The Masuna found themselves being questioned intensively about how the planetary political system operated. As a people they were slightly xenophobic, but something about this young human woman radiated authority, and they found themselves opening up and describing their problems in detail. Iain sat on the opposite side of the table, and listened with great interest.

Meanwhile, Robert Gatsby was able to introduce the other human members of the group to the various Masuna he knew. Conversation was much more general than with Sienna's group, and the conversation quickly turned to Datura. The film of the dinner on Crystal had been seen by everyone present, and the two officers found themselves being questioned in detail. The locals were particularly interested in knowing more about the Empress, especially when they realised this human group had been on the senior table with her.

Robert Gatsby suddenly remembered the pictures of Sienna and Iain.

Towards the end of the meal, Ergan stood up.

He said, "I would like to thank the human group for coming here and talking to us. It is important that people from elsewhere in the Federation learn about our planet.

"Mrs Taylor, I understand you are quite close to the Empress.

"One of the problems the nations on our planet have, is that we cannot find anyone acceptable to all the nations to whom we can delegate the task of arbitrating our differences fairly.

"Up to now, we did not consider anyone the Federation has sent sufficiently senior to act in that position."

Robert Gatsby was stunned. He suddenly realised why all the attempts to arbitrate the problems on the planet had failed; they had not considered the sociological structure of the species. They would only accept as arbitrator someone with really senior stature. Also, that arbitrator had to have authority to rule decisively.

Whatever he and his Ambassador negotiated, had to be referred back to Nova for final approval. From the Masuna point of view, that made arbitration decisions ineffectual.

"If you were such an arbitrator, being closely related to the Empress, would she accept your rulings?"

Siena stood up, and somehow she dominated the room.

"If your nations were willing to accept me as an arbitrator, I would operate the arbitration as a Contract of *Sirt* with my Empress, with all that implies. I am completely confident that Sylvia will accept my rulings and implement them by decree as a Federation Emergency. Your seas are far too cold for a swim.

"However, before I would accept that position, the vast majority of your nations must be in favour of this, and all the nations involved must give me an undertaking that they will abide by the rulings.

"Otherwise, sadly, we will leave you to resolve your differences by war, and at the end of that process the Empress will probably change your status to Protectorate and endeavour to fix the damage.

"She believes strongly in the Federation Constitution, and will not act by decree until you have inflicted severe damage on yourselves."

Ergan nodded. He said, "We have taken the liberty of recording this meeting and your comments. With your permission we will circulate it to all the polities on the planet.

"If the vast majority agree, the arbitration will occur under your control."

Robert Gatsby was both elated and alarmed. This human group seemed to have achieved more in the last two hours than the Federation had achieved in years. His alarm came from the extreme youth of the person who seemed to be volunteering to be arbitrator.

He was nowhere near as confident as this young woman that the Empress would simply accept whatever had been decided.

He decided that his next conversation with his boss was going to be interesting.

The recording was passed around all the polities on the planet.

The Federation had been quite wrong when they assumed that the Masuna collectively were spoiling for a fight with each other.

While huge political, economic and religious differences were present between the groups, apart from a small militaristic minority the majority of the leaders recognised that war would be a planetary disaster.

It would also be deadlier, as even without the use of nuclear weapons and the Federation insistence on the code of *Intranu**, destruction and casualties using modern weapons would be horrible.

There was an active debate across the planet for a day, before acceptances began to trickle back to Ergan.

* * *

After the dinner with Ergan, Peter had suggested to Sienna that it would be sensible to take Robert back to the Nova Embassy in the yacht shuttle. The Embassy shuttle would follow them.

He added, "Since I am a little lacking in the bravery department, it would be good if you could explain what you are going to do to the Nova Ambassador and the Admiral!"

His Empress looked at him with annoyance for a moment, and then laughed.

"Fair enough. Unfortunately, I think we will have to show your orders to the Admiral and the Ambassador on a strictly confidential basis. I better see if Katie is around, as I would like to try to maintain our anonymity!"

---

* *[Author's note: Intranu is a **Fighting Honour Code** used to prevent major casualties amongst noncombatants and is incorporated in the Federation Constitution]*

The Nova Ambassador had been enormously relieved when he heard that his deputy was being brought back on the shuttle from the yacht, together with its human group.

When he heard, the Admiral insisted on coming down by fast military shuttle together with his flag captain and a squad of marines. He had decided to simply arrest the human group for interference, without worrying too much about the legalities.

As a result, when the shuttle arrived at the Embassy, all its passengers found themselves being "escorted" by marines into a large room.

The Admiral was incredulous when he saw two officers in the group in Federation Fleet uniforms.

"Consider yourselves under arrest", he said brusquely.

Robert was about to interject when Sienna said, "Admiral, before you do anything further Robert Gatsby needs to talk to you and the Ambassador privately."

He saw that she was a Shepherd, which meant something in the fleet.

He nodded, and the Ambassador said, "There is a small drawing room through that door."

Five minutes later, the door opened again, and Peter and Louise were ordered into the room.

The Admiral put out his hand, "Let's see this data chip."

As on Datura, the sealed orders were verified, printed, and read with complete astonishment.

Robert Gatsby watched the process with a certain satisfaction. He was looking forward to seeing how they would react when they heard about the arbitration. At this stage, it was by no means certain that a sufficient proportion of the polities would accept, but he thought the chances were reasonable.

The Admiral looked at the pair of officers. "Under the circumstances, you are no longer under arrest. Since we now appear to be under your orders, what do you want us to do, Commander?"

Peter said, "First of all, it is really important that knowledge of the sealed orders goes no further than anyone this room.

"Secondly, Sienna has volunteered to explain her role. We are all going to support her absolutely in this. It is by far the best chance we have of sorting out the political mess here.

"It is not certain that she will succeed, but she is determined to try.

"We will make the conversation brief, as she is pregnant and tired and we need to get her back to the yacht."

The thought occurred to the Ambassador and the Admiral that their Empress was also known to be pregnant. They wondered about the probability of two pregnant Shepherds being in this distant part of the Federation at the same time.

When she came in, Sienna said, "I'm worn out, and I'm going to sit down. The remote will run the recording, which it will leave with you."

As this was done, like his deputy the Ambassador experienced a mixture of elation and alarm.

He had immediately drawn the same conclusions as Robert. He hoped Sienna would be able to handle the stress.

The Admiral's thinking was on different lines: he was reflecting on the girl's absolute confidence that the Empress would support her.

When the recording was finished, Sienna said; "We will return at about 11 o'clock tomorrow morning, when we will do some serious planning.

"Between now and then, I would like the Embassy to get together a written briefing on all the polities and their leadership. I apologise for the late night this is going to create."

"Finally, I would like Robert Gatsby to be attached to my group if this arbitration goes ahead. He can liaise with the Ambassador if we need anything, and I think I would value his on the spot input."

The Admiral remarked, "Young lady, I assume that your confidence that the Empress will support you is justified. Swimming in these waters is dangerous! If I heard the recording correctly, you are absolutely committed to abide by the *Sirt* convention."

Sienna nodded. "She will; now if you don't mind I need to get back to Cheetah."

20 minutes later, all the staff in the Embassy were being roused. It promised to be a busy night.

The Ambassador, the Admiral, and Robert Gatsby were enjoying a quiet coffee while the staff organised themselves.

The Admiral asked Robert his impressions of Sienna.

He said, "She was exhausted when she came in here. When she was talking to the Masuna, she was completely convincing and most impressive. The recording did not do her performance justice."

The Admiral nodded, "If you add to that a set of most extraordinary orders, not to mention an impossibly powerful interstellar yacht, I think we will treat Sienna Taylor with maximum respect."

He turned to the Ambassador, "Henry, if you wish I can immediately delegate 20 or 30 officers to digging out basic information for your staff. That will speed matters considerably, as your people can concentrate on data checking, formatting, presentation and making sure the package is coherent.

"I suspect that whatever is prepared will be subject to sharp questioning tomorrow, and I do not think it would be good to provide second-rate data to our young lady. My colleagues on Nova have warned me about this family!"

The different nations on Masun noted the shuttle leaving the Embassy for the luxury yacht.

Shortly afterwards, they realised that the entire Embassy appear to have been roused, and a plethora of coded messages were being passed to and from the Federation Fleet.

Ergan was pleased; Sienna Taylor clearly wielded enormous authority.

Over the next two days, many nations who were unsure whether to agree to this arbitration decided participation was preferable.

A trickle of acceptances became a flood.

7c – Negotiations

The shuttle from Cheetah returned just before 11 o'clock the following morning.

The presentation and report that had been prepared overnight was read carefully. The embassy staff saw that all of the group from the yacht participated, and were making notes on the copies.

Sienna said to Robert, "This is an excellent piece of work. We've got a whole lot of questions, but that reflects the amount of work which has been done.

"I would like everyone involved including yourself and the Ambassador to assemble in the auditorium in 20 minutes. Please also arrange a video link to the Fleet, and ask the Admiral if the officers who participated can listen in."

Robert realised no one had told Sienna that the Fleet had been involved.

20 minutes later, with preparations complete, Sienna walked to the microphone on the stage of the auditorium.

"Good morning everyone, I am Sienna Taylor.

"I would like to thank all of you who worked overnight to prepare the presentation, including the Fleet officers who were also involved. From my first read, it is an excellent piece of work.

"As I said to Robert, we've got a whole lot of questions, but that can wait for the time being.

"We are working on the assumption that the Masuna nations will agree that I arbitrate under *Sirt* rules.

"There is a reasonable chance of this occurring, but even if it does not the work will not be wasted. When she gets here, Sylvia will be most interested in looking at what has been done.

"As she said on Nova about five weeks ago, she is determined to see that the problems which are cropping up in this far-flung region of the Federation are fixed. It is just as important to her as much closer parts which have been members for longer."

As the Admiral watched from the office on the flag battleship, he realised that Sienna radiated authority. He had rarely seen an audience so interested in lapping up every word.

He was more than ever convinced that she was the hidden Empress. Sienna continued, "For the arbitration, I also need a summary of the possible political models, with subjective summaries of their advantages and disadvantages.

"I would like the Masun nations to be involved in the choice. However, if they can't or won't agree, I will decide for them. Fortunately, I have some training in this area.

"As part and parcel of the same exercise, a new constitution needs to be framed, with appropriate variations for the different models. The existing version was cobbled together too quickly, and its deficiencies have become apparent.

"Accordingly we need to set up two groups to look at these questions. After this meeting, I will ask for volunteers who have applicable interest or knowledge in those two areas.

"Major Louise Moore will chair the group looking at political models, and my husband Iain the other group looking at constitutions. He has legal training.

"Commander Peter Moore and I will try and keep tabs on the whole process. Also, I will be getting answers to our questions on last night's work.

"I think the whole process needs to be completed within 48 hours.

"I'm afraid I need to take some exercise every day, and have a sleep most afternoons as I am pregnant, which will limit my availability. Peter will deputise for me when I am absent.

"Are there any questions?"

There were several questions, which Sienna handled quickly and tactfully.

As soon as the presentation was finished, the Admiral called his Fleet Captain, who had also been watching. "Round up two suitably qualified groups to help with Sienna's next projects. Perhaps your XO could coordinate with the Embassy, Major Moore and Iain Taylor on how this is to be organised. This has an extremely high priority.

"Also, tell everyone concerned that for the purposes of this exercise, they are to obey instructions from those two whatever their rank."

He decided that he would like some more information on the Taylors. He sent a search request to the planetary databases, and was a little disconcerted when the message came back; "You are not authorised for that information".

A few seconds later, he was still staring at the message with some frustration, when his screen cleared and a new message appeared. "The computer complexes have been overridden. Admiral, you have a limited clearance for background information on the Taylors. Please keep it to yourself."

He wondered who or what could have overridden the complexes. There were literally only a handful of entities who had the authority.

With a 48 hour time limit, the groups collecting the information that Sienna wanted worked extraordinarily long hours.

For Iain, finding himself in an executive position was a new experience, and he floundered a little at the start. Peter spent some time with him providing discreet guidance, and privately wondered to himself if Sienna had decided to give her husband some executive training.

Louise was a natural organiser, and the group preparing descriptions of the various possible models found she was well organised, helpful and supportive.

They also found she could be quite caustic about sloppy work.

The Ambassador had a chance to have a quiet word with Sienna.

"Sienna, may I suggest that you use the next two days to get yourself completely rested. We can cope here. Matters are likely to become most stressful after that, and I don't think you can afford to be anything but fresh.

"I might add, that although I was initially horrified to hear about the arbitration process which you have volunteered to manage, I now think this may be by far the best chance we have of sorting out this planet."

Sienna decided to take the advice.

At the end of the two days, a substantial paper had been prepared. As copies were being handed out, a message came through from the Masuna known as Ergan.

"18 out of the 20 national groups have bound themselves to accept Mrs Sienna Taylor as arbitrator for a new planetary governance model under a Contract of *Sirt* with the Empress Sylvia."

Sienna said, "Send my formal acceptance to Ergan, and ask him to forward it to all the groups.

"Also, tell them that the formal arbitration will occur in fourteen days' time at a suitably large venue. It may take several days to complete. I intend to talk individually to all the groups in the near future.

"Please provide the leadership contact points."

Back on Cheetah that evening, she said to her group. "Well done everyone; we have now got to first base.

"As I intimated, the next stage is to talk individually to all the national leaders. We will start first thing tomorrow morning, working down the list in order of size.

"Right now, I think we should have some supper, and then get some sleep."

7d – Arbitration

Matters did not go to plan.

Just before an early breakfast, a message was received from one of the large groups called the Hatua, who were angry at what they regarded as outside interference.

"We are completely opposed to arbitration by this unknown human. We demand to see her to express our views."

Iain saw his wife looking cross for a moment. She said something, which sounded like a muffled swearword. Sienna rarely swore, and when she did it meant trouble for someone.

"Peter and Louise, change of plan.

"Cheetah, tell the group we were planning to see at 10 o'clock that we will be unavoidably an hour late, with suitable apologies.

"Tell the Hatua we will see their leaders at 9:30."

Peter said, "Sienna, for once I must step in and talk about security. The easiest way for this group to fix matters the way they want is simply to have you killed.

"No doubt they will be deeply remorseful, and plausible deniability will be the theme, but the result will be satisfactory to them."

Sienna looked absolutely furious with her Commander and was about to say something cutting, when Cheetah interjected; "Sienna, stop and think. Peter is absolutely correct. We must insist on a high level of security."

Cheetah paused for a moment.

"Otherwise, technical problems will occur with my shuttles rendering them unusable."

Once again, Sienna started to say something when Iain chimed in, "Sienna, Peter and Cheetah are trying to protect you, and you need to take their advice.

"We're not saying you can't go, but you must listen to your staff! And me."

There was a long silence, as Sienna glared at the group. It was unfair that her husband had joined the chorus as well.

Then she said rather reluctantly, "OK, what do we need to do?"

A few minutes later, in a rather mercurial change of mood, she smiled.

"I admit I have played the spoiled brat, and I apologise. The suggestions are sensible."

An hour later, Cheetah's shuttle landed at the Hatua main government building. He had used the half an hour travel time to seed all parts of the building with surveillance devices.

As the humans disembarked, the small group of officials meeting them noticed the party included two large remotes.

In a small anti-room, after they had been seated at a table, the Hatua leader gave Sienna a withering tirade about the inappropriateness of her interference in a planet's affairs. A small remote provided an immediate translation in English.

She listened in silence.

The leader was just about to finish talking, or rather shouting, when there was a disturbance at the entrance, and three heavily armed Masuna burst in. The security officers in the room started reaching for their weapons.

One of the combat remotes encased the human group and the Hatua leader in a force shield, visible as a slightly opaque screen.

The other remote opened fire with a powerful concealed laser weapon. The three Masuna crumpled with grotesque burn marks on their chests.

There was complete silence for a few seconds, as the scent of incinerated clothing and flesh filled the room.

The Hatua leader looked shocked. Peter wondered whether it was because of the sudden deaths, or because the attack had failed.

Sienna had turned quite pale, but still remained silent.

As soon as Cheetah decided that no threat remained, the force screen lifted.

The Hatua leader says, "Mrs Taylor, I am profoundly shocked by this, and must apologise."

Colour returned to Sienna's cheeks, and standing up she said; "This attack was stupid, and the perpetrators have been killed. Take no further action. The planners behind this attack, whoever they might be, will be embarrassed, and it will be regarded as deeply shameful by the other Masuna nations.

"Sir, you have completely misunderstood my role as arbitrator. In my view, it is vastly preferable that the Masuna nations agree between themselves what needs to be done. I have no wish to impose anything that does not have the concurrence of the majority.

"All the groups which have agreed to the arbitration need to talk between themselves, and suggest reforms. They need to understand clearly that changes which are obviously partisan will not be acceptable. Your nations must learn to communicate even if there is a history of hatred and war.

"There will be points upon which they can agree, and there will be areas where fundamental disagreements will persist, which is understandable. That is where I can step in as an arbitrator. Some of my rulings will be hard to accept for some of the groups, but that is my function. You can be certain there will be no historical bias.

"Separately from this, the Nova Embassy has prepared a paper on various types of political model and associated constitutions, with a note of the advantages and disadvantages.

"The planet from which my species originally hailed experimented with a wild variety of political systems, some of which were successful and some of which were utterly disastrous. It is unlikely that anyone from your planet will suggest a model which had not been tried on Earth at some stage.

"I intend to circulate this paper as a discussion focus."

Sienna paused from moment, to study her audience. She did not know that much about Masuna psychology, but it seemed to her that hostility had lessened and they were starting to listen seriously.

"If you stand aside from the arbitration process, you will have no influence on the results.

"When the Empress Sylvia arrives, you can be sure she will support my rulings. She is enormously powerful, and she will not permit dissident minorities to hinder the process. If they resist, they will be subject to punitive sanctions, and will not be allowed to unilaterally start wars."

"Sir, I request that your nation reconsiders its decision not to participate."

As she met his eyes, the Hatua leader recognised that the young human woman in front of him radiated authority.

He had suspected that an assassination plan was being considered, but had taken no action to investigate, which was likely to prove most embarrassing.

Mrs Taylor's comments had made him feel acutely uncomfortable, and ashamed.

He bowed, "Your request will be seriously considered, Mrs Taylor."

When they left, they were escorted by a full honour guard as well as the Hatua leader.

News of the attack was filtering out, when a complete recording of the whole event including Sienna's comments was released from an unknown source.

Shortly afterwards, there was a statement from the Nova Embassy regretting the attack. It attached the political model paper to which Sienna had alluded.

All the Masuna leaders studied the recording of the attack and this new information with great interest.

When the Admiral and his Flag Captain had finished watching the attack recording, they looked at each other thoughtfully.

The Admiral said, "That was one of the more impressive impromptu speeches I've ever heard. I am no expert on Masuna facial expressions, but I reckon the Hatua leader was shaken to the core. I suspect the hidden message was 'I'll forgive the attack if you front up'.

"In a strange way, I think the chances of getting this planet fixed just improved."

His Flag Captain nodded, and added; "By the way, I thought the performance of those two combat remotes was remarkable. Those that we have on board here would not have been anywhere near as efficient. In fact, they reek of Habitat or Palace technology.

"I'm beginning to wonder about that strange yacht out there."

Later on that morning, Sienna and her group started visiting the major nations.

Since the leaders had all watched the events at Hatua, she found that what she needed to say had been considerably shortened.

Her basic message was, "You need to consider how you wish to manage yourselves politically. Use our models paper as a reference, and talk to the other Masuna nations, and particularly your enemies.

"It would be vastly preferable to go to the arbitration process with a clear preferred model across all the groups. I can decide the boundaries where differences exist.

"Above all, start to think of yourselves as a single species which needs to interact with the rest of the Federation as a stable entity.

"My group would be delighted to talk further with any nation during the next few days."

As a result of Sienna's urging, the Masuna nations started to talk to each other seriously.

With groups which were recognised as enemies, this was hesitant at first, and then much more lengthy discussion started. This was bilateral at first, and then became multilateral.

The human group was frequently asked to participate in discussions where evident difficulties existed.

Unfortunately for Sienna, three days later she ran into a period of horrible morning sickness. This "illness" had to be explained to the Masuna, who had nothing similar in their biology. She was frequently only available in the afternoon, and looked tired, drawn and pale.

The Embassy staff and the Cheetah humans had to assist negotiations without much help from Sienna.

As soon as he heard, the Fleet Admiral insisted that a doctor and nurse from the flagship be sent across to look after her. They were told they could take as long as needed, and the Admiral had added that it would be a good idea if the nurse stayed on the yacht.

When he contacted Cheetah, he said; "Sienna, I gather you are suffering badly, and in nine days you are going to have to front up to a major gathering. We need to do everything possible to make sure you're healthy.

"Peter and your husband are happy with this. The nurse can stay with you on the yacht, assuming there is accommodation available."

Sienna was feeling so miserable, she accepted without a murmur.

When the doctor and the senior nurse arrived, Peter told them at the entrance: "You must not say anything to anyone about what you see or hear on this yacht. This is really important.

"With the attack, the Federation press has suddenly become aware of what we are doing here, and they are doing everything possible to dig out further information.

"Safety lies in saying nothing at all!"

The doctor was surprised at the sophistication of the small medical unit, and Sienna was given a comprehensive examination.

He said, "Mrs Taylor, your pregnancy is progressing normally. Unfortunately, your body is adapting to its new situation with an excess of pregnancy hormones. Centuries of medical practice have indicated that doing nothing with morning sickness is absolutely the best policy.

"Some previous medications that alleviated symptoms were disastrous.

"Felicity Corning is a senior staff nurse, and has specialised in pregnancy, although not much of that happens in the fleet. She will stay with you here, and help. I suggest she comes with you whenever you travel, and take her advice if she says you need to rest."

Sienna said wanly, "Thank you, Doctor. Oh, I'm going to be sick again ..."

She found having the nurse present helped.

Felicity was more than impressed with the yacht. She was talking to Iain later on that day.

He said, "We are really grateful for your help. Sienna has accepted your instructions with hardly a murmur – she must be feeling really bad as that is not like her at all. By the way, call everyone here by their first names.

"Also, the yacht is called Cheetah, and you can talk to him at any time. You will find him marginally intelligent!"

A male voice said. "Hello, Felicity. Ignore the rude comment which Iain just made!

"If you need anything, please ask. Also, there is an extensive entertainment library on board if you just want something to keep yourself occupied."

7e – Masun Fix

The news about the attack on the human group took two days by foldspace to reach Nova.

Admiral Jenna had an immediate discussion with the Governor. "Sienna is really stirring things up on the planet. I am most concerned about that attack, although it looks like my officers were wide awake.

"There is a substantial Federation battle group exercising in the area, with about 150 vessels.

"Do you think it would be appropriate if it appeared in the vicinity of Masun?"

Caroline agreed, "That sounds like a good idea. This might suggest to the Masuna that we are taking reform of their planetary political system rather seriously, and we really don't like attacks on Sienna.

"It will also send a message to Sienna that we are quite worried about her!"

The Admiral in charge of the battle group was ordered to postpone the exercises and move his group to Masun as quickly as possible. He was to liaise with the local fleet, and wait for further instructions. He was also advised by Admiral Jenna that this was a "showing the flag" exercise, as a serious attempt was being made to resolve the political impasse on the planet. A little strangely, he was given permission to enquire about a Commander Moore and Major Moore when he arrived.

When this happened, he was immediately briefed by the local Admiral, together with three of his senior officers. They were quite astonished when they watched the recordings about Sienna, and were given a copy of Peter's sealed orders.

The local Admiral told them, "Sienna Taylor is quite young but is showing immense maturity and courage. The fact that Admiral Jenna and the Governor immediately despatched you here when they heard about the attack on her, indicates that they are seriously concerned.

"Absolutely don't quote me on this anywhere, but I'm reasonably confident we are watching our hidden Empress."

The political process on the planet was already seething with activity when the battle group arrived.

The Masuna interpreted this move as a signal that the Federation was committed to supporting the arbitration proposal. It was also clearly annoyed by the attack on Sienna.

It had been a long time since a battle group had assembled in a solar system anywhere except Nova. The Hatua realised they had mis-stepped badly, and joined the process together with the other dissenting nation.

There was a view crystallising that Sienna had spelt out the position exactly when she said their planet would be reduced to a protectorate if they inflicted severe internal damage on themselves through a war.

All the nations accelerated efforts to formalise in general terms exactly how a new Constitution and political model should operate.

The Federation journalists were fascinated by the developments, and particularly the appearance of the Federation battle group in the sky.

They found the name Sienna Taylor kept cropping up, but the computer complexes refused to provide any data whatsoever on her.

The Hatua and Ergan's Confederation were trying to start a dialogue. It was not going well, and Sienna was asked to attend.

She agreed, but said it would have to be early in the afternoon. Over lunch, Felicity had managed to cajole her into eating some broth, with a great deal of encouragement from Iain.

The Masuna were perturbed when she appeared, with a woman who was clearly a medical attendant lurking in the background. Even to their eyes, she looked frighteningly pale and ill.

She was seated immediately, with a microphone to amplify her words. The nurse placed a rug around her shoulders, and gave her a bottle clearly containing a nutritive fluid.

After apologising for her personal condition, she said; "Please summarise your discussion. It would be helpful if a large whiteboard was brought in. I would like someone to note down the key points as they are made, and also where you have differences.

"You can take turns explaining why you think the differences exist."

The process took about an hour, while the first whiteboard was covered with notes, and a second one was needed.

All Sienna did was ask occasional questions, which were utterly to the point. She never ventured an opinion. Unknown to the Masuna, in some cases she was being quietly prompted by subvocal communication from her team and Cheetah.

Answering the questions forced the Masuna on both sides to modify their positions. It was clear that the basis for a set of compromises was being outlined.

At the end of the hour, Felicity said, and it was the first time she had spoken, "I'm sorry, that is enough for today. It is time Sienna went back to her yacht and rested."

Sienna started to protest, but the nurse firmly overrode her. "Sienna, you must rest."

As she stood to go, all the Masuna rose and clapped. In their culture, this was a gesture of great respect. Sienna said briefly, "Thank you. I'm sorry, but you will have to finish without me."

Peter took over from her.

Once again, a recording of the whole process was circulated.

It was watched by two Admirals and a small group of senior officers.

Back at the yacht, Felicity made Sienna take a little food and drink, and then settle down for a sleep.

When she returned to the lounge area, she thought for a moment she was seeing Sienna again, when she realised it was a young woman who looked extraordinarily similar to her charge.

She said, "Hello, I'm Felicity."

Katie smiled, "I am Katie. I'm pleased with the care you are taking of Sienna. I'm a doctor, and will have a look at her when she wakes."

At that moment, Iain and Peter emerged from the kitchen area, where they had been helping themselves to a snack.

Felicity could see their faces brighten when they saw Katie, "Katie, we are really glad to see you!

"Things have been getting a little out of control here, and it is great that you are back."

The nurse was astonished that the Commander did not know that Katie was on board his own yacht.

At that moment, Sienna's cat wandered in and with a loud purr leapt onto the newcomer's shoulder, licking her ear enthusiastically.

Katie laughed, "It's nice to see you too, Yelli!"

She turned to Felicity. "Felicity, it is really important that you never, ever, mention that you have seen me aboard this yacht.

"I am Sienna's great-grandmother, and to protect the Taylors' privacy, it is essential that no one knows I'm around."

Felicity's eyes widened as she realised Katie's identity.

"You have probably guessed by now that Sienna is the Empress. When the Crystal Palace arrives in two or three weeks' time, I can pretend to be Sienna, while Sienna aka Sylvia takes on her formal role.

"We are all hoping she will have gotten over this bout of morning sickness by then, as otherwise we might have a problem."

* * *

Over the next week, the staff at the Nova embassy noticed that the Masuna collectively were gradually coalescing on a preferred governance model. The areas of disagreement between the groups were relatively sharply defined, but small in extent.

This was a startling improvement over the previous position.

Fortunately, it was also apparent that Sienna was starting to recover.

A large hall was chosen as the venue for the arbitration process.

On the day, representatives from all the Masuna nations collected, and the proceedings began.

Sienna sat on a raised pedestal at the end, surrounded by the human group from Cheetah and Robert Gatsby. There were three large remotes at the side and behind the group. There were few illusions about their function.

At 10 o'clock precisely, she hit a small bell on the table, and the sound resonated through the hall.

She said in a clear voice, "In accordance with the agreement with all the Masuna nations, I, Sienna Taylor, open these arbitration proceedings under a contract of *Sirt* with the Empress Sylvia.

"There is general agreement on a new political model and constitution, with some clearly defined differences.

"It is my view that these represent honestly held differences of opinion. It is most satisfactory that a large part of the previous differences have been removed by concessions on all sides.

"Your peoples are learning to compromise.

"I accept the broad framework of the consensus which has been presented.

"I have been given a list of the areas where differences persist. I propose to tackle these one by one.

"I will ask each group or nation disagreeing to provide one representative to summarise their view in one *tend,* which for our audiences elsewhere represents about 15 minutes. The representative can expect to be questioned seriously, and for the responses time will be added.

"The questions do not represent criticism, but I need to understand the basis of difficulty.

"At the end of each item, I will confer with my colleagues on this podium, and I will arbitrate the difference. The ruling may prefer one side or the other, but I guarantee no historical bias."

The list ran to a dozen points, and took two days to consider.

At the end of the second day, Sienna rose, holding a paper summary of the totality of the revised position.

"The new political system for Masun has been settled, and I so arbitrate."

She took a pen from Iain, and signed and dated the document.

She said, "The Crystal Palace is now arriving on the outskirts of the Masun solar system."

A little later the Masun nations each received a message.

"There will be a Federation Dinner on the Crystal Palace in three days. Please select two representatives to attend".

The Nova Ambassador could not help sending a message to Crystal.

"The timing was impeccable".

Crystal placed herself in low orbit, in the centre of the battle group.

She was easily visible with a set of low powered binoculars, and the Masuna were collectively awed.

* * *

As usual, the Empress greeted her guests as they entered, with a golden cat on one shoulder, and with the Nova Ambassador next to her. The cat's eyes were glowing faintly.

A little later, Sylvia sat at a slightly raised table, with her Ambassador, the leaders of the three largest Masun nations and Ergan, together with their wives. It was recognised that the inclusion of Ergan reflected his initial input to the arbitration process.

The group from Cheetah plus Robert Gatsby were on a separate table. Felicity was surprised to find she was included, together with Robert's wife.

Otherwise, the other Masuna invitees, the two Admirals and a number of senior Fleet officers were scattered among another dozen tables together with six more junior officers chosen randomly. The final table held press representatives, who had also been chosen by lot.

The Admirals, the Ambassador, and Robert were quite confused: they had been convinced that Sienna was the Empress.

Halfway through the first course, Sylvia stood up.

Silence spread throughout the hall.

She waited a moment, and then began; "My people, I greet you.

"I am completely satisfied with the arbitration process which has occurred. It is my belief that a much more efficient structure has been established. If the Masuna nations feel it needs to be amended in the future, I'm willing to assist.

"In achieving this, I am grateful to my support group," and she smiled in the direction of the Cheetah group table. The camera carefully panned over them. Iain, conspicuous with his plaster and sling, leant over and gave the fake Sienna a kiss on the cheek dangerously close to her lips.

"Cheeky!" Katie murmured, amused.

Sylvia continued: "I am also grateful to the staff at the Nova Embassy, and the fleet officers who assisted.

"However, and most of all, I am grateful to the Masuna nations who were able to put aside their differences and design something which needed little amendment. They should be proud of what they have achieved. I expect them to start to wind back the militarisation which has occurred.

"In the future, it would be good if more of your young people studied at the universities at Nova and elsewhere.

"I am sure this will gradually break down barriers between your species and the other members of our Federation.

"The Fleet would also value more recruits from your planet."

As she was speaking, a giant semitransparent cat's face appeared in the air, with faintly glowing eyes. A distinct purr was also audible throughout the hall. Most of the people present looked at it with amazement. A few remembered that the same face had been seen in a Stortin stadium many decades previously.

Sylvia paused for a moment, and looked around the hall.

"People of the Federation, I am every bit as interested in the outer planets as those closer in, and I would like the gap in general welfare and income between the regions to diminish steadily.

"Particularly in the case of health, a great deal still needs to be done.

"My best wishes to you all."

At that, Sylvia smiled and sat down, as applause echoed through the Hall. The giant cat face disappeared.

Ergan murmured, "The Empress mispronounced slightly the name of our people in exactly the same way as Sienna Taylor and had a tiny insect bite on her neck which I also saw on Sienna. Apart from the colour of their hair, otherwise the latter and the Empress appear absolutely identical."

A quiet conversation was also going on between the two admirals.

"I wonder whether we are seeing what we think we are seeing. The Empress and Sienna Taylor have my unbounded admiration, but this has the look of a beautifully orchestrated show.

"However, I think we should keep any speculation on how it was arranged strictly to ourselves."

The journalists on the press table thought they had nailed down the identity of the hidden Empress. To see their candidate sitting at a table listening was a profound disappointment.

During the main course, Sylvia moved around the room, spending a few minutes at each of the tables. The journalists enjoyed a little more of her time.

She was asked which planet she would visit next.

She laughed; "To be honest, I'm not sure. I think the glare of publicity which you lot are helping to provide, is persuading several planets in this region to fix their problems. I will just watch things for a bit.

"Health issues in this region would make a good subject for journalistic investigation!

"I'll tell you what: the best article I read on that subject in the next five months gets the journalist a conducted tour by me of the Crystal Palace, plus a pictures exclusive for a month on the twins when they are born!

"By the way, I would be truly grateful if the press stopped trying to find out where I live most of the time. You have no idea how much my husband and I value our privacy."

* * *

Later on that evening, a tired group of humans returned to Cheetah. Felicity insisted that Sienna ate something before she went to bed.

"My Lady, you were so busy dazzling your audience that you ate almost nothing. I know, because I asked Crystal to keep tabs!"

At that moment, Katie walked into the room.

"Congratulations Sienna, you seem to have successfully re-organised another planet!

"I listened to some of the journalists after you left their table. I think your tour and pictures offer is going to their collective heads. I think health issues are going to be a major publicity area for the next few months!

"The journalists want to see you and the more private parts of the Crystal Palace, while their editors want the pictures!

"More seriously, the historical databases have diverged again, and I must leave for a while.

"I think you should go to bed, together with that rather forward husband of yours!"

The following day an invitation was sent to Cheetah inviting the group to a farewell lunch with Ergan and his family, and several other leaders of his Confederation and their wives. The furs dealer called Er would also be present.

When they arrived, they were taken to a luxurious room in a private house, and the foodstuffs and drinks from Cheetah were unhitched from the accompanying remote.

Halfway through the first course, Ergan rose and made a short welcoming speech.

He then said "Sienna, on behalf of all the Masuna nations, we would like you to accept a small present. We are immensely grateful for your help."

Er's wife reached down to a box next to her, and took out a beautiful hooded fur coat in a thick white fur with silvery guard hairs.

"The animals from which this fur derives are extremely rare, and only a few are allowed to be taken each year."

Sienna stood up and thanked him profusely. The Masuna could see that tears were forming in her eyes, which she wiped away.

The coat fitted her perfectly.

After the meal as they were returning on the shuttle, Louise remarked, "Sienna, I think the Masuna were telling you something with that most beautiful coat.

"When I was researching the planet I came across an article on the fur. Apart from being staggeringly expensive, it is almost unheard of for it to be made into a coat. It is normally just used for trimming."

At its first sitting, the re-organised Masuna Parliament voted to erect a large statue of Sienna.

The caption read "Sienna Taylor, Ruler of our hearts"

Chapter 8

TWO GENERALS AND A SCIENTIST

WITH HER BEARING GROUP, KATIE STUDIED the new divergence of the earth-based history.

It was immediately clear that the Duke of Wellington was no longer part of the army.

The British – Portuguese armies in Portugal in 1807 had been heavily defeated in his absence, and the British army forced to leave the country. French occupation of the whole region had been rapid, ruthless and efficient.

With the whole Iberian Peninsula under their control and no visible opposition, residual resistance in Spain and Portugal to the French had spluttered on for a few months and then died away. This was despite a hatred for the invader amongst the people generally.

In the 'safe' history, guerrilla action over the next six years had cost the French on average about 100 soldiers a day. This 'running sore' had materially weakened their army.

In the new history, with most of the French safely garrisoned in the towns and not trashing the countryside in military campaigns –French armies at war mostly depended on foraging – there was much less inflammatory behaviour to stir up guerrilla movements.

With the south-western portion of his realm secured, Napoleon had been able to turn his attention to consolidating the rest of his empire.

Meanwhile, back in Britain the Whigs had taken over government with the failure of the British Army on the continent, and a reluctant truce had been agreed with Napoleon. Effectively, Napoleon allowed a resumed trade with Europe, and Britain agreed to stop subsiding opposition to the French.

The key point about this tacit agreement, was that Napoleon no longer felt obliged to invade Russia to enforce his "continental" anti-British trade system.

In the 'safe' history, it was the disastrous attack on Russia in 1812 which had broken his power. Nearly 700,000 soldiers had invaded Russia, and two thirds had died or been captured. Only a comparative handful of effective soldiers remained in 1813. France's reluctant allies Austria and Prussia had changed sides on seeing the size of the defeat.

Without this military catastrophe, the Bonaparte dynasty entrenched itself.

Mount Tambora in Indonesia erupted in April 1815, and 1816 became known as the "Year without a summer". European, North American and Asian harvests were disastrous, and terrible famines developed.

Napoleon tackled famine in his Empire with great efficiency, and the death rate in Europe was much lower than might have been expected. A large degree of underlying support developed for the Bonaparte dynasty even outside France. When Napoleon died in 1823, his son inherited his position without noticeable dissent.

With the wealth of their European Empire and a population nearly twice that of Britain, the French competed for outside territory much more effectively than in the 'safe' history.

A sort of Pax Français spread across Europe, the Middle East and a large part of North America. Britain failed to oust the French from India, and French influence spread across a large part of south-east Asia.

Eventually, the major opposition to France appeared in China. An efficient right-wing leader took control, and the energies of the Chinese people concentrated on development.

Although scientific development had been slower in the 19th and 20th centuries than under the 'safe' history, nuclear weapons were eventually invented in the 21st.

Major rivalry between the French Empire and a resurgent China led to a nuclear war, which devastated most of the developed world.

8a – Wellington

It did not take Katie's group long to find out why Wellington had failed to appear.

His brother was retiring as Governor-General of India in March 1805.

Wellington had left India with him, but the Royal Navy ship carrying them had foundered off the Indian coast. Two sailors had been the only survivors.

All the latter could say was that in the middle of a comparatively minor storm, there had been an explosion below the waterline, and the ship had sunk almost immediately. There had been no time to release the ship's boats. The sailors had been on deck, and had clung to wreckage, which had enabled them to survive.

Once again, Katie was forced to endure the temporal shock of returning to the early 19th century. This time, she arranged to be "found" in Dublin. The country had managed to stay relatively prosperous, and its Catholic institutions were adept at looking after orphans. There were many of these from the Irish who had died fighting in Europe over the past few years.

Fortunately for her, on this occasion the symptoms were quite mild.

When she had recovered, she moved herself in time and location to the Indian port where the Royal Navy ship carrying Wellington was leaving harbour. He was then known as Arthur Wellesley. Katie and her cat set up a full time watch for Aon.

She thought to herself that it was fortunate that Aon had limited time to identify key historical moments before she would run out of energy at any particular locality, and would be forced to move downtime again. She had to locate herself at known locations and times, within quite narrow margins. This had made the task of thwarting her far easier – if she could have attacked someone like Wellington anywhere in his life, she would have been impossible to stop.

Katie had decided that her enemy had simply translocated some matter into the ship's keel, causing a large explosion. That would have sunk the ship too quickly for boats to be launched.

Two days later, there was a large thunderstorm off the Indian coast.

In the middle of this, Katie detected Aon's approach. Linking up with her cat, she blocked her.

Once again, there was a furious exchange of energies, before Aon realised she had insufficient power to break through.

"Katie Shepherd, once again you block me. I assume my previous attempts to change history have failed. This will not be tolerated."

Aon vanished. Katie remained in place for another three days, to ensure her enemy did not return.

Her Bearing group confirmed that history had returned to the safe path.

8b – Trap

Back in her normal quadrant of the galaxy, Katie decided to visit her human support group.

Cheetah had moved to a planet called Mor, well-known for its beautiful climate and scenery. Sienna had decided that her party needed a holiday on an all expenses paid basis. Felicity found herself included in the group, about which she was delighted. The yacht was beginning to feel like home.

The Taylors were lounging in deckchairs on a beach on a tropical atoll, together with Felicity. Sienna had covered her face with a large straw hat to protect it from sunburn.

Peter and Louise were being taught to sail on a small catamaran. They had capsized twice, which had not diminished their enthusiasm. Their instructor had not been pleased, as his pupils had pushed the boat beyond their ability limits, and capsizing even small catamarans was dangerous to both crew and boat.

After a quick check with Sienna, Peter had told the instructor; "If we hurt ourselves, that is our problem. Also, if the boat is damaged, you will be completely reimbursed."

Sienna heard a deckchair being pulled up.

A familiar voice said, "I'm glad to see the Taylor family is enjoying itself!"

Iain groaned theatrically; "Great grandmother trouble again! Hi Katie! "Successful trip?"

Katie laughed, "Spoilsport. I'll tell you about it later, on the yacht."

"Hello Felicity. Your charge seems to be doing well, hiding underneath that hat."

Felicity said, "Thank you, My Lady. I've had worst patients, but not many!"

Sienna said without moving, "I heard that even though I'm asleep! I hope the chattering class – which doesn't mean the press – lets me stay that way!"

Meanwhile, out on the bay, Louise as helmsperson had once again capsized the boat. This time, Peter appeared to have sprained his wrist, which concluded the lesson.

The instructor was secretly pleased – he was starting to worry about someone being seriously hurt. His sailing students were altogether too adventurous.

A shuttle was called down, and the Moores and Felicity were collected.

As Felicity bandaged the wrist, she was given a brief outline of what was involved with Katie's visit, and she was warned again never to repeat anything she heard.

* * *

In the evening, Katie re-appeared just before supper.

Louise and Peter still looked excited, and both were clearly a little sunburnt. Katie looked at them and laughed; "I trust your recklessness today doesn't extend to other parts of your personal lives!"

Louise blushed, which led to more general laughter.

With all the group assembled, Katie described her trip in detail.

She added, "I wish all these time excursions were as easy. For once, everything panned out pretty much the way I hoped."

Peter had been looking thoughtful. "Katie, can you repeat exactly what Aon said?"

When this had been done, he was quiet for a few seconds and then said "When I was a kid, some of the books I read were adventure stories where the hero was being chased.

"In some of the cases, the best way to escape was to arrange some sort of ambush.

"Katie, I hate to ask this, but is there any way you can be injured or killed by this Aon?"

Katie considered for a moment, "For a direct physical attack, the answer is probably 'no'.

"When I am in foldspace, I'm almost invulnerable, and in my human form my body will revert to foldspace automatically if too threatened."

Peter persisted, "But what about a temporal attack?

"From my primitive and simplistic human point of view, what would happen if Aon arranged the equivalent of a deadfall. For example, he could do this by arranging for two temporally significant events close together.

"As you were fixing one, the chronon results of a major history change could be used to threaten you with a chronon temporal disaster.

"I have no idea whether this can be done, or what the result might be."

For the first time in anyone's experience, Katie looked uncomfortable, and there was a long silence.

"Peter, you have posed a disturbing question. I don't know the answer, and I will have to talk to my Bearing group.

"Thank you for the idea. You and Louise are definitely earning your bread and cheese!"

Afterwards, Felicity said to Sienna while checking her blood pressure, "It's strange listening to Katie. She seems so – ordinary – despite the fact that she has almost unlimited power.

"I have to keep reminding myself that she was the key individual in a large part of the history of the Federation."

Sienna smiled. She had decided she really liked Felicity. She had grown much more comfortable with Louise, but the latter never seemed to entirely shed her military persona. The blush earlier on in the evening had been a rare chink. She wondered about the reason.

"I am truly grateful that she cares enough to keep visiting us. I was terribly unhappy when I was told that I would be the new Empress when she abdicated. Even now, I sometimes feel quite disturbed at the influence I have on my peoples. With Katie around plus someone else, I have two advisers who stand at a completely different level.

"Having said that, I am so glad that I have Iain, the Moores, Cheetah and yourself around. It helps to keep me feeling that I am in a sane environment. Also, it is good that I have people with me who will occasionally tell me I've gone off the rails. It would be so easy to allow myself to be surrounded by total sycophants, who simply agreed with everything I suggested!"

Felicity felt deeply honoured by the conversation. She felt an enormous sense of loyalty, if not devotion, to her slightly built Empress.

She said, "Thank you for the comment, My Lady. Putting on a different hat, it is now time for some exercise!"

* * *

Katie described Peter's comments to her Bearing group.

There was a thoughtful silence when she finished.

Iva said, "We need to research and collect our thoughts. We will meet again in one period.

When the group reconvened, Iva said; "Katie, we have checked the databases, and what we have found is disturbing.

"There are no recorded examples of the situation which the young human called Peter postulated.

"It could be argued that the prohibition by the Oldest of almost all time travel was responsible, but even so some examples might have been expected to exist.

"It occurred to one of our members that when our time shift device was being designed and tested, this type of situation would have been examined.

"When we looked, although a database folder existed with the name 'Testing and research results', it was empty. So were all the backup locations.

"It appears that they have all been deliberately cleared, many millennia ago.

"Once again, we suspect the Oldest was involved, but we have no idea why."

There was a sense of worry within the Bearing group. The uneasy feeling that they were not fully in control of events was strengthening.

Iva continued, "Turning to the temporal trap idea, we can only speculate. The incompleteness of our theory of time is becoming serious.

"We know the following facts;

> Two versions of the same person can exist in the same time stream. If they meet, the older version is eliminated from history at that point.
>
> We have no historical examples of two individuals existing in the same time sequence for any length of time.
>
> Time Shift Devices will not move into the future after the time they were created.

"In our admittedly inadequate theory of time, there are indications that having two versions of the same person in the same time stream is not stable. There appears to be a statistical probability of the older version disappearing, the probability being dependent on the distance and time apart of the two versions. Close proximity means an almost immediate trigger for the process. This also means that as an older version approaches the time when the younger version existed, the probability of spontaneous erasure increases systematically.

"In the case where one of the versions comes from a totally different time stream, it is not at all clear what might happen. The possibilities ranged from behaviour similar to what occurs in the 'normal' case, which was our assumption when we used delays in the effect to transfer information when you were talking to Albert Einstein, to a violent ejection of both versions from all time streams. Once again, likely there is a probability effect operating, which has protected you when you emerged into the old earth time stream.

"There are suggestions in our theory that the 'violent ejection' mechanism is also probability based, and runs concurrently with the ordinary mechanism. Perhaps we were just lucky in the Einstein case, that both inserted versions of yourself were not erased.

"We think it would be most unwise for you to experiment further."

Iva paused from moment.

"Turning to the deadfall effect speculated on by Peter Moore, we simply don't know what would happen if a sentient from outside a time stream was directly affected by a dramatic shift in the chronon flow. Where you effected major changes, you were the cause of the change, and not directly in the flow.

"Our recommendation is that at the next history shift, you do nothing for a while. If there is a further shift, the latter change should be tackled first, and then the uptime effect. Bear in mind, that Aon will have difficulty in locating two significant historical events sufficiently close together to operate a deadfall, especially with her energy limitations.

"This also means that you should not return to the present, but wait in the past. That would also help you avoid temporal shock."

8c – Aon

The alien entity known as Aon was deeply perturbed.

Intellectually she realised that the Qui disdain for other species, and their refusal to comply with the Bearing requests to cease expanding, had led to their extinction.

However the psychic jolt which had erased her sanity when the Qui species was exterminated had given her mind a permanent hatred of the Bearing in general, and the human species in particular.

As she had started to move back in time, the psychic comfort zone produced by her species was perceptible in foldspace, but the effect was greatly enhanced every time she dipped back into normal space. Combined with the knowledge that her race was going to die if she did not succeed in changing history, this had only increased her bitterness.

She was being careful to suppress as far as possible her personal psyche; if it was perceived by her younger self, or any other Qui, a meeting was likely to result between her younger and older selves leading to elimination and the end of her quest.

Her species was technically proficient, and many millennia previously she had been quickly recognised as extraordinary even by Qui standards. This had eventually led to the offer to join the Bearing Community. Over a long period, she had studied the many technologies available. In particular, she had a comprehensive understanding of the time shift device.

It was a matter of immense frustration to her that withdrawal from the Community had barred her from using many of the better components available within the manufacturing centres. The device she had managed to build had serious limitations. It had a total inability to stay outside foldspace for more than a short period without losing its connection to its supergiant sun energy source, and needed to move back in time to accumulate energy. Even worse was its inability to move into the future again - it could only go backwards in time.

This had caused her to only attack or change individuals or events which had a relatively closely defined position in time and space. Her flexibility was impeded by the poor state of the records to which she had access.

She thought to herself, "That young human Bearing Katie Shepherd has clearly been staying in the vicinity of my targets while suppressing her Bearing attributes. That is why I have not detected her until I was ready to attack.

"Going through my memory of the last encounter, there is an anomaly. That strange creature accompanying the young human is far more than it appears. When I tried to perceive it properly, my personal scan was almost completely blocked. What little I could glean represented totally unfamiliar engineering. I do not believe it was built by the Bearing.

"What is visible is little more than a facade to something much greater.

"Katie Shepherd does not have the knowledge or experience to recognise that feature.

"This suggests to me that there is another entity involving itself with time travel.

"Setting this aside, I must now consider how to set a chronon trap for my young enemy."

8d – John Churchill, Duke of Marlborough

The parents of John Churchill had been prosperous landowners in Dorset in the early 17th century. In the English Civil War, Winston Churchill had been part of the royalist cavalry, and when King Charles 1st had lost his war and his head, he had been heavily fined by the parliamentarians.

This left the family in dire straits financially, not a comfortable position in the 17th Century.

As a result he had been forced to live with his wife's mother in Devon, who had been a supporter of the parliamentarians. This led to a legacy of residual bitterness within the family. Both the parents and the children learnt to be careful of what and to whom they said anything.

When King Charles II regained the monarchy in 1660, there was a little royal preferment in order to provide some compensation for the family loyalty.

Winston Churchill's eldest son John was the second of nine children, of whom four died in infancy.

Arabella, his older sister, had been given a position in 1665 as a lady in waiting to Anne Hyde, the Duchess of York, whose husband James was the King's brother.

It did not take long for her to be noticed by the Duke.

Her family were so strongly royalist, that when they discovered she had become a mistress to the Duke they were delighted. No one was ever quite sure why the Duchess of York tolerated this, especially as Arabella eventually bore him four children, two while the Duchess was still alive (she died in 1671 from breast cancer).

John had grown into a good looking teenager, and there was a strong mutual affection between him and his older sister.

In 1666, after a particularly enjoyable tryst with the Duke, she was asked if there was any favour she would like.

"Sir, I have a younger brother who is quite desirous of seeing the Court. Would it be possible for him to become a page?"

* * *

John Churchill arrived in London with a steely determination to improve his position in life. Apart from the scarcity of money, he had not enjoyed watching his father suffer from the indignity of having to live with his wife's mother, who had been angry when Charles II was brought back as King. She rarely missed an opportunity to insert a jibe into a conversation.

He decided at a quite early age, that he was going to be wealthy and powerful.

While initially overawed by the sheer size of London compared to the country towns where he had been brought up, he rapidly adapted to his new environment. His sister and parents had given him enough money to ensure he was reasonably clothed, and he soon demonstrated that he was efficient and conscientious.

The Duke of York was so pleased with this new page – not to mention his sister – that he gave him a free commission in the Army a year later, which started John Churchill's military career. He saw service in the Mediterranean where he learned basic soldiering skills.

When he returned to England in 1671, the bronzed and dashing young soldier started a liaison with the voluptuous Barbara Palmer. She was King Charles 2nd's favourite mistress, and eventually bore him a number of children. This did not seem to have stopped her taking a series of lovers on the side. The young Churchill must have really impressed her, because she gave him £5000, an absolutely enormous sum in those days. Apparently, King Charles was quite amused when he heard, and this did not stop him eventually creating her Duchess of Cleveland.

Instead of spending the money, John Churchill bought himself an annuity to provide for his financial future. Clearly, a determination to secure his position was already showing.

A little later he went to France and saw action with the French under Turenne. His bravery and enormous charm produced praise on all sides.

Subsequently, his political and military club career prospered, particularly with the assistance of is eventual wife Sarah Jennings whom he met in 1675.

When Charles II died in 1685, Churchill's patron the Duke of York, became James II of England. He had two legitimate daughters Mary and Anne from his first wife, who were both Protestant, and in 1688 a young son was born by his second wife. His daughter Mary married William of Orange in 1677.

Unfortunately for James, John Churchill had become increasingly disenchanted with his liege lord because the latter had begun to promote Catholics and Catholicism on all possible occasions after his conversion.

The birth of James' son, who would be brought up a Catholic, was the last straw for Churchill and a large part of the Protestant nobility.

When he changed sides in 1688, the King was doomed and the so-called "Glorious Revolution" led to the installation of William and Mary as King and Queen of England.

James's daughter Anne would become Queen on the death of William and Mary as part of the settlement.

Fortunately for John and his wife Sarah, the latter had become a bosom friend of Anne.

John Churchill's political and military career eventually blossomed with the War of the Spanish Succession. Effectively, the death of King Carlos 2nd of Spain, with Louis XIV of France a strong claimant to the Spanish throne, led to the possibility of the French and Spanish Crowns being united. This was absolutely unacceptable to the rest of Europe, as the combined populations and military capability of the two countries would have dominated Europe.

When the war started in 1701, John Churchill was appointed to lead the British contingent of the coalition which was formed to oppose this combination.

In a series of campaigns stretching over the next decade, John Churchill led the coalition armies to a series of glittering victories. This was despite huge political and leadership problems within the coalition itself.

He demonstrated that he was arguably England's greatest ever general, and was eventually created Duke of Marlborough.

* * *

Aon read this with great satisfaction. She found the moral and political behaviour of the human species quite strange, but it was immediately obvious to her that a tiny mental push on her part would change human history. She would be able to almost immediately move on to another target nearby in time whose demise would have an equally great impact. It would take some time for the Bearing in general, and Katie Shepherd in particular, to find her extraordinarily small change. She was completely confident that the latter would be irretrievably buried by a chronon disaster as she combed through the reign of Charles 2nd looking for the alteration.

8e – Isaac Newton

Once again, the earth-based historical database veered wildly. Katie and her Bearing group did nothing, and waited.

They did not have to wait long; a few periods later another major change occurred, and it appeared that the scientific and engineering revolution which started off in England in the 18th century had been delayed. It did not take much study of the databases for the cause to become apparent; one of the greatest mathematicians and scientists had failed to appear. There was simply no historical record about Isaac Newton. Without his input, a substantial part of the mathematical basis for engineering had been seriously delayed, in particular the application of calculus. His introduction of methodical scientific study was also critical. His book Principia Mathematica had provided a focus for discussion on a large range of scientific and mathematical problems, and history rated it one of the greatest intellectual achievements.

Curiously, the initial historical effect was quite small, probably because the activities of a small group of mathematicians and scientists in London were not significant politically or economically in the 17th century. It was not until the late 18th and 19th centuries, that the scientific impact became large.

Katie asked her Bearing group about this; "It seems to me that whether or not Newton had been present would not have had much impact in the 17th century.

"Would this have meant that I could have immediately tackled the first historical change?"

Her Bearing friend Iva answered, "Again, it is vexing that our theory of time is incomplete. However, it appears that somehow the chronons are 'aware' of the future impact of quite small changes even if that impact takes a long time to become apparent. Where those are significant, there is a real change in the flow of time which is immediate. When you were dealing with Einstein, this was a good example. His impact on history was a long way in the future.

"This is quite paradoxical. Possibly it is analogous to the paired slits experiment, with electrons fired at those slits. You will be aware that they can behave as either particles or waves. The moment an observer tries to check which slit an electron passed through, the interference pattern when the electron was acting like a wave which interfered with itself, disappears. Somehow the electron 'knows' that it is going to be checked in the future, and behaves like a particle rather than a wave."

It was hard to investigate what had happened to Newton. The historical record had been mangled, particularly with no great historical need to encourage the collection and maintenance of interesting background information. The only relevant items which could be found were marriage, birth and death records from the Colsterworth parish church near the Newton family home at Woolsthorpe in Lincolnshire. These records were in poor shape, and only passing references to Newton's parents could be found. His scratched signature on a wall at the King's School in Grantham had disappeared.

After a few periods of intensive study, Katie said to her Bearing group; "History has been so grotesquely changed that we really don't know what has happened. It looks like I will simply have to be present when Newton was born, and stay completely incognito until Aon appears.

"My cat can bring along a store of baby food, antibiotics, and nanobot immunity enhancers."

A little later, an idea occurred to her. She still remembered clearly the question that Sienna had raised; *"How different do you have to be to avoid the 'older version disappearance' effect?"*

She had a strange conversation with her alter ego. "If I reduce myself, with your help, to not much above the level of a simple village girl and stay in the Newton household, can you maintain a continuous hidden monitoring operation and control my ability level?"

The reply was; "Yes. This is effectively what has happened in the past. I remain aware even when you're suffering from temporal shock and memory amnesia. By the way, I have decided I would like to be called *Alte*. I think it will help anchor me as a separate personality."

Following on from this, she asked her cat; "If my alter ego Alte is left totally in control, with my personality totally submerged, would the chronons perceive her as a different person?"

There was a long pause before her cat answered, "Possibly."

Katie continued, "Since I seem to be in some sort of time loop – you remember that I apparently changed history on my own at Waterloo – this offers a possible way of exiting.

"When I did the warning thing with Einstein, it could be Alte who talks to me beforehand. If she then escapes obliteration, she could return to this time and move into the future. This presumes of course, that I can trust her to 'resurrect' me!"

From the depths of her mind a reply came back, "That is not fair. It is hard for me to completely dominate your personality, which is powerful, but I can suppress your persona completely for a period. It is far more comfortable to remain in the background in my corner of our mind. I can influence the Newton family to make sure that we are accepted into the household.

"The idea is worth trying; we have nothing to lose. However, it is not clear how we retain a memory of this plan so we can implement it at our presumed next iteration."

Her cat immediately responded, "I will retain a memory of the conversation, and will brief you appropriately when the time comes."

A little later when Katie reflected on this strange conversation, she realised there were interesting implications to her cat's last statement. She was horribly reluctant, possibly scared, to follow up those implications.

It also occurred to her that Newton had lived until he was 84 in the 'safe' history, which was an extraordinary age for that era. She wondered if it was her immunity enhancement in a previous loop which had contributed.

* * *

Geographically the hamlet called Woolsthorpe was almost in the centre of England, in an area mainly covered by low rolling hills. In his time it was heavily forested. Small farms were located in most of the valleys, and wool production was the principal cash source for most farms. At the time, it was a prosperous area. The Normans had built a small fortification called Belvoir near the village on the most prominent local hill.

In the 17th century, the dwellings of most farm labourers were awful. The expense of glass meant windows were slits to try and minimise wind draft, and only a few had proper fireplaces and chimneys. In most cases, fires were simply lit in the centre of the one and only room and the smoke allowed to swirl up and disappear through a hole in the roof. This generally left the rooms in a haze of barely tolerable smoke. Proper hygiene and water supply were almost unknown. People generally slept in their clothes on crude mattresses filled with straw or hay, with some rough blankets. Winter cold from an era known as the Little Ice Age, appalling hygiene and diet, and lung damage from smoke meant that early death was almost inevitable for farm workers.

Newton's father, also called Isaac, was a prosperous middle aged local farmer. His stone built house was quite grandiose by local standards, with four rooms on two stories. It even had glass in the windows, with the peculiar thickening in the centre due to its production from opening out a blown glass bulb. There were proper fireplaces and two chimneys. Behind the house, there was a walled kitchen garden, and several farm buildings including a hayloft.

He married an 18-year-old girl called Hannah in late 1641, and had been pleasantly surprised at how quickly she had taken over the management of his household and several servants. She was a much stronger character than he had expected.

In the early spring of 1642, Hannah had woken at dawn, and when she had gone downstairs to light the fire, she heard sobbing by the back door.

On looking, she found a thin young girl sitting with her back against the wall. She was covered in a ragged and dirty greatcoat many sizes too large, which looked like it had been rescued from a rubbish tip. Her forehead was badly bruised and her hands were scratched and dirty. What had once been good shoes were covered in mud.

The child looked up, and said; "Please, please can I come inside for a few minutes as I'm terribly cold and hungry."

There was a desperate appeal in her eyes.

Hannah slightly reluctantly said, "All right, come and sit by the fire which I'm about to light."

She gave the girl a little water to drink, and the congealed remains of the stew which she and her husband Isaac had eaten the previous evening.

She was surprised that the girl managed to say "Thank you", before wolfing the food. While this was happening, Hannah rekindled the fire with some twigs, and then added some more wood from the log basket.

"Where did you come from and what has happened to you?", she asked when the girl had stopped eating.

The girl started to cry again and then said between sniffles, "All I can remember is that I was travelling with my parents in a cart, which overturned when we were crossing a river. I managed to scramble ashore, but there was no sign of them."

"I think my head got banged a bit, and I can't remember anything about my other name or where I came from, except I think I was called Katie".

"This all happened three days ago, and I was lucky to find an empty barn each night. I – borrowed – this coat off a scarecrow I saw."

Theft of even minor items was taken seriously in the 17th century. The girl was obviously aware of this despite her apparent age of about eight.

Hannah thought about this for a minute or so, as she watched her fire gain strength.

"All right, you can stay here for the time being, while we try and find out where you came from.

"My maid will be coming in soon; she is called Sarah. Explain who you are, and then you can help her prepare breakfast and do some other chores round the house.

"I'm going upstairs now to finish changing, and I will be down with my husband in about 20 minutes. I think I know where some dry clothes are stored which might fit you."

Unknown to Katie or Hannah, Alte had discreetly influenced the decision.

Back in her bedroom, she explained to Isaac what had happened. He just nodded, and then started coughing.

Over the next week, Hannah was pleased that the girl tried hard to help around the house. Attempts to find out what had happened to her parents drew a complete blank.

Eventually she said to the girl, "Katie, you can stay here permanently, and help the maid in the house and her husband in the walled garden and orchard. There is a bed in the shed next door, and I will get you some blankets."

Katie was still distressed that nothing could be discovered about her family. She now knew the hamlet and the nearby village of Colsterworth well, and had been taken several times into Grantham, a small market town a few miles away. Some children she had met had shown her where they stayed in the town orphanage. She had been horrified by their living conditions. There was a pervasive stench of urine and faeces, and the rooms were damp and cold. She heard that the food varied between bad and awful, and in the winter there was almost no heating. For warmth, the children shared the filthy beds, which had straw mattresses and blankets which were thin and worn.

Katie realised she had been incredibly lucky to come across Hannah Newton and her husband.

She also joined the village school, where the old teacher was astonished to find the girl could already read and write, and understood basic arithmetic. He often enlisted her to help some of the other children.

Apart from assisting round the house, she found that she particularly enjoyed going out with Isaac into the fields and orchard. She liked helping with the animals, as the farm's main income was wool from the large flock of sheep. There was also a small dairy herd, and two large horses. Katy never quite understood why the farm cats and two dogs never attacked the chickens or each other – there seemed to be a sort of cautious truce between the three groups. Vegetables grew in the walled kitchen garden, and there were espaliered apple and pear trees on the South facing wall.

For his part, the farmer enjoyed her company, and as his cough grew steadily worse, found that an extra pair of young hands was really useful for the collection of fruit, cabbages, carrots and turnips.

On one occasion, he found her dragging a bag of old oats which was far too heavy for her size.

"Katie, don't handle things as heavy as that – you will hurt yourself."

She laughed a little, "I don't find it too bad, and I'm sure it's not hurting me at all."

He discovered that she appeared to be much stronger than he expected, and all the family noticed that she never seemed to become ill.

She also had an affinity with the animals, and seemed completely unafraid of the dairy herd's cantankerous old bull, with whom even Isaac was careful.

One morning he saw her in the small field where the bull was kept on its own. As he froze with horror for a moment, he watched her reach through a hole in the fence, break off a little clump of juicy grass, and feed it to the old bull. The animal had licked the grass from her cupped hand with surprising gentleness, showing none of the bad temper or dangerous behaviour for which it had become notorious.

Isaac was worried that if he disturbed the pair, the animal would react and seriously hurt Katie even if it was accidental, since it weighed many times as much as the child.

After a couple more handfuls, which cleared all the readily available grass, Katie gave the bull a little rub on its forehead then ran over to the gate which she climbed over with great agility.

Alte had laid a compulsion on the larger animals to like her and be careful – it would not suit the script if Katie was injured.

Afterwards, Isaac told her; "Katie, you must be careful with the bigger farm animals. I saw you feeding the old bull, but that animal is dangerous. Several of the villagers have been hurt by it."

The girl looked at him, clearly a little puzzled. "But he is such a nice old bull, and he really likes me. I'm sure he wouldn't hurt me!"

After a little while, Isaac gave up and Katie was allowed to feed the bull, or move it wherever it needed to go. The animal seemed to need little encouragement to be led by the girl on a short rope to a new field, and always seemed to be on its best behaviour. The same was true of the pair of Clydesdale horses, which were used for ploughing and pulling the farm carts.

The only part of her daily routine she disliked, was the so-called wash cycle.

Personal washing was not a high priority in the 17th century, but clothes still had to be occasionally cleaned.

A large wooden tub was filled with water, slightly warmed with a kettle boiled on the fire, and all the clothes were tipped in. A few flakes of rough soap were added, and the whole stirred and prodded with a stick.

Any item which was particularly dirty, had to be extracted, placed on a board and scrubbed with a little more soap.

The whole process was incredibly boring, and Hannah found she had to bring a little pressure to bear to get Katie to concentrate. She didn't particularly mind, as otherwise the girl was a joy to have around.

One morning she was surprised to find Katie looking at one of the few books owned by the family. The girl was reading each page. In the 17th Century, outside the nobility and the wealthy middle classes, literacy was rare. She noticed that her hands were quite clean.

She said, "I am pleased that you are being careful with the book, Katie, but I am surprised you can read each page."

The girl looked up, with quite a worried little frown; "It is not reading which is difficult Hannah, but the words and writing itself. The spelling, letters and the wording seem quite unfamiliar."

The day turned quite warm and sunny for early May, and Katie decided to wander over to the village once she had done her chores. She saw that the local blacksmith was working hard making something. She came over to watch. A thick white-hot iron rod had just been pulled out of the fire, and the smith was clearly shaping what looked like a scythe blade. His assistant, a large and solid boy of about 15, had paused from operating the big bellows which blew into the charcoal furnace.

She watched in fascination as blows from a heavy hammer first curved the rod and then thinned the metal into a blade. After about a minute, it was put back into the glowing charcoal, and the assistant pumped furiously again. The process then repeated several times, the smith gave a few final blows, and then the still brightly glowing metal implement was plunged into a barrel of water with a furious hiss.

The metal was taken out and heated more briefly, and then once again plunged into the water. The edge was sharpened on a grinding wheel.

Katie asked, "Please Mister Worrall, why did you put the blade into the water barrel twice?"

The old blacksmith looked at her, and smiled. He had been a little intrigued by the girl, especially as her eyes had seemed to be glowing slightly as he worked. He had decided it was just a reflection from the charcoal furnace. However, no other child had ever asked him that question.

"Katie, the first time I plunged the tool into the water it was nearly white hot, and the process is called quenching. It makes the metal extremely hard, but also brittle.

"The second time, I was careful not to heat it so much, and the second plunge is called tempering. It makes the metal a little softer, but also far more flexible. This produces a much better tool, as it is less likely to break.

"By the way, this is my new apprentice Adrian. He comes from Nottingham."

Katie said, "Thank you for telling me that."

She nodded to the boy, and then skipped away down the street. She was not particularly keen on talking to him. She had listened to some of the other village children the previous day; apparently Adrian had used his large size to bully some of them, and the girls were quite frightened of him.

The smith was aware of this, and was wondering whether he had made a mistake in taking on the boy.

* * *

A few days later, the Newton family and Katie came back from church late morning. Hannah asked her to collect some vegetables from the wall garden, and some mint and thyme.

As she walked back, she saw the village children in a nearby field and decided to join them after she had delivered her two baskets. When she reached the group, matters were not at all as she had expected. The blacksmith's apprentice Adrian was slapping one of the younger boys on his face.

Apparently there had been an argument. The other village boys and girls were looking on quite fearfully, obviously scared to intervene.

Katie had no such qualms. She shouted at him; "Adrian, stop hitting Mark. He is much smaller than you are, and you could really hurt him."

Adrian turned, annoyed. "Shut up Katie, or I'll give you a belting too!"

The other boy took the opportunity to run away.

Katie said, "That was an awful thing to do. It's not fair to attack someone much smaller than yourself."

Adrian said, "Right, a beating its going to be!"

He had decided that it was time he became gang leader of the village kids, and no challenge to his authority was going to be allowed.

Alta had watched this little pantomime with some concern. Although generally aloof from human sentiments and emotion, she decided she really did not like this boy.

She unblocked Katie's unarmed combat abilities.

None of the other children were quite sure what happened – and certainly not Adrian – but as he raised his hand to slap her hard, instead of running away she kicked him savagely in the knee.

As his leg gave away and he fell forward, she hit him as hard as she could on the side of his face with the edge of her hand.

He crumpled to the ground, and suffered a further heavy kick to his ribs.

It was fortunate for him that she was only about half his weight.

She was about to complete the damage with some more kicks, when something told her to stop.

"That's enough Katie, or you will really hurt him."

The other village children looked at her in awe. Two minutes later, Adrian stood up shakily and shuffled off towards the blacksmith's shed.

When he arrived, he was asked "What happened to you?"

All he could say was, "The village children ganged up on me and beat me up."

In fact, an alternative story was quickly doing the rounds of the village, to general astonishment.

From that moment, Katie became the effective leader of the village children. Adrian's behaviour improved markedly. It was noticed that he was quite scared of her.

Harvesting of the early summer hay crop needed several workers to be employed from outside, as Isaac was no longer strong enough to wield a scythe. With the hamlet and village children, Katie helped by first of all regularly turning all the grass to dry it, and then helping to collect and stack it in the hay barn. Fortunately, the weather was kind and the process was completed without trouble. However, everyone worked from the moment the dew had dried until dark, with only brief breaks for food and drink. As it was nearly mid-Summer this made for a long day, but getting the hay stored while it was dry was critical for the animals in winter. Katie was utterly exhausted when they stopped each night.

Isaac said, "Hannah and I are pleased with the help you are giving us, Katie. We have decided to let you come and live in the small bed in the other room downstairs. It will be much warmer there."

Katie realised that effectively she had been admitted permanently to the household.

Hannah discovered in the summer that she was pregnant. Her delight at this was overshadowed by worries about her husband. Also, even in this secluded part of England it was apparent that the country was becoming bitterly divided politically.

Katie listened to the conversation over supper in mid-July. She didn't really understand much about what was being said, but even to her the Newtons sounded most concerned.

Isaac was saying, "I heard from one of the grain merchants, that Parliament and the King are really disagreeing. I fear that this could easily come to civil war.

"Bill Worrall was telling me that he has just been asked by the Earl to make a number of halberd heads.

"Also, I hear the King's officers are looking all over the country to find new supplies of gunpowder. London is solidly for the Parliamentarians, and that is where most of the powder mills are located."

Katie asked, "Please Mister Newton, what is a halberd?"

The farmer looked at her rather grimly, "It is a type of long spear – a stick with a sharp point – which also has an extra bit like a small spiky axe at the end. It is used in wartime to make holes in people, or cut them badly.

"However I don't think you should worry about that. I really hope that nothing comes of this."

However he thought to himself, "The way things are going, I don't believe my own reassurance to Katie."

Two days later, things suddenly looked even more concerning to the family.

There was group of tradesmen called saltpetermen. So desperate was the need for gunpowder, that the rulers of most European countries had provided licences to these people to enter and dig up any private property in search of potassium nitrate, known at the time as saltpetre. They were far from popular, especially as they frequently profited from a little graft on the side. A suitable bribe would often divert them to someone else's property. The excesses of the men involved in this trade were a significant source of grievances in the Parliament.

Typically, nitrate was found in ground which had been heavily contaminated with urine such as animal barns in the country and public latrines in the towns. Animal manure or bird droppings were also usable. The soil or manure would be dug up and placed in a heap or large container with some sort of relatively waterproof base. Water would be dripped slowly through the material, where it would dissolve the nitrate and then be collected through a channel or other outlet. Boiling down with ashes to provide the potassium, would eventually lead to contaminated potassium nitrate precipitating out after cursory filtering and cooling. Re-dissolving in clean boiling water and better filtering led to a much purer product crystallising out when the solution cooled. The remaining liquid was recycled to an earlier stage as it still held nitrate.

Katie had just finished lighting the fire early in the morning, when she heard a loud rapping on the front door. Looking through the window, she saw a group of rough looking men with several large carts.

Frightened, she shouted up the stairs, "Mister Newton, there are some nasty looking men at the door!"

Isaac came down, took the iron poker from the fire, and then shouted through the door "Who are you, and what do you want?"

The answer came back, "We are the King's saltpetermen, and we are going to dig up your main barn."

Katie saw that Isaac looked really worried, "But we need the barn to store the oat harvest which is about to start."

The leader of the men, who had once been a farmer himself, said "That's too bad.

"However, if you provide us with lunch for the next two days, we will be out of here by tomorrow night."

In the circumstances, all Isaac could do was agree. It would be quite stupid to get on the wrong side of this sort of gang. There had been some ugly stories circulating about some saltpetermen groups. He took care to stay around the house all day, and warned the women in the household never to be on their own with these men.

Katie had become leader and chief organiser of games and the like for the village children. One of the games was a sort of hare and hounds chase. Someone would be delegated to take a bag of ashes and every 20 meters or so drop a little heap to indicate the trail. With a few minutes start, the game was to find how quickly they could catch the hare. A good pursuit meant lots of tricky detours and going through interesting parts of the countryside.

The children quickly found that Katie made a good hare; for a girl she ran fast, and had a talent for inventing interesting routes.

Katy had seen charcoal delivered in rough bags at the smith's shed, and had vaguely wondered where it came from. That morning, Isaac had mentioned that a group of charcoal burners were setting up in a patch of wood which he owned near the local river.

"There are only a few types of wood which are suitable, and they will move on after about a month. What they are doing is quite skilled. The wood has to be cooked in heaps for several days, and must be watched night and day to make sure it only ever smoulders as it is reduced to charcoal.

"Our part of the deal is that they will leave the area clear felled, with the unsuitable wood as logs for us. That way, we get a new field and firewood for free!"

Katie had been elected hare again, and decided to use the charcoal burners as the destination.

When she started, she created three interesting zigzags, and then as she went over a low hill, she was surprised at what she saw.

There were men felling trees in the area immediately in front of her. The axemen were bringing the trees down, and trimming off the loose small branches. Another group were using enormous two person handsaws to make logs.

A little further away, there was a rough line which started as freshly dug shallow round pits, moved on through conical piles of wood being carefully stacked to nearly twice a man's height. Once the pile was complete it would be covered with earth and ashes, and set alight leaving thin spirals of smoke coming out of a sort of small chimney at the top.

She watched as one of the earlier conical piles was rapidly pulled apart and spread as quickly as possible to cool the charcoal. This was being helped by men sprinkling water out of rough leather buckets. A little further away, cool and dry charcoal was being raked and collected into bags. A thin smoke haze covered the whole area.

As she watched, the other children caught up with her and the group watched the charcoal burners for a few minutes.

Then one of the boys said, "Last one back to the village is a ninny!", and the whole group rushed off.

Later on that day, Katie came back on her own. She was quite interested in the process.

One of the men asked his fellow worker, "Where does the girl come from?"

The answer was, "She lives with the Newtons in the village. The smith told me she was an orphan with unknown parents."

Katie asked one of the men, "Please sir, does the covered wood ever catch fire properly?"

The man laughed, "Yes lass, that's why we have to watch the piles night and day in relays. If that starts to happen, we immediately pile on more earth. Otherwise we just end up with ash rather than charcoal!"

As she passed one of the crude shelters the men lived in, there was a piteous mew from the side, and a small cat came up to her cautiously. Something about the animal reached out to her, and she carefully reached down and picked it up. It purred.

When she got back home she said to Hannah, "Mrs Newton, I found this cat in the woods. Can I keep it please?"

Farm cats generally looked after themselves. In return for shelter and occasional stroking, they kept farmyards more or less clear of rats and mice.

Hannah laughed, "Of course you can, Katie. However, don't be too disappointed if our resident cats and dogs chase it away. They are all quite territorial, and don't like newcomers!"

However, when Katie cautiously introduced the animal to the other cats, it seemed to be accepted immediately. The same happened with the dogs, except they seem to be even more enthusiastic. There was much wagging of tails, purring and mutual sniffing.

After a little while, Hannah noticed that Katie's cat seemed to be hanging around her in the house most of the time.

Alte had a hidden conversation with the cat. "Katie seems to be well established in the village, and she is pretty well indistinguishable from the other village children.

"I will have to be careful that she does not become too distinctive. Smothering her intelligence is difficult."

The cat answered, "From a camouflage point of view, this is a good environment for me. I have reviewed and supplemented my scanning shields, and without a careful in-depth look Aon will not be able to perceive me.

"I am now watching Hannah Newton effectively on a full-time basis."

Unfortunately, over the next few weeks, Isaac's cough grew steadily worse and he was clearly ailing.

* * *

At the beginning of August, Isaac Newton had discreetly contacted the local Parliamentarians. He had been angered by the saltpetermen, and believed the King and the county nobles were extravagant and inefficient.

He was barely on speaking terms with the Earl of Rutland who owned Belvoir Castle.

When she heard, Hannah was most annoyed with her husband.

"Isaac, I know you want to join the Parliamentary militia, but may I point out as your wife that I am pregnant, and you have a large farm to manage!

"Also, I think you need to look after yourself with great care. That cough of yours is getting really bad, and I noticed you were spitting a little blood this morning."

Unknown to the Newtons, Katie was within hearing distance. Something inside her told her to stay completely out of sight, and not to interfere.

During August, King Charles moved himself to Nottingham and formally raised his standard against Parliament. His noblemen scoured the country raising recruits.

The Parliamentarians were based in London, and they also started raising armies.

The first rather small and inconclusive clash of the war took place at the Battle of Southam, about 80 km south of Nottingham. Fortunately for the Newtons, this was also a long way from Woolsthorpe.

The Earl of Rutland had collected a small militia on behalf of King Charles, and Katie saw the group riding towards the village. On the outskirts, he was surprised to see a young girl leading an enormous bull with what appeared to be little more than a piece of string. Three cows were following.

The girl paused to let them pass, but he stopped and asked, "Where are you from, young lady? I don't think it's safe for you to be leading such an enormous animal."

She replied, "I'm called Katie, and I live with the Newtons. Everyone tells me that the old bull is dangerous, but I don't think so at all. I think he is lovely and he will never hurt me.

"By the way, if you're going past Mister Newton's house, please be quiet as he is trying to sleep. I think he has a nasty illness."

The Earl paused and considered, surprised by the girl's confidence and authority. While he was not on good terms with the farmer, there was a certain mutual respect and he had heard about his health. He had been planning to confiscate some of the food on the farm, but decided in the circumstances to give the place a miss. He did not know that five years later, with the bitterness of a civil war infecting the nation, his own home at Belvoir Castle would be burned down by the Parliamentarians.

As the group cantered away, Alte thought to herself, unbeknown to Katie, "Once again, we seem to have influenced history. I have to wonder what would have happened if the farm had been raided for supplies. This meeting seems to have been enshrined in the record."

Three weeks later, Isaac Newton was clearly dying and in severe pain. When Hannah was outside, Alte took over completely and went upstairs with her cat on her shoulder.

Isaac heard her come in, and watched her sit on the bed. His chest hurt terribly.

He had come to really like the girl, and said; "I'm afraid I'm not long for this world, lass. Hannah has assured me that you can stay at our house for as long as you like if you are worried about that."

To his astonishment, he saw that the girl's eyes appeared to be glowing.

She said, and the timbre of her voice was completely different from its usual tone, "Isaac, I regret your condition, and I have decided to alleviate your pain as I appreciate the kindness your family has shown. Katie does not know about this conversation, as I stay hidden all the time. We are from the far future, and we are a sort of bipartite personality."

Isaac was surprised to find he believed the girl, if that was what she was, and said, "Why are you here?"

Alte said, "We are fighting a war in time, and we have an enemy who is determined to destroy the human race. Your unborn son is important in that context, and we are here to protect him.

"You will not be able to repeat this conversation to anyone. I will leave you now."

As she and the cat left the room, he felt the pain in his lung fade away.

* * *

Towards the end of September, Isaac died. Hannah was almost paralysed with grief, and kept on breaking down and crying. The first time this happened, she was firmly told to sit down by the fireplace by her young guest.

Katie said, "I am so sorry Hannah, but there was nothing that could be done about Isaac."

The girl gently stroked her hair, and Hannah found herself crying with her head on the girl's shoulder.

Strangely, she found that Katie just took over and made sure the household and farm kept on running. Even the other workers on the farm accepted her instructions.

This was just as well, as Hannah was finding the late stages of her pregnancy were not going well. She went into labour on Christmas Day by the old calendar which was followed at the time, just after dark in the afternoon.

It was snowing heavily outside with a howling wind, and the village midwife lived a twenty minute walk away even in fine weather. Sarah's husband attempted to fetch her, but came back almost immediately. "Its pitch black outside and the snow is so heavy and is drifting so badly that I can't see where I am going. I won't be able to get through."

Hannah was desperate, and said "Katie, get Sarah straight away. I hope she knows something about childbirth!"

She grimaced in pain again, as another contraction struck.

Katie quickly located Sarah, who looked absolutely panic stricken when she came to the bedroom. "Hannah, I don't know anything about being a mid-wife!"

To the astonishment of both women, Katie spoke again in a tone of voice they had never heard before.

"Sarah, go and boil a large pot of water and locate some clean rags or shirts. I know what to do, and will look after Hannah."

Thankful for a positive instruction, Sarah rushed off to complete her assigned task.

It was quickly apparent that despite her young age, the girl knew exactly the procedure to be followed. This was just as well, as it was a difficult birth.

When the child finally appeared, it was apparent that it was premature and tiny. Unnoticed by the two women, Alte injected nanobot immunity enhancers and some vitamins. She left the baby with Hannah to feed, although it was clear that the woman was in poor shape. History said it would take her some months to fully recover.

Both women discovered that they were unable to talk about Katie's assistance with the birth. Alte had placed a block on their minds.

In that day and age, premature babies rarely survived. However, with discreet help from Alte, Hannah was surprised and relieved that her baby was doing well.

* * *

According to the records that she had seen, Aon had learnt that Isaac Newton was born on Christmas Day, 25 December 1642.

As a technologist and engineer, she had always liked changes or items she produced to be elegant. For her, a change which was more complex than needed, or an engineering component which was unnecessarily elaborate, was fundamentally dissatisfying.

She had studied human biology, and was aware that human medical knowledge in the middle of the 17th century was primitive. Reading that Newton was a premature baby suggested to her that an efficient method of interfering, with minimal external impact, would be to make sure the child died at or shortly after birth. Tiny changes to biological function would be all that was required, and there would be almost no sign of external tampering.

The day before Christmas, Aon scouted the village to locate the Newton household. She also wanted to make sure that her Bearing enemies were absent. She went round the hamlet and nearby village making sure that every mind she came across was ordinary. She took particular interest in females of childbearing age. Finding everyone and everything looked completely normal, she left with the intention of returning briefly late the following day.

Two hours after Newton's birth, Alte and her cat perceived Aon's arrival within the house. The cat had detected her presence the previous day, and had warned Alte to make sure they were hidden unless Hannah was threatened.

Aon was totally disconcerted to discover that her enemy was present; after a furious exchange of energies, which achieved nothing, she said; "Katie Shepherd, once again you thwart me!

"You will not be able to stop me next time we meet."

Aon moved downtime again; the storage system on her time shift device needed to be fully charged for what she had in mind. She was going to abandon elegance. If there were other consequences, she no longer cared.

As she disappeared, Alte thought at her cat, "Have you any concept of what Aon meant when she said she would be unstoppable next time?"

Her cat said, "It will have to be fairly drastic for us not to be able to reverse the change or stop Aon.

"In the meantime, I suggest we investigate what caused the non-appearance of John Churchill, and then move out of this time stream completely while we await Aon's next move."

They waited a few more days to ensure that Aon did not return, and that the baby Isaac Newton was thriving, before moving up time about 18 years. Alte moved her persona into the background, and Katie took over again.

* * *

From 1660 onwards, they carefully stepped through the Churchill family history in short time intervals, to find where history had diverged. This took a significant amount of time. If Newton's nonappearance had not been tackled first, there was no doubt that a chronon disaster would have overwhelmed Katie, with unknown results.

Everything proceeded normally, and in 1665 John Churchill's sister Arabella took up her position as a Lady in Waiting to the Duchess of York.

Aon's change was so subtle, that Katie and her cat overshot by several weeks before they noticed the divergence. Returning was difficult as they had to ensure they kept away from their earlier versions.

They discovered that Arabella had never become a mistress to the Duke of York. Aon had made another Lady in Waiting the target of James's affection with a tiny change to the Duke's mindset. Arabella had been completely ignored.

As a result, she never had the opportunity to bring her brother to court. John Churchill had eventually trained to be a lawyer, and never left South-West England.

Katie removed herself completely from the scene, and the cat simply merged into the background in disguise. It was quite confident it was undetectable unless Aon tried a really deep scan, and it had no intention of being anything but totally inconspicuous. It settled down to wait for perhaps several weeks.

* * *

A tall, rather thin girl, Arabella Churchill was delighted to have at last arrived at the Court.

Her family had given her sufficient money to make sure she was reasonably dressed, and she was careful to be most respectful to the Duchess of York Anne Hyde, when she was first introduced. The Duchess took an immediate liking to the girl. She found her intelligent and perceptive, and from her own slightly impoverished background she appreciated that Arabella's family were not in a position to provide much support.

Two days later, Arabella was talking quietly to another lady in waiting, called Elisabeth. The latter was quite short, but had a figure much more in keeping with the ideals of the age. In other words, she was plump and full figured.

Elisabeth suddenly stopped talking, looked slightly excited, and curtsied. Turning, Arabella saw a distinguished looking gentleman pause as he was about to walk past.

Elisabeth said, "Good morning, My Lord; the Duchess is looking forward to seeing you."

Katie's cat saw Aon place an attraction on the Duke's mind for short plump women, with a corresponding disdain for tall slim girls.

The Duke said, "Good morning Elisabeth; your outfit suits your complexion admirably. By the way, I shall be taking a short walk in the rose garden after lunch."

He nodded to Arabella, and then walked past in the direction of the Duchess's rooms.

Realising his identity, Arabella was rather irritated that she had not been introduced.

She noticed that her companion was more than a little distracted.

Elisabeth said, "Arabella, when you see her later on this morning, please give my excuses to the Duchess. I've just remembered I need to see my dressmaker this afternoon."

Arabella knew that her companion came from a wealthy family, but rather sourly thought to herself that it was unlikely to be the dressmaker she was meeting.

* * *

Katie studied the video of this meeting. She said, "We'll give it a couple of days to make sure that Aon has slipped down time, when I will move in and invert the changes that Aon made.

"On further consideration, I think I will also make sure that the Duchess keeps on liking Arabella even after she becomes the Duke's mistress.

"I suppose that will explain the historical anomaly that Arabella produced two children while the Duchess was still alive, but was not returned to her parents."

When this was done, the pair moved back to the vicinity of Nova.

At a meeting with her Bearing group, Iva said, "Once again, history seems to have settled back on the safe path, despite Katie's additional adjustments. Or was that, 'because of'?

"However, the comment that Aon made about her next change being irreversible is disturbing."

Chapter 9

POLITICAL SETTLEMENT

S IENNA AND HER GROUP WERE IN a relaxed mood after their holiday. She had been considering longer term plans, and had discussed these with Iain. She realised that she was more than happy with the support group which had gelled around her. She had also decided that she wanted to have Felicity around permanently, or if not, for as long as possible.

She asked the nurse directly, "Felicity, would you be interested in staying with us on a long-term basis? Obviously, this would eventually lead to you helping bring up my children.

"Don't worry about future pay and conditions. They will considerably exceed naval norms, but it would probably be better if you actually stayed in the service."

Felicity, both surprised and delighted, said; "My Lady, that would be wonderful!"

Sienna said, "Good. Cheetah, can you please link Felicity into our communications network, and provide her with the requisite training."

She had a similar conversation with Peter and Louise.

"You have both been enormously helpful, and I find that having you here and occasionally disagreeing with me, is good for my sanity. I don't know how this fits in with your personal plans, but I would like to have you around for a long time. You would be responsible for the personal security of all my family, any dignitaries who come to Nova, and act as an interface between myself and the Fleet.

"You would be in command of appropriate detachments from the Fleet and marines. In fact, whatever you think you need! You would retain the authority over the Federation military forces and the diplomatic service that you currently hold. Only Aunty Caroline as Governor and Admiral Jenna as Admiral of the Fleet could overrule you.

"Please talk about this between yourselves, and let me know in due course."

Peter looked at Louise, who nodded slightly.

He said, "My Lady, we would be honoured to serve you directly for the foreseeable future."

9a – Kenta

Back on her yacht after supper, Sienna said to her group, "I think we will have to head back to Nova in about six weeks. In the meantime, where did you think we should go next?"

Iain replied, "Just for once, I anticipated that question. With some help from Cheetah, I have been researching the news databases.

"Right at the edge of the Federation boundary, there is a planet called Kenta which has only been a part of the Federation for about 10 years. It managed to acquire Federation technology some decades before then.

"Their solar system is interesting in that there is an enormous asteroid belt. The three gas giant planets deflected two planets about half Nova's size into a grazing collision. The gravitational and frictional stresses shattered both of them. Gravity interactions with the gas giants ensured that the smashed pieces did not coalesce together into another large planet. Instead, they formed a dense asteroid field. Eventually, it is thought that random interactions will bring enough of the fragments together for a new planet or planetoids to start forming as gravitation attracts more material, but this might take many hundreds of thousands of years.

"This happened almost yesterday in geological time; the ice age which destroyed the civilisation of the Kenta inhabitants appears to have been due to huge amounts of dust from the collision obscuring their sun. While the dust has mostly cleared, it is believed that it might have been a long time before the ice age finished.

"At the moment, the computer complex is in the process of arranging the manufacture of a large set of solar mirrors. In a couple of decades, it is forecast that the extra energy will be starting to clear the ice properly.

"The difficulty with the process was that huge shields have had to be built to protect the solar mirrors from the large supply of asteroids. Even now, these make night-time on Kenta spectacular, as the planet is still being bombarded with specimens of all sizes.

"The planet dropped into this ice age about 2000 years ago, but its inhabitants had developed a sufficient level of sophistication to survive. However, that did not stop terrible wars and huge depopulation before they managed to stabilise their civilisation. Mostly, they went underground to avoid continuous asteroid bombardment and warfare.

"Only a small part of the planet is habitable around the equatorial belt. Ice sheets cover a large part of the rest.

"The small amount of arable land left has been cultivated intensively, and there are laws against using it for anything except food production.

"These days, cities are being built on parts which are totally unsuited for farms, using powerful shields to protect from asteroids. While not as frequent as a few centuries ago, the latter still represent a significant hazard.

"The availability of fusion power, powerful shield generating technology and gravity control has led to active colonisation of the asteroid belt. Most of the fragments are metal rich, as most were formed from the liquid metal cores of the planets and solidified with relatively smooth surfaces.

"There are zillions of these ranging in size from inconsequential to mountain sized or larger.

"Describing this asteroid belt as lawless does not even begin to convey the position. Hundreds of entities have sprung up which do not acknowledge any authority. In a number of cases, miniature federations have formed. They all protect themselves militarily, and piracy is almost a way of life for a number of the communities. Apart from this, external revenue comes from selling processed metals.

"Having said this, a large part of the dynamism of the Kenta civilisation seems to have migrated to this belt. The communities are brash, lawless, inventive and innovative. Their cultural achievements are considerable in terms of music, writing and the arts generally.

"The control problem from the point of view of the main Kenta government on the planet surface, is that these groups are impossible to police successfully. Their colonised asteroids drift randomly through the belts, shielded by clouds of smaller pieces and dust. It is easy to plant anti-ship and antipersonnel missiles on nearby rocks which makes military options difficult.

"Not to mention that the asteroids do not have settled orbits through the asteroid belt. Unless observed continuously, they simply disappear into the surrounding obscurity, which covers an enormous volume of space. In some cases, this is helped by small foldspace drives running continuously.

"To even travel through the asteroid belt requires heavily reinforced shields. Cheetah and our shuttles would be okay, because of the extraordinary strength of their shields.

"Otherwise it is dangerous for anything less than a Federation cruiser to travel through the belt."

"The inhabitants use vessels where over 90% of the engine power is used to reinforce their shields. Nonetheless, a small percentage of their vessels are destroyed every year.

"The Kenta government has appealed for Federation assistance in managing the position, but any sort of physical invasion of the belt is likely to result in huge civilian casualties.

"Military losses are also likely to be significant if the asteroid groups decide to resist, even assuming that a feasible plan can be devised.

"Active discussions with Federation representatives are continuing, but no one has any clear idea of how to fix the position. At the moment, the possible cures look far worse than the disease!

"Off the top of my head, once again I have no idea how we would begin to solve this problem."

Iain distributed the data on the planet, and there was a pause for about half an hour as the information was studied.

For once, it was Felicity who spoke first.

"I have not told anyone, but one of my personal hobbies is ballroom dancing. For the last two decades, dances derived from those of Old Earth have become fashionable, and the activity has been sweeping the Federation.

"For some reason, the Kenta caught on to this quite early on, well before they joined. Because they have adapted to underground living, they built a large number of underground dance venues.

"Getting to the point, in just over three weeks' time, they have a grand Midwinter Ball.

"Apparently the acoustics and design of the cavern they use for this is fabulous. It is now famous in ballroom dancing circles. There is a growing view that it should be the permanent location for Federation Ballroom Championships.

"My lady, entry to this event is by invitation only, but I'm sure you could arrange that! You and Iain have become quite famous in this part of the Federation!

"This would enable you to meet unofficially most of the more powerful figures on the planet. I'm not sure whether this will help, but it seems to me to be at least a starting point."

Sienna looked thoughtful for a moment, and then said; "The main problem is rather simple; we can't dance!"

Felicity smiled a little impishly, "It will take us 10 days to get to Kenta, and we will have a little time after that for polishing. That is enough time for everyone to reach an acceptable standard if we work hard!

"It will also be good exercise, and much more fun than our gymnasium!

"Of course, I would expect Peter and Louise to participate as well!"

The dancing classes started the following morning, and the group discovered that Felicity was a rather determined and talented teacher. Iain found the cast on his wrist and lower arm inconvenient, but Sienna and Felicity were so quick and light on their feet that he was able to manage the dancing. In fact, he found Felicity was a better partner: while still relatively lightly built, she was heavier than Sienna and her greater strength and experience enabled her to lead him effectively.

It was unfortunate that the covering was not due to be removed until about a week after the Ball.

Cheetah sent a message to the Federation Ambassador, requesting that invitations be arranged for his entire human group. This was well beyond what Sienna had suggested. Separately, he instructed the computer complexes to forge a message from Nova strongly suggesting the same action, using his override codes.

The Nova ambassador on Kenta was a little put out to receive these instructions, but he had heard about the Taylors. He did not know anything about the rest of the group, but the instructions seemed to be clear.

As he told his secretary, "Michelle, I'm not at all sure we will be able to get these invites, but I'll try. Put a call through to the Minister for Home Affairs."

To his surprise, the Minister immediately agreed to consider the request, and said he would take it to the planetary Premier and the Cabinet.

The Kenta government was uncertain of the relationship between the Taylors and the Empress Sylvia, but a powerful connection clearly existed.

The sweeping changes which had occurred since this human group had appeared in this part of the Federation had been widely noted.

Everywhere they went, the Taylors seemed to be agents of change.

While the asteroid communities were outside the control of the government, they also represented a vital economic and social part of their civilisation. There was a huge drift of their best and brightest towards the belt, which had a dynamism that the planetary Kenta lacked.

The government was desperately keen for someone to suggest how they could move the asteroid populations back into their main civilisation without serious violence. They had even extended an unofficial welcome by inviting three of the larger groupings to send representatives.

They decided that a Midwinter Ball invitation to the Taylors and their group was an excellent idea.

* * *

Cheetah interrupted the evening meal.

"You will all be pleased to hear that formal invitations to the Midwinter Ball have been issued by the Kenta government. These include Peter, Louise and Felicity.

"An itinerary and a list of the dances has also been forwarded. These include the Empress Waltz, the Viennese Waltz, the Alpha Waltz, the Modern Waltz, the Carousel, Quickstep, Rumba, Samba and the Argentine Tango. You will note the heavy emphasis on the waltzes!

"Co-incidentally, the Admiral who was in charge at Datura has been moved here, which might be helpful."

Iain said, "Thank you, Cheetah. That was well beyond what Sienna requested, but I won't ask how you engineered it!

He looked at Peter with a big grin, "Peter, you're really going to have to try a lot harder!"

The target of his jibe visibly squirmed.

When Felicity had started her classes, she had quickly realised that Sienna had a natural talent for dancing. She seemed to remember dances almost effortlessly, she was quick on her feet and had a natural feel for musical beat. Louise was also quite good despite her solid build. She managed her weight and balance beautifully. Iain was a good average despite his injury, but Peter was a complete disaster.

Felicity had a little talk with Louise. "Louise, at the moment I'm arranging three practice sessions a day. I'm afraid to say that Peter is in need of further coaching. If you don't mind, I would like the pair of you to have an extra session late each evening."

Louise realised that Felicity was telling her that Peter was likely to be an embarrassment if he did not improve.

The two women cornered Peter, who reluctantly admitted that it was a good idea.

9b – Arrival

When they arrived at Kenta, they discovered that the Fleet detachment had been considerably reinforced. Clearly the difficulties being experienced by the government had been noticed although no practical solution was apparent.

The senior officers of the detachments in this far-flung part of the Federation had been communicating with each other, and they had privately agreed between themselves to watch out for Cheetah and her passengers.

As a result, soon after Cheetah had arrived, an invitation was received from the local admiral for the entire group to come over for a dinner.

When they arrived, they were formally dressed, with the Moores and Felicity in their full dress uniforms.

There was a small honour guard at the shuttle bay. Despite the visual evidence to the contrary, there was still a strong suspicion in the Fleet that Sienna was actually the Empress. The Admiral had decided that the best compromise for greeting her respectfully while maintaining anonymity, was to meet her himself.

Peter said to the Lieutenant in charge of the entrance, "Permission for my group to come aboard, Lieutenant?"

"Permission granted, Commander. Admiral Hargreaves is waiting with the honour guard by the bay exit."

Sienna and Iain took the lead, and as they came up to the honour guard, which stiffened to attention, Sienna said "Admiral Hargreaves, I'm delighted to see you again, and thank you for the invitation to my group.

"You know Iain, Commander Peter Moore and Major Louise Moore, and standing next to them trying to look inconspicuous is Senior Staff Nurse Felicity Corning."

The Admiral laughed, "Sienna, thank you for accepting my invitation. Since I met you on Datura, you and your group appear to have made even more waves!

"By the way, you will be glad to hear that most of the problems in the other regions of this part of the Federation have evaporated.

"Sylvia's offer of a conducted tour and free pictures, has led to an army of journalists scurrying around all the planets looking for health and other issues. Fear of publicity has led to most of the problems being fixed.

"Of course, the most obvious exception to all of this is Kenta.

"Doubtless, that has nothing to do with your arrival here!"

Iain and Sienna saw gentle amusement in the Admiral's face as he looked at them.

As the group left, the honour guard was put at ease.

The young lieutenant in charge asked, "Sergeant, can you remember when and who the Admiral last met at the bay entrance?"

The reply surprised him, "As I recall sir, only the Nova Governor, Admiral Jenna, and one head of state."

* * *

The Nova ambassador and his wife were amongst the guests, which also included the Admiral's wife. The ambassador was surprised at how young Sienna appeared when he first saw her entering the dining room. However, as he greeted her, he saw two young eyes appraising him, which seemed to be looking into the depths of his being.

A sense of awe permeated him, despite his veteran status in the diplomatic corps. His wife had always been regarded as a formidable character in her own right, but he noticed that she was rather overwhelmed as well.

A small voice told him to be extremely careful with this woman.

After seating at a large ovoid dining table and more general introductions, Iain explained to the flag captain that they had been on holiday on a tropical island on the planet Mor.

He continued, "Sienna, myself and Felicity basically lounged on the beach. While we were hard at work doing this, Peter and Louise were demonstrating that it was just as well that we have a space navy rather than one which relies on sails!"

There was some laughter at this, and Peter saw a way of teasing his wife a little as revenge for the dancing lessons.

He provided a rather exaggerated description of how Louise as helmsperson had managed to capsize the catamaran.

"The wind was quite strong, but Louise was nicely balancing one pontoon and myself just above the water, when she was distracted for a moment.

"The pontoon flew up as the cat tipped over; I'm sure she said 'Eek' as she bellyflopped into the water next to the instructor!"

There was laughter all around the table at this, including Louise.

Recovering strongly she said, "I did not say 'Eek' – it was a lot ruder than that!

"Besides which Peter, your bellyflop was rather more spectacular than mine as you had further to fall from the upturned pontoon!

"Also, you omitted to mention that you had capsized twice a little earlier!"

The Admiral really laughed at that; "Commander, I think you should have formed a Board of Enquiry to apportion blame there!"

A little later, noticing that Felicity was rather quiet, the Admiral's wife asked her how she found living on Cheetah.

Felicity looked thoughtful for a moment and then smiled, "The yacht is quite small, but it is extraordinarily comfortable and well equipped. I have my own room and bathroom, which are rather larger than would be the case on a Navy ship.

"I feel I am associated with a most interesting group of people, and I never feel left out of conversations.

"It now feels like home."

On the other side of the table, Sienna asked the Admiral directly why there was such a problem policing the asteroid belt. Iain had provided a good description, but she was interested in hearing a military view.

As he thought about his answer, he realised that the whole Cheetah group were listening carefully.

"Sienna, the first thing you need to appreciate about the asteroid belt is its sheer size. Two moderately sized planets effectively disintegrated about 2000 years ago into multi-trillions of fragments ranging from dust to thousands of cubic kilometres.

"The shepherding influence of the gas giants and the planet Kenta has created a flattened blob – no, a better description would be a flattened fat sausage - of asteroids, meteoroids and dust. This has spread around about

15% of the orbital around the sun. The approximate dimensions in millions of kilometres are 80 by 20 by 5. That represents a huge volume, and does not include the fuzzy edge all the way around it.

"The spectacular meteor showers we see every night on Kenta demonstrate that there are still plenty of escapees from this asteroid cloud, but otherwise the belt is surprisingly stable.

"Continual collisions ensure there is plenty of dust and it is hard for agglomerations to be created.

"Statistically, this will eventually occur as enough mass will randomly collect in one place to be relatively stable and with enough gravity to start to pull in and retain more fragments. At that point, we expect planetoids to form.

"Visually, the belt becomes opaque to visible light after about 50,000 km. Since a large proportion of the fragments are metallic, radar is also nearly useless.

"The belt is an easy place in which to disappear.

"Of course, without exceptionally powerful shields, it is also a highly dangerous location for a spacecraft. Even then, larger asteroids have to be avoided.

"Returning to your question, with Federation mining technology it is easy to tunnel into the larger asteroids and become almost invisible. This also means that the little city states which have formed are completely protected from external meteorites. It is easy to hide anti spacecraft missiles locally. Summing up, the locations of the communities are uncertain, they are fiercely independent, will only obey their own rules, and are quite well armed.

"We see no easy way of changing the political position."

As these comments were considered, there was a pause in the conversation.

Peter added, "That is a serious problem for the future. I hope our Empress has some ideas!

"At the moment, we are being focused by Felicity on the Winter Ball in a week's time!

"Speaking personally, I have rarely been pushed so hard!

"When we have some free time, which parts of the planet are worth visiting?"

Conversation then broke up into smaller groups around the table, and food arrived.

* * *

The following day, serious preparation for the Ball began. Felicity had located the best clothing and footwear suppliers, and she insisted that Sienna and Iain needed proper ball outfits.

She told Louise and Peter, "Our formal dress uniforms are acceptable, but everyone will need more suitable footwear."

Cheetah was quite concerned about the shopping.

"Because of their history, the majority of the shops are deep underground. This means that my monitoring of your surroundings will be handicapped.

"The immediate solution would be to include a combat remote, but it will not act as efficiently as normal as it will only be able to rely on its internal programming. The signal links I can establish do not have enough bandwidth for direct control."

Iain said, "The planetary cities of Kenta have a reputation of being completely law-abiding. Including a combat remote – and remember a certain video of those remotes in action has been widely circulated – would probably be regarded as rather insulting by the government and population.

"Is that what we want at this stage, even assuming the locals would agree to the presence of what amounts to an advanced military machine?"

Louise added, "Peter and I can obtain permission to be armed, and we would stay with Sienna all the time.

"Having said that, I am also uncomfortable about not having Cheetah at full effectiveness.

"Actually, it would be sensible to request help from the Admiral in terms of having some armed female plainclothes security officers present."

Sienna thought about this.

"We have to move around on the planet, and we know that a large part of the culture is underground.

"I accept the need to have Louise, Peter and the security officers present continuously. If nothing else, that will help when I have to go to the loo!

"Cheetah, do you think this would be sufficient?"

The yacht AI reluctantly agreed to these arrangements.

9c – Ball

The three female security officers that the fleet had supplied still looked a little military despite civilian clothing. They had been instructed that their primary function was to guard Sienna.

The commander in charge of naval security had said to them, "The Admiral told me that Sienna Taylor is extremely important; she is to be protected at all costs. Two other married senior officers are permanently assigned to her yacht. You will be reporting directly on this assignment to Major Louise Moore.

One of the security officers asked, "Sir, may I ask why Mrs Taylor is so important?"

"Lieutenant, since the Cheetah group arrived in this quadrant of the Federation, they have been at the centre of some major political changes.

"Sienna Taylor is a Shepherd and has a close but undefined relationship with the Empress. Despite film evidence to the contrary, there is a school of thought in the Fleet that believes she is Sylvia. For Admiral Jenna to assign two senior officers to her permanently is extraordinary.

"However, you are never to repeat those last comments."

As a result of this conversation, the three officers were a little nervous when they first met the Taylors.

Louise took them in hand straight away; "Relax, and fade into the background. You need to practice a less military look. Don't worry, it took Commander Moore and I a little time to learn to play act. However, don't for one moment stop watching Sienna's surroundings."

In fact, the group as a whole enjoyed visiting the surface of Kenta. Although in places the cities were starting to develop externally with the aid of powerful shields, most of the population still lived underground.

The availability of Federation mining technology – especially rock shattering equipment – had led to a great expansion of the space available. Enormous caverns had been built, and filled with small cities.

It had helped that the Kenta were also an artistic species, and they wanted their cities to remain attractive.

The cavern they visited was half a kilometre underground. It rather reminded Sienna of the habitat reserve on Sheila, except that it was filled with buildings of various shapes and sizes in circular rows. Studded around the roof were large lighting disks interspersed with air vents. Consistency of style between the buildings was noticeable, and they had been designed to fit in with their surroundings. There were tiny gardens associated with most of the houses. There were large numbers of shuttles moving in a clockwise flow pattern around the cavern. At regular intervals around the side, there were the entrances to large tunnels. The guidebooks had said that most of the population actually lived in the smaller houses in the tunnels; those in the main cavern were too costly.

The main shopping parade was front and centre. The shops themselves looked well-stocked and expensive.

Three hours later, the group had been equipped to Felicity's satisfaction.

She thought to herself, "It's just as well Sienna is picking up the tab; the prices were astronomical, although the quality was good."

There had been refreshment break halfway through the shopping. The Fleet security officers were happy to find that they were included in the coffee and cakes order.

When Sienna needed to go to the toilet, Louise insisted that two of the security officers searched the area first, and then went in with her together with one of the officers.

She said, "I'm sorry Sienna; with Cheetah unable to provide a blanket security cover, we need to be around."

They were unaware that their procedures were being watched.

* * *

The leadership of two of the larger asteroid belt communities had been quickly alerted to the arrival of Cheetah.

In common with the government of Kenta, they were uncertain what this really meant, but were quite determined to maintain their autonomy. Their own experts had studied the security arrangements and how they had located their communities in their asteroids. These experts were convinced that there was no satisfactory way they could be forced to participate in anything.

"Short of a campaign of total destruction, there is no way anyone can easily subdue us. Attacking us would be dangerous for even powerful Federation forces.

"Locating us would be difficult, and even Federation battleships would have difficulty fending off our missile salvos at point blank range from the ambush asteroids.

"Lightly shielded assault craft would be unlikely to survive frequent collisions with small asteroids, and assaults by space suited Marines would be suicidal."

* * *

The previous evening Cheetah had surprised her group by saying rather more formally than normal, "My Lady, I have taken the liberty of fabricating a small pendant to go with your outfit."

Sienna had always shown a considerable disdain for wearing any form of jewellery.

A remote brought in a jewellery box, which it placed in front of Sienna. She opened it, and gasped.

"Cheetah, it is absolutely beautiful!"

She held up the pendant by its silver chain. It consisted of a round diamond about 3 cm across, surrounded by seven emerald cut diamonds in a starburst pattern. The diamonds were held together by a light platinum frame, and were clearly flawless whites.

"I will be delighted to wear it tomorrow, although wearing jewellery goes against the habits of a lifetime!"

On the day of the Winter Ball, Felicity inspected her group before they left Cheetah. It was clear that she knew a great deal more about major dancing events than she had admitted, and she had quietly taken control.

She inwardly nodded to herself. Even Peter had raised himself to a nearly acceptable standard of dancing. For the rest, she had been astonished at how quickly Sienna learned the routines.

She thought to herself, "If I had been given another two weeks to train the Empress, she would have reached a championship standard."

Two officers from the fleet had been invited, and it had been agreed that Cheetah's shuttle would stop to pick them up together with a full security detail. The latter would follow in another shuttle.

At the flagship entrance, as the Admiral and his wife stepped into the shuttle, he paused in astonishment.

Sienna was wearing a silvery ball gown, and round her throat was a diamond pendant with the largest stones he had ever seen.

Federation technology could synthesise diamonds with relative ease, but they were always slightly flawed and never completely clear. Also, they were never as large as these.

His wife reacted more quickly, "Sienna, you look magnificent. The pendant suits you absolutely!"

Sienna laughed, "Good evening Matilda, and thank you for the compliment. I am not accustomed to wearing jewellery, but I couldn't resist it!"

* * *

The whole group looked around as they entered the underground ballroom. As Felicity had indicated, it was an inspiring construction. Apart from standard lighting and air vents on the hemispherical roof, the Kenta had taken a leaf from the pictures they had seen of Old Earth and hung the room with giant chandeliers. All around the base of the roof, large triangular mirrors had been inset into the wall, with the point aimed at the centre of the roof. At the far end there was a stage and a sunken area where an orchestra was assembled.

As they entered, their names and titles or rank were announced.

Sienna noticed there was a little stir when Felicity's rank and name were announced.

Before the formal dancing started, drinks and some light refreshments were offered. Sienna and Iain found themselves talking to the Admiral and his wife, with no-one else within earshot.

The Admiral said, "You would not know this, but my wife was a professional jewellery valuer before we were married. As a sort of hobby, she has maintained an interest in the area, despite my inability to finance almost anything she looks at!

"She would have heard if any pendant like the one you are wearing was for sale anywhere in the Federation, My Lady."

Iain said, "Admiral, you and your wife must not repeat those comments or use that title for Sienna. It would be most inconvenient for us."

There was no levity at all in his tone.

"Anyhow, I think we are being called to order for the first dance."

The middle-aged Kenta who was in charge of proceedings for the evening had walked across to the microphone.

"To our local people and visitors from the asteroid belt, and nationals of other species visiting us today, the Government and Ballroom Association of our planet greet you.

"In particular, we would like to welcome the group of people from the yacht Cheetah.

"Apart from Mrs Sienna Taylor, who has already made a considerable impact on other planets in this part of our Federation, we are pleased to see that Miss Felicity Corning is also present.

"For those not in the dancing world, you should be aware that she and her dancing partner were one of the winners in the Federation Amateur Ballroom Championship last year."

Felicity blushed, as the remainder of the Cheetah group looked at her in surprise.

The compere continued, "I would like to invite Miss Corning to open proceedings with an Alpha Waltz, with a partner of her choice."

Felicity smiled; this was absolutely her world.

She held out her hand to Sienna who took it rather shyly.

"I've never danced in public before, Felicity."

"Just think of it as a practice session, with your teacher and your favourite dance!"

In Federation dancing circles, it was not at all unusual for pairs of dancers to be of the same sex.

As the floor cleared, Felicity led Sienna into the middle of the floor, took a ballroom hold, and nodded to the orchestra.

The Alpha Waltz starts off with five simple waltz steps, and then morphs into a series of checks and turns, finishing with a spin.

From an initial moment's nervousness, Sienna found herself being lifted by the live orchestra. This waltz had always been her favourite dance, and in a moment she relaxed and let herself enjoy the movements.

To the experts in the ballroom, it was obvious that Felicity was the championship dancer, but somehow it was Sienna who held their eyes. This was helped by the magnificent pendant she wore, which scintillated as she moved and spun in the brilliant spotlight which bathed the pair.

The Admiral's wife murmured to her husband, "Sienna's pendant is amazing; I would love to buy something like that!"

Her husband replied, "I'm sorry dear, but I think that item of jewellery is unavailable at any price!"

The dance display was also being watched by two representatives from the larger of the asteroid belt communities.

He murmured to his companion, "Sienna Taylor is already too conspicuous. She may be influential enough to motivate action against us. We need to consider how to neutralise her political effect. Regrettable as this may be, we should talk to the Fer Community."

This was a small asteroid belt community known for kidnapping, piracy and extortion. It was well hidden in the heart of the asteroid belt. It had connections with the criminal element on Kenta.

When Felicity and Sienna had finished their exhibition dance, there was prolonged applause, and then more general dancing started.

Sienna and Iain participated in a number of the slower dances as the evening progressed – but it was obvious that his plastered arm was quite a severe handicap.

There were regular refreshment breaks, during which Sienna and Iain wandered from group to group.

The Nova ambassador and the Federation fleet admiral noticed that wherever she went, Sienna immediately became the focus of the group.

The ambassador said, "That young woman has the most enormous presence. I'm beginning to understand why the Taylors have had such an impact wherever they have been!

"I'm sure even the Kenta have noticed that if she changed her hair style, she would look exactly like the Empress Sylvia!"

His colleague replied softly, "John, I think that both Sylvia and Sienna would be annoyed if you repeat that comment."

9d – Disaster

As they embarked on Cheetah's shuttle at the end of the evening, Louise said "Congratulations Felicity, it was a good idea to participate in this event!

"By the way, are you going to spring any other surprises on us?!"

Felicity looked a little embarrassed; "Not immediately!"

The following day, Sienna was feeling distinctly the worse for wear.

Her nurse told her, "I'm sorry My Lady, but my instructions are that you simply have a quiet, boring day. You over-exerted yourself yesterday!"

Sienna rather grumpily accepted the comment.

"OK. I am beginning to really dislike being pregnant."

Then she added, "Iain wanted to visit some camera shops this morning, and I think you were planning some shopping."

Her husband had maintained a keen interest in amateur photography.

"Why don't you both go planet-side this morning? I am sure I can look after myself for an hour or two!

"You can borrow my brown Masuna fur coat if you like."

Iain and Felicity happily agreed to this, but Louise added immediately.

"That's fine Sienna, but I must still insist on some protection. I'll come down as well, and we will bring the Fleet security officers."

Iain protested, "That's complete overkill, Louise. Surely we don't need all of them!

"You and a single security officer will be more than enough. We aren't really targets!"

Louise could hardly disagree with this, and they set off an hour later.

In an underground shopping mall, a camera shop and a glove shop stood side by side. The latter was tiny, and fitted the "boutique" label. Because of the planet's recent cold history, Kenta gloves were apparently the best available.

The camera shop was enormous. Like most of the larger shops, it had several back doors to the maze of tunnels the Kenta had built underground over the millennia.

Kenta shops were cold by human standards, as the species was comfortable at a distinctly lower temperature than human norms. Felicity kept the hood up on her coat. After about half an hour in the glove shop, together with the Fleet officer she wandered back carrying her purchases to where Iain was cheerfully discussing the comparative merits of two different cameras with the shop assistant.

* * *

It was an easy mistake to make.

Iain was clearly identifiable with his plaster cast, and even humans might have mistaken Felicity for Sienna. They had similar hair colour and the distinctive Masuna fur coat had been seen being worn by Sienna several times.

The eight heavily armed Fer gang members had been waiting impatiently for Felicity to return from the glove shop. Small shops were not connected to the tunnel network.

They had access to nearly all the larger outlets, and they just needed Sienna Taylor to visit such a shop.

Louise and the security officer were alert, and as the back door of the shop sprang open with Kenta armed with handguns appearing, they were already reaching for their weapons. The Kenta assistant dived to the floor behind the counter.

Louise was hit by two bullets, one in the chest and one in the thigh, but returned one shot. She collapsed onto a display cabinet and slid to the ground badly injured.

The security officer was hit three times in her chest, and died instantly.

Iain was also badly hurt, with bullets through his shoulder and arm.

Felicity screamed, but that did not stop her leaping over Iain to protect him.

As the gang members were under orders that Sienna was under no circumstances to be harmed, they ceased fire.

Their leader said, "Grab the pair, let's get out of here. Pick up Raten; the bitch shot him dead."

As he passed Louise, he kicked her hard. She moaned softly.

In fact they were a little shaken. They had expected to simply face down the group with levelled arms and overwhelming numbers, and kidnap Sienna and if possible Iain.

They rushed through the door, bolting it shut behind them. A gang member attached a timed explosive charge to the roof.

The tunnel behind sloped downwards at a steep angle. 200 metres further down, there was another steel door, which was slammed shut behind them.

As they continued, there was a rumble as the explosive charge brought down the roof of the tunnel near the shop.

* * *

The communications relay from the small remotes that had been tracking the Cheetah group had passed back high quality images of what was happening. These ceased as the tunnel collapsed.

As Cheetah had said, there was too much iron in the rocks for accurate tracking or much signal bandwidth. Normal defensive responses were impossible.

The local police and authorities were immediately informed, and armed groups rushed to the shop. Crystal emerged from foldspace near the planet, to the astonishment of the local Federation Fleet.

She immediately sent a message to the Fleet flagship, "Major Louise Moore will be transferred to your medical unit. Warn your surgeons to expect her almost immediately."

The police were shocked to find the dead security officer and Louise badly wounded.

As she was brought up on a stretcher, a shuttle was waiting. A remote said, "Place the major inside".

The moment the stretcher was inside, the door shut, and the shuttle rocketed upwards.

In fact, the moment the inside was invisible from outside, Crystal transferred the stretcher and Louise via foldspace to the main surgical unit of the flagship. She hoped no-one would notice the timing. She would tell the Admiral and doctors not to reveal the transfer.

Back on Cheetah, a horrified Sienna and Peter were brought up to date with what was happening.

Sienna was almost frantic with worry about Iain.

She said –almost shrieked- "Cheetah and Crystal, why can't you locate them!?"

She knew the answer, but she had to say something.

Crystal answered, "The depth underground of the area plus iron rich rock have crippled our search ability. It has also cut off our private communications net.

"Cheetah and I are deploying search drones everywhere possible, but apparently there are hundreds of kilometres of unmapped and unused tunnels under the city.

"We cannot clear the tunnel until part of the city has been evacuated because the explosion has dangerously weakened the rock foundation of that portion of the city complex.

"If we just remove the rock, we may collapse the floor over a substantial area."

Crystal paused for a moment, and then added; "Also, the kidnap group have just told the authorities that they will detonate a fusion device under the city if they are pursued."

Peter found that Sienna was gripping his arm with both hands so tightly it was painful. Worry about Louise gripped him.

"Sienna, I must go to the flagship to be with Louise; from what I saw, she is desperately injured".

She replied, as she started to sob, "Oh, I am so sorry Peter – you must be terribly anxious as well.

"We will shuttle over straight away.

"Those kidnappers, and whoever they represent, are going to regret this. If Louise and Iain don't survive, I may obliterate their people. I am also worried about Felicity."

Sienna was realising that she was nearly as concerned about Felicity as about Iain and Louise – she realised that she had come to love the woman like a sort of elder sister.

Sienna had never felt so angry in her life, although she realised fury was colouring her judgement. She realised she had inherited the same mindset and anger response as her grandmother.

As they shuttled across to the flagship at emergency speed, with Sienna looking white and strained, Peter said; "Did you see that Felicity rather heroically threw herself over Iain as he fell. That seemed to stop the shooting.

"I think you were the real target.

"I also saw the leader of criminal group kick Louise as he passed her. I will not forget that."

His Empress looked at him; "As I said before, some people somewhere are going to really regret today."

The trip took about ten minutes. Peter saw that despite the strain on her face, Sienna's eyes seemed slightly unfocussed, and she said nothing further.

In fact she was talking to her monitoring Bearing.

"Can you help locate Iain, and is he OK?

The answer did not re-assure her. "Iain is critically ill and is only alive because of Felicity and her medical skills.

"As a matter of policy, I have been told I must not intervene directly, which I regret; this is a Federation problem that you must resolve."

However the Bearing was thinking to himself. "It would be a bad outcome if Iain died. Sienna might do something unfortunate. Also, we owe Katie a favour for what she is doing for the Community. She likes Iain, and she does not need any more grief.

"I will modify my instruction and ensure Iain survives".

* * *

The Admiral met them as they arrived.

"Commander, my lieutenant will show you to the hospital straight away. If you need anything, including some food and drink, please let him know."

Peter said, "Thank you, sir".

As he was turning to leave Sienna said, "I will be along as soon as possible, after talking to the Admiral."

The latter said, "Sienna, can I suggest we go to my office for a brief discussion."

Neither said anything as they hurried through the vessel.

When they reached his office and sat down, there was silence for a moment. Sienna looked at him, and he could see the fury in her face; "Admiral, I really liked your murdered security officer. I will be sending my personal condolences to her family.

"A group of people somewhere are going to regret this. I am more than annoyed.

"You should be aware that Crystal has sent an Imperial Decree from 'Sylvia' to Admiral Jenna ordering him to assemble two Fleet Battle Groups here forthwith."

The Admiral paled. 300 Fleet ships in one place was the largest assemblage since the Xicon War.

Something burned in the face of the young woman in front of him, and he realised that epic decisions were about to be made. Shepherds had a reputation for staying angry, or grieving, for a long time. Her grandmother had disappeared for many decades when her husband died.

He feared for anyone connected in any way to the kidnapping group if Iain died. His Empress might simply destroy everything, which would be a ghastly stain on her reputation and could imperil the Federation.

He said, "My Lady, there is an emergency meeting of the Kenta leaders in progress. I gather they are furious at this attack."

Sienna was so upset that for the first time she did not correct his use of the title.

He continued, "I will let you know anything I hear, if that is necessary."

The young woman in front of him said, "Thank you. I must go and keep Peter company now. Until we hear something from the kidnapping group, or Crystal finds something, we must wait."

When she arrived at the surgical unit, she found Peter looking through an observation window at the operating area.

"Have you heard anything?" she asked.

Peter said, "One of the surgeons came out briefly to tell me Louise would likely survive.

"She was only transferred here just in time. She would have been dead in another five minutes."

Sienna held his arm tightly again, and said softly, "Thank goodness something has gone right today."

* * *

In a well-stocked cave deep underground, Felicity was doing her best with Iain.

There were basic medical supplies and equipment, but most of these were aimed at Kenta physiology.

Iain had lost a lot of blood. Her pleas with the gang leader had finally made him stop moving long enough to allow her to bandage Iain sufficiently to stop the bleeding. However according to the Kenta equipment, his blood pressure was alarmingly low.

She said to the gang leader, "Iain must have a blood transfusion, or he will die. He has lost too much blood, and his system is unstable. He is on the edge of what we call major shock symptoms."

"Since you will not let him near any real hospital, I will have to improvise. Fortunately, my blood type will do, as it is O negative. That is a universal donor type. You need to delegate someone to help me collect some of my own blood, and then I will transfuse it into him.

"As soon as his blood pressure rises, I must remove the bullet from his shoulder."

It took twenty minutes to extract enough blood, and then Felicity was able to start the transfusion into Iain. It was lucky he had survived long enough for her to start. She felt distinctly shaky, as she had donated an unsafe amount too quickly.

She told the gang member helping her, "I must drink some more water, have something to eat and lie down. Otherwise I may pass out.

"Let me know when the blood bag is nearly empty."

She was given a large drink of water and some survival rations to eat.

After that she lay on the floor, still in her bloodied fur coat, with a small blanket as a head rest, and closed her eyes.

She was roused half an hour later, and she disconnected the transfusion gear.

She was pleased to see that some colour had returned to Iain's cheeks, so far as she could judge from the camping lights. His blood pressure had risen to a safer level.

She said, "I must now remove the bullet from his shoulder".

A curious feature of personal arms in the Federation, was that old-fashioned pistols using explosive propelled bullets were still favoured by both security staff and criminals. The guns were small and discrete, with ten round magazines.

The laser rifles and pistols used by soldiers and police were far quieter and more lethal, but they were also substantially larger.

The calibre of the bullet in Iain's shoulder was small. Felicity injected a little anaesthetic around the area, dusted the wound with Kenta antibiotic, both of which she hoped would be safe for humans, and with the help of a scalpel and small pincers pulled out the bullet. It had been lodged against a bone, which she suspected was broken. However, there was nothing she could do about that.

She sewed up the wound, with more antibiotic, and firmly bandaged the area. She was pleased to note that further blood loss was minimal.

As she finished, she saw Iain's eyes flicker open.

"Felicity, where am I, and what has happened. I feel so weak!"

Looking down he saw the blood on his trousers and shirt.

He continued weakly; "Oh, I remember the door at the shop opening, the Kenta men rushing in, and guns firing........

"Is Louise all right?"

The leader of the Kenta group had been watching Felicity's highly competent performance as a nurse.

A horrible suspicion had been growing on him.

He angrily asked Felicity, "What is your name, human woman?"

She looked him straight in the eye.

"Felicity Corning.

"You've kidnapped the wrong person.

"Heaven help you and the people you represent when Sienna finds you".

The last was spoken so softly the Kenta could only just hear it.

His eyes narrowed. "But we do have you and Mrs Taylor's husband.

"We have heard that she is devoted to him. I must contact my leadership."

As he left, Felicity told Iain, "You need to be fed and hydrated. I will slowly spoon feed you some soup."

Crystal and Cheetah could detect the encrypted signals that passed between somewhere deep below the Kenta city to the asteroid belt, but they were too brief for the source to be located.

Sienna and Peter were waiting in a small office near the surgical unit, with both nursing a coffee.

Cheetah had kept them appraised of what was happening using their hidden communications net.

Shortly after, an anonymous message was received on the equivalent of the local internet;

"We are an asteroid freedom group. We hold Felicity Corning and Iain Taylor.

"The latter is injured. We demand that Sienna Taylor leaves this system and guarantees never to return. We will hold Iain Taylor and Miss Corning as security for this for some time."

Sienna listened to this message in stony silence.

Peter and her AIs waited for her to respond.

After two minutes she said, "First of all, they must prove they hold Iain and Felicity.

"Ask the anonymous channel two questions.

- for Iain, where did he first meet two Shepherds
- for Felicity, roughly what did I say when I was under a hat on Mor when we had an unexpected visitor

"While we are awaiting a response, on the assumption that they are the gang responsible, any suggestions?"

An hour later, Peter and the two AIs had made a number of suggestions. However, no-one was convinced that Sienna had been listening that carefully.

A message came back; "In a cafe on Nova, and a request to the chattering classes to let her stay asleep".

Cheetah remarked, "That at least proves that Iain is alive and conscious."

A few minutes later, Sienna seemed to stir herself slightly, and come out of her reverie.

"This is what I am going to suggest to the gang, as somehow I have to get Iain into a hospital and recover Felicity.

"I am going to offer to exchange myself, Cheetah and my pendant for them both.

"Crystal will guarantee she will not monitor the trade or what happens before I reach the asteroid belt. She will move herself into foldspace. I am sure they are unaware of Cheetah's capabilities.

"To ensure honesty, I will offer to pilot Cheetah on my own some way from Kenta, having visibly removed the combat remotes.

"One of their unarmed people can search the vessel. I will be armed. It looks like a luxury yacht to a cursory inspection. Once Iain and Felicity are in space in their own shuttle, and have spoken to me, I will surrender my weapon and the other gang crew can then travel to my yacht and board. I will tell them I will not release the electronic lock to them until Iain and Felicity are completely safe."

Peter immediately started to protest, but both AIs were silent. They could see the logic of the position.

He asked "But what if they simply take you captive and refuse to release Iain and Felicity?"

The answer was unambiguous. "In that case, the deal is terminated. Our people will be rescued by Crystal. All gang members who can be identified will be captured.

"Obviously, Cheetah will take measures to protect me."

She added, so softly that Peter could only just hear her; "If they refuse, or at that stage Iain and Felicity are dead, more drastic action will be taken."

Raising her voice, she continued; "However, this is not what I want. I would rather Cheetah and I are taken to the heart of the asteroid belt, enabling identification of the criminal community.

"They will then have to comply with other conditions. Again, drastic action is an option."

There was silence for a few minutes, as her comments were digested.

Peter asked, "What sort of drastic action had you in mind, Sienna?"

The answer shocked him. The AIs said nothing. Sienna had already discussed retribution with them.

Sienna's suggestion was passed through the anonymous channel.

In the cave, the gang leader was delighted. The primary target had always been Sienna Taylor. A luxury yacht and a certain diamond pendant would be a bonus. Details were sent to the asteroid community in an encrypted compressed format. Agreement was received almost immediately from its leadership.

He came over to Iain and Felicity.

"Mr Taylor, your wife has offered to swap herself for you and Miss Corning. I have heard from my leadership that this will be acceptable."

Iain was horrified, and said, still rather weakly, "Oh no! Sienna shouldn't do this!"

Felicity said, "Iain, you really need to be in hospital. I have patched you up, but things could easily go wrong. You need to be monitored properly.

"Sir, would it be possible for just Iain to be released. I am Sienna's nurse, and I should be looking after her."

The gang leader looked at the human woman with a certain respect. He could recognise raw courage and loyalty. He thought to himself that having two hostages rather than one would definitely be an improvement.

"I will send a further message. I am not sure that the suggestion will be accepted. I will offer to release you in two shuttles. If Mrs Taylor agrees, you can pilot one of the shuttles. If you wish, there will be nothing to stop you going to the yacht's location, following us. The other shuttle with Mr Taylor will be despatched to the Federation Fleet. Be aware that explosive devices will be placed in the shuttles, in case of treachery."

The message was sent straight away through the anonymous channel.

On hearing it, Sienna said "While I'm not at all happy with this idea, there is some sense in Felicity's position.

"I must admit it will be good for my morale to have her around."

Crystal said, "On balance, this is a good suggestion. Sienna, I recommend you signal acceptance."

The message went back, "Agreed. Specify a location for the yacht and an approximate transfer time. Iain Taylor needs to be removed to a hospital as soon as possible.

"My yacht's three combat remotes will leave, together with Commander Moore, in a shuttle.

"The Crystal Palace will depart immediately into foldspace."

20 minutes later, a message came back.

"We accept this proposal. Have media channels monitor and transmit the removal of the three combat remotes and Commander Moore in the shuttle.

"We have anonymously contacted a group we know, and they will send a member in a shuttle to check that the yacht Cheetah is empty apart from

Mrs Taylor. On verification, he will send a coded message which we will understand.

"Arrange to have three shuttles available by the Kenta city. Mr Taylor and Miss Corning will be given a shuttle each. Be warned that remotely controlled explosive devices will be placed in the shuttles as a precaution against treachery.

"All three shuttles will move together towards the yacht, and at the halfway point two will be released. One will be programmed to head towards the Federation fleet, and Miss Corning will have control of the other. If she wishes to follow us to the yacht, that is fine.

"This should happen in three hours' time."

A space coordinates location was provided as a destination for Cheetah.

9e – Asteroid Belt

Sienna sent a message to Admiral Hargreaves requesting an immediate meeting in the small office. When he arrived a few minutes later, he was given a quick summary of what had happened.

He was horrified at the implications for Sienna's safety.

"My Lady, this is a terrible risk for you. Putting yourself into the hands of these people could have alarming implications for the Federation!"

Sienna looked at him, and there was steel in the tone she used; "Do not use that title in public, Admiral. My anonymity is important. Also, do not repeat this conversation anywhere.

"If this plan is unacceptable to you, Peter will issue formal instructions to you. I might add that I'm not suicidal, and measures to protect me will be in place."

He nodded reluctantly; "I will cooperate under protest, My Lady."

Sienna replied, "Good. Now, how are we going to handle the Kenta government? We need to have these arrangements in place almost immediately."

When the Kenta government was advised at these arrangements, they were furious that they had not been involved with the negotiations.

However, the Admiral said to them, "First of all, the Federation fleet is the legal authority in this case under Federation protocols as kidnapping of foreign nationals is involved.

"Secondly, you should be aware that Admiral Jenna has been commanded by our Empress to send two battle groups here immediately. We expect them in about 10 days. That is about 300 vessels.

"Please arrange for immediate media coverage of the yacht Cheetah. Commander Moore and Mrs Taylor will return there now, and Commander Moore needs to be filmed leaving the yacht together with the three combat remotes.

"The Crystal Palace will also visibly leave this area, after announcing she will not participate in or monitor the transfer to the asteroid.

"Finally, park three standard shuttles near the main entrance of the city where the attack took place, and remove all police and surveillance devices from the area forthwith. Public announcements of this should be made as soon as arrangements are complete."

Two hours later, a group of masked Kenta appeared, with their two hostages crowded in the centre of the group. Iain was being carried on a crude stretcher as he could not walk. A number of guns were seen to be pointed in their direction.

A gang member placed parcels in the back of two of the shuttles, and Felicity was told to enter one and wait at the back. She should tell the shuttle AI to follow the other shuttles when they launched. At the approximate halfway point to the yacht, she was told she would be allowed to take charge of the shuttle and either follow the group or leave. The parcel was a large bomb which would explode if she did not follow the instructions.

The stretcher holding Iain was placed in the other shuttle, and the small control AI was told; "Follow the other shuttle which the group of Kenta is about to enter until you receive permission to take your passenger at maximum speed to the Federation Fleet flagship, which is hovering 50,000 kms above us."

While this was happening, a shuttle from the capital city on Kenta was seen approaching Cheetah.

It was admitted to his reception bay, and a rough looking Kenta man emerged. Sienna was standing at the side of the entrance looking rather nervous, and holding a small gun. She had never fired any weapon, and hoped the way she was holding it looked convincing.

She was wearing quite drab clothing, because Cheetah had told her firmly; "Sienna, I know this goes against the grain, but the safest course is for you to play the part of a scared and nervous girl. You must suppress your instinct to dominate!

"I will also be pretending to be a simpleminded yacht AI!"

She said to the Kenta man, "I will show you everything in the yacht, including the engine area. I will surrender this weapon to you when a conversation from my nurse and my husband is relayed through to me which indicates they are free and clear in shuttles. You can then tell the gang that there is no one else aboard and I am disarmed."

The Kenta made a thorough search of the yacht, and then inspected the engine area. He had little engineering experience, and it appeared normal.

He had noticed the diamond pendant on the table in the lounge area, and looked at it longingly for a moment. However he knew it was too conspicuous, and the anonymous group had told him to leave it alone if he saw it.

He had a strong suspicion of their identity. Crossing the gang involved would be hazardous, and he was being well paid.

He looked at the young human woman. She looked subdued and downcast, and he doubted that she had ever fired a gun. As he had searched the vessel, he could have disarmed her on several occasions.

He said, "Give me the gun, and I will send the all clear message. By the way, I have no connection with the people who are coming aboard. I was contracted by an unknown party for this task.

"It is a beautiful yacht, and I would imagine the gang with whom you are dealing will be delighted to capture it. I have some suspicions about their identity. If I am correct, be careful with them; they are extremely dangerous."

A few minutes later, Cheetah said in a standard computer-generated voice, "Voice messages being received from two shuttles. Do you wish to listen and respond?"

Sienna was able to have a minute's audible conversation with Iain and Felicity. They confirmed they were in separate shuttles, one of which was already approaching the Federation fleet. She actually knew this from their hidden communications net, but this had to remain disguised.

He saw the girl place the gun on the table and then sit down, and start to sob.

She looked at the Kenta, "Take my gun, and confirm to the group that I am disarmed."

The Kenta took the weapon, and said "Human woman, I regret that I have also been instructed to tie you to a chair to ensure you do not pick up another weapon. I apologise for this."

Without a word, Sienna sat on a suitable chair to which she was bound.

The Kenta then left, having sent a brief message.

Cheetah continued; "Two shuttles approaching who request entrance. Please advise."

Sienna said, "Computer, admit shuttles. Allow existing visitor to leave as they arrive."

5 minutes later, there was a noise at the door, and the Kenta group entered, followed by Felicity.

Sienna was released from the chair, and flew into the arms of the nurse, again sobbing slightly.

"Felicity, I am so glad to see you. I've been scared out of my mind!"

Felicity just held her tightly, and could not resist gently stroking the back of Sienna's hair.

In fact, Sienna was having a hidden conversation.

"Cheetah is acting the part of a simpleminded AI, and I am pretending to be a scared nervous girl, which is not that far from the truth.

"Felicity, I'm so grateful to you, as I am told on good authority that you saved Iain's life on at least two occasions. Play the part of being the dominant nurse, which won't be difficult for you!

"I have just heard that Iain has arrived at the flagship, and is being bundled into their hospital for a complete checkup."

At that point the Kenta leader said to one of his subordinates, "Check the vessel and particularly the girl and that necklace for any hidden location or signalling devices. The rest of you, search the vessel thoroughly.

"Mrs Taylor, release the vessel controls to us."

Sienna detached herself from Felicity, and looking as nervous and subdued as she could manage she went up to the master control seat.

"Computer, open protocols for changing vessel control authority."

Cheetah's artificial sounding voice said, "Input master password into keypad".

Sienna tapped a 10 digit number and letter sequence into the keypad, purely for show.

The computer voice continued, "Master password verified. Specify new control authority of vessel."

She said, "Any of the Kenta who've just come aboard are fully authorised to operate the controls. Provide each of them with a master password. Remove my control."

The computer voice said, "New authorities activated."

The Kenta leader said to one of his subordinates; "Penda, take control and steer us to the asteroid belt and our rendezvous. Let me know if you have any problems."

Turning to Felicity and Sienna he said, "You have been allocated the small bedroom and bathroom which I assume Miss Corning occupied. My people will occupy the rest of the space.

"Prepare some food and drink for yourselves, and then confine yourself to that area. It will take about four hours to reach our community."

One of the Kenta had been systematically moving around Cheetah with an electronic detection wand. He was particularly careful to check Sienna and the diamond necklace.

"No signalling devices or location devices detected."

The two human women quickly prepared some food and drink, and moved to Felicity's room.

As they walked across, Sienna saw piles of her own and the Moores' possessions being collected from the other rooms, obviously to be kept as loot.

One of the gang was waving a white fur coat.

He was sharply reprimanded by his boss, "Put that fur coat down carefully. I think it is from Masun, in which case it is worth an absolute fortune!"

The gang leader picked up Sienna's pendant. Having spent a lifetime in the robbery and extortion business, he had a good working knowledge of jewellery values. However, the diamonds in the pendant were so fabulous that they would have to be cut to smaller sizes to be saleable.

He thought to himself, "That's a pity, as the pendant is quite amazing."

Sienna watched him for a moment, and fury boiled up in her again.

She grabbed Felicity's hand and almost dragged her into the bedroom, slamming the door behind them.

Turning, Felicity almost stepped back, such was the fury evident in Sienna's face.

She hissed, "Felicity, those creatures are going to roast in hell! That goes for the rest of their community! When I have located them, I'm going to systematically obliterate their asteroid and any connections."

Felicity looked at her Empress in dismay. Sienna's family had a reputation for being people not to annoy. This was quite difficult, but once it occurred it had been observed that anger management was not one of their strengths. A furious Shepherd stayed that way for a long time.

She went over to Sienna, and took her in a careful hug. "Oh Sienna, My Lady, there is almost nothing I would not do for you!

"But if you have any gratitude for what I have done for Iain, please, please do not just exterminate the Kenta in the asteroid belt.

"Many of them are entirely innocent, and this would indelibly stain your future, and the future of the Federation!"

She could not help gently stroking the back of Sienna's head and the top of her neck again.

Sienna started to cry.

The Kenta outside could hear her.

The leader had observed how subdued the woman seemed, and the way she always seemed to try and stay in the shadow of Felicity with her eyes down.

He wondered whether they had not made another terrible mistake. The Empress Sylvia and Mrs Taylor were known to be almost identical. Perhaps it was Sylvia who reorganised the planet Masun, and not this woman.

However, he still worried about the soft comment he had heard from the nurse about what would happen when Sienna found them.

The nurse's evident devotion to Sienna was puzzling; perhaps this was a human trait and there was a family or clan linkage of which he had no knowledge.

He did not know that both Cheetah and Felicity had told Sienna that unless she kept her eyes down and acted in a totally subdued fashion, her internal rage would show.

About five minutes later, Sienna detached herself from her nurse and lay down on the bed with her eyes shut.

When Felicity brought across a glass of water, she murmured.

"Thank you again, Felicity. You have brought me back from the brink of insanity.

"When the dust has settled from this miserable affair, please let me know two things you would really like which I can reasonably arrange. Iain and I are enormously in your debt."

* * *

On the flagship, the shuttle was allowed on board in a remote bay, Iain was carefully removed, and then a volunteer bomb disposal expert moved the vessel outside the flagship and disarmed the explosive device. Security wished it to be intact, to try and trace its origin, although simply destroying it in space would have been much safer. There was a grim determination to find the associates of the group who had murdered and injured their officers.

Iain was given a comprehensive checkup, but the surgeons were satisfied that he was recovering.

They told him, "You have a broken collarbone which is going to be uncomfortable. If it does not heal properly with simple immobilisation, you may require some minor surgery a little further down the track. However it looks like the staff nurse who cared for you did excellent work, and we would prefer to avoid further trauma for the time being. We are changing the bandages, and you're being given a further course of antibiotics and an extra blood transfusion."

Back on Cheetah, Felicity shed her bloodied and dirty garments, and enjoyed her first decent wash for several days. She also decided that wearing her full professional uniform as a navy staff nurse was appropriate.

Just outside the asteroid belt, a huge old freighter was waiting. Cheetah was moved into the hold of this vessel. While this was happening, Crystal arranged for three combat remotes to be moved through foldspace transfer into an inaccessible area of the yacht. She told her fellow AI; "You will observe that these remotes are slightly larger than the previous version. I have rebuilt them and each contains a multi cored computer complex which will enable them to act with much greater sophistication than most combat remotes when you do not have satisfactory control capability. They have been programmed to make protection of Sienna, and then her surrounding group, their absolute priority."

A message was piped through to Sienna, "Mrs Taylor, we are now in the hold of a large freighter. This will take the yacht to our community.

"It has extraordinary shields. Your vessel would not survive exposure to space in the asteroid belt on its own."

It was Felicity who answered, "Thank you for telling us. Mrs Taylor is lying down, exhausted. She is in a most depressed state, not helped by her pregnancy."

In fact, Sienna was having a long conversation with Iain. He was describing in detail everything that had happened under the Kenta city after he regained consciousness.

He added, "Darling, without Felicity I think I would have almost certainly died. We must think of some way of rewarding her."

His wife answered softly, "I agree. When I have dealt with this mob, we will think of something appropriate if Felicity does not have any ideas! I already told her that."

A few hours later, there were some heavy bumps and loud clangs. A message came through the loudspeakers in the room, "Human women, we have arrived at the community dock. We have decided that you should stay aboard this yacht for the time being. The temperature is more suitable for your physiology, and there are appropriate food supplies.

"Three female guards will be on board at all times.

"We are negotiating with the planetary government and the Federation. This will take some time, but there is sufficient entertainment available aboard the yacht, together with exercise facilities, to keep you occupied and healthy."

Cheetah had already quietly assured Sienna that he was close enough to maintain active monitoring.

He added, "You're doing well playing the scared girl. When you change to your normal self, this will come as a shock to the criminal leadership.

"I am breaking the encryption on the majority of the computers in this community. What I have discovered already is more than interesting. In particular, the approximate locations and movement vectors of a large number of the other communities are now in my possession.

"I have passed these across to Crystal, who is embedding permanent location markers.

"By the way, I'm keeping your fur coat and diamond pendant under observation. It will be interesting to see where they are sent."

* * *

News of the kidnapping and murder had led to a rapid concentration on Kenta of every available journalist in that area of the Federation. The event was turning into a media newsfest.

Discovering that Mrs Taylor had swapped herself for her husband led to yet more interest.

As a human story, it was unbeatable.

The negotiations between the kidnap group, the Kenta government and the Federation fleet did not seem to be achieving a great deal.

The government was demanding that the two kidnapped humans be released and anyone connected with the murder of the Federation security officer and the kidnapping of the human group should be handed over for trial.

A blunt comment was added, "All other discussions are terminated until satisfactory resolution of these matters."

The Federation Fleet simply said, "We agree with the position of the Kenta government."

After a few days, the Kenta leadership of the two asteroid communities who had arranged to kidnap Sienna were becoming concerned.

Holding on to Mrs Taylor did not seem to be providing the pressure point they had expected.

Moreover, there were persistent rumours that an enormous Federation Fleet force had been dispatched to the area.

They decided to bring matters to a head. They were still convinced that military action by even a large force within the asteroid belt would be prohibitively costly, even if their location was known.

Sienna and Felicity were warned that they were going to be placed on public display in front of the leadership group of the asteroid. Video of the event would be sent out live.

The senior Kenta female guard had made sure that they were well treated by the other members of her team and the shift replacements.

She said to them, "This meeting will be in two hours' time, and you will be taken from the yacht a little before that. I personally regret that it appears our leadership is planning to treat you far more severely in order to bring pressure to bear on the planetary Kenta government and the Federation fleet."

"A live video feed of you both is going to be fed to the planetary news channels. May I suggest that you plead for mercy?"

Sienna answered softly, "I appreciate the information, and the good treatment provided by you and your people. I think you were personally responsible.

"That will be remembered."

Sienna and Felicity dressed with considerable care, with the latter in her full uniform and Sienna in a long silvery dress with white gloves.

In due course, they left the yacht and sat down in a small transport shuttle together with the three guards. It travelled down a long tunnel, then through a large cavern which was clearly the commercial hub, and stopped next to an imposing building set into the asteroid rock on the far side.

As they travelled, Cheetah set up a continuous line of tiny communication remotes. When the building was reached, he found an empty room with plenty of air space and the three combat remotes were moved in by foldspace transfer. Massive thicknesses of iron rich rock would make foldspace transfer of Sienna and Felicity imprecise and dangerous unless the remotes were present to provide exact location co-ordinates. If matters did not go as intended, he was now in a position to rescue Sienna and Felicity.

In a large room, Sienna and Felicity were asked to stand on a small stage, which was brightly spot lit. It was seen that Felicity was slightly in front of Sienna, who had her head down and looked totally subdued.

The leaders of the community were seated at a large table further back, and a number of cameras were clearly focused on the stage. The leader of the kidnap gang was also present together with several of his colleagues.

Back on the flagship, Louise was still seriously ill, but stable. She was conscious and had indicated an interest in watching when told what was happening.

Iain's bed had been wheeled in next to her, and the Admiral, his flag captain and Peter were also present. A large screen had been set up.

The flag captain remarked when the video images first started to appear; "Mrs Taylor looks remarkably subdued."

Iain answered, "Captain, she is absolutely furious, and does not want anyone to get a good look at her face and eyes, it is so obvious. I gather Felicity managed to get her to modify her original plan.

"Apparently, she was contemplating arranging for 'Sylvia' to obliterate a substantial part of the asteroid belt.

"Even to me, she has been tight lipped since then."

Peter added, "I think the asteroid community leaders are going to get a considerable shock in the near future. They've given Sienna the perfect platform – I think most of the Kenta people are watching this performance!"

The asteroid leader stood up, but only his voice was audible with no video images.

"Mrs Taylor, images and audio linkage to the planet and all other communities in the asteroid belts are now live."

He did not know that the same was true of Cheetah's recording devices.

"We are free communities in this area of the asteroid belt, and we are determined that this will continue.

"Because we believe you are influential and connected to the Empress Sylvia, we intend to hold you as a guarantee that no further action will be taken against us.

"We have decided that the life of luxury you have been leading on the yacht we captured will stop. You and your nurse will be given basic accommodation in our penal areas.

"We will not allow anyone ....

At that moment, Sienna raised her face for the first time, and stepped forward to be slightly in front of Felicity.

In a voice which rang out across the chamber she said, "That is enough!"

The community leader stopped speaking in astonishment.

Sienna continued, "This sorry affair ends here.

"The lawlessness of this community and others is intolerable. You have seen fit to murder one of the security officers from the Fleet, severely injure my husband and one of our friends, and kidnap nearly everyone else in my group.

"My great-grandmother told the Federation that as a result of two mistakes she made – Europia and Xicon - all planets within our colonised envelope should either be Protectorates or self-governing Federation members. She accepted that this would result in some injustices, but without this change the security risk was too high.

"The Federation Constitution was duly amended.

"The accuracy of her statement is now being demonstrated.

"Considering this asteroid belt as a sort of planet, the Empress has asked me to pass on to this community and others in this area, three alternatives.

"These will ensure compliance with the Federation Constitution."

Sienna completely dominated the group of people in the room and the multi millions of others who were watching.

There seemed no suggestion in her posture that she was a kidnapped captive, and at severe risk.

She surveyed the group in front of them, and noted with savage satisfaction the look of horror which was spreading over the gang leader's face. And elsewhere.

"These are the alternatives;

"Firstly, that the asteroid group communities form themselves into a confederation, with their own laws and policing in conformity with Federation norms. They become a Protectorate.

"Secondly, they negotiate with the planetary Kenta, and reintegrate themselves into the political setup of this solar system. This would include policing and laws consistent with those on Kenta. This is the alternative favoured by the Empress."

The asteroid leader found his voice at last, and said "These alternatives are unacceptable, and unenforceable."

His notional captive smiled at him rather grimly.

"The third alternative is regrettable. A substantial part of the vitality and resourcefulness of the Kenta people have migrated to this asteroid belt.

"The belt will be divided into five notional bands.

"Communities in any particular band who agree to the first two alternatives will be allowed whichever option they choose. That agreement must be unanimous between all the contained communities.

"Other bands will be destroyed in stages.

"You should be aware that two Federation Battle Groups have been ordered by the Empress to this area. They will arrive in a few days.

"In turn, around the circumference of each of those bands, the Fleet with technical assistance from the Crystal Palace will interlock force fields and move inwards. The contracting enclosure will push the asteroid material towards a centre point. The Federation fleet will not be needed after about two months at full power as a sufficient mass will be gathered to continue to collapse under its own gravity. At that point, the process is irreversible. A half melted planetoid will form as the collapse finalises.

"It is unfortunate that the blameless communities of Hiron, Foret, Gilo, and Won, and many other smaller groups, would all be in the first band to be treated as they are close to you, if no agreement has been reached. The Federation Fleet would assist communities in evacuating their people if requested."

It was a considerable surprise to the communities mentioned that their location was known.

"The fleet will then move on to the next non-compliant band.

"The Empress has no intention of committing the Fleet and the Kenta authorities to a guerrilla war."

There was a vast silence throughout the room.

Sienna added, almost as an afterthought, "It is expected that all those involved with the murder and kidnapping on the planet will be handed over to the Kenta authorities for trial under planetary law.

"The rest of the communities in the asteroid belt, and perhaps the people here, might care to consider how to handle the leadership of this community and any others which have been implicated. They have precipitated vast political change or complete destruction.

"The asteroid belt communities have 28 Kenta days to make collective decisions and present firm proposals to the Empress.

"Preparation for the enclosures will start soon after the Fleet reinforcements arrive.

"Sylvia is most annoyed and will not discuss changes to these alternatives.

"I would now like to be escorted back to my yacht, as I'm feeling quite weary".

The group of Kenta in the room had been so stunned that they had forgotten that the cameras had been running throughout Sienna's speech. They belatedly realised that they had provided a perfect platform for a specific set of messages.

There was complete silence as Felicity and Sienna walked across to the guards, and then left the room. Then the shouting started.

While they were returning, the three combat remotes were returned to the yacht hold.

As the humans stepped out of the shuttle in front of Cheetah, a guard operated the command to open Cheetah's door.

Just inside, with the doors shutting, the combat remotes appeared and placed themselves in front of Sienna and Felicity.

Sienna turned to her escort. "We are now returning to Kenta, which will only take a few minutes. Computer, escort the guards to the spare bedroom where they will remain confined. Disarm them if they resist."

The senior guard bowed her head to Sienna, and said to her subordinates. "Follow me. I am quite certain that any resistance would be useless."

The moment the door was shut, Sienna said; "Let's go. While that is happening, I need to lie down".

A few minutes later, a disorderly debate in the community main conference room was interrupted.

A senior guard rushed in, and gave a cursory salute. "The yacht we captured has gone, presumably by direct foldspace transfer. We thought this was impossible inside a large solid body.

"A large part of our community has armed itself and is demonstrating in front of this building. They are demanding that you all resign."

A certain gang leader remembered the human nurse's soft comment about what would happen when Sienna located his group. He realised that he had utterly misunderstood Mrs Taylor.

* * *

Back on the flagship, as Sienna's little speech concluded, the Flag Captain remarked, "I could almost feel sorry for the asteroid Kenta. The last alternative was definitely a new variant on being between a rock and a hard place!"

The Admiral said, "Take note, Alan. That young lady is not a person to annoy."

"Up to now, I think she has relied on subtlety to effect change. Physically attacking her people meant she switched to a sledgehammer approach. Having said that, it is likely to be no less effective and if we are lucky, casualties should be minimal."

Iain suddenly looked happy. "Cheetah has returned, and Sienna is coming over with Felicity to collect me. She wants to say hello to Louise, and thank her. Peter, she suggests you stay here until your better half is pretty well on her feet.

"Admiral, there are apparently three Kenta guards on the shuttle which she would like to offload on you."

The Admiral laughed, "I always suspected there was a hidden communications network.

"Alan, organise a full honour guard by the shuttle entrance, and we will go down and collect our mistress."

He was pleased that decisive action was being taken, without the necessity of the Fleet being involved in a murderous confrontation with the asteroid communities from within the belt. No effective opposition to the enclosure process that 'Sylvia' had specified appeared possible. He suspected his technical people would be interested in the suggestions that the Crystal Palace would make as to how to improve the interlocking of force fields.

He thought to himself, "I'm not sure which of the alternatives the asteroid Kenta will choose, but I'm certain they will not wish to see the belt eliminated. That would just force them back to the planet with their asset base gone."

At the bay entrance, a hastily convened honour guard came stiffly to attention as the shuttle entered.

A significant proportion of the Fleet's personnel had watched Sienna's presentation, and Sienna Taylor had acquired a huge following. No-one had been relishing the thought of a possible direct intra-belt military confrontation with the asteroid communities. Casualties on both sides would have been enormous.

Some regretted she was not the Empress.

As Sienna and Felicity walked down the exit steps, the honour guard and all the officers saluted. Following an ancient naval tradition, a hornpipe was played.

She mischievously asked the nervous officer on duty at the entrance, "Permission to come aboard with my nurse, Lieutenant?"

"Certainly, Ma'am, My Lady", he said, fluffing his lines completely.

She saved him from further embarrassment by walking across to the main group of officers.

"I'm delighted to see you again, Admiral.

"Three Kenta guards are still in the shuttle. Get someone to bring them out. They are to be well treated as they were good to me and Felicity on the yacht. They are to be released with enough money to go where they wish, and no charges are to be preferred.

"I will come over for a serious talk with you and your staff tomorrow. Right now, I want to see Louise, collect Iain, and get back to the yacht."

She added, more softly, "And tomorrow, you can dispense with the ceremony!"

In the hospital ward, she kissed Iain gently and said, "I'll be back in a few minutes to take you to Cheetah. Now I must go and say hello to Louise."

Half an hour later, she and Felicity had carefully manoeuvred a floating stretcher carrying Iain onto the shuttle, and Felicity was fussing over him making sure he was entirely comfortable as they left the battleship.

Iain looked at her with a smile, "Thank you for everything you have done, Felicity. I owe you my life, and Sienna is enormously grateful to you for other reasons as well.

"For each of those, we would like to give you a present of anything we can reasonably supply.

"What would you suggest?"

Felicity looked strangely troubled for a moment, with eyes downcast.

"There is something you should both be aware of about me.

"I am not at all attracted to men, which I suppose means I am a lesbian."

Sienna quickly moved across to her and put her arm around her shoulder, "Felicity, I think I already knew that, and it does not worry me or Iain at all.

"What would you like us to do for you?"

Felicity said nothing for a moment, then murmured; "I would like to have some children. Could, could Iain donate some sperm samples in due course?"

Sienna and Iain looked astonished, and then both smiled.

Iain said, "As soon as I am up to it," and reddened slightly as both women laughed.

Sienna added, "Felicity, we will give you some time to think about what else you would like us to do for you!"

* * *

On the planet, the Kenta leaders had watched Sienna's speech with astonishment, and then deep satisfaction.

Curiously, although no-one had actually seen the Empress despite the unexpected appearance of the Crystal Palace, there was no doubt that her message had been passed on exactly, and the technical ability to arrange the enclosure existed.

Two days later, messages were received from several of the larger communities suggesting that discussions with the planetary leadership should start immediately. After a brief and fierce debate, the communities collectively decided that they had to negotiate. They had been so overawed by Sienna that the 'Empress's' expressed preference for reintegration had become the preferred option. Endless debate and doing nothing was not a good default choice.

The message added, "The leadership group on Fer has been killed by its own people.

"In apology, that community wishes to return Mrs Taylor's fur coat and diamond pendant and sundry other goods.

"The gang who kidnapped her have been goaled, and will be returned to the planetary authorities as soon as possible."

* * *

A few hours later, the first of the Federation battle groups emerged from foldspace near the outer part of the Kenta solar system.

The message came through to Cheetah, "Sienna, Admiral Jenna and I would like to see you for dinner on the flagship with Admiral Hargreaves, together with your group. Best wishes, Caroline."

A message went back agreeing, but Sienna added; "Only Peter will be coming as Iain and Louise are still too weak to be moved, and my nurse Felicity needs to look after Iain. Admiral Hargreaves knows my real position, but tell him a full honour guard every time I appear is entirely unnecessary."

Soon after they arrived, Admiral Jenna and Caroline had been briefed on everything which had occurred while they were in foldspace. They then sat down to watch a recording of Sienna's speech in the asteroid belt.

When it was finished, Caroline looked at her Admiral with a faint smile; "Sienna is maturing fast. The distinction between her and 'Sylvia' seems to be increasingly blurred.

"I think the jungle drums will be sending the message across the Federation to be extraordinarily careful not to annoy Sienna Taylor or 'Sylvia', even when she disappears into the background again. They are being given an object lesson in the use of raw power.

"I hope Katie is around to fill in when we get round to having a formal dinner for the politicians on this planet and the asteroid belt".

A day later, technical specifications for the hardware and the necessary software for contracting enclosures were supplied by Crystal.

These were eagerly studied by the engineering staff. Interlocking of shields had been understood even before the Habitat left Earth, but it was obvious that the new methodology would be far more efficient, and the interlocking between ships could occur with much wider spacings.

Admiral Jenna ordered the two Battle Groups to each separately practice the enclosure and contraction manoeuvre.

He decided that competition would sharpen the training, and after a brief discussion with the AI announced that the Crystal Palace would oversee the efficiency of practice sessions, and would announce a winner when they ceased. The prize was an extra day's shore leave for the personnel of the winning group.

When the practice sessions started, the enclosure area included several largish asteroids. It was quickly found that the procedure was more complex than realised. Where a large mass impacted interlocked shields, its movement vectors and mass had to be taken into account, and either the spacing between the fleet ships had to be reduced or an extra vessel had to be inserted to maintain consistency. These required accurate, and above all quick, manoeuvring, which stressed the crews.

Although algorithms were quickly drafted, it was discovered that the optimum response was still more an art than science. It was found that some tactical officers had a much better 'feel' for the process than others, and control authority was rapidly centred on those staff.

Crystal provided a nearly continuous update on the relative ranking of the two Battle Groups, including individual critiques. These were studied with great interest from the lowest ranks upwards. Personnel or vessels which made a mistake became the subject of sharp criticism by their own group.

In fact, the process began to resemble that of the finals of a serious sports competition.

The manoeuvres were conducted in the vicinity of the asteroid belt, and were observed with alarm. Negotiations were accelerated.

After a week, Admiral Jenna ordered the manoeuvres to take place at a much greater distance, at the outer edge of the Kenta solar system.

This time, 10 small craft from each of the battle groups were ordered to try and break the enclosure from the inside of the other group. Subject to certain safety restrictions, fusion weapons were allowed to be used, with the agreement of the Kenta government.

The asteroid Kenta had been wondering whether it was possible to break such enclosures. To see the Federation Fleet practising manoeuvres to prevent any such action snuffed out any residual hope that this policy might be workable.

Admiral Hargreaves and his flag captain had also been studying the progress of the training exercises with interest; it was clear that setting up the enclosures for the asteroid belt would now be little more than a routine exercise. As Sienna had indicated, there had not been a hint of any softening of her viewpoint from the Empress.

As the flag captain remarked, "You were right, Admiral. The Empress is not a lady to annoy. It is going to be a long while before anyone challenges our mistress again."

Chapter 10

NEMESIS AGAIN

WHEN SHE WAS NOT IN ACTIVE discussion with her Bearing group, Katie had based herself on Sienna's tropical island on Nova.

While only a tiny part of her was still human, she still enjoyed playacting the tourist. Sybaritic pleasures like sunbathing and swimming in the coral cove were quite satisfying.

In the meantime, her background intelligence was considering what Aon might do next. She was uneasily aware that the entity was much older, more experienced, and had a technological understanding vastly greater than her own.

Her Bearing partners had put themselves in the shoes of their enemy, and had come up with a dismaying list of possibilities. For several of them, they were uncertain that a defence existed.

Two weeks later, her holiday ended. The historical databases had again veered wildly.

Studying them it became clear that the focus was an obscure battle in France at a place called Bouvines in 1214, between the French and an alliance of nations including the English, the Dutch, the Germans and the Portuguese.

In the original historical database, winning this battle established the French monarchy as the strong central control point for France.

It also resulted in King John of England returning to his country seriously weakened. A year later, he was forced to sign the Magna Carta, which has always been held as one of the iconic steps in the development of English law. That it was more a defence of the rights of the Church and the nobility against arbitrary Royal decisions did not diminish the significance of the document.

In most English history books, the Battle of Bouvines is hardly mentioned, which is common for cases of inglorious defeat. However in France it is recognised as a major victory and one of the decisive turning points of European history.

Aon had moved history by giving the French King a severe case of diarrhoea on the day of the battle. Without his rallying influence, his army had suffered a disastrous defeat as it was seriously outnumbered and the retreat point was one small bridge. This radically changed European history.

As usual, Katie had to move back in time with its customary problems. This time, she appeared outside a nunnery in France, and was taken in suffering severe temporal shock. When she had recovered, she was pleased to note that this time she had immediately recovered her memories.

She thought to herself, "I must be getting used to this temporal movement."

The method that Aon had used was straightforward. After the customary tasting of the French King's food for poison, she had introduced into it a small quantity of a chemical called phenolphthalein, which is a powerful and long lasting laxative. As there was only a short time interval during which this action could be taken, it was clear when Aon had to appear.

Katie was unsure where the chemicals for its production had been sourced, as they were unavailable in that era. She thought to herself, "It is possible that Aon had enough forethought to bring along a supply of basic chemical building blocks of high activity."

She decided that the best way to thwart her enemy was to simply block her when she materialised.

However, when she and her cat detected her arrival, she was concerned to find that the Qui Bearing was almost gleeful as she appeared.

"Ah, Katie Shepherd, right on time! You're so predictable! I will now obliterate your history with a method you cannot stop. I thought it both appropriate and satisfying that you should be a witness to this.

"I am going to move to one of your cities called Rome, and destroy it by translocating a substantial amount of mass underneath it.

"This method lacks subtly, but I do not think you can prevent it. Its destruction at this time will transform human history."

At that, Aon reverted to foldspace where, as she started to move slowly down time and alter her location to be above Rome, she had full access through her machine to its supergiant solar energy supply. Due to her great age and experience, she was fundamentally stronger in foldspace than Katie

Shepherd and her cat, and did not believe that the human Bearing could stop her proceeding.

Katie frantically reverted to foldspace as well, and latched herself onto Aon. Somehow, anyhow, she had to be stopped.

As they "grappled", they drifted down time and their location moved significantly. Katie tried everything she knew to try and block the Bearing, but she realised Aon was stronger and as she "tired", she felt her grip weakening.

Aon remarked, "You are now too weak to prevent translocation of the matter.

"I will now move to the location above your Italian city."

Katie realised she had one desperate expedient left. She had no idea what would happen, or what effect it would have, but she had to try. It did not even occur to her that it might be suicidal even to her.

She translocated her time device into Aon's machine.

For a moment, a significant part of the energy output of two supergiant stars merged, and there was a colossal explosion in foldspace. There was wild, random movement in space and time.

So great was the impact, that a minuscule fraction of the energy even passed through to normal space.

A tiny, tiny fraction of the energy leakage appeared in a volcanic magma chamber at a place called Santorini at around 1600 BC. The small but rapidly improving civilisation on Crete known as the Minoan Era was obliterated as the volcano exploded in a catastrophic eruption.

There were huge effects elsewhere on earth, well documented in the historical and geological record.

10a – New Beginning

For an immeasurable period of time, there was nothing. Then Katie felt her personal energy system starting to pull itself together.

For a little while, she just collected her energy and then started to study her surroundings. Initially, everything was opaque. Then a thought came through to her from her cat.

"Awake at last! There are limits to patience even with an electronic entity like myself!"

Katie remembered the statement that her cat was linked to her in space and time. Apparently, this included surviving catastrophic explosions in foldspace.

"Where, and perhaps more to the point, when am I?"

Her cat answered, "You will find the answer to the second question disturbing.

"As to where, you are actually quite close to your own planet.

"However, ... it is just over 2 billion years younger."

For a moment, Katie thought she had misunderstood. Then she opened out her perceptions, and started to study her surroundings properly.

Looking at Earth, it was obviously completely different. A massive glaciation was in place covering nearly the whole planet, and it was spinning at a much greater rate. The moon was much closer to Earth; transfer of angular momentum from the planet had not yet pushed it out to the distance to which she was accustomed, and increased the length of the days.

The sun was much dimmer.

"What happened to Aon?"

The cat answered, "Unknown. She could have been dispersed over all of space and time, or shifted to another Galaxy completely. At any rate, no trace of her has ever been found."

Katie's perceptions focused, "What do you mean by 'ever been found'?"

Her cat hesitated for a moment, "Katie, you need to understand that we are participating in a time loop cycle which has had a large number of iterations.

"It is possible that we have now found a way of exiting this process.

"The first time this occurred, I was not present – or built – and your many-times predecessor had the task of constructing a technology from scratch.

"Even with her Bearing abilities, this took a huge length of time. In effect, she had to reconstruct an advanced computer technology from a zero base single-handed, inventing some of the technology herself. It took her about 100,000 years, and nearly drove her insane from loneliness. We are still not entirely sure how she achieved this, and if the intelligence of which I am a tiny part was human, we would be quite awed.

"However at that point she was able to construct artificial intelligences, which could provide serious assistance and company.

"The first major achievement was to move her operations to the cold side of a planet on a star close to the Galactic Core. Radiation levels are such that it is totally hostile to any organic life form. It seemed unlikely then that anyone, including the Bearing as we now know them, would ever find this base, and that remains the case. This base is known as the Construct.

"This was needed to ensure that we would not be affected by chronon effects from possible future loops.

"We then moved a small device rather similar to this package – your cat – to an era just before now to start building a comfortable and sophisticated habitation for you when you arrived. It then moved itself back to a location near Earth so you could be guided to the core star.

"Obviously, in the thousands of iterations of the time loop since then, the Construct has become more and more sophisticated, and we now have a deep understanding of time theory. Our technology is also far beyond what the Bearing have ever achieved; this little device known as your cat carries information about advances from the previous cycle back to the start. Effectively, each of the thousands of cycles started on the shoulders of the previous loop with 2 billion years of incremental knowledge included.

"To preserve your sanity over the time period before other sentient beings develop, we have a time stasis device which enables you to leapfrog time periods for up to fifty million years."

Katie thought about this for a little while.

She suddenly realised why the Oldest had seemed so familiar. *It was her, billions of years older.*

The reason the Oldest had disappeared, was that she had effectively met herself which the chronons would not allow.

Suddenly, it all fitted together so neatly. Obviously, over the multitude of iterations, many different historical paths had been tried. One way or another, all except one had ended disastrously. Subtle assistance had obviously been applied on many occasions, presumably using her cat as the agent.

She also realised that her alternative personality, Alte, would have been gradually developing. She had now reached a point where there was a possibility that the chronons would differentiate her from the 'real' Katie Shepherd.

"All right, a lot of things have now become clear. You had better guide me to the Construct."

10b – Escape

During the current cycle, for the first time Alte had taken over completely just after Katie had completed consulting with her Bearing group, Sienna and Iain about Einstein's disappearance in Zürich.

For Katie [older version] it was the morning before she had made her last comments to Einstein which had changed the future.

Katie [younger version] had just finished breakfast when a duplicate of herself appeared.

The duplicate said "Just listen. When Einstein asks you about the photoelectric effect later on today, say the following;

'What might happen if light was considered as a particle rather than a wave?'

'What energy effects might be relevant for this theoretical particle?'

"Don't move in time before then. This is so important ...."

As the duplicate finished the word 'important' she simply vanished. Strangely, a small area where her feet been touching the ground had also vanished.

This time, as Alte had reached the word "important", she had displaced herself away.

For a picosecond reality wavered, and then she realised that the chronons had distinguished her from Katie. She had not been obliterated.

She was much less emotional and far more alien than Katie proper, but for a small moment a sense of relief flooded her. She moved herself back to the Construct, and placed herself in the stasis device. There were fundamental theoretical reasons why time machines constructed in any one era would simply not move into the future. Natural time had to be allowed to pass.

When she reached the date of Katie's abdication, she emerged from the stasis device and brought herself up-to-date with everything that had occurred subsequently.

Before she had completely submerged Katie, she had been asked to give Sienna some additional assistance if it was required.

* * *

Sienna, Iain and Felicity were just finishing breakfast when her cat suddenly sat up and hissed, with its fur standing on end.

Sienna had never seen it behave like this, and was looking at the 'animal' with some alarm, when Katie walked in through the door. At first glance, she seemed rather sombre, and her eyes were glowing faintly.

The human group all heard the message from her cat, "That is not Katie. The entity you see in front of you is not known to the Bearing Community.

"This is a matter of concern, and I have sent a request for help."

The junior Bearing who was acting as Sienna's cat was more than just concerned. All an initial exploratory probe had discovered, was that the being that had appeared was completely impenetrable. It was also utterly alien even to the Bearing.

As the local community assembled, a high-level conversation occurred. Strangely, Sienna was included, but not the rest of her group.

"Alien entity, what is your relation to Katie and where are you from?"

The reply alarmed them still further, "My name is Alte and I/we are a personality related to Katie Shepherd, but now distinct from her. I/we are also linked to an intelligence of enormous power located elsewhere. I/we are here as the successor to the Oldest, who understood our nature and to whom I/we are related.

"Katie Shepherd is far more human than the entity you sense.

"To prevent the statistical chance of chronon obliteration, she cannot be allowed to return for a long period.

"It is not safe for you to know more, and be aware that the technology I/we represent is further ahead of your own than you are ahead of the Federation species.

"I/we have been requested by Katie to finish assisting Sienna Taylor. When that is done, I/we will more fully engage with the Bearing Community, with the understanding that information restrictions will remain. I/we will not say more at this time."

All the Bearing present left, sending out a description of the meeting to their colleagues throughout the galaxy. They were deeply disturbed; discovering that they were not the pinnacle of power in the galaxy was more crushing to them than it would have been to a human group. They had enjoyed the sensation for aeons.

When they had gone, Alte turned to Sienna.

"Greetings, Sienna. As I/we told the Bearing, Katie has asked me to assist. When you get round to holding a Federation dinner, I/we will take your place as complete knowledge of your past is held. I/we will keep a watching brief on you, and may return on future occasions. However, these will be rare. You have matured sufficiently to require little further assistance.

"You should also be aware that you will not see your great-grandmother again for a number of decades. If she returns prior to that, she risks disrupting the time stream again and personal obliteration."

From moment, Sienna felt a huge wave of sadness. The entity with which she was 'conversing' felt completely different from her great-grandmother, and there was absolutely no sense of empathy.

Curiosity took over for a moment, "Can you say what you are, Alte?"

Alte's eyes flared brilliantly, "It is not safe for you to have that knowledge. I/we are intensely disturbing even to the Bearing. Do not reveal what little you know of us to anyone else in the Federation.

"By the way, your pendant has been slightly modified to make it more impressive.

"Farewell for the time being."

* * *

A few days later, the last of the asteroid Kenta groups announced that they would reintegrate with the Kenta planetary government. Apparently, there had been quite violent confrontations with two of their smaller communities, which had been effectively invaded by the other groups when they absolutely refused to cooperate. For reasons which no-one could understand, their leadership groups simply would not believe that the Empress would carry out her threat.

Negotiations were concluded with three days to go before the deadline.

Caroline in her role as Governor had a long talk with Sienna.

"Congratulations Sienna, you seem to have completed the reorganisation of this part of the Federation!

"More seriously, my read of the political vibrations across all the planets is that you have firmly established yourself as an entity which must not be annoyed.

"There is vast confusion between your Sylvia identity, and that of your persona as Sienna Taylor.

"I think we need to have a Federation dinner shortly. Will Katie be able to stand in?"

Caroline saw tears form in Sienna's eyes. "Another entity will appear. Apparently, for reasons I have been forbidden to mention, I will not be able to see Katie again for many decades."

There was a short pause, and then Sienna's mood seemed to brighten a little.

She looked at her aunt rather mischievously; "There is some further information which I would like to announce at that dinner, which I have not yet been authorised to impart to anyone.

"I apologise for this, but the Bearing community is quite disturbed at the moment, and my local representative is temporarily absent."

While Caroline was a little irritated at the comment, another part of her was satisfied that her Empress was now universally accepted as the ultimate authority in the Federation, and was clearly an effective interface with the Bearing.

* * *

A Federation dinner hosted by the Nova Ambassador was held two weeks later in the main ballroom Hall in the Kenta underground city.

Louise had recovered sufficiently to be able to attend, with Crystal providing special wheelchair seating. It locally reduced gravity, to make her more comfortable.

Sienna had transported herself across to the Crystal Palace three days previously. She had told her group, "As you shuttle down to the dinner, you will be joined by a Sienna lookalike. She is not Katie, and I'm told that she has a total knowledge of my past.

"Try and act completely naturally with her, and don't allow yourselves to be overawed, although that would be justified. She has even disturbed the Bearing.

"Iain, I doubt you will be even tempted to try anything cheeky with her!"

As promised, Alte appeared in the shuttle on the way down to the dinner.

For a moment, even Iain was fooled by the likeness to his wife, until she started to speak.

In a strange timbred voice unlike anything they had heard before, she said "Greetings, group from Cheetah. In a moment, I/we will complete my Sienna simulation, and no-one will be able to tell the difference.

"As a group, you have done well. Your support to Sienna was important, but the help you gave Katie Shepherd was pivotal. I/we have given each of you and Sienna a small present, but it will be some time before its nature is appreciated."

Alte's voice then changed, to an exact simulation of Sienna, and she smiled.

"Let's just enjoy the dinner!"

A number of the more prominent Federation journalists had been invited, and one of those was seated on the Cheetah group's table, together with two representatives from the asteroid community. Other senior journalists were scattered elsewhere in the Hall.

This journalist had studied the career of Sienna Taylor discreetly but in depth. He decided he would allow himself one question to satisfy his own burning curiosity as to whether she was really Sylvia.

The Empress was the last guest to arrive, together with the Nova Governor and Admiral Jenna. Apart from her normal silver outfit and hair, it was noticed that she was wearing a diamond pendant which appeared identical to that which had been worn by Sienna Taylor, except that the central diamond glowed faintly and the surrounding diamonds kept on emitting little flashes in a synchronised and coruscating pattern.

Caroline had laughed when she saw the flashes. She was heard to remark, "My Lady, I see you are determined to upstage Sienna!"

At Sienna's table, after a little initial hesitancy, the asteroid Kenta found themselves talking freely to the humans.

They apologised to Iain and Louise for their injuries, and were relieved when Louise said "While I appreciate the apologies, it was really not your fault. The direct perpetrators are now in the hands of the planetary Kenta authorities, and I'm sure justice will be done."

Peter added, "The clip of Louise being kicked while desperately injured is probably going to limit the result of any appeals for clemency. It appears that was totally disgusting to the people generally. Personally, I admit that I would have preferred to watch Louise beat up the gang leader quite thoroughly when she is fully recovered!"

One of the Kenta asked, "Mrs Taylor, the Fer community were amazed when your yacht was able to enter foldspace from the centre of the asteroid. As far as we were aware, this was beyond the technology of any Federation craft. Even Fleet ships have to be in the vacuum of space to achieve this safely. Where did you acquire the yacht?

Sienna laughed, "Please call me Sienna. Actually, the yacht is not mine but was given to Sylvia as a belated wedding present by the former Empress Katie. It was built by the Bearing, and apart from being extremely fast with extraordinary shields, they used much more advanced technology. You will not see that yacht in any Federation repair yard!

"Since the objective of my group was to assist Sylvia in this area of the Federation, she passed it over to me for the trip."

At that, there was a brief lull in the conversation.

The journalist on the table saw the chance to ask the question which he had prepared. Assuming it was the real Empress who had just seated herself at the head table, the woman at the table had to be some sort of stand-in. He was convinced that any Shepherd stand-in, no matter how identical, had to possess a limited knowledge of fine detail from Sienna Taylor's past.

"Sienna, you will be aware that I am a senior journalist from the Nova Times. I'm embarrassed to admit that I have made a discrete but reasonably thorough search of your past."

He saw Iain and Peter frowning slightly at that comment.

He overrode a slight feeling of internal anxiety, and pressed on; "I apologise for this, but there is something which has always puzzled me a little.

"As far as I can see, you topped your year at Melbourne University. Why was the gold medal for best student in your field given to a student from Stortin?

Sienna looked at him from moment, "Apart from it being a bronze medal, I admit the University planned to give me the honour. However, I spoke to the Chancellor Gene Robinson and explained that I thought it was better it was placed elsewhere. Shepherds on Nova have altogether too much prominence, and I felt that there would be a feeling of unfair preference if I was given the award. A Stortin student had rather similar results, and had worked with extraordinary enthusiasm and dedication. He was selected to be the recipient. Actually, I knew Fel Tand quite well, and we were friends. When I last heard, he had just been promoted to a senior HMC position on Cordia.

"Having said that, I trust you will cease any further researches into my past, or that of any other Shepherd. You will find that Sylvia will be quite annoyed with you if that is not the case.

"You might pass that comment on to the other journalists."

The journalist was astonished; he had been absolutely convinced that Sienna was actually the Empress. The answer he had received was convincing, and actually included more detail than he had researched. In his own mind, he had no doubt that Sienna's comment was exact.

Sienna Taylor was not Sylvia.

At that moment, the Empress stood up, and a wave of silence spread across the Hall.

She looked around for a moment, and then began, "My people, once again I am delighted to see that a region of my Federation has resolved its problems.

"I must thank my close relative and friend Sienna Taylor and her group from the yacht Cheetah for their contribution.

"I was absolutely furious to hear that two of them were seriously injured, but are now well on the way to recovery. I admit that anger management is not one of my strengths, and if either of them had died I might have done something which I would have subsequently regretted.

"Having said that, much credit needs to be given to the asteroid Kenta groups for acceding to my desire for a more settled political system in this area.

"In gratitude for this, Admiral Jenna has been ordered to pass some details of the improved shield locking technology that Crystal provided across to the Kenta asteroid communities. This will greatly improve the efficiency with which they can fend off errant asteroids, and make their space vessels much safer."

In fact, Admiral Jenna had resisted that command. He had believed the technology gave his fleet a significant military advantage. However, his Empress had overruled him ruthlessly, about which he was quite disgruntled. She had told him that only part of the material that Crystal had passed over needed to be released, and had added that giving the asteroid Kenta a reason to appreciate the Federation was important. He had reluctantly accepted this, realising his Empress likely had a better feel for the politics of the area than his own.

Sylvia continued, "On a wider tableau, I am permitted to pass on some information about my great grandmother."

She paused from moment, realising that everyone in that Hall was hanging on her every word.

"The good news is that Katie has been successful in her war. This has concluded, but some of its results are disturbing even to the Bearing.

"However, in the process she has suffered more than anyone in my Federation can possibly imagine."

People close to Sylvia could see that tears were forming in her eyes, and her voice turned slightly gruff; "One result is that it will be many decades – and those were the exact words which were used – before I can see her again."

Her audience could see that it took a moment for Sienna to recover herself, before she continued.

"Finally, Sienna and I are now planning to return to Nova, and we plan to merge into the background completely.

"Our priorities will be centred on our family and future children for some time to come.

My best wishes to you all."

* * *

As Sienna's group were returning to Cheetah on the shuttle, Louise looked at the entity which was simulating Sienna and said, "Whoever or whatever you are, thank you for your assistance."

The entity replied, "I/we appreciate the thanks. Such a comment is rare," and vanished.

A little later, they were joined by a tired Sienna.

She had acquired the habit of having a bedtime cocoa before retiring.

A subdued discussion of what had happened occurred, with a general feeling of relief that it had ended well.

After a pause, Sienna remarked; "One being we never considered as a divertant was Aon, who was amongst the most important figures in the drama we have just experienced."

Overviewing the group from her hidden position, Alte could only agree.

She thought to herself, "The Construct and the Bearing would not exist without Aon's intervention. How the time loop was first formed remains unknown."

Sienna continued, "History had to be nudged in certain directions by Katie as she moved to neutralise her changes."

"From my perspective and from what little we understand of this whole affair, to succeed in her quest to destroy existence as we know it, all she had to do was absolutely nothing."

THE END

Glossary

Aon: Member of the Bearing promoted from the Qui species

Bearing: Communal group of entities inhabiting higher levels of existence known as foldspace. Overarching intelligence of the galaxy

Calai: Militaristic species inhabiting a number of planets known as the Calai Federation. Invaded Earth shortly after Katie Shepherd fled with her group in the Habitat

Cheetah: Space yacht built by the Bearing with Artificial Intelligence and given to the Empress Sylvia as a wedding present by Katie Shepherd.

Chronons: Fundamental particles of time

Crystal: Controlling Artificial Intelligence of a giant spacecraft and palace of the Empress.

Datura: Federation planet

Divertant: Key individual in history whose actions changed the flow of time

Europia: Federation planet inhabited by earth derived nations

FAC: Federation Administration College. Being a graduate nearly mandatory requirement for entering Federation civil service.

Foldspace: Higher planes of existence, key to interstellar travel and gravity control

Ghost Fleet: Hidden robotic fleet built by the Bearing and controlled by Artificial Intelligence known as Avenger. Commanded by the Empress of the Federation

Habitat:	Planetoid sized spacecraft controlled by Artificial Intelligence known as Sheila
HMC:	Habitat Manufacturing Corporation. Commercial operation owned by Sheila manufacturing fusion drives, gravity control machinery and advanced computer chips, and other advanced technology
Iain Taylor:	Husband of Sienna Taylor, the latter better known as the Empress Sylvia
Katie Shepherd:	Empress of the Outer Arm Federation until she became a junior Bearing
Kenta:	Federation planet
Masun:	Federation planet
Nova:	Sparsely populated planet, capital of the Outer Arm Federation
Oldest:	Most senior and oldest member of the Bearing
Outer Arm Federation:	Federation of planetary species set up by Katie Shepherd with the assistance of the Bearing and associated artificial intelligences
Qui:	Xenophobic and expansionary species exterminated by the Bearing
Sheila:	Artificial Intelligence controlling the Habitat
Shepherd:	Group of humans related to Katie Shepherd with a peculiar chromosome complex
Sienna Taylor:	Shepherd member who became the hidden Empress of the Outer Arm Federation
Sylvia:	Empress of the Outer Arm Federation, aka Sienna Taylor
Xicon:	Advanced and arrogant species who challenged the Federation in the Xicon War. Defeated by Katie Shepherd and the Ghost Fleet
Yelli:	Personal remote provided by the Oldest to Katie Shepherd in the form of a cat

Printed in the United States
By Bookmasters